PITS & POISON

THESE GODLY LIES

R. RAETA

Atera Books

Book Two

Pits & Poison

THESE GODLY LIES

R. RAETA

Pits & Poison: These Godly Lies by R. Raeta

Published by Atera Books

First paperback edition June 2024

First hardcover edition November 2024

Character Artwork by mahsa.gallerry

Paperback ISBN: 979-8-9855547-5-5

Hardcover ISBN: 979-8-9855547-6-2

www.rraeta.com

For the ones we've lost and the threads of change their memory weaves within us.

A NOTE FROM THE AUTHOR

Dear Reader,

This book's setting travels throughout the globe at different moments in history. While there are references to historical events and places, please know that they are depicted through a creative lens. While I strive to be as accurate and as respectful as possible with the historical facts sprinkled in, I am by no means an expert and this is first and foremost a work of fiction. It is my hope that these references can be used as a starting point in learning more about the world and the history that has helped shape it.

As always, it is my greatest wish for my readers to stay safe. Please visit my website at www.rraeta.com for a full list on some of the content to be mindful of.

Eternally grateful,
Rachelle

CHAPTER ONE

Once, he kept his memories close—shielded them with a fierceness that betrayed their value. Now, he wraps each one like a gift and watches her face as he peels back the layers of who he is. Only she could make feeling exposed feel like relief.

CALIFORNIA, UNITED STATES
1955

HE TELLS HER STORIES.

The kind woven with truth and fibers spun from memories so old they've faded. For her, he knits together his past and delivers every dream, every fear, one story at a time—tells her everything she's always wished to know, even when it's the answer to a question she never knew to ask. Anna holds each one close, the patchwork of his life growing stitch by stitch until it becomes something she can wrap around herself.

1

At night they curl up together, sometimes in the bed, sometimes on the couch. Occasionally in the meadow, where the native wild-flowers tickle her skin, closed petals kissing her cheeks, as she stares up at a blanket of stars and traces the ones that carry his names.

Tonight, they're in the living room sprawled beneath a quilt of Anna's making and nothing else. The fire crackles in the hearth, flooding the room in warmth and light while the wind whistles through the trees, autumn rain pelting her windows as if the storm were trying to force its way in. She's curled up against his chest, her breath whispering over his heart as his fingertips trace the curve of her shoulder blade lazily, each pass slower than the one previous.

"I used to love sitting in front of the fire as a child," he murmurs, the words teasing her hair before he shifts, placing a kiss to her crown. "I used to lie in front of the hearth and watch the flames dance until the warmth of it lulled me into sleep."

"It's hard to imagine you as a child." The confession is as soft and languid as the fingers now playing with the ends of her hair.

"Most days it's hard to remember," he admits. "I suppose that happens when you become too busy to reflect on things. The memory of it fades until the only thing left is the bones."

Anna thinks of all the things she's lived through; all the connections she's made. The only ones she fully remembers are the ones she's held on to. Her early years in England, the hardships she faced in France, the only parts of it she remembers clearly are the moments that involve him and Piers. All the hurt, the things that ate at her, have rotted away until all she recalls is that, at one point, it was *there*.

Time changes everything. Sometimes, it erases things too.

"My earliest memory was of being taken—the smoke and the fear. I don't remember so much as know it, now." She tilts her chin, meeting his gaze. "It's strange to realize such a crucial event in my life stopped being important enough to carry."

Khiran's hand leaves the small of her back to coax an errant curl from her face. His touch lingers, tracing her brow. "We have mirrored beginnings. Your story starts with being stolen and mine with being abandoned." He leans in, their noses brushing. If she wanted to, Anna could count every one of his eyelashes. "I came into Eira's care because I was unwanted. I never knew why—I was too young to understand. I'm not sure Eira did, either. I just know I was alone and then I wasn't."

Anna's brow creases, her mind replaying the words as she lifts her head, leaning on her elbow and hovering over him. "You were a child when you met Eira?"

He's never talked about his life from *before*. She had never even thought to ask. In the beginning, she looked to him the way mortals look up to the sky and find their gods in the stars. He was ancient and powerful, the idea that he was ever anything other than that seemed impossible. Later, after she had experienced dozens of lifetimes, her own beginnings had become so distant that she never thought to wonder about *his*.

"Did you not know?"

"How would I? You never told me."

He shrugs a shoulder. "I expected Eira to take great pleasure in sharing embarrassing stories of my youth, if I'm honest." His nose wrinkles in irritation. "She certainly enjoyed making *me* suffer through them."

Anna scoffs, her hair spilling over the rug as she lays back down beside him and folds her arm beneath her head as a pillow. "She avoided talking about you. I think she was afraid she'd slip and say something you wouldn't want me to know."

"Like embarrassing stories of my youth?"

She kicks his shin, but there's no strength behind it. More a scolding than a punishment. "Maybe if you hadn't kept so many secrets, I would have had the pleasure of hearing some of those."

Khiran's smile wanes, sobering. "Does it still bother you?"

"Yes." There are a dozen things she wished he would have done differently, but none of it changes the end result. He will always believe he was acting in her best interest the same way she will always believe he was wrong. What matters is that it's done—that he trusts her to bear the burdens *with* him going forward. "Does it scare you? Not having secrets with me?"

"No," he murmurs, placing a gentle kiss on her forehead. "You were right to demand it. It feels... freeing. Not having to measure my words with you."

She bites her lip, a poor attempt at smothering her smile. "That's a good answer. Almost perfect."

"Only almost? Perhaps I should have rehearsed it more. Added in some poetic musings on your superior judgment and divine beauty?" He grins crookedly.

"Mm," she hums. "It couldn't have hurt."

"I will make a note for next time," he promises.

Anna looks at him, committing to memory every fleck of green in his irises. It's a habit she's developed recently. Her heart's way of coping with having lost him for over a decade. There is still a nervous itch under her skin every time he leaves. It hums in her ears, settles over her heart. Sometimes she lays her hand over her chest and the ache is so great she can imagine the vibrations against her palm as clearly as if she placed it on one of her hives.

She thinks that, maybe, he feels it too.

There's a shadow at the edges of his farewell smiles, cast by the looming presence of his past mistakes. It doesn't matter that she's forgiven him—doesn't matter that she believes him when he promises *never again*. Part of her still fears that he will leave and not come back. She suspects it might take decades before it fades completely. Silas was right when he told her that trust takes more time once it's broken.

Anna frowns, the thought pulling at her. It's not any of her business, not really, but the question nags her. "Silas mentioned something to me, back when he was helping us rehouse children during the famines."

Another kiss, this one to the corner of her mouth. "The Shepherd?" he murmurs. He seems more concerned with tracing the line of her jaw with his lips than their conversation.

"He prefers Silas," she huffs. "I don't know why you and Eira are so stubborn about using his name."

"He has yet to earn the privilege."

"Keeping our secret isn't enough to earn your respect?"

"He has my respect as well as my gratitude," he corrects, a sigh

4

in his voice. He pulls away just enough to meet her eyes. "My *trust* is not so easily given. I don't offer my friendship as easily as you do, Anna."

"Perhaps that's why you have so few."

"Better a lonely fool than a dead one."

"You can't die." A reminder, for both of them.

His lips twist, a resigned sort of half smile. "There are different kinds of death," he murmurs, his palm cradling her jaw. His thumb traces the line of her cheek, his eyes dark with nightmares that carry her name. "Ask your question, Anna."

Swallowing down the impulse to chase away the shadows in his gaze, Anna wets her lips. "What happened to Eira? All Silas would say is that she was right to be distrustful of him—that she had been betrayed." She frowns, trying to recall the memory. "It felt like he was implying that you both were."

Khiran releases a long sigh, pulling away from her and laying flat on his back. "I was expecting a different line of questioning."

"But you'll answer it?"

"Yes. I just don't know how well I *can*." He stares up at the ceiling, brow creasing in thought. "I was there when it happened, but I was still young. I didn't understand it all." He shakes his head. "Or maybe I did, once, but it wasn't a memory I held on to."

Young. The word rings in Anna's ears. Somehow, she knows even before she asks. "It was when you were still mortal."

He looks at her, the crease in his brow deepening. "He really didn't tell you anything else, did he?"

"He said it wasn't his to tell." She shrugs a bare shoulder, pulling the quilt closer to her chest. "I suppose it isn't yours, either. It's Eira's."

"You're wrong." Behind him, the log on the fire shifts, sparks erupting from the bed of embers. "It's mine more than anyone's. It was the betrayal of Eira's trust that put immortality in my hands."

Once, when the world was young, so was Eira. They called her by many names—Eir, Hygieia, Panacea—but they all called her merciful. She healed their sick and aided their mothers. She was beautiful, and her soul was vibrant and full of hope. Most of all, she was *happy*. She cared for the people and the people cared for her.

Until they didn't.

The world changed. Slowly, the number of mortals seeking her help waned and the voices of skeptics rang louder than the truth. The remedies she provided went from wanted to scorned. All that hope she once carried for humanity and their potential withered and, with it, so did she. Her golden hair turned gray and her hands became as weathered and gnarled as her heart. Bitter and wounded, she shut herself away.

Some say she found the cottage in the meadow, others say she built it herself one stone at a time over years of heartbreak. Either way, she stayed. Put all the love and care the mortals refused into the soil and treated her sorrows with the warmth from her hearth until the home she made became as much a part of her as her own heart. The magic she held, the same magic she once used to ease other's pain, evolved to provide mercy for herself.

For years, no one looked for her. The paths leading to her became overgrown; the forest swallowing it up as if it never existed. A century passed, then two, then three. Soon, only one trail remained—so narrow the forest reached out and brushed one's shoulders with every step.

Every season, Eira planted her seeds and tended her garden, but there was no love in it. No pride in the meals she cooked or the bounties she harvested. No joy. She went through the motions and every year felt like the one previous. Until one fall morning, she woke to the frost dusting the meadow in a layer of glittering ice, and the monotony of her life was broken by the discovery of a set of small, shuffled footprints.

Somehow, a child had stumbled down her path. A waif of a thing, wearing nothing but tattered clothing and filth, curled up amidst the woodpile for shelter. Eira thought he looked more like a frightened animal than a child.

"What is your name?" she asked. "Where did you come from?"

The child did not answer.

Eira tried again, and again, in every language she knew. Despite looking as old as four summers, the boy showed no sign of having understood any of it. The hardened shell protecting Eira's heart cracked. "Let us warm you up," she soothed. "Get you fed."

She held out her weathered hand, waited for him to take it. Some things are universal. Her smile, her patience, needed no translation. He put his hand in hers and didn't flinch when she led him to the door.

From that day, Eira found new life. The masses no longer wanted her help or her mercy, but the child *did*. She fed him and bathed him, taught him what she knew about language and healing and *love*, and the creases in her face smoothed and the silver in her hair warmed until it was as blonde as honey. By the time the child grew a few years older, only the lines around her eyes and the calluses on her hands remained.

And they were happy.

The child grew from an illiterate half-starved creature to a boy that questioned everything. With a warm bed and a full stomach, he began to see beauty in the flowers he once trampled without thought, admired the way birds dipped and swerved in flight without scheming for a way to catch them. He learned to smile. Learned to laugh. Under Eira's care, he found the childhood life had denied him.

They spent four years like that—finding happiness and connection in each other. Four years of plucking fruit from the trees and harvesting roots from the earth, of meals shared and evenings sprawled in front of a fire while Eira wove stories for the boy to get lost in.

He never realized what she was—never knew enough to question the differences between them. When people gradually began stumbling down her path again, he didn't understand how strange it was that they spoke different languages and prayed to different gods.

7

The world he knew fit in the cradle of Eira's meadow. How could a child comprehend the scale of the world outside it?

So he learned their languages and their customs, began to recognize the deities they worshipped. His young mind rationalized it—looked at his life, his experiences, and fit them into the mold he knew. When your world is small, it's easy to find strangeness in differences. To put your likeness on a pedestal. When you're young, though, those differences don't carry the same weight.

The boy did not see Eira's visitors as strange or *other*. He only assumed that differences were the natural order of things—that neighbors sang different songs but gathered at the same table. That the outside world operated in the same laws as the meadow. Everything grew under the same sun: the flowers and the trees, the grass and the seeds sown in the garden. The boy decided early on that people must be the same.

It was, of course, incredibly naïve, but it was a beautiful belief. One he'd struggle to shed. Belief can be tricky like that—it can burrow itself so thoroughly that it becomes part of you. Centuries of horrors could never burn it out of him. Even when he saw that the world wasn't what he thought, that small part of him never stopped believing that it *could* be. Eira's care had doomed him to forever hope for the best, while the world prepared him to expect the worst.

But there, in Eira's meadow and with a childish understanding of how the world worked beyond it, the boy feared no one and no thing. It never occurred to him that something as innocent as truth, as well meaning as good intentions, could lead to a sinister outcome. So, when he met the only woman his caretaker called a friend, he held her in the same regard as the healer herself.

Seeing her for the first time is a memory he held on to—hard to forget the way she came to The Meadow not by path but by river. She emerged from the deepest part with the water rushing around her, frigid and unforgiving from the snowmelt, but her steps were sure. Confident in ways that commanded. The river bent itself to her whims, curling around her feet like a cat begging for affection. Over the tall green grasses, the spring flowers he'd collected in his hand, he watched as she made it from river to shore with no more than a wet hem to show for it.

She returned his stare with eyes reminiscent of the night sky, dark with pinpricks of light. When she smiled at him, her round face reminded him of the moon set against inky black hair.

She only spoke to Eira, that first time. Her lips moved around a language that was new to him, but Eira understood and responded in the same tongue with the same ease she seemed to carry with every other dialect that happened to come through her door. Later, he would ask to learn it and she would tell him dead languages weren't worth teaching when he still had so many living languages to master.

A year passed, and the friend returned. The boy met her at the door, Eira busy with a laboring mother in the back.

She asked him a question in a language he couldn't interpret. When he didn't answer, she studied him a moment longer before trying again, in English. "You were here before."

It was only an observation, but the boy heard the question in it. "This is my home," he answered.

"Home." The way she echoed the word was odd, as if it tasted strange on her tongue. Foreign. "How long have you called Eira's home your own?"

The boy hesitated, not because he sensed danger in the question, but because he simply didn't know the answer. "For as long as I remember."

She stared at him a few moments longer, a crease developing between her brows. The boy thought it looked a little bit like worry. "How many summers are you?"

He shrugged. It never seemed like an important thing to know. "Seven?"

She gave a slow nod, as if tucking the information away. Later, the boy would catch them talking quietly amongst themselves in that same language he had no hope of interpreting. His name was never used, but he knew by Eira's shadowed glances that they were speaking of him. The stranger's voice was soft, coaxing, but there was a tension in his caretaker's shoulders, a bite to her words, that set him on edge.

Eira refused to tell him what it was regarding, even after her friend returned to the river and let the current carry her away. He wouldn't understand, not until months later, when Eira left to get supplies and never returned.

One day stretched into two. Then three. Then four. Worry was a weight on his chest as he watched her trail slowly get swallowed by the forest. On the seventh day, he found Eira's friend on the shore with her hand outstretched and a promise on her lips. "I can take you to her."

For the first time since luck had him stumbling into Eira's meadow, since he found a home under her roof, he found himself following a stranger out of it. With his small hand in hers, the woman led him into the river and into a world that looked so unlike his own. A world made of branches instead of sky, of roots so large they rose from the earth like twisting paths all leading to the same destination—a tree so magnificent, he knew it must be one of myth.

Then he saw Eira—saw the heartbreak in her expression—and any sense of wonder left him.

She was surrounded by strangers, but there was only one she knelt before. Only one she begged to leave him be. A man of white— white hair, white skin, white robes. A man of snow and ice.

He didn't look at her as he reached his hands into the branches and pulled a golden fruit from its limbs. Didn't look at her while he inspected it. "Really, Eira," he crooned, but there was cruelty coiling beneath the words. A slow poison disguising itself as a cure. "You should be thanking me. Imagine how hard it would be for a heart as tender as yours to say goodbye once his time came? I am giving you a gift."

The boy watched the woman he knew as family, stomach twisting and heart in his throat, as Eira's knees remained firmly planted. Her voice was raw in ways that felt as futile as begging for rain from a clear and cloudless sky. "Please, at least allow him the chance to grow," she pleaded. "Allow him to choose it."

When The First laughed, the boy felt it in his chest. It snared around his heart like iron left in the snow, the sound of it so bitterly cold it burned.

He pressed the fruit into the boy's hands. "Eat." When the boy hesitated, he added promise to the command. "Eat it, and you shall be able to stay by Eira's side forever. You would like that, wouldn't you?"

It was, of course, the right thing to say—there was nothing the boy wanted more.

So he brought the peach to his lips, took a bite, and tried not to notice the look of defeat deepening the lines of Eira's face when he swallowed it down.

ANNA LAYS, THE ECHOES OF THE STORY STILL SETTLING AROUND HER. There are so many questions clamoring around her mind, but the unnamed character stands out the most. The betrayer. The one Silas must have been speaking of when he told her that trust takes more time once it's been broken. "Who was she?"

"Kaia," Khiran murmurs. There is a sadness in the way he says her name. A regret. "She and Eira were best friends before it happened."

She studies his expression in the dimming light. The fire needs to be fed; the last of the flames are listless with hunger, but she makes no move to get up. "You feel bad for her."

"She didn't mean the harm she caused," he says, fingers trailing absently over Anna's skin. "She confessed to me, much later, that she was a mother before she was a god. She knew the heartbreak Eira would face and tried to protect her from it. Unfortunately, intent weighs little when faced with the consequences."

"You forgave her." A statement, not a question. His words are too rooted in certainty to be anything else. Anna recognizes it in the softness of his expression, the truth of it folded between words spoken and words held back.

"There was never anything for me to forgive. I was never angry with her." Under her palm, his chest rises and falls with a hollow laugh. "What child doesn't revel in the thought of playing at something they're not? To have the power to follow the threads of their curiosity no matter how many miles or oceans it may cross? No. I could never regret the door Kaia opened for me. Not as a child, and not now. She gave me an existence I never knew to dream of."

"Is she one of the few you call a friend?"

"No, friend isn't quite the right word for her," he confesses. "I suppose, if I were to call Eira a mother, Kaia would be an aunt. Things were... *difficult* after I gained immortality. The Meadow was my home, but The First knew where to find me. After that, he had someone capable of retrieving me when he wished. Kaia was the only other one to offer me a haven when she saw I was in need of one."

Anna frowns. "Difficult how?" When he hesitates, she knows it was the right question to ask.

The smile twisting at the corners of his lips is sharp with resentment. "The First wasn't as pleased with my capabilities as I was." The hand at her spine stills, fanning between her shoulder blades. Anna wonders if he can feel the ache of her heart beneath his palm. "He was hoping for power and was instead delivered a boy with parlor tricks."

The need to see him, to gauge his expression and measure his hurt, is too heavy to ignore. She sits up, the quilt pooling at her thighs as she straddles his waist. His eyes drag down, admiration intertwining with devotion. Anna has lived through more lifetimes than any mortal should, but she has never felt like a goddess, not until Khiran started looking at her like this. She waits for his gaze to meet hers, fingers slipping between his own until their palms kiss, before she speaks. "He's a fool."

His eyes spark, as if she has discovered one of his favorite pastimes. Perhaps she has. "Wise words for someone who has never met him. I wholeheartedly agree."

Anna leans forward, their noses brushing and their clasped hands pinned on either side of his head. So close, she can see the shadows in his eyes—the ones he wishes to hide even from himself. "Then why do you sound as if you believe him?"

He stares up at her, gaze hooded and lips turned up in a somber smile. "I know what I am, and what I am not." He sits up, their chests touching as his fingers slip from hers, trailing up her arms with a whispered softness. "I am a master of deceit, of plucking and pulling at strings and making those in power believe it was choice and not influence that shaped their decisions." His palms cradle her jaw, thumbs stroking the ridge of her cheeks. Outside, the thunder rumbles a split second after Anna catches the flash of lightning reflected in Khiran's eyes. "I'm not a soldier, Anna."

She frowns, hands reaching for his wrists. The fire is only a lick of flame, more light than heat. Without it, she's starting to feel the chill seeping between the crack under the door, but his palms are warm against her cheeks. "Why should you need to be?"

"Because, when the time comes, that is exactly who he will send. Soldiers."

CHAPTER TWO

His hatred for them is a raw, burning thing kept alight by all the ways
they've wronged him. Right now, he hates them for putting fear in her eyes.
For forcing him to be the one to put it there.

THE STATE BATTLES RECORD FLOODING THAT WINTER. THE NEWSPAPERS print stories about levees breaking—water spilling into valleys and leaving homes and farms under water. Khiran has already warned her not to attempt going into town—the San Lorenzo river has spilled over into the lowlands and completely cut her off. Even once the water recedes, it will be weeks before the ground dries enough for the skinny wheels of her cart to make it without sinking.

Spring, she knows, will arrive faster than she's ready (it always does). As soon as the storms ease and the soil begins to resemble dirt more than mud, she forces herself to go out and start clearing some of the garden beds.

Anna rises, leaning on her heels and adjusting the scarf around her neck. The morning is clear and cloudless, but the wind is bitterly cold. Looking over her shoulder, she's unsurprised to find Khiran watching her. The pages of his newspaper lie forgotten in his lap, the corners fluttering. It's a game he's made—reading the papers just so he can point out the fallacies. One point for every omission, five points for shameless propaganda, and ten points for blatant lies. Yesterday he had awarded himself ten points when *The Alabama Journal* went as far as to claim Montgomery police were "protecting" participants of the bus boycott.

Anna crosses her arms over her chest, raising an eyebrow. "If you're not reading, you might as well help."

He hums, tilting his head. "I could."

"But you don't want to," she says, filling in the part he purposefully left unsaid.

The grin he wears is crooked, but the warmth in his eyes softens the teasing edge. "Not in the least."

Anna huffs on a laugh, shaking her head and brushing the dirt from the knees of her overalls. "Yet you still sit there and watch me."

"You're a pleasure to watch." He folds the paper and sets it aside, the breeze teasing the pages. "You enjoy this life. It looks beautiful on you."

"I'm covered in dirt."

When she steps close enough, he laces his fingers with her own, not shying away from the soil blackening her fingernails. Despite being without a jacket, his hands feel blissfully warm. "Hence why I have no plans of joining you. I will, however, happily run you a bath when you're finished."

"How chivalrous."

"My motivations are much more selfish, I'm afraid. I have high hopes of joining you."

She shakes her head, but her cheeks ache from the force of her smile. "I haven't finished clearing out the beds. I want them to be ready for spring."

"Spring is months away."

"But it's dry *now*." She grants him a quick kiss before returning to her work. "I only have a few more to do, anyway."

The sigh he gives is petulant. "Very well." He eyes the way she's bundled in her coat, the scarf high on her neck, and the humor in his voice drains away. "You look cold."

"It *is* cold," she laughs, already wrapping her hands around a stubborn stalk and pulling it up by its roots. "But I'm fine." She sets it aside and moves to the next one. "I'm just thankful the temperature never drops low enough for it to snow."

She can feel his eyes on her, but the weight feels different. More studious than admiring. "Gloves would help," he suggests, the offer unspoken but audible all the same.

He would bring her everything she could ever need or wish for if she let him. Since he's returned to her, the garden has become more of a passion project than a chore; the food she gathers more for pride than necessity. She's already had to remind him several times that she *likes* providing for herself in at least some capacity. Likes the way it fills her days and rewards her efforts with results she can measure.

"They're cumbersome," she says, but the words don't fully capture her feelings. Her hands feel clumsy in gloves and, while they would provide her with warmth, they do little as far as protection. She can sink her hands into the earth without fearing what might be hiding beneath it. Once, her hand closed on a rock so sharp she's certain her palm would have split if not for the immortal magic that flows through her.

The prick of pain only lasted a second. She'd much rather risk the occasional jab if it means being able to take comfort in the feel of soil parting around her fingers. Gloves may save her some discomfort, but they rob her of the feeling of connection, too.

"Why don't you tell me a story?" she says, sending him a smile, her cheeks flush from the chill. "It'll keep my mind off the cold."

"You just want to keep me busy so I'll stop needling you about going inside."

Anna doesn't bother denying it. "That had crossed my mind."

His lips thin, but he leans his chin on the heel of his hand as he watches her. He's silent for so long, she begins to think he'll refuse. When he does finally speak, his voice holds a weight that makes her go still.

"The First's favorite son is his strongest," he says. "Malik controls fire, births it from his palms and breathes it off his tongue the way dragons of myth and legend burned cities down to ashes." He shrugs, leaning further into his seat and looking out over the horizon. "Dragons aren't real, of course, but the damage he left in his wake was. He would burn his way across countries before The First finally put him on a shorter leash. He is the weapon he cannot control."

"He's also what Eira feared I would become," he confesses with a wince. "The First gave him power before he was old enough to wield it. A child prone to destruction. No one could touch him without paying a price for it. According to Eira, he set fire to everything he touched his first century, and with everything that burned his anger grew."

Anna swallows. Her hands lie limp in her lap. She's not sure when they stilled, when she became more engrossed with Khiran's words than the work in front of her. "Why are you telling me this?" The story feels too pointed, too random, to be without purpose.

"Because that's one of the soldiers he will send." The answer is wrapped in resignation. His gaze slides away. "And because I realized I have allowed my bitterness to leave you completely unprepared. You should know who we will be facing."

Anna turns, sits with her back against the wooden trusses of her raised bed. The cold from the ground seeps through her denim, but with the anxious, prickling heat she feels in her chest it's almost welcome. "Who else?"

He tells her of The Huntress and her ability to track magic the way a hound tracks a scent with just a touch. The Bladesmith who melds metal with her own blood to create weapons that can pierce gods. The Heartsinger who can snare any heart and play them like a puppeteer plucking and pulling at strings. The Timekeeper who can make a moment stand still.

Something nags at her. "Does Malik not have a title?"

He pauses, eyes dark with memories she's afraid to know. "The Calamity."

There's an edge in his voice, a tightness in his expression, that sets her on edge. "You fear him."

"We all do. He's quick to temper and always catastrophic. There's no controlling him. No reasoning with him. He's a bomb waiting to go off and none of us are immune to his flames."

"The First, too?"

He goes quiet. "No. I suspect fear is an impossible feeling for someone whose power is beyond everything."

Anna frowns. Khiran's words are soft, but they ring with the bitter edge of belief. Still, she can't help but feel that they don't ring quite true. "Not everything," she muses, her eyes tracing the limbs of the branches overhead. "How could he possibly be stronger than the source?"

Khiran follows her gaze. "A tree is still just a tree, Anna." He shakes his head, his words laced with regret. "Even when its roots cradle the world."

Anna keeps staring, watching the way the naked branches sway, a whisper in the wind. "I disagree."

There are questions in his eyes, but they lack the serrated edge of skepticism that would make his gaze feel mocking. His voice is soft, open and curious, when he asks, "What makes you say that?"

It's silly, but she knows he'll trust the truth of it, anyway. "It's just a feeling."

He tilts his head, studying her. "Try to explain it to me."

Anna sighs, looking up at the sky as if she could find the answers in the clouds. "Power isn't always loud; sometimes it's quiet. Subtle. You have the ability to sway the course of history with the right face and some well placed words. Maybe you aren't a soldier, but not all battles are won by brute force alone."

"Try," he corrects, voice soft. "I have the power to *try* to change minds. My failures outweigh my successes."

"Your successes save more than my hands ever could," she counters. A reminder, because there are moments where she's certain he forgets. It must be hard to measure lives when he saves them from so far—when they are numbers and not names. Not faces.

His expression darkens. "And my failures lose twice as many."

Anna has stopped thinking of the moments he was unsuccessful as failures. Every life saved is a life that would have been lost were it not for his influence. The only way he could fail, in her eyes, would be to sit by and do nothing.

She nods toward the old oak at the back of the house. "That tree has stood for at least a century," she murmurs. "It's survived that long without magic and on its own strength. It has shaded this patch of land, has sheltered and fed generations and generations of wildlife, which in turn fed countless people. There's a power in that. Even if it's quiet. Even if we can't see it." She turns back to him. "Maybe The Tree is like that. Like *you*."

For a moment, he's silent, his eyes measuring hers. "Maybe," he concedes. "But it isn't sentient. It doesn't choose the hands that pluck its fruit from its branches any more than it can choose to do something about it. In The First's care, it is a tool and nothing more."

Anna doesn't argue. He's right on every point and she has nothing to counter with. Still, she can't seem to shake the doubt rooted in her heart for reasons she can't explain.

THAT NIGHT, SHE DREAMS.

She's in the ground, thick roots twisting and spider webbing through the earth. They're everywhere. Tangling in her hair, twining between her fingers. She can feel them fanning across her back and curling around her chest like a rib cage fashioned of gnarled wood instead of bone. She looks down, feeling some of the fine roots along her jaw snapping like a thread pulled too tight.

A root, as thick as her arm, coils across her chest and over her shoulder, pinning her in place. Beneath it are clothes worn thin and centuries out of style. Her toes curl, sockless, in shoes that feel three sizes too big. She hasn't seen it in nearly a millennium, but she knows with a level of certainty only possible in dreams that it is the exact same thing she wore when Khiran offered her forever in the shape of a peach—henna swirling over his hands and bangled bracelets winking as brightly as his dark gaze when he promised death would never come for her.

Around her, the roots pulse.

The rhythm is too familiar to mistake—she hears it every time she presses her cheek to Khiran's chest.

A heartbeat.

It is not roots that surround her, but *veins*. Arteries.

They all lead back to her.

CHAPTER THREE

He knows it can't end well—it never does—but she is still achingly human in ways he finds simultaneously frustrating and admirable. It is a strange thing to love the heart that invites pain under their roof.

CALIFORNIA, UNITED STATES
SPRING 1956

ANNA DOESN'T MAKE A HABIT OF GOING INTO TOWN.

The cottage and the gardens she's surrounded it with provide her with most of her needs. The fields, forests, and coastline are bountiful with the rest. However, there are some things she simply isn't equipped to provide for herself—flour and rice, fabric and thread. Since Khiran returned to her, he's made a point to bring whatever she needs just to spare her the necessity of the journey. It's unfortunate that she hadn't realized she was low on sugar before he left yesterday, but she supposes it gives her the chance to see how the town has changed since she's last visited in the fall.

She hooks Loki to a post outside the convenience store, petting the donkey on the nose and feeding him a carrot from her pocket before heading in. Above her, a bell chimes as she opens the door.

"Ah, Miss Anna! Haven't seen you for a while. Was starting to worry the storms got ya."

Anna offers the balding man a smile. "I'm well enough. Loki has been getting older, poor thing. It's getting harder for him to make the journey." A lie. The donkey is just as stubborn and prone to trouble as the first day she brought him home. Still, it's a better excuse than the truth—that she has no need to make the trip when Khiran brings her whatever she wishes. She changes the topic before he can inquire further. "How is Susan doing? And the kids?"

Carl catches her up—Susan is obsessing over the quilt she's working on (she shows one at the county fair every year, you know) and he's certain his girls are solely to blame for all his hair loss. Anna nods and hums in interest when the conversation calls for it, all while plucking goods off the shelf and into her hand basket.

"I don't know what's gotten into kids these days," he grumbles, as she sets her purchases on the counter. He rings up the items, his gold watch winking up at her with every twist of his wrist. "Gayle's got it in her mind that she wants to go to college, of all things. Can you believe it?" He scoffs, shaking his head and repeats the word as if it's personally wronged him. "*College*. I tell you, Anna. The world is changing something awful. What's a girl going to do with a college education? Waste of money is what it is."

Good for her, Anna thinks. What she says is, "The world is always changing. Could you kindly add today's paper to the order? You know how out of touch I get up there."

"Eh? Oh, yeah. Of course." He ducks below the counter, grabbing a paper from the top and handing it to her. "Not a whole lot of folks buying them these days. What with television and all. You know, I got a cousin who's a rancher that'd be willing to buy that old place up from ya."

Anna tries to smother her smile. He's brought it up multiple times. Nearly as often as his insistence that she should retire her cart and get a car. "Yes, I believe you've mentioned."

Carl has the decency to look embarrassed, scratching at the graying stubble of his jaw sheepishly. "It's just not right, is all. Little lady like you living all the way up there by yourself."

She could ask why his cousin would be any different, but she knows a tired conversation when she sees one. "How much do I owe you, Carl?"

"Oh, that'd be, uh— " He squints at the numbers on the register. "A dollar twenty-eight."

She rests her bag on the counter, fishing for her coin purse. Behind her, she hears the bell of the shop door chime.

Carl's face darkens. "You again?! You got some nerve, kid!"

Anna turns, curious. The person in the doorway is, in fact, a kid. He's scrawny, beanpole thin, and can't be older than sixteen. His eyes, so dark they're nearly as black as his chin length hair, narrow in rebellion. "I have money!"

"Yeah? You got enough to cover that loaf of bread you stole from me last week?"

"I didn't—"

"I'll pay for him," Anna says, severing the argument before it can escalate. Carl's face has turned a curious shade of violet. "The loaf of bread, too."

"Miss Anna, that's—you shouldn't—"

"He can grab what he needs while you bag up my things. We'll do it all in one transaction. It'll hardly take you any extra time at all." The boy is staring at her from the doorway, unsure. Anna holds out her now empty shopping basket with a smile. "Go on and fill it up, but let's try not to keep Mr. Robinson waiting."

Tentatively, he takes the offered basket, giving her one last assessing look before turning toward the aisles. Anna doesn't miss the way he continues to look back over his shoulder, as if waiting for her to change her mind.

Carl is already leaning over the counter. "You got a good heart, a real good heart, but I'm telling you he's wasting it." Despite the hiss in his voice, every word rings with a volume that matches his angry flush. "Kid has been a right nuisance ever since he showed up here. Picking pockets, lifting goods, the works."

Anna looks from Carl to the boy, watching the way his shoulders hunch and his hand shakes as they grip a jar of peanut butter. "Yes, you mentioned he stole... what was it? A loaf of bread? Please make sure to add that to my bill."

He must notice the edge of judgement in her voice. "Well, it's not about—"

Anna knows exactly what it's about. Knows it the same way she knows Carl wouldn't have questioned her kindness if the boy had been white. "Are you turning down my money, Carl?"

As suspected, his stream of protests abruptly cease. Anna can see him chewing on the words, though. They must be tougher than leather for how the muscle in his jaw spasms as he finishes bagging the rest of her items. When the boy comes back, Carl grudgingly punches in the additional items on the till and places them in a separate bag.

Bread, peanut butter, and two cans of beans.

Anna has to force a fragile smile just to hide the depths of her worry. "Are you sure that's all?"

He doesn't meet her eyes. His gaze settles lower, near her chin, when he nods. "Yes ma'am. Thank you."

On the other side of the counter, Carl scoffs under his breath. If she wasn't already biting her tongue, Anna may have given into the temptation to insist the boy grab more. As it is, she can't trust that she won't have a few extra words for the grocer as well. So, with her lips pursed, she silently pays the total.

On her way out, she hesitates, her hand lingering on the doorframe as she waits for the boy to be out of earshot. She offers Carl some final, parting words in the hopes that they'll sink in when he finds himself alone. "Of all the things he could have taken. Did you even once ask yourself what kind of teenager steals bread?" she asks, suddenly tired. He doesn't answer. Anna hopes it's because he feels embarrassed. Shame is a powerful motivator for change. Yet, she has the distinct sense that Carl will fail to learn or grow from any of it.

She shifts the weight of the bag on her hip, letting the door close behind her. The tiny brass bell above her rings as it shuts.

The boy is waiting by her cart, staring at Loki with an odd expression as he clutches the paper bag to his chest. It's not until she places her items in the back that he turns to look at her. There's a stubbornness in the set of his brows, a determination in the way his chin tips. "Thank you," he says, as his hand pulls some coins from his pocket before holding it out for her to take. "Here. For my things."

Anna considers refusing, but she gets the sense that it would wound his pride. She accepts the money, the coins warm in her palm. "I'm sorry I had to step in for you to get them." She places the money in the pocket of her dress. "What's your name?"

He hesitates, just long enough that Anna thinks he might not give it. "Jiro. Jiro Okino."

"It's nice to meet you, Jiro. I'm Anna." She lets her stare linger. "Do you have somewhere to go?"

"Yeah," he says, but the tired shrug of his shoulders contradicts the word. "There's this old boat shored up on the beach." He scuffs the toe of his shoe against the sidewalk, the grip on his bag tightening until Anna catches the sound of crinkling paper. "It's close to the docks. Sometimes I can make a bit of money helping the fishermen. It's not a lot, but they're the only ones willing to hire me."

Anna considers him, mind turning over the idea for a few seconds before she commits to offering it. "I could use an extra set of hands at home, if you're willing. Help in the garden, the kitchen, things like that." She gives Loki a scratch behind his long ear. He lips at the hem of her shirt. "Of course, I'm a ways away. It would have to be a live-in position. But I could give you meals and a room in addition to a weekly payment?"

He frowns, his brows lowering and eyes narrowing. "I don't want your charity."

Anna tilts her head. "Is it charity if you're providing me a service?"

He adjusts his hold on the bag, eyeing her cautiously. "What if you decide to fire me?"

"Then I suppose I'd bring you back on my next trip into town. Assuming that's where you wished to go."

He considers it, lips thin and brow furrowed. "Yeah. Alright."

Anna hides her relief behind a smile. "Come on then. We'll swing by the pier so you can grab your things."

THE FIRST HALF OF THE RIDE HOME IS QUIET. FILLED ONLY WITH THE creaking of wheels and Loki's petulant sighs as he stubbornly makes his way up some of the steeper hills. Once, when she was younger, Anna might have been tempted to fill it with questions just to save her from the awkward edge of silence. She feels no such need, now.

The centuries have given her the confidence that comes with knowing the fragility of a moment—taught her to recognize the insignificance of some and the importance of others. She senses, instinctively, that she has more to lose with the boy beside her by pushing questions than she does by embracing his silence. So she steers Loki around some of the bigger rivets on the dirt road leading to home and watches the landscape slowly change from the comfort of her seat until Jiro chooses to break the silence.

"You didn't give a last name."

"You're right," Anna hums. "People in town know it as Spector, but I ask that you not call me by that. I only borrowed it for the sake of avoiding questions."

The suspicion in his gaze is as evident as the edge in his voice. "So what's your *real* last name?"

"I don't have one." She shrugs. "Hard to have a family name without a family."

The confession seems to snag his interest, but he doesn't continue the line of questioning. There must be a thread of understanding, of likeness, because the tension in him relaxes, the rigid set of his shoulders slowly melting. The silence between them feels less forced now.

When he breaks it for the second time, it feels more candid than accusatory.

"A car would drive this a lot faster, you know."

Anna doesn't bother to hide her smile. "A car would," she agrees, "but the trip keeps Loki young. He's more prone to trouble when he's bored." She also has no interest in troubling herself with the process getting a driver's license would entail. Besides, she doubts a car would make it past the redwood grove where the trail thins and winds between the giants.

Loki's ears swivel back, hearing his name. Jiro frowns at him. "What kind of weird name is that?"

She glances at him from the corner of her eye, weighing his interest. "It's the name of a Norse god. I could tell you about him, if you'd like?"

A moment of hesitation. Anna gets the sense that he is weighing her as carefully as she does him. He must find her offer sincere, because he eventually nods. "Yeah. Okay."

She spends the next two hours telling him the stories of Loki and his mischief. The entire time, she thinks of blue-green eyes—of how they would light if he heard her spinning the same stories he once wove for her.

ANNA KNOWS NEXT TO NOTHING ABOUT JIRO'S PAST, BUT IT QUICKLY becomes apparent that her lifestyle is vastly different from what he knows. He regards Loki with a curiosity that borders on distrust, as if waiting for the animal to bite him the moment he turns his back. When the chickens rush him, eager for their meal, there is a shadow of panic in the way he tosses the table scraps as far away from himself as possible. Still, if he complains about any of his tasks, he only does so out of earshot.

He takes to cooking much easier.

When Anna shows him the garden, points out the herbs and the

R. RAETA

vegetables and explains which of the scattered fruit trees grow what, she can see the interest in his dark eyes. Sometimes when they cook, when he doesn't notice her looking, she catches his lips moving soundlessly around the words as if trying to commit each recipe to memory. On a whim, she offers him a cookbook from her shelves and lets him choose their evening meals. He pours over the pages with an enthusiasm only matched by the excitement that lights his eyes when it's time to eat it. She has a sneaking suspicion that, with time, he will become more adept in the kitchen than she is.

The apiary also seems to spark an interest. Though, to be fair, Anna suspects part of his curiosity is fed by the honey they lick from their fingers when they harvest. Still, he listens as she explains things. Looks when she points out the differences between the workers and the drones, squints when she points out the queen hiding amongst them.

"Why does she have a blue dot on her?"

"It's just a bit of paint. It makes her easier to find," she explains, tilting the frame as she examines the brood cells. "See the ones that keep following her? Those are her attendants."

"The queen has attendants?"

Anna hums an affirmation, distractedly checking the other side of the frame. "They clean her and bring her food so she can focus her energy on laying." She frowns, noticing a bulb of wax in the corner. "Though she might not be for much longer. Do you see that? It's a queen cell."

"What does that mean? That there would be two queens?"

Anna shakes her head. "It would be her replacement. I noticed a decrease in how much she was laying in the last few weeks. They must be rejecting her."

The bridge of Jiro's nose wrinkles. "They can do that? I thought the queen controlled all of them?"

"No," she murmurs, putting the frame back into the box. "A queen doesn't command the hive—she's a slave to it." The moment she's born, her life becomes dependent on how well she does her job. If she does it poorly, the hive will build a special cell for her replace-

30

ment before swarming her. The needs of the many will always outweigh the needs of the one.

Anna has always admired that about them. She can think of more than a few monarchies that would have done well to learn a few things from the lives of bees. Anna doesn't hesitate to voice the thought and is rewarded with one of Jiro's rare smiles. She can't help but notice how much younger he looks when there's a hint of laughter lighting his eyes.

They've only shared a roof for just shy of two weeks, hardly enough time to truly know the other, but Anna already finds comfort in his presence. It's nice, not being alone between the sometimes long stretches of Khiran's absences.

Jiro, she knows, is still struggling to settle. He walks through the house like a stranger. There's a hesitancy in his touch. Anna gets the sense that he is perpetually waiting for it all to be taken away. The first week, whenever she said his name—to ask him to bring something from the garden, to stir the pot of stew on the stove—his spine would straighten. He stared at her, breath held, as if preparing for the worst.

Anna understands that feeling. She has lived it every time the hem of her sleeve rose too high or her collar slipped. Has spent centuries avoiding communal baths and swimsuits on the beach. There is a torture in waiting for the fall; an agony in understanding that the world has given you every reason to expect it.

TWO DAYS LATER, THEY'RE CLEARING THE BED OF BROCCOLI AND CABBAGE to make room for tomatoes. Spring has started to warm into summer, too hot for her winter crop to thrive. She rolls up her sleeves, pulling the old plants from the soil and places them in the wheelbarrow to compost later. There's dirt everywhere by the time she's done. It stains the knees of her overalls and powders her skin—she's certain she'll feel it on her scalp when she bathes later.

Anna knows it's not the dirt that keeps snaring Jiro's attention.

She pretends not to notice the way his stare lingers on her exposed arms—lets him have a moment to gather his question before deciding whether to voice it or hold it close.

"Are you sick?"

Anna thinks of another boy she brought under her wing lifetimes ago—the only one to ever call her mother. Piers had been so much younger than Jiro is now, less hardened, but there's a subtle thread of concern in the teen's voice that reminds her of the terror that had rimmed Piers' eyes when he first spotted the marks on her skin. She remembers how her heart shattered when he asked, *"Are you dying?"*

She spares Jiro a glance. Long enough to read the crease bridging his nose and the furrow in his brow as curiosity and not fear. Short enough that he won't feel embarrassed for asking. She pulls a stray weed from the bed, then another. "Do I look sick?"

A moment of silence. When Anna dares to look, he's watching her as if she's some kind of puzzle he can't quite solve. It's only when she offers him a small smile of encouragement that he finds the courage to answer. "I guess not." His gaze lowers back to her arms, a frown teasing the corner of his mouth. "What are they?"

Her hand sinks into the soil, cupped palm making a pocket as her left tucks a seedling into the dirt. "Vitiligo," she answers. The word still tastes strange on her tongue, despite Khiran's assurances that its origins are older than she is. After enduring centuries of accusations ranging from leprosy to witchcraft, that particular bit of knowledge still feels like a slap in the face.

She brushes the soil from her hands, dirt smudging her gardening apron. "It isn't contagious. It doesn't even hurt." Shrugging, she straightens and admires her work. The seeds she started in the greenhouse had a high turn out this year. She'll likely have to thin things out later, but for now she can at least let each seedling have a chance to thrive.

"I used to be ashamed of it," she admits. The confession pulls at her chest, a string still stubbornly twining around her heart no matter how many times she's tried to cut it loose. "Maybe I still am, just a little. It's hard wearing our differences with pride when the world looks at them with contempt. It took me a long time to realize that it's not my skin that's the problem, but *people*."

She looks at him, sees the way he shifts, the way his eyes go dark with memories and nightmares. Anna thinks of the way Carl saw him as a thief before a starving child. Thinks of the pier full of jobs and the dock workers—the ones that turned him away and the ones who offered him only a fraction of what they should—and she knows that Jiro understands what it is to be *other*. To be ostracized for something as out of his control as where his ancestors came from.

Gently, her hand rests on his shoulder with the softness the world has robbed him of. Connection in the form of touch. She's prepared for him to pull away, to curl inward the way he always does when he feels the need to shield himself, but he leans into her hand. The tension in his shoulders relaxes beneath her palm as if her touch is balm on a wound that was left to fester longer than it should.

Once, so long ago it has become more fact than memory, she lived a life alone in the woods. A life where the only words spoken to her were threats and the only touch she received was the feeling of rough hands dragging her away. Until a stranger with dark eyes and sun-kissed skin pressed a peach into her palm and soothed the oppressive silence with a kindness Anna hadn't felt in years.

It dawns on her, with a swiftness that temporarily robs her of breath, that her presence in Jiro's life may very well hold the same earth shattering impact. She thinks of the way she once looked up to Khiran, idolized and feared him, and her stomach twists uncomfortably.

Jiro doesn't know of her immortality. It's Anna's hope that he never will; that he'll spend a few years growing under her roof, so he can build up the strength to take on the world once he leaves. She hopes, with a fierceness that makes her pulse hum, that Jiro will only ever see her as a woman and nothing more. That he'll see her flaws —see that the empathy that guides her actions is entirely human.

He doesn't have the centuries she did to learn the difference.

IN THE END, IT TAKES JIRO FIVE WEEKS TO FINALLY START TREATING HER home like his own. Anna discovers her suspicions were correct about his talent in the kitchen. Where he once seemed uncomfortable making meal suggestions, he's begun taking it upon himself to plan their weekly menu. Anna chimes in occasionally, but for the most part he takes charge.

He seems to thrive when given the opportunity to control some things for himself. Anna suspects it's been a while since he's had the luxury of choosing his meal versus making do with what he was given. It is, again, something she understands more than he knows. There is a freedom that comes with knowing you won't go to sleep hungry; a weight that's lifted from your spirit. She has never had to remind him not to be wasteful—he's as conscious as she is over every scrap of food.

Anna washes a few carrots in the sink, her hands working out the bits of soil clinging stubbornly to the gnarled roots. "Jiro," she says, tipping her head in his direction. "Could you grab me some rosemary from the garden?"

He pauses, his knife still in the process of peeling a potato as his brow furrows. After a moment of quiet frustration, he asks, "Which one is that again?"

Anna tries to hide her smile as she cuts the top off a carrot. The herbs she grows seem to be very different from the seasonings he grew up with. It's one of the few things he still feels uncertain about. With how chaotic her herb bed is, she can't altogether blame him. "The one you said looks a bit like pine needles."

He sets the potato, half-peeled, on the table with the knife, wiping his hands on the apron Anna helped him sew last week. "How much?"

"Just a stem should do," she hums, cutting the carrot lengthwise into long spears.

He leaves the kitchen door wide open when he leaves, the early summer breeze brushing against her skin like a cool kiss. It's a habit Anna's noticed but chooses not to comment on. Deep fears have a way of manifesting into small, but telling, actions. She suspects it will take months before Jiro will close a door behind him and trust it to open when he returns.

She's gathered the lengths of carrot together on the cutting board, just beginning to dice them into finer bites, when the sound of Jiro shouting drifts from the open doorway. There's an edge to his voice, fear masquerading as bravery, that makes her heart jump.

Anna thinks of Khiran's warnings, that it's not if but *when* they're found, and feels her heart plummet. The knife drops from her hands, her feet quickly taking her through the open door. Her mind scrambles for another line of reasoning, but she doesn't get any visitors, not this far up. The only people that wander these hills are her and—

The garden comes into view and, with it, the sight of Jiro brandishing a shovel like a weapon. The man at the other end is as familiar to her as her own heart.

Relief comes as a sigh painted with the colors of his name, the tension in her shoulders relaxing. "Khiran."

He glances up at her, a question in his gaze. He's wearing tan slacks and a tweed vest over a cream shirt. It isn't unlike something she would see a banker wearing in town, but the indigo fabric wrapping the package he holds clashes against the western style.

Jiro points the end of the shovel towards Khiran's chest. The expression he wears might be more intimidating if worn by an adult, but the bravado lacks strength when the top of his head barely reaches Khiran's shoulders. "I don't know who you think you are or what you're selling, mister, but you should leave!"

She moves quickly to Jiro's side, resting a comforting hand on his shoulder. "I'm so sorry," she apologizes, the anxious edge in the boy's eyes stirring guilt. "I should have warned you. Khiran visits often."

Khiran meets her gaze, eyebrow raised. She can practically hear his thought: *Visit?*

Anna pointedly ignores it. Instead, gently coaxing him to lower the shovel. She notices, with amusement, that he still has a stem of rosemary clutched in one of his hands.

Jiro pins him with a distrustful look but dutifully lets the shovel drop, the blade giving a metallic twang when the tip strikes a rock. He glances at the fabric bag hanging from Khiran's crooked finger. "What are you? One of those door to door salesmen, or something?"

Khiran's answer is glib. "Not in this life, anyway."

Anna interrupts before Jiro can speak the snarky retort she can practically see him holding. "Let's take this inside, shall we? Jiro? Would you be so kind as to put the shovel in the garden shed for me?"

Jiro doesn't seem thrilled by the request, but he nods before handing her the sprig of rosemary. "Here."

Anna takes it with gratitude. "Thank you."

Once Jiro has walked the first few feet toward the garden, she links her arm through Khiran's as they head towards the house. She can feel the weight of his questions the entire way, but he doesn't speak until after they're well out of earshot.

"I've only been gone six weeks," he accuses, but there's a thread of laughter in his voice that makes the words sound more amused than angry. "When, exactly, did you take it upon yourself to adopt?"

"I didn't adopt him. I *hired* him." When he looks no more convinced, she raises her chin pointedly. "He helps me around the house."

"Ah," he breathes. "And I suppose he has to live in, what with the journey being so far."

"Exactly."

He hums. "His clothes look new. Suspiciously similar to that fabric I brought you last spring. A uniform, I suppose?"

She smothers a smile, releasing his arm to enter the kitchen. "I'm so happy you understand."

He grabs her hand, forcing her to face him. Whatever amusement that lit his eyes only a moment before has extinguished, leaving a quiet regret in its place. "He can't stay, Anna."

She frowns, lips parting—ready to protest—but Jiro is coming in. The sound of the door shutting cutting her off before she can start.

She sends Khiran a meaningful look that promises they will continue this conversation later.

He answers with a subtle nod. *Later.*

Jiro has yet to shed his scowl. "You just come whenever you want, then?"

Khiran sets his package on the counter before shrugging out of his coat. "One tends to do that in their own home." He holds the coat, momentarily uncertain. Anna realizes he's not sure what to do with it now that he's unable to make it disappear with a bit of magic and a flick of his wrist.

She quickly steps forward, kissing his cheek and taking it from his hands. "I'll put it in the bedroom. How was your trip?"

Khiran glances at the stranger in his kitchen. "Apparently not as eventful as your time at home."

Jiro looks between them, blood draining from his face. "Wait. You're *married?*"

Oh.

Anna's lips part soundlessly. They've never discussed how to refer to each other—they've never *needed* to. They're tied together in ways that went beyond mortal ceremonies and vows.

The corner of Khiran's mouth twitches, a suppressed smile. *"What do you think?"* he asks in perfect French. *"Shall we admit to living in sin, or will you drag me to the nearest chapel and make an honest man out of me?"*

Anna rolls her eyes, swatting his arm. *"I'm a modern woman. I demand a proposal on bent knee."*

His eyes darken, the curl of his mouth turning suggestive. *"You know I have no qualms kneeling for you. Shall I remind you of my devotion tonight, my love?"*

Heat rushes to her cheeks. "Yes," she blurts, fingers twisting in her apron as she wills her blood to cool. Jiro looks at her as if he's never seen her before. "I'm married. *We're* married. Jiro, this is my husband, Khiran. Khiran, this is Jiro. He's been helping me here around the cottage."

"A pleasure," Khiran says, warm enough to convince Anna that he means it. He takes a seat in his usual spot at the kitchen table, setting his attention to the parcel he'd brought with him. His long fingers work at the knot tied at the top, the fabric falling away to reveal lacquered boxes.

Anna already knows what it is. The little tradition they started centuries ago in the mountains of Genoa has continued. Whenever he returns home, it is always with some sort of food for her to try. Though sometimes he forgoes the guessing and brings her something she's enjoyed in the past. His last trip, he had brought her feijoada—a Brazilian stew with black beans and different meats. It made her think of the day trip they made to Salvador, the way the stew felt warm and comforting in her stomach after having made the journey with his magic.

She can tell by the lacquered boxes and the shade of indigo of the fabric that today's dish has more than likely come from Japan. He's brought several meals from there over the last year as he carefully watched the aftermath of the nuclear bombs dropped on Hiroshima and Nagasaki. Anna has seen the images of the distinctive mushroom cloud, read the articles that headlined every major newspaper across the county.

Khiran described the horror of it, pale-faced and ashen. Of civilians dying months after the bombs dropped, plagued with strange and horrible symptoms. How the bomb sites stopped any type of life from taking root for miles. Of all of man's weapons, Anna knows this one scares him the most.

Jiro eyes the box, a strange look of recognition and suspicion pinching his face. "Where'd you get that?"

Khiran opens the lid, tactfully ignoring the question by offering one of his own. Lined neatly inside are some fish shaped pastries. "Would you care for some?"

"That's taiyaki."

"It is." Khiran's brow ticks upward, a subtle challenge.

"Do you like taiyaki, Jiro?," she asks, deliberately ignoring the tension between them. "I've never had the opportunity to try it."

"I haven't had it since I was a kid." The edge in his voice, the skepticism stubbornly heating his eyes, makes it clear that his questions won't be cowed by Khiran or redirected by her. "Where did you get it?"

"I had some business in Monterey."

Anna knows the moment he says it, that it's a lie. The answer is too fluid, too smooth, for it to be the truth. Still, paired with his easy confidence and Monterey's history, it's believable. Before the war, the canneries had been supplied fish and abalone from the Japanese divers and fisherman that had built their businesses there. Some of the families returned after the war, but few of them had the means to rebuild the businesses the government stole from them. The town and its fishing industry have been slowly dying ever since.

Jiro falters, grudgingly accepting Khiran's answer. Unfortunately, he seems no closer to trusting it.

ANNA CLOSES HER BEDROOM DOOR, LEANING BACK AGAINST THE WOOD.

Dinner was an awkward affair. As was the time spent in the living room after. Jiro had been a bit prickly with her in the beginning, but it pales in comparison to the outright needling remarks he shoots at her so-called husband. Khiran takes it all in stride, but Anna catches the way his jaw flexes when Jiro finds a particularly sore spot to prod.

"So you just leave for weeks, come back for a few nights, before you leave her again?"

Anna flinches openly at the memory of it. She had thought Jiro might retreat into his defenses, particularly once Khiran's relationship to her was clear, but instead he seems more combative. Unfortunate, since she can tell by the way Khiran sits at the edge of their bed, his hands folded between his knees and his attention solely on her, that the conversation they put off till *later* is now.

"He can't stay," he repeats, soft but firm. "You know he can't."

She studies his expression carefully. "This isn't about what he said, right? Please don't hold his actions tonight against him."

Khiran frowns. "I like to believe I'm above begrudging a child for throwing a fit." He scoffs, the sound soft in the dark. "Besides, it is apparent that he adores *you*. How he feels about me is irrelevant."

Anna doesn't deny it. "I care for him, too. In time, I'm certain he'll—"

"That's not the issue. He could worship the ground I walked on and it still wouldn't sway my opinion on this. He shouldn't *be here*, Anna."

Her arms cross over her chest, a stubborn lift of her chin. "He was homeless, Khiran. And that town is so full of bigots, people would rather chase him away than help him."

His stare doesn't falter. Doesn't flinch. "Then we will find him another town."

"If that's what he wants, then that's fine. But I promised him a roof and a job for as long as he wants it."

He shakes his head, the first traces of frustration sharpening the edge of his voice. "He'll be caught in the middle, Anna. You can't possibly wish that for him."

"Of course I don't, but we don't know if that will happen months or decades from now! You're asking me to turn him away on the chance that it comes sooner than later."

The way he stares at her makes her skin flush. It's the same look he's given her in the past, the one where she feels exposed of secrets she never even knew she held. He still sees right through her. She suspects he always will.

"You were afraid," Khiran says, the words soft. "When he shouted. Those moments before you saw it was only me."

Anna flinches, unable to deny it. Discreetly, she thumbs at the ring on her right hand—the one that connects them. Her fear must have been strong enough, *real* enough, for him to feel it. "Yes," she admits, "but that doesn't mean I'll cater to the fear of what could—"

"Will," he corrects. "What *will* happen. It is inevitable. We need to treat it that way."

She deflates, feeling chastised. "What will happen," she echoes, voice soft, before adding, "*Someday.*"

"Anna—"

"Jiro needs help now," she stresses. "You told me once that you gave me immortality because you saw the good that I could do. Please don't ask me not to do it. Not now. Not after everything."

He runs a hand over his face, fingers massaging his temple. "And if they come while he's here?"

Her eyebrows rise in challenge. "Do you have any reason to believe they will?"

His mouth thins. "You are relentless."

Anna's lips curl, her smile triumphant as she pushes herself from the door. Her hands rise, reaching for him. "Maybe a little."

He groans, falling back onto the mattress. His forearm rests over his eyes. "Absolutely insufferable."

She joins him, straddling his hips and kissing the exposed skin under the line of his jaw. "Am I?"

"Without question."

She grins against him, her hands lowering to his belt. "I don't believe you."

"Damn it, Anna," he mutters, breath hitching. His fingertips trace a path up her arm before sliding into her hair. "You're being terribly distracting." He turns his head, catching her lips. "I'm trying to be angry with you."

She hums against him, successfully undoing the catch of his belt. "Be angry tomorrow," she sighs, eyes fluttering shut as his lips move over her jaw. Nipping at her pulse. "I missed you."

His hands roam her back, settling on her hips as he rolls them over. He hovers over her, a breath away. Anna can see every fleck of green swimming in the blue of his irises. Can see every regret. He places a kiss at the corner of her mouth, the ridge of her cheek, her closed eyelid. "I'm sorry," he murmurs. "I would come more often if I could, but if they notice—"

She hushes him, her hands curling in the fabric of his shirt. "I know."

Fingers trace her brow, sweeping a stray curl to the side. Another kiss, this one lingering longer, to her forehead. It feels like an apology.

CHAPTER FOUR

The boy hates him. He can live with that, truly. There are moments—when he observes her happiness, when he's holding her in his arms, when he's tasting her skin—that he remembers it can't last forever. And he hates himself, too.

CALIFORNIA, UNITED STATES
WINTER 1956

JIRO SPRINGS THE QUESTION ON HER MID DECEMBER, THE RAIN OUTSIDE thunderous and his voice deceptively casual. "Is your husband going to be here for Christmas?"

Seven months.

It's been seven months and they still don't get along.

Anna's eyes lift from the page of the novel she'd been reading, studying his expression. He doesn't return her stare, instead flipping the page of the cookbook he's been looking over the past few days

43

while they've been avoiding the torrential downpour outside their walls. Jiro has probably looked over that same recipe a dozen times over by now. Certainly enough that it can't possibly be holding his attention the way he pretends it is. He's more invested in her answer than he wants her to know, but Anna's not sure *why*. She gives him the most honest answer she can. "I'm not sure."

The holidays were never something they bothered to celebrate. The meaning and spirit of them was lost to Anna over the centuries. Occasionally, she would find herself enjoying the festivities when whatever life she had built called for it, but it had always been social rather than spiritual. She participated, but the holiday held no personal meaning to her.

His lips thin in response, glowering into the open pages.

A thought occurs to her—one she kicks herself for not recognizing sooner. "Jiro, do you celebrate Christmas?"

He shrugs. "We used to. My mom used to take us to church every Sunday. Would decorate the house and convince my father to get a tree." A frown pulls at his mouth, bitter longing at the edges. "I think a lot of it was just her trying to fit in, but it was fun."

Anna closes her book, looking around the living room thoughtfully. "I've never had a tree of my own," she confesses, measuring the room and rearranging furniture with her eyes. "Would you be willing to share some of your traditions with me?"

She catches the tiny smile curling his lips. "Sure."

KHIRAN BLINKS, FROZEN IN THE DOORWAY AS HE SURVEYS THE CHAOS. "There's a tree in our living room."

Anna hums, threading a needle through a piece of popcorn. There's a pile of popped kernels in the lap of her dress that she's been alternatively eating and decorating with. Jiro decided to brave the rain to try to find more red hollyleaf berries, so he can finish the strand he started. "There is."

"It's rather large."

She glances at the tree, its peak so tall it curls against the ceiling. "It looked smaller in the forest."

"I see," he murmurs, setting a box labeled *Moulin de la Vierge* beside her before joining her on the floor. "I suppose this is for the boy?"

"A little," she admits, shrugging. "He asked if you would be here for Christmas."

He raises a brow. "Would you like me to be?"

"It might help. Maybe it will encourage you both to connect."

He shakes his head, laughing under his breath. "Your optimism is charming. Hopelessly blind, but charming."

Anna huffs, her needle pausing as she lets her hands drop to her lap. She leans her head against his shoulder. "I just don't understand it."

He reaches for the box between them, opening the lid to reveal neat rows of colorful macarons. When he holds it out to her in offering, Anna closes her eyes and selects one at random. Yellow. She takes a bite, savoring the citrusy sweet taste of lemon.

Khiran selects a green one. "Don't worry yourself over it."

The sound of the kitchen door shutting and the quick fall of footsteps announces Jiro's return. He comes from around the corner, his dark hair wet but his grin bright. "I found some!" His expression falls flat when he sees who sits beside her. "Oh. Your husband's here."

He avoids Khiran's name as much as Khiran avoids his. A petty game they seem wholly uninterested in ending anytime soon.

Khiran's brows rise. "I am."

Anna holds out the pastry box, not above bribing Jiro's mood with sweets. "Macaron?"

He frowns at the rows of colorful cookies as if weighing whether to say no strictly because Khiran brought them. In the end, he grudgingly accepts a raspberry flavored one. Taking a small nibble from the corner, he makes a show of chewing thoughtfully before shrugging. "It's alright, I guess."

Khiran's lips twitch in the corners. Anna can't be sure if it's a smile or a grimace.

Jiro pops the rest of the cookie in his mouth, lips stained with the smug shadow of a grin as he chews.

Khiran returns home late Christmas morning.

Anna knows without asking, that he timed his arrival purposefully. That he took her wish for them to get along to heart, regardless of how little faith he has in it. Under his arm, two gifts wrapped in red paper and gold trimmings snag her attention the moment he walks in the door.

Her lips are turned in a frown when he greets her with a kiss. They had agreed not to exchange.

Khiran smothers a grin. "Don't scold me too severely. I consider yours to be a gift for both of us. I merely had it wrapped for the occasion."

Yours, he had said, which means... Anna glances at the packages, the red paper winking up at her. "And the other one?"

His smirk sours into something that looks suspiciously like embarrassment. Glancing away, he sets the presents beneath the tree. Anna suspects it's strategic; a reason to avoid her gaze when he admits, "I figured it couldn't hurt."

A huff of laughter, and he shakes his head. "I couldn't exactly acquire what you really wanted. Not on my own." He runs a hand through his hair. "I thought perhaps an olive branch might inspire him to meet me halfway."

Warmth curls in her chest, a gratitude that goes beyond what words can convey. She takes his hands in hers and tries, anyway. "Thank you," she murmurs. "Thank you for trying."

The breath he releases is sharp with doubt. "Don't thank me yet. I'm half expecting him to lob it at my face. Or use it for kindling."

Anna knows he won't. For all Jiro's stubborn refusal to give

Khiran an inch of a chance, he won't refuse a gift out of spite. Not when he lived so long with so little. Whether it is received with gratitude or suspicion, however, is a question Anna doesn't know the answer to.

Silently, she desperately hopes for the former.

That hope dims when Jiro comes in from gathering herbs from the garden and greets Khiran with a snide, "so you decided to show up?" in lieu of a hello. Even more so, when their lunch is fraught with tension instead of merriment. Khiran excuses himself to the living room while she cleans up the dishes and Jiro prepares the chicken. Anna suspects his leaving was more for her sake than his own—it's only after he leaves and the tension in the small kitchen eases that she realizes her neck and shoulders are taut with it.

She sets the first plate on the drying rack before moving to the next. The water is warm on her hands, bubbles tickling her wrists, as she runs the dishrag over the china. Anna used to think they were too pretty, too fragile, for their lifestyle—the delicately painted florals twirling around the gold rims. Now, despite having broken several pieces over the years, she's glad for them. The bit of color has grown on her; a spark of joy mapped in scrolling vines.

"There's something for you under the tree," she says, breaking the casual silence. "Perhaps when we're done here, we'll open gifts?"

Out of the corner of her eye, she sees his spine straighten, his head swiveling to face her. "I thought we weren't exchanging."

"It's not from me."

A beat of silence, two, and Anna looks up from her washing. Jiro is frozen, his mouth parted and his eyes searching. There's a confused furrow creasing his smooth brow, but it's eclipsed by the suspicion shadowing his gaze. "Why would he get me anything?"

Anna shrugs, pulling the final plate from the water and setting it on the rack before grabbing a towel for her hands. Turning, she faces him fully, leaning against the apron sink. She can feel the chill of the enameled cast iron through her dress as she dries her hands. Weighing her answer, she eventually settles for the truth. "He understood that what I wanted most is for you two to get along."

Jiro flinches. The trembling beginnings of guilt darken his eyes as his jaw works around words he can't seem to bring himself to speak. Anna suspects they probably resemble an apology.

She sighs. "I don't expect you to like him. There's always going to be people we simply don't get along with—"

"It's not that," he interrupts, the words leaving him in a rush and a flush rising to his cheeks. "It's not—I just don't like how he treats *you*." Anna recoils, but he continues before she can speak. "I know he's not actually your husband."

Anna's lips part, but the only thing that escapes is a soft, "Oh."

Jiro's face flushes, voice hissing like a pot under pressure. "You said you didn't have a family name. Which means he didn't *give* you one." He gestured to her right hand. "And you wear that ring, but it's not on your wedding finger."

Anna blinks, too stunned to feel embarrassed. "You think I'm his mistress?"

Jiro flushes scarlet. "Well, aren't you?" He makes a wide gesture to the walls. "He has you out here all by yourself in the middle of nowhere. And he leaves you alone for weeks, sometimes *months* at a time. He says he's traveling for work, but he's probably got a whole other family on the side!"

Anna brings a hand to her temple, feeling foolish, because of *course* that's what it looks like. She takes a breath, bracing herself. "We aren't married—not in a way the church or government would recognize—but he is mine and mine alone. We never needed a ceremony or a ring to symbolize our commitment to each other, and Khiran doesn't have a family name for the same reason *I* don't. We were both orphans in this world. He didn't—"

"He leaves you up here, all by yourself, for weeks at a time." Jiro interrupts, face twisting as he looks away. "I mean, you went out and hired a stupid kid even though you didn't actually need help, just so you wouldn't be alone."

Anna's heart drops. Tumbles. "Is that what you think?" she breathes, the words bruising on her tongue. "Jiro... I didn't bring you here because I was tired of being alone. I brought you here so *you* wouldn't be." She catches his gaze, holds it with a desperation she knows he must feel. "And Khiran—"

She swallows, wets her lips. The hand towel is twisted in her hands, the embroidered flowers she stitched straining in her grasp. "I can't explain to you the lengths he would go for the sake of my happiness, but please understand: if I wanted him to stay, he would. Even when he shouldn't. Even when he *can't*."

Jiro goes quiet, his righteous confidence melting away into something uncertain. The firm line of his narrow shoulders sags. "I told you I didn't want charity."

"It was never about charity, Jiro. How could it be when I'm gaining something too?" Her chest heaves with the force of her exhale, as if she could breathe out the noose around her heart. "I don't mind being alone, but that doesn't mean you being here hasn't brought me so much joy."

For a sliver of a moment, she thinks he'll argue—that those stubborn defenses she quietly convinced him to shed will rise up stronger than ever. Instead, he looks around the kitchen, eyes lingering on the meal they've been preparing since morning. "So this is my home?"

It breaks her heart that he feels the need to ask. "Yes. For as long as you want it."

He nods, tongue in his cheek. When he meets her eyes, there's a determined edge to his stare. "Then I don't want any more of your money."

Anna blinks, her lips parting around a gentle protest, but he doesn't give her the opportunity.

"If you pay me, it's just a job that happens to come with meals and a roof," he says, voice firm. "I don't want that. Not anymore. I just—I want to be home for Christmas." He takes a deep breath, swallowing, before he adds, "Please."

Anna gives him a trembling smile, her eyes glassy. "Welcome home, then."

WHEN THEY'RE IN THE LIVING ROOM, PRESENTS IN THEIR LAPS, JIRO hesitates. His eyes flit between Khiran and the red wrapping paper. As Anna predicted, he doesn't refuse it, though she's almost certain there would have been a snide remark or two had it not been for their conversation in the kitchen. He rips the gold ribbon, pulls back the paper, and pauses. In his hands is a stack of paper. Anna can make out Khiran's loopy scrawl from the couch.

"The chef at a patisserie I frequent was kind enough to share some of his recipes," Khiran explains, his fingers laced in his lap. "I took the liberty of translating them."

Jiro is silent, removing the rest of the wrapping paper and thumbing through the pages with careful precision. Anna doesn't miss the subtle tremble of his hand. "It's French?"

Khiran breathes a laugh. "Yes. Considering the amount of macarons that mysteriously went missing, I took the risk of assuming you might have had a change of heart."

Flushing, Jiro sets the bound pages on his lap. He glances at Anna, sees the warmth and happiness in her expression and swallows thickly before dropping his gaze to his lap. To his gift. "Thank you," he mutters, the words thick and awkward but no less genuine. "That's... really thoughtful."

Khiran clears his throat, shifting his weight. "Some of the ingredients are harder to come by, but if you're in need of something, I'll do what I can to provide it."

Jiro nods, shifting awkwardly. "I'm... gonna go check on the chicken."

Once he's left, Khiran releases a sigh. "At least he didn't burn it."

Anna shakes her head, placing a tender kiss in the hollow of his cheek. "It was perfect. I'm not sure I could have thought of something better suited." She studies his face. "I had assumed *your* sweet tooth was responsible for my missing macarons. How'd you know Jiro was the one who ate them?"

The corner of his lips twitch into a smile. "You savor your sweets. That box didn't make it forty-eight hours. It was fairly easy to deduce." He nods toward the thin gift in her lap. "Go on, then."

Anna opens it slowly, peeling the paper with careful hands and growing pleasure. "It's a record!" She beams up at him, the light in her eyes teasing. "Were you getting tired of the same ones?" They already had several they played regularly, but the music collection was vastly outnumbered by books.

He takes the album from her hands, grinning as he stands. "I'm afraid my motives were much more selfish."

"Oh?" she asks, laughter coloring her voice.

He pulls the record from the sleeve, the black vinyl winking at her in the light. "Do you remember The Cotton Club?"

The club in New York. Where she danced with him in a dress made of silver beads and magic. Sometimes she thinks about that night and swears she can still remember the sound those beads made when scattered across the floor of her old flat. "Of course I do."

He puts the record on, the empty static from the needle replaced with trilling notes from piano keys followed by a deep, crooning voice. "I've been thinking..."

Anna smiles. "Have you?"

"Yes." He turns to her, taking her hand and coaxing her from the sofa. Anna lets him lead her to the center of the cozy living room. He adjusts his hold on her hand, his long fingers folding over hers while his other splays over her waist. "It's been far too long since I've danced with you."

Her cheek rests against his shoulder, her smile so wide she's certain he must feel it. "I think I stepped on your toes at least five times that night."

"I think I counted seven," he teases, grinning against her crown. He shifts, giving her hand a squeeze and placing a kiss to her temple before dropping his voice to a murmur only she can hear. "Holding you is still worth every bit of pain."

She holds him closer, closing her eyes and enjoying the feel of their bodies swaying. When she opens them, she catches sight of Jiro hovering in the doorway—an odd expression creasing his brow. Anna pauses, lifting her head from Khiran's shoulder. Jiro shifts his weight, awkwardly gesturing to the kitchen. "The chicken is done, I think. If you wanna check it?"

Anna lets her hand fall from Khiran's shoulder, offering him a tender smile. "Save me another dance?"

The scoff that leaves him is warm. "As if I would have anyone else."

She brightens, giving his hand a squeeze before releasing him. "I'll go take a look," she tells Jiro, motioning toward the sofa. "Why don't you and Khiran set up one of the board games? Maybe Scrabble?"

Jiro frowns. "He always tries to cheat!"

Khiran is already fishing the box from the cabinet, rolling his eyes. "I'm telling you, *chapeau* is a type of hat."

"It's French!"

"So is the word *menu*, but I'm certain you'd allow it."

Anna shakes her head. "Jiro, grab the dictionary, would you? Khiran, if it's not in there, you can't play it."

"It would've been there if it were a newer edition," he grumbles weakly.

She turns, heading toward the kitchen, but she catches Jiro's retort (*"then buy one"*) before their voices become too muffled to interpret. Taking a meat thermometer, she checks the internal temperature before deeming it ready to remove from the oven. She sets it on the counter, covering the dish with a lid. She'll let it rest a bit before they carve it and serve dinner. It should give them enough time to at least start a game.

Heading back to the living room, she notices with no small amount of apprehension that they've gone quiet. The only thing she hears is the hollow click of the wooden tiles being set on their trays. She braces herself, fully expecting to find their silence to be anything but comfortable.

Then Jiro's voice, soft as it is, reaches her before she turns the corner. "You really do love her... don't you?"

Anna stills, listening for his response.

Khiran breathes a laugh. "Love is too small a word," he murmurs, "but I suppose it will do."

A smile tugs at her lips, and Anna takes a moment to lean against the wall and *hope*.

THings are improving.

Jiro still tosses an occasional jab Khiran's way, but they feel more pushing than painful. As if the game he started no longer holds any stakes, but he's still playing out of sheer stubbornness. He no longer prods at the parts that hurt—no longer mentions the time Khiran's away or mocks him with a laundry list of the things he missed.

It's a subtle truce, but it's enough to smooth the tension between them into something comfortable. Anna still occasionally catches the teen casting skeptical looks at some of the things Khiran brings home —he was particularly baffled by the samosas. One day, when they're in the garden, he summons the courage to ask her where it all comes from.

"Khiran travels a lot," she answers, a truth so thin it feels like a lie. "The city offers a lot of food options we don't see around here. It's why he makes a point to bring it. He knows I enjoy trying new things."

Jiro frowns, obviously unsatisfied with her answer, but doesn't push. Anna suspects it's only because he doesn't have a better explanation. Three days later, when Khiran brings home a tteokbokki— boiled strips of rice cake served in a spicy red sauce—he makes no comment. Even though Anna can see the questions in his eyes.

Then spring arrives as it has a habit of doing—seemingly overnight and far before Anna feels prepared for it. Most days are spent between the garden and the greenhouse as they fold small plants into the earth and sow new seeds into the tiny pots they've left behind. In the meadows, flowers carpet the landscape in shades of purple and orange. Seeds that laid dormant revitalized by the heavy rains brought by winter. When the weather is especially welcoming, they picnic among the blossoms and watch the clouds move across a crystalline blue sky.

Today, Anna cuts thin slices of cured ham for their sandwiches. Khiran looks through a newspaper in a language she's unfamiliar with at the kitchen table. In front of him are the tiny cucumber finger sandwiches she had put him in charge of. Jiro had snickered at how messy they look—the cucumber sliced in a variety of different widths and the bread trimmed in lopsided triangles. Anna just hopes he followed the recipe card she gave him. The last time he helped in the kitchen, he had put so much garlic in the spaghetti sauce it *burned*.

Anna frowns, looking out the window. "Jiro has been gone for a while."

Khiran turns the page, his face growing darker with every article he scans. "There's more propaganda in here than news," he grumbles. "It's no wonder nobody ever knows what's happening."

Shaking her head, Anna dries her hands on a dishtowel. "It shouldn't have taken him this long to grab some oranges."

A whispered rustle of paper, another page turned. "Perhaps he got distracted." He sets the newspaper down, folding it carefully, before meeting her eyes. "We would know if one of the others was here."

"How?"

"Those with power rarely wield it quietly." There's a bitter edge to the words. It matches the sneer teasing the corner of his mouth. When she still looks concerned, he sighs, standing. "Very well. Let's have a look."

"You think I'm being silly."

"I think you worry because you care," he counters, placing a kiss at her temple. "It's an admirable quality."

The moment they step outside, Anna knows there's something off. It's a feeling on the back of her neck; the emptiness of the garden. She and Khiran share a look. She can tell he feels it, too. Then, she sees the tail end of a path trailing just behind the apiary. It isn't of her making, but she recognizes it instantly. "Khiran?"

"I see it," he mutters.

She looks up at him, a sense of foreboding making her mouth go dry. "Do you think—"

"Everything's fine, I'm sure. Last I visited her, she mentioned wishing to see you. I'm sure that's all this is."

"You've been visiting?"

"I always do, from time to time."

Anna stares down the trail, a thought winding around her ribs like a noose. "Jiro's not in the garden."

One moment, two, and Khiran curses.

EIRA'S HOME IS, AS ALWAYS, THE SAME AS THE LAST TIME ANNA LEFT IT. Smoke curls up from the chimney, the meadow grasses tall and peppered with flowers nurtured by spring rains and budding warmth. Decomposed leaves from seasons past slip, still wet from the morning mist, under Anna's heel.

Jiro is at the edge of the forest, his brows drawn tight as he stares at the house. Hearing them approach, he allows them a quick glance before returning to the meadow—as if it being out of his sight risks it disappearing. "You don't have any neighbors," he says, a tremor of nervousness making his voice shake. "I've been back here with you gathering firewood dozens of times. There's not supposed to be a house here."

The sigh Khiran releases sounds like both defeat and acceptance. "Come on, then. It's too late to hope for discretion now."

Anna winces, watching his back as he follows the trail without them. This wasn't part of their plan. Jiro wasn't supposed to know about this side of their lives. Doubt chokes her, curdling in her gut like old milk. Maybe Khiran was right. Maybe she should have let him find someone to take Jiro in before he could have the chance to get wrapped up in their mess.

"What's he talking about?" Jiro asks.

Anna hates the suspicion in his eyes.

She breathes around the weight on her chest. "You're right," she says, swallowing. "I don't have any neighbors." Because it is far too late to keep this secret.

Jiro studies her. His favorite mask—the one of cool, stubborn indifference—slowly fades into one of wonder. "So this place is...?"

"Magic." The word tastes strange in her mouth. Like it somehow says too much and not nearly enough. "Come on. I'll tell you more once we're inside."

He follows her, his gaze flitting over the meadow as if every facet of it is something to be studied. Khiran has already gone inside without them, but it's just as well. It gives Anna more time to think of how much and how little information she's willing to part with.

"The sun is in a different position," Jiro notes, his eyes wide with fascination.

"We're not in California anymore."

"Where are we, then?"

Anna doesn't have an answer for him. Eira's home has always been a place that folds itself between nowhere and everywhere all at once. It's only the length of the trails and the flora that give her the sense that it lies somewhere on the European continent, but she can't even be sure if that's entirely true. "The Meadow," is the only answer she can give him that feels like truth.

When Anna opens the door, Eira's cornflower eyes immediately go to the extra person in her threshold, frowning. "Well, this is a surprise."

Anna flinches. There is a word hiding between the others, silent but somehow ringing through her chest with the clarity of a bell. *Unwelcome.* "He found your trail before we did."

Eira hums, studying the boy with the same calculating gaze she once pinned on her. Anna remembers the feel of it, the way she wanted to curl into herself in hopes of hiding the worst parts of her.

Eira sighs, turning to Khiran with a scowl of disapproval deepening the wrinkles around her mouth. "I expect this from her, but you should know better."

When he says nothing, she shakes her head. Her gray hair, twisted into a braid at her back, moves with her. "Never mind. *I* should have known. Of course, you couldn't say no to her. Lovesick fool that you are." She pins Jiro with a hard gaze. "Follow the trail back home, boy. I'm afraid this conversation isn't for your ears."

He looks ready to argue, but Eira's stare sharpens before he can voice a complaint and his outrage quickly sobers into resignation. Still, he glances to Anna first.

She offers him a fragile smile. "We'll be home soon. Would you mind getting dinner started?"

Hesitantly, he nods, giving them all one last parting glance before leaving. Eira barely waits for the door to close behind him. Her sigh is like leaves on gravel. "Sit. I wish the issue of the boy was my greatest concern, but it isn't." She pins Khiran with a meaningful stare. "There's news from Edun."

The change in him is instant. His spine straightens, tension plucking at his shoulders, but it's the way his attention sharpens—as if Eira's every word could spell out their future—that alarms Anna the most.

"Edun?" she asks, carefully sinking into one of the chairs. The word somehow sounds both foreign and familiar at the same time. She thinks of the stories about a garden and a serpent, of golden apples and eternal youth.

Khiran wets his lips. He has yet to sit. "It's where The Tree grows."

Anna doesn't need to ask which. When it comes to them, there is really only one.

Eira's scowl could curl paint. "I thought I said to sit? I won't have my neck suffer because you can't be bothered to take your seat."

There's a retort teasing his tongue, Anna can see it in the way his eyes narrow and his lips thin. He manages to chew on the words until they leave him as something different entirely. "Very well," he says, complying to her demand and sitting in the chair opposite of Anna's. She can feel his boot gently toe hers beneath the table. "What news?"

"It's about The Tree," she starts, suddenly looking unsure. Anxious. "They say it's dying."

Khiran's denial is immediate. "Impossible."

"I believed so, too. Had it not come from someone I trust, I might have written it off as a rumor." Her eyes meet Anna's. "But the word came from Silas."

Anna inhales sharply. "You still see him?"

Eira nods. "We've come to an understanding, him and I. We save more together than we do alone."

Khiran laces his fingers, resting pale knuckles against his mouth. "It can't be true. Those were his exact words?"

"He says its limbs are barren of the leaves to shade it. That it looked more skeletal than alive." She leans back into her chair, fingers drumming on the tabletop. "There have been rumors circulating for centuries, but I never paid them much mind. Now, I'm not so sure."

His face darkens. "About the fruit?"

"So you've heard them, too," she hums.

Anna frowns, her brow creasing as she looks between them. "What about it?"

Sighing, he runs a hand through his hair. "I had heard whispers that the fruit was tainted in some way, but it could still just be that. Whispers."

Anna has heard several stories about the tree from which her immortality stemmed. Sometimes Khiran tells it like that—a story. Other times, it will feature in a memory he recalls for her. He has always described it as mighty, but she's never thought to wonder about the logistics. "Does it not have periods of dormancy?"

Eira shakes her head. "Never. Not in all the thousands of years I have seen it."

The silence that falls between them is heavy with questions. Hesitantly, Anna gives the most pressing one a voice. "What does it mean?"

The look Khiran and Eira share, the quiet searching, answers her question before he can. "I don't know, but it has to be a sign that something has changed."

CHAPTER FIVE

Sometimes, he fears her heart as much as he loves it. Fears the way it puts others first and herself second. There is nothing more terrifying than knowing she would put herself at risk to save him.

CALIFORNIA, UNITED STATES
SPRING 1957

JIRO IS WAITING FOR THEM WHEN THEY GET HOME.

Khiran's favorite reading chair, a deep leather wingback, has been dragged across the room and placed right in the entry. When Khiran opens the door, the first thing they see is Jiro's frame sunk into the leather. He's gained weight in the year he's lived with her, but he still manages to look dwarfed in that oversized chair with its polished brass nailheads and lion heads carved, mid-roar, from the armrest. It's a physical reminder that, regardless of how mature he feels, he's still a child.

The second thing she sees is her shotgun—the one she kept in the closet for hunting grouse—across his lap.

He holds it with both hands, ready to snap it up to his shoulder. His finger is painfully close to the trigger as he stares at Khiran. "What are you?"

From his lips, the question feels like a wound. The distrust in his eyes feels like salt. "Jiro—"

"Immortal," Khiran says, cutting her off before she can string her feelings into words. He gestures to the firearm, voice steady but firm. "If you feel safer holding a gun, so be it. But know that while it hasn't a chance of killing me, it *will* hurt, and I will be *incredibly* displeased."

Jiro wavers, a moment of hesitation, before the flash of uncertainty is stubbornly snuffed out by resolve. His grip flexes on the stock. "So, what? You're some kind of god?"

Khiran's answer is carefully neutral. "Something like that."

"Anna named the donkey Loki after the god of lies. Is that you?"

The muscle in his jaw jumps, but Khiran doesn't deny it. "It's one of the many names I've earned over the centuries, yes."

In her chest, Anna's heart gives a painful twist. "Those are myths, Jiro. Stories. They aren't the truth," she explains gently. "Khiran isn't your enemy any more than I am."

For the first time, he looks at her. "He can be anywhere, right?" He spits the question with vehemence, as if the words themselves are coals that have sat in his heart, simmering and waiting to catch. To *burn*. "Isn't that how it works? Why he's always bringing different food home, and it's always still warm?"

Anna doesn't understand the source of his anger, but she knows a lie now would land like dynamite. Cautiously, she nods, grateful when Khiran seems to accept her leading the conversation. "That's one of his abilities, yes."

"Must be great," he sneers. "Like one big party all the time, right? Eat what you want, be where you want. Watch the stupid little humans kill each other for entertainment."

"Jiro—"

"Why do you always defend him?!" he shouts, standing. The

barrel of the gun hits the wood floors with a dull thud. Anna's just relieved his finger is no longer near the trigger. "He's a god! So why the hell isn't he doing anything?"

"He is—"

"Then it's not enough!" He looks at Khiran, anger and pain making his eyes glassy. "Why weren't you there?! Why didn't you stop it? They put us in horse stalls like we were animals! When they finally let us go, we didn't have anything to go back to!"

Understanding softens Khiran's expression into one of pity. "You were forced into one of the internment camps."

With one sentence, Anna sees where his anger stems and the poison starts. There is a feeling of emptiness in her chest, a hollow echo chamber of regret.

"Yeah, I was!" Jiro snaps. "So where the hell were you?!"

She knows exactly where Khiran was.

He was in Germany inspiring mutinies and deserters. Gathering secrets to slip to allied code breakers like buried treasure. Whispering in the ears of journalists and photographers, turning their eyes towards the horrors in hopes that they would tell the world in words and pictures. In China, Korea, Indonesia—bearing witness to horrors he refuses to share even with her.

She knows, because it was her he came home to. Tired and beaten, he'd fold himself into her arms and tell her all the ways he had failed while he was gone. Anna had held him, listened to all the ways the world tore itself apart from the comfort of the little home she had made herself.

Khiran had been overseas, killing himself trying to make a difference. Anna had been here, living her life of gardens and honey, painting and reading. Enjoying a peaceful life in the same state that rounded up anyone of Japanese ancestry and stripped them of everything in the name of national security. It's not Khiran who deserves Jiro's resentment, but *her*.

She tries to swallow, but her throat is so tight it feels like swallowing sand. There's an apology on her tongue that she can't bring herself to speak. It's too weak. Words are too weak.

"I was in Washington," Khiran answers. "In London, Paris,

Osaka, Hong Kong, Berlin. There is nothing entertaining about witnessing what humans do to each other." He softens, resigned to a truth Anna has known for decades. "I cannot be everywhere. Not at once."

Jiro picks up the shotgun, resting the wooden stock against his shoulder and looking down the barrel. Straight at Khiran. "I don't believe you."

Anna steps between them, her hands open. Placating. "It's the truth. We aren't without limitations, Jiro."

His face changes. The hot fury that burned so brightly goes out, his face paling in realization. "You're one of them."

It isn't until the words leave him that Anna realizes what she probably should have from the beginning. He had thought her to be like him—mortal and suffering under the same cruel neglect from gods he didn't believe existed until today. How would he have thought her to be anything else? She has no power, no magic, like the others. Aside from her immortality, there is nothing that excludes her from being strictly human.

"Yes," she murmurs. "And no." She lowers her hands, lets them hang limp at her sides. "I live a very human life, but I don't... I don't *die* like one." Her chest aches around the words, but she can see Jiro struggling to understand the difference. "I've been alive for more than eight centuries. I've helped those I can, how I can, but I only have mortal means in which to do it."

She gestures to Khiran behind her, not daring to take her eyes off the boy she's come to love as family. "Khiran helps how he can, but he does it on a bigger scale. One we can't see, because if we did, it wouldn't *work*."

She takes a step toward him, but Jiro only raises the barrel higher. He aims it at her chest, tears streaming down his cheeks. Anna softens, fingers gently curling around cold steel. "I'm sorry we weren't there to help you when you needed it."

Jiro's teeth clench so hard, Anna can almost hear them groan. "Didn't you hear us praying?"

"No." She hopes he can hear the regret that saturates the word as easily as she can taste it. It sits on her tongue, oily and bitter. "It doesn't work that way."

Even if it did, she knows it wouldn't change the outcome. Their ears would ring with a world's worth of prayers they couldn't heed. Couldn't answer. Anna doesn't need the whispers of more ghosts to drown in.

"Give me the gun, Jiro." It's a request disguised as an order. Anna's voice is too soft, too gentle, to be a command. "We both know you won't shoot me."

"Why not?!" he shouts, voice cracking like glass under pressure. Splintering into a thousand shards, each as sharp and as dangerous as the other. "My father stopped fighting. Gave up. But I'm not like him. I'm not weak." The tears come faster, breath hitching, face crumpling. When he repeats the words, they come out as a sob. "I'm not!"

"No, Jiro. You're not. You've been so strong. That's why you're here. That's why you're still alive." She offers him a smile, a timid, haunted thing that carries more suffering than it should. "Living takes strength, but that doesn't mean you have to do it alone."

A second, then two. The barrel of the shotgun trembles with how violently he's shaking. Then it drops away, the steel thudding against the floor. In the morning, when she looks, Anna knows she will find an imprint of the muzzle on the wood—a scar more visible than the ones on their hearts. For now, she focuses on the boy leaning into her, his forehead against her collar and his tears soaking into the cotton of her dress. Her arms wrap around his shoulders, folding him into her embrace until the firearm drops from his grip completely. His empty hands fist in the cloth at her back as if she's the only thing mooring him. As if letting her go would mean being swept off into the sea.

It's a feeling she knows—*understands.* She holds him closer, tighter, just so he'll know he's not alone in holding on.

Silently, Khiran picks up the abandoned shotgun from the floor. His movements slow and careful as he goes to empty it of ammunition. His brow furrows, eyes meeting hers over Jiro's dark hair, before he angles his body so she can see the chamber.

It's empty.

THAT NIGHT, KHIRAN LAYS WITH HIS BACK TO THE MATTRESS AND HIS gaze on the ceiling. "How did you know it wasn't loaded?"

The question is so soft, it floats. Anna thinks of the hard steel pressed against her chest, of the years of pain that drove it there in the first place. Thinks of the box of birdshot that sat in the same closet as the shotgun. "I didn't," she admits. The confession sounds louder in the dark. "I only—" She pauses. *Knew* isn't the right word —doesn't do the feeling in her chest justice. Knowing implies facts and certainties. Knowing is simple. Easy.

Belief is harder.

"I had *faith* that he wouldn't pull the trigger."

He turns to his side, facing her. She can feel his gaze on her cheek, questioning. Mirroring his position, they lay face to face, with only a sliver of silver moonlight streaming through the window to see by. So close they share the same breath. "It's not your fault."

"I know," she murmurs, but the words are fragile. Weak. Knowing is different from believing. Just because she knows it to be true doesn't mean she *feels* it.

Khiran's fingers thread through her hair, curling at the nape of her neck. "You put yourself between me and the end of a shotgun."

"I don't bleed." The color of his eyes is lost in the dark, but she can see the way they spark. She doesn't let his displeasure shy her from the truth. "You do."

"Don't do it again."

Anna reaches for the hand tangled in her hair, thumb brushing soothing circles over his pulse. "You know I can't promise that."

"Won't," he corrects, the word a resigned grumble against her lips.

She considers it, turns the differences around in her mind the way a child holds a crystal to the window just to watch the light bend and refract, showering the room in a galaxy of rainbow colored stars.

"Won't," she agrees, because choosing him has only ever felt natural, never forced. "And can't." Because shielding him from hurt, from pain, was as instinctual as breathing. She could have hung back, could have held her breath, but her heart would have burned and her lungs would have starved. "Would you do any differently?"

"No," he sighs. "But we've already established that I'm a fool when it comes to you."

Anna's smile is heavy, weighed down by heartache. "Then let us be fools together."

CHAPTER SIX

Never has a choice hurt him so terribly. The goodbye, the forgiveness, in her
*eyes will haunt him—**burn** him—like live coal nestled behind his ribcage.*
The temptation to let it consume him is terrifyingly real, but he smothers it
before it can catch. To stop fighting now would mean losing her, too.

CALIFORNIA, UNITED STATES
SUMMER 1958

WHEN THE DAY COMES, ANNA ISN'T READY FOR IT.

Together, they had made plan after plan for how they would
proceed when The First sent someone looking for them. Years of
discussing and fine tuning an escape, so they could sleep easier at
night. They couldn't be more prepared and, yet, the moment Anna
spies a pale blonde stranger's silhouette approaching their home is
the moment she realizes that—for all they spoke of it—she never
really believed the day would come as soon as it did.

Jiro has been with them for a little over two years. Khiran brought her all the ingredients she requested so she could make him galette des rois for his eighteenth birthday in two weeks, because she knows he's been eager to try it since he stumbled on a recipe in the French cookbook Khiran brought back for him. They're getting along, have grown on each other the way time and circumstance nurtures. Anna is so happy with where her life is, she had stopped believing in the possibility of it ending before it could well and truly *start*.

Khiran never had such difficulties.

He's by her side in an instant—no doubt feeling the fear lancing her heart. One look at the stranger, still only a silhouette of dark leather against pale skin, and he steps in front of her. Shielding her. "Get Jiro. Now."

Questions buzz like a hive in her lungs, urgent and pointed, but she knows better than to release them. There is a time for questions and there is a time for trust. Anna knows exactly where this moment falls.

She runs into the house, her throat tight and her heart drumming in her ears. Jiro's in the kitchen, just like she expected him to be. He looks up from the garlic he's mincing, his expression hardening into a scowl when he sees her.

"What's wrong? Why—"

"You need to come with me," she urges, voice hushed.

It feels like they've talked about this moment a dozen times over, but Anna still flips through her memories of the conversation as if she doesn't know his instructions by heart.

Go to their room. Hide in the crawl space, directly under their bed. Wait for Khiran to find her to either tell her it's safe or to whisk her away.

Jiro's hand is sweaty in hers as she leads him down the hallway. She doesn't release it until she opens the closet and lifts the hatch in the floor. "You go first," she whispers, trying to keep her voice steady. Jiro's expression pales. If he didn't know the severity of their situation before, he certainly does now. "I'll close it behind us, okay? But we need to move quickly."

He swallows thickly, but gives a jerky nod before lowering himself beneath the floorboards. Anna quickly follows, feet first, before reaching up to close the door over their heads. It takes a moment for her eyes to adjust to the dim light, the smell of wood and earth thick in the small space. She's not certain if it's the dark or her rabbiting pulse, but it feels more claustrophobic than she remembers. The timbered floor joists hang so low, she has to go on her hands and knees to clear them.

She finds Jiro's face in the dark and tips her chin in a silent order to follow. As she shuffles through the dirt, the occasional stone biting uncomfortably into her knees, she tries to measure how far to crawl. From the vents under the front porch, she can catch the sound of voices but can't interpret the words. Khiran sounds steady, though. That alone reassures her that, at the very least, they have some time.

After about ten feet, she stops, turning her body so she can lie on her back. Above her head, a chalked 'x' marks the trusses, assuring her that she's in the right spot. Jiro follows her lead, settling beside her. In the dim, his eyes are wide and wild with fear. She grasps his hand, giving it a comforting squeeze while bringing a finger to her lips.

Stay quiet.

He visibly swallows. Nods.

Together they wait, muffled voices the only clue to their fate. Anna stares up at the trusses, her heart beating against her ribs like a drum. Silently, she counts, her lips moving with each number.

Twenty seconds in, the voices quiet. For a brief, blessed moment, she thinks the danger is past.

Then Khiran appears from nowhere, one arm winding around her waist while the other grabs a startled Jiro. Anna sees a flash of blonde hair, hears a furious curse from behind him before space folds in on itself. Jiro's yelp is lost in the nothingness, twisting until it sounds like it comes from another world entirely. Then their backs hit the ground with wildflowers tickling her cheek and Khiran panting over them with eyes so wide, Anna can see her own fear reflected in them.

Jiro pushes himself up, his hair as windswept and wild as his expression. There's an unsteadiness in the way he's standing, a sick sheen to his complexion that tells her his stomach feels as twisted as her own. His legs falter, his body disappearing, half hidden by the tall grass as he retches.

Anna rolls over, bracing herself on her hands and knees and wills her stomach to settle and her vision to stop spinning. Khiran's hand is at her back, rubbing small, apologetic circles.

He releases a breath, the sound so sharp, Anna wonders if he must have been holding it. Standing, he offers her help up. There's a jerkiness to his movements, an anxiety still trembling beneath his carefully controlled mask. "I'm sorry. I know this way of travel is harder on you."

Jiro groans from his spot in the grass. "What the *hell* was that?"

"We're at Eira's," Khiran answers, even though they both know that's not what the teen was asking. "If you're ready, we need to move. Eira's magic will fight against her following, but we don't have long before she forces her way in."

Anna thinks of the stories he's told her—of how the betrayal Eira felt was sharpened by the consequences she had to live with after. Thinks of the flash of blonde, of the way Khiran insisted she hide *beneath* the house, and knows The Huntress does more than track his magic, she's able to *follow* it. This meadow is a reprieve, not a sanctuary. Her heart lurches, her hand finding the crook of Jiro's arm and helping him up. She's still dizzy, her steps clumsy and her world tipping, but she doesn't dare waste time waiting.

They need to get Jiro to safety before securing their own.

"It will pass," she promises. "Come on."

He's still lanky, but the years under her care have added height and muscle to his frame. Anna feels the weight of it now as he bumbles, steps slurred. She pales, turning to Khiran fearfully. There's no comfort in his expression, only mounting horror. This wasn't something either of them had planned for.

Jiro is mortal. The effects of travel are more poignant and lingering longer.

Khiran grabs him, mumbling an apology under his breath and hoisting him over his shoulder.

Jiro groans, his words muffled by the hand covering his mouth. "If I throw up, you'll have deserved it." It's uncertain if it's more a joke or a threat. Khiran doesn't pause in his stride.

Eira meets them at the threshold, her blue eyes assessing the tightness in Khiran's expression and the fear painting Anna's gaze. She looks to Khiran, searching. "Who was it?"

"The Huntress."

"Did she come alone?"

"Yes."

"Good. The last thing we need is to battle time along with her blades." She ushers them inside, nodding toward the boy slung over Khiran's shoulder. "Set the boy in the chair. I'll assist him while you grab what you need."

Anna's hand reaches out, snagging the ancient woman's sleeve. "I don't think he'll make it down the path. Not on his own."

"Silas is already here. We've been expecting you."

Anna's first reaction is one of relief—the uncoiling of a breath held too tight. The second is more subtle. A trickle of unease that grows stronger the longer it sits with her. She has no idea how Silas would have known to be here, but the fact that he is can't possibly be good.

She swallows, nodding, and lets Eira usher her inside. When she meets her old friend's dark gaze, he doesn't smile. There's a tension in the line of Silas' spine, one that echoes danger. The last time she saw him wear such an expression, they were dodging discovery in Louisiana and waiting for the moment their luck was sure to run out.

Jiro sits in an upholstered chair in front of the empty fireplace, his elbows planted on his knees and his head cradled in his hands as he releases a miserable groan.

"The room is still spinning."

Anna flinches. "I know, I'm sorry. I promise it will pass." Her eyes lift to Silas, an unspoken plea.

Watch him?

There's a promise in the solemn dip of his chin. "Go. Khiran is in the bedroom gathering what you'll need."

The tone of his voice, the lack of warmth, makes her blood run

71

cold—the chill of fear dipping so low it *burns*. She releases a stuttering breath, her skin prickling with nerves as she rushes to the bedroom. Khiran is already pulling a bag over his shoulder, a long charcoal coat she doesn't recognize draped over his frame. In his hands is a similar one a few sizes smaller. "Put this on," he says, with the edge of an order. As he helps her pull it over her shoulders, Anna's surprised to find it feels heavier than it should. He catches her look. "I had Eira sew gold into the hem."

Of course. They don't know where they'll be going, let alone how long they'll be able to stay there. Gold is a currency that has no nationality—no borders.

Coat settled on her shoulders, Khiran takes her hand. There are warnings in his eyes, fear tightening the line of his jaw. "We cannot linger, Anna."

She nods, trying to swallow past the tightness in her throat. There can be no long, drawn out goodbyes. No lingering embraces. The safety of everyone hinges on how quickly they leave. "Jiro first," she murmurs. "Silas needs to take Jiro first."

He doesn't deserve the mess he's found himself in—a mortal caught up in the pettiness of gods.

Khiran's hand squeezes her own, the anxious edge of his expression softening. "Of course."

The living room is silent when they return, tension blanketing the room so thickly it's suffocating. Jiro still looks pale and clammy, leaning his weight on the back of the chair, but Anna is relieved to find him standing. She knows Silas' speed and strength is no more than a mortal man's. Had he needed to physically carry Jiro to safety, it would have slowed him down considerably.

Anna takes the teen by the shoulders, tries to commit him to memory while bracing herself for the likelihood that memory is all she'll ever have of him. "Silas has agreed to take you somewhere safe."

Jiro looks between them, shock bleeding into disbelief. He recoils from her touch. "Wait. What are you talking about?! If you think I'm not going with you—"

Anna breaks his hopes before Khiran can. "No." The word is

weighted with regret, heavy on her tongue, but she wills it to hold firm. She can crumble later, when he's safe from all the danger she would bring him. "We're running, Jiro. I don't know when or where we'll stop. *If* we'll stop." The smile she offers is weak. Strained with bittersweet goodbyes. "We—we aren't coming back."

He stares at her, his eyes wide with the trembling beginnings of grief. He's gotten so much taller over the years, they're now eye to eye. His lips part, silently, around words he can't find. After a few failed attempts, he gives up, his mouth closing around a hiccoughed sob as he launches himself into her arms.

Anna's throat goes tight, wishing she had more time to make this farewell last. She hugs him back, her arms winding around his shoulders. Jiro cries into her shirt. Anna tries to find the strength to hold in her own. "Silas is a dear friend of mine," she murmurs, like a promise. "He'll make sure you're taken care of. Don't be afraid."

His lip curls, bitter and full of a pain that echoes her own. "I'm not worried about that. I'd rather be on the run than—" His voice cuts off, the words too heavy to shape. Anna knows what they are without having to hear them.

Than be alone.

There is an ache in her heart, one she knows she will carry with her until the end. She knows how deep a wound loneliness can carve, has spent centuries healing from the scars it had left on her. The few years Jiro had in her care wasn't enough to heal the hurt he's suffered, but Anna can hope that it was enough to give him a fighting chance at finding happiness for himself.

She has to believe he will.

Quickly, she pulls herself from his embrace. Khiran's warning words are a sharp and brittle echo over her heart. *We cannot linger.* She looks between Eira, holding her head high and her expression strong. "Jiro and Silas go first." Her voice holds no room for arguments. Even if it did, she's already hugging Silas goodbye before either of them can protest. She murmurs in his ear, too soft for Jiro to catch it. "Take care of him."

When she steps back, he rests his hand on her shoulder, giving a reassuring squeeze. It feels like a promise. He looks to Khiran. "Seek out Cassius. He'll provide you shelter."

Anna doesn't know who Cassius is, but the effect it has on Khiran is immediate. His eyes sharpen with distrust, the muscle in his cheek jumping with the strain on his jaw. "You're mad," he spits, the words dipped in tar, dark and molten. "If you think—"

"I know it," Silas interrupts, his voice an anchor of calm in the storm of Khiran's fury. "I would not lead her somewhere unsafe."

The stare they share is heavy with a history she doesn't know. Anna folds her hand around Khiran's wrist, fingertips brushing over his erratic pulse. She waits until Silas meets her eyes, softens under her gaze, before speaking. "You're certain?"

His eyes hold no hesitation. "My friend, I would lay my life on it." When Khiran gives no answering protest, Silas meets Eira's impatient gaze. "Chicago."

"Chicago?!" Jiro parrots, the city leaving his lips like a curse. "I'm not—"

"It's done," Eira snaps. Her eyes keep darting to the windows. "Grab the boy and take it."

Jiro flushes. Outraged. "I won't! I refuse!"

"Then you damn both of them!" The words, her voice, are serrated and sharp—biting—in ways only the truth can be. "You will live out the rest of your short, mortal life knowing they will suffer for your stubbornness long after you're in the ground."

The anger drains from him, the flush in his cheeks fading until he's so pale he looks almost ghostly. When he looks at her, horror dilating his pupils, Anna wants to comfort him, wants to scold Eira for her cruelty, but she can't. She can't, because they have no time for convincing. No time for gentle explanations.

"We need to leave. *Now*." Silas says, voice sharp with warning. He holds out his hand, palm up. "We need to run."

This time, Jiro doesn't argue. There are tears clinging to his eyelashes, a thousand apologies and a million regrets that will never be said shining in his gaze.

Anna hears them anyway.

She smiles, hopes he sees the love she has for him. Hopes he can carry it with him.

Jiro takes Silas' hand, lets the god shepherd him out the door. Anna releases a shaky breath, the knot in her chest slowly loosening. He's going to make it. Silas is going to find somewhere safe, and Jiro will have a chance to live the rest of his life without running. Without fearing the retribution of gods he never believed in until that awful moment the truth was forced on him. He can--

"She's here. At the south edge of the forest." Eira stiffens, her eyes finding Khiran's with despair. Her face is ashen. "She's not alone. She brought Malik."

Khiran pales. "The path—"

"Silas is still traveling. I can't change the course until he reaches the end!" Her hands tremble as she ushers them out, her expression stricken in ways that make Anna's heart race. The beat of it so loud she struggles to hear over the pounding beat in her ears. "Start running!" she snaps. "Go north, follow the river! I'll open your path the moment Silas steps off his! Go! Go!"

Khiran's hand clasps her wrist, running to the back door faster than her legs can catch up. She stumbles after him, heart in her throat. Outside, the sun is bright enough to temporarily rob her of sight—a wash of light before bleeding away into reality as her heart knocks against her rib cage.

Over the meadow, a voice echoes. "Still trying to run, Liesmith?" A laugh, sharp as a blade and just as threatening, rolls from her lips. "We both know hiding behind Eira's skirts won't protect you."

Anna looks over her shoulder, searching, but the house blocks her line of sight. Her foot catches on a rock, sending her stumbling, but Khiran's grip is as firm as Eira's scolding.

"Don't look! Just run!"

A groan, earth deep, trembles under their feet. The meadow shivers, an invisible vibration in the roots shaking its grassy heads. It reminds Anna of the husky, rattled warnings of the vipers she'd occasionally find hiding in the rocky outcroppings back home. Then she looks over her shoulder and understands why the ground shakes and the meadow trembles.

Eira's house is rising, lurching and peeling from the earth and leaving behind a crater in the shape of its foundation. It staggers, river rock slipping loose from its bed of mortar on the chimney and rolling off the roof. It hits the ground, shattering like a grenade. Beneath the dirt clogged joists, a pair of legs unfold—thin and wiry things that resemble twigs more than branches beneath the bulky shadow of the cottage.

They look suspiciously like chicken legs.

"What did I say about looking?! Stop gawping like fools!" Eira snaps. A quick glance proves that Khiran looks just as shocked as Anna feels. "Keep moving!"

Anna catches sight of the house charging the intruders, its bulk swaying with every lanky step, before Khiran pulls her away. A few yards and Eira shouts. "The path is open—there!"

Anna can see it. It's just ahead, a stone's throw away. Her lungs burn and her legs ache, but she pushes to go faster. Safety is on the other side of that path, a few more moments of pain in exchange for the freedom to hold on to each other longer. Just a little bit—

A violent crack splits the air, a wave of heat crashing like the tide at her back and sending them sprawling. When she looks up, the cottage is on fire, an inferno of embers and flame. A screech emits from the windows like a serrated whistle of a teapot bursting under pressure.

Eira is already up, dirt streaking her skirt. She pushes against Anna's back, urging her forward, as Khiran pulls her to her feet. "Run, you stupid girl! Before the path closes. *Run!*"

Eira's hands are hot.

Burning.

Anna's eyes find hers. There are cracks appearing over her skin, like pottery left too long in the kiln. They lift away, peeling and floating away like ash on the wind, making her disappear flake by flake. Anna's voice catches, stuck in her throat the way her feet stick to the ground. Eira's words from a lifetime ago ring in her memory.

This house is my heart.

Khiran's grip is tight, a bruising pressure, as he pulls her away.

He knows. He sees it, too. He *must*. "Eira's right," he rasps, "We need to run."

There are tears in his eyes, pooling and unshed. Anna can see the fire, can see Eira, reflected in his gaze.

She looks back at the woman who taught her how to live instead of survive—registers the softness of her smile and the goodbye in it.

"No," Anna says, but her voice is lost in the chaos. She feels Khiran's arms slip around her waist. Feels him pull. "No," she repeats, louder this time. He must hear her—he must—because even she can hear it over the static crackling in her ears. His grip only grows tighter, his steps faster.

Anna fights. "No! We can't—" She gasps, the air knocked from her lungs as her stomach meets Khiran's shoulder, his fingers bruising her thighs with a desperate grip. The trail is a blur under his feet. Anna cranes her neck, searching the stretch of trail behind them.

There is only flame and smoke—only ash.

Anna's hands fist in Khiran's shirt, a sound she doesn't recognize clawing up her throat.

Khiran doesn't slow. Doesn't stop.

Doesn't *look*.

Somewhere between the suffocating pain and numbing grief, Anna thinks it might be better that way.

ANNA DOESN'T KNOW WHERE THE PATH ENDS, ONLY THAT THERE ARE beech trees as far as her eyes can see and the sun looks higher than where it was when they left.

Khiran walks another yard, his steps dragging through the dried leaves littering the forest floor. Finally, he sets her down.

Blood rushes back to her legs, the sensation of pins and needles pricking at the bottoms of her feet. She flinches, leaning her forehead against his chest. She can't bring herself to look at him. "We left her."

Her voice breaks, the words bitter and dark on her tongue. "We *left her.*"

The hands lingering at her hips tighten. "We had to. It was too late. The fire—"

"We didn't," she cries, fists curling against his chest. "We shouldn't have left her!"

"Do you think you're the only one who loved her?! The only one who's *gutted*?! She raised me! I—" A growl, dark and tainted with grief and rage eclipses the words. He turns, his fist pulling back before cracking against the nearest tree. "Damn it!"

Another strike, weaker than the last, and suddenly the coiled tension in his body eases. Wilts. His hand drops away, blood smearing a crimson stain over the pale bark. Slowly, he sinks. Knees planted on the forest floor, he stares at the split skin of his knuckles. "Damn it," he repeats, a murmur brittle with grief.

Anna hears the way his voice catches, can feel the exact moment his pain eclipses his fury. She kneels in front of him, hands shaking as she reaches for him—pulls him into her until his face presses into the curve of her shoulder. There are tears trailing her cheeks, despite her efforts to bite them back. "I'm sorry," she croaks. "I'm so sorry. I —" She can't force the words past the sob clawing at her throat.

It dawns on her that they have never suffered a loss together. In all their centuries, one of them has always been the grounding force to hold the other. Khiran's bloodied hands lift, one fisting in the stretch of fabric between her shoulder blades and the other at the base of her spine. In her arms, he breaks. He breaks and she isn't strong enough to hold the pieces of him together. Not when she's broken, too.

Together, they fall apart.

CHAPTER SEVEN

He knows the woman who raised him. He knows, without a shadow of doubt, that she chose this path for a purpose. Can see the direction she's leading him in as clearly as if she pointed it out with her own gnarled hand. It is only because he knows her, trusts her, loves her, that he follows.

Balkan Mountains, Bulgaria
Summer 1958

Grief is a strange thing. Some moments it's a weight on her chest, a pressure behind her eyes and glass in her throat. Then, when the tears slow and her breath no longer feels like it's being torn from her lungs, everything starts to feel *less*. Numb. It's the difference between fighting against the current and letting the river sweep her away. Struggle and surrender.

Anna thinks it feels a little bit like drowning.

Limbs weightless and cold. Suspended in time while the world continues to turn.

It's hours before they resurface. Anna only knows because the shadows have lengthened, reaching across the landscape like the grasping fingers of a ghost chasing the last rays of light.

Khiran's breath fans over her collar. His arms encircle her, but his hold lacks the urgent pressure that left phantom bruises on her skin. "We can't stay here."

Anna swallows, eyes drifting shut. She doesn't know how she can possibly move when it feels like she's still being dragged down, down, down. How can she run when it feels like she's still pinned down by the weight of an ocean?

He lifts his head from her shoulder, the palms of his hands sliding along her jaw. Red rims his eyes, making the blue of his irises look glassy. "We have to."

"I'm so tired," she says, but the words crack and crumble. They feel as weak as she is.

"Look at me," he murmurs, a thread of a command lacing his voice. It sounds strained. Fragile.

One wrong move and it feels like they both will shatter, but there are no hands Anna trusts more than the ones that hold her now. She looks at him. Sees all the ways his pain matches her own.

His thumbs brush over her cheeks, wiping at tears that have long since dried. "It can't be for nothing, Anna. You have to try. If you don't, if they find us here and they take you, I will never forgive you. Do you understand?" Gently, as if the pressure alone could break her, he kisses her. "Please," he murmurs, the word whispering against her lips. "Tell me you understand."

Raising her hands to grasp his wrists feels like moving through mud. It's so heavy. She's *so tired*. Still, his pulse is a steady beat beneath her fingertips, a reminder that giving up now means giving him up forever. "Where should we go?"

A moment of silence, and Anna feels the fracture on her heart widen. He doesn't know either.

She wets her lips, giving his wrists a small squeeze. "Pick a direction," she offers, with more faith than she feels. It sounds frail even to her own ears, but she's *trying*. Perhaps that's the first step. Blindly choosing a path and pretending to hope there's something brighter at the end of it.

He scans the trees, as if looking for an answer in the maze of swaying branches. "East. We'll head East."

East, Anna thinks, where the setting sun will be at their backs and they can avoid watching the last glimmers of light slip away.

KHIRAN SAYS LITTLE WHILE THEY WALK, BUT HE TELLS HER WHAT SHE needs to know.

The woman hunting them has a name and limits just as he does. Marcia can follow magic to its maker, can twist it into a pathway she can travel, but only if she's ready to catch it while it's in use. As long as he doesn't use his magic, she'll only have mortal means in which to reach them. It means they have time, but Khiran warns that Marcia will know where Eira's path ended. If she gets close enough, she'll still be able to track them the way a dog follows a scent.

They only stop once it becomes too dark to travel. Wherever they are, the night is warm even when the moon paints the landscape in cool silver. It's a small blessing... Anna isn't sure she could have summoned the willpower to build a fire even if it were freezing. Laying on a bed of pine needles, she curls into Khiran's side in a desperate attempt to find some comfort in his touch.

"Do you know where we are?" The murmured question sounds loud in the dark.

The silence that answers her is long enough to make her doubt if he's awake, but the sigh she feels beneath her palm gives him away before his voice does. "Bulgaria. Judging by the beech trees, I'd guess we're in the Balkan Mountains."

She's unfamiliar with this part of the world. If she's ever stepped foot here, it was only ever under Eira's powers. The trip too short to ever get her bearings. "Is one of your hideouts here?" She can't bring herself to say the word *home*.

"No."

Anna remains silent. There's a question burning on her tongue, but she can't bring herself to speak it. Not when they're suffocating beneath the weight of their grief. Not when the sound of Eira's name still twists at her heart.

Somehow, Khiran hears the question she's left unsaid. A grimace pulls at his mouth, the hand on her hip clenching in the fabric of her dress. "We're going to Const—no, they're not calling it that anymore. Istanbul. We're going to Istanbul."

Anna studies his face, measures the way his heart pounds beneath her open palms. "What's in Istanbul?"

Beneath her hand, his chest moves around a sigh. "Cassius."

Anna stares, the meaning behind his words slowly sinking in. It can't be a coincidence that Eira would send them here—so close to where Silas urged them to seek shelter. Anna thinks of Eira's hand, outstretched and disintegrating like ashes on the wind, and feels her throat close and her stomach sour. She suspects the path would have led them all the way to Turkey had the flames not interrupted. That the path stayed open long enough for them to get this far... Eira's magic must have held by sheer will alone even after her body couldn't.

She tries to hide the hitch in her breath, fists her hand in the lapel of his coat to disguise the trembling. It doesn't work. In the moonlight, the pale ivory of her ring glows against the charcoal fabric twisted in her grip, and Khiran folds himself around her. Holds her closer.

Anna wonders how it must hurt—feeling her pain curling in his chest when he's already drowning in his own.

THEY FIND A ROAD THE NEXT MORNING.

Khiran convinces an elderly woman into driving them five hours to Istanbul with charm and a few pieces of gold. The truck is cozy, certainly not ideal for three adults. Anna spends most of the ride on Khiran's lap just so the woman—Albena—has plenty of room to change gears.

Khiran does all the talking, his tongue curling around a language she doesn't understand as they approach the city. He must say something amusing, because Albena's lips pull into a leathery, wrinkled smile as her head tips back. Grey hair peeks out beneath the red scarf tied securely over her head and knotted beneath her chin. She drops them off in front of the arched entrance of the Bazaar, the network of winding streets filled with swaths of people and the heavy scent of spices.

Khiran bids Albena farewell for the both of them, their lone bag slung over his shoulder. The smile he wears drops the moment she pulls her truck back onto the busy street. Replaced by a fatigue so bone-deep, Anna worries it might cripple him.

She takes his hand, their fingers lacing. It's not enough to erase the shadows under his eyes, but she hopes it's enough to remind him that he's not alone. Not here and not in his grief. He gives her fingers a gentle squeeze. It feels like gratitude.

"We need some provisions." He glances down at her, a frown creasing his brow. "When was the last time you ate?"

The smells wafting from the various restaurants have been teasing her since she opened the truck door. "Yesterday morning." She doesn't remind him that it was his last meal, too. She suspects she's not the only one whose hunger was swallowed by despair.

He nods. "Food first, then." A moment of consideration, and he adds, "And coffee."

She's not sure what she was expecting, but the Baazar is huge. A network of brightly painted domed ceilings and a labyrinth of narrow streets filled with everything from a kaleidoscope of mosaic glass lanterns to spices. Large arched windows let in a stream of light over their heads. Cats roam freely, some of them curling up contently in the booths—napping on heaping stacks of vibrantly colored rugs.

Anna takes it in, momentarily breathless by the unexpected beauty of it.

"It's grown over the years, but the oldest parts of the Baazar have been here since the 15th century." Khiran tells her, allowing her a moment to let her eyes wander.

"Grown?" Anna echoes, turning to him curiously. "How large is it?"

He frowns in thought. "If memory serves, there's over several thousand shops." Anna blinks, stunned, and his eyes soften—the corners of his mouth twitching in a shadow of a smile. "I'm afraid you won't be able to appreciate it fully. Not today."

She nods, her eyes scanning the faces in the crowd. "Do you think we're safe here?"

Khiran hesitates. "Marcia will have already followed us as far as the Balkan Mountains. She'll be tracking us from there. As long as I don't give her magic to trace, time is on our side. Our dear friend, Albena, did us a greater service than she realizes in driving us as far as she did."

"Good. That's good." The tension in her shoulders, the unspoken fear coiled around her heart like a noose, goes slack. "Because food sounds like a really good idea."

He breathes a laugh, the sound weak and rough around the edges, but honest.

They stop by a jeweler first. Khiran sells a bit of gold in exchange for lira, the local currency, before he leads them down the winding streets in search of food. At a bakery stall, he purchases a ring of sesame crusted bread called simit. With it already being late afternoon, it's a few hours old and no longer warm, but Anna still enjoys the taste of the molasses dipped bread on her tongue and the crunch of sesame seeds between her teeth.

When they sit for coffee, Anna admires the way it pours from the copper kettle. An orange tabby winds between her ankles, purring when she reaches down to scratch beneath its chin. "There are so many cats."

Khiran sips his coffee, sighing against the rim as the heat curls against his tongue. "They're revered in Islamic culture." He glances down at the tabby, offering his hand. A trilling meow, and the cat pushes its cheek into his crooked fingers. "The people of this city care for them—feed them, provide them shelter. They roam freely and are treated with kindness."

She brings her own cup to her lips. It's thicker than the coffee she's had at diners. It proves to be exponentially stronger, too. She swallows, the rich and earthy taste sitting on her tongue. "It's... bracing."

He takes another sip, his expression as dark as the coffee over the rim of pale china. "Bracing is exactly what I need at the moment," he grumbles.

ANNA FEELS HERSELF GROW INCREASINGLY UNCOMFORTABLE AS THEY GET closer. The grounds are large, the landscaping manicured, but it's the sprawling villa that makes her hesitate. "This is..."

"Excessive," Khiran grumbles. "It suits him."

Anna measures the tension in his shoulders, the hardness of his gaze as he stares ahead. "You're worried."

"I don't like trusting our safety to someone else."

She shakes her head. "It's more than that. The moment Silas suggested it, you hated the idea."

"Cassius is no friend to me," he grumbles, jaw tight. "I have doubts over whether he will help."

Anna watches him, noting the way he doesn't return her stare. "You think he'll turn on us."

Khiran's lips thin. "I think it's *possible*."

"Silas wouldn't have sent us here if he had doubts," she reassures, but the words feel like they're for her as much as they are for him. "That's his gift, right? Knowing when and where to seek safety?"

"Figured that out, did you?"

She shrugs, her eyes drifting back to the Roman style pillars lining the villa's entrance like the ivory keys of a piano. "Once I knew he was like you, it wasn't much of a leap. The way he would stand so still... it was like the swamp itself was speaking to him."

"That's part of it," he admits. "I always believed he was touched by luck as well."

Anna frowns. "Believed?"

"The gifts we receive don't come with guidance. I know I can change my appearance, travel to the other side of the world, merely by wishing for it, but I couldn't tell you how or why." He shakes his head, looking tired. "The Tree gives, but it does not guide."

She lets herself process the information, the sound of their footfall filling the silence between them. Anna hadn't considered that the others' gifts were learned and not taught—that Khiran must have fumbled those first few years to discover his capabilities and limitations. She remembers his confession the night they laid bare beneath her quilt with a storm pelting rain at their windows and a fire crackling in the hearth.

The First wasn't as pleased with my capabilities as I was. He was hoping for power and was instead delivered a boy with parlor tricks.

How hard—how *far*—had The First pushed him in order to pull each and every one of Khiran's gifts to the surface? How long did he continue before he accepted there weren't more hiding away? Anna swallows, her throat dry and her chest tight.

How long was Khiran punished simply for being different from what The First wanted?

His hand finds her elbow, stopping her. There's a question in his gaze, threaded with concern. "You're upset—don't be. It's as you said, Silas wouldn't direct us here if it wasn't safe. Any concerns I have are rooted more in fear than fact."

She searches his gaze, unable to bring herself to correct him. To admit it wasn't the present she was mourning, but his past. Instead, she nods, heart in her throat, and tells him a truth that's easier to part with. "I believe you."

CASSIUS IS THERE TO GREET THEM IN THE COURTYARD, HIS CLOTHING AS decadent as his marble statues and fountains. Gold hoops adorn his ears, a metallic glint in a sea of soft golden curls. His velvet brocade shawl hangs off his shoulders, the ornate trim delicately embroidered with tiny beads and sequins that shine off the rich purple fabric.

His arms outstretch in welcome, his smile blinding. There are dimples playing at the corners of his full mouth. "Brother! What brings you to my corner of paradise?"

Anna falters, but Khiran is already shaking his head. "Not that sort of brother," he grumbles, as if the title is one he'd rather be without. Voice rising, he addresses the blonde. "I'm sure you already know why I'm here."

His smile grows sly at the corners, crooked in ways that tease. "I might, but please don't stop on my account. I'm truly looking forward to hearing it."

Khiran mutters darkly under his breath. Anna can't be certain, but she's fairly sure one of the words uttered was *insufferable*. "I am seeking shelter and your discretion. The First isn't pleased with me at the moment."

"*We*," Cassius corrects, his hand flicking between them pointedly. "I assume you don't intend to leave your lady love out in the cold? Seems wasteful, considering how far you've already gone for her."

Khiran's expression darkens, clouded with warnings. "I am asking on both our behalfs. Any debt owed will be shouldered by me alone."

Cassius chuckles, the sound lighter than the storm darkening Khiran's eyes. "You are ever so careful with your words. I've always adored that about you, you know." His gaze flits over Khiran's shoulder, meeting Anna's stare. "Well, don't be shy. Introduce me to your lovely lady."

Khiran steps to the side, effectively shielding her from the other man's view. "Don't."

His answering smile is coy. "Surely you wouldn't come to my door asking for help but deny me the simple pleasure of at least *looking* at the woman you're so ready to die for?"

Khiran's hand twitches against her own, fingers flexing.

"Don't be so cross, I won't touch," Cassius chastises but doesn't wait for approval. He circles them, crystalline eyes assessing. "She is a tiny thing, isn't she? Like a bird." His gaze flits up, meeting Khiran's bitter glare through impossibly long lashes. "Marcia would find great pleasure in breaking her. You know how she is with her toys."

Khiran says nothing, but Anna can hear the grinding of his teeth —see the way the muscle in his jaw spasms.

Cassius must find it to be as telling as she does. "But you know that, don't you?" He tsks, his stare still entirely too sharp. "That's why you hid her. That's why you're here."

"The Shepherd's suggestion," Khiran grinds out. "I wouldn't have trusted you otherwise."

The shift in Cassius is immediate. "Silas sent you?" Lips thinning, he gives a quiet scoff. Somehow it sounds more fond than irritated. "Of course he did. He knows I have a soft spot for star-crossed lovers."

He crosses his arms over his chest, leaning against the wall at his back. "I'm surprised you listened. I never knew you to be friendly with anyone other than—"

Khiran flinches, the tendons in his hand straining as his hands fist so tightly, Anna wonders if half-mooned bruises will line his palms once she coaxes them open. "I'm not," he snaps, before Cassius can let Eira's name slip past his lips.

Cassius looks skeptical, but then his gaze shifts, looking at Anna with new light. "You?"

She tips her chin proudly. "He's my friend."

A bark of laughter, so sharp it makes Anna jump. "Friend?" he drawls, the word steeped in a sarcasm so thick, Anna can almost feel it. "You are but a moment to him, Little Bird. Not all of us are so foolish as to hand our affections over to someone so fragile."

Anna blinks, lips parting. Khiran must see the confusion in her expression, because he whispers her name like a warning.

She doesn't heed it.

"Fragile?"

Beside her, Khiran curses under his breath as he quickly places himself in front of her—blocking her from Cassius' view. Anna peeks over his shoulder, standing on her toes, and catches a glimpse just in time to see Cassius' smile fall.

"Whatever accommodations you can spare would be most appreciated. We—"

Cassius waves a hand as if sweeping the conversation away entirely. "No, no. Forget all that. Bring back your lady friend. I want to speak to her."

Khiran's jaw flexes. "No. We need shelter. You will either grant the request or turn us away. There is nothing else to discuss."

Hands covering over his closed fist, Anna steps out of his shadow and stands at his side. "Silas trusts him," she says, a quiet reprimand. "We can too."

He disagrees. She can see it hardening the edges of his gaze, drawing his brows into a furious frown. In her hands, his fist trembles. She gives a gentle squeeze, holding his stare. "Together," she whispers. A promise and a reminder.

When she turns to face him, it's clear Cassius has watched the interaction with rapt attention. His blonde brows rise, equal parts invitation and dare. "Who are you?"

"I'm... just Anna."

"Don't be coy. As lovely as it looks on you, I'm not in the mood for games. Particularly when you come into my home claiming friendship to someone I hold dear."

"It's the truth."

"Is it? Why should I believe you?"

Anna frowns. "Why wouldn't you?"

Cassius tips his head in Khiran's direction without breaking eye contact. "Do you know what we call your lover? The *Liesmith*. He's been here less than five minutes and he's already proving worthy of his title. Why should you be different?"

Beside her, Khiran bristles. Anna's stare hardens. "He's trying to protect me," she counters. "Honesty is an easy sacrifice when you're afraid."

Cassius studies her. "But you're not afraid, are you? Why is that?"

She shrugs. "Silas trusts you. I trust Silas. Even if we weren't friends, he would never lead me to harm. It isn't who he is."

"How… simple."

Anna thinks of the evening Khiran came back to her, a peach in his hand and an apology in his gaze. She glances at him, relieved to find him more resigned than angry. She offers him a small smile. "The truth usually is."

"Adorable." The word falls flat. "In a naïve, mortal sort of way." Cassius looks between them, no less wary. "Very well, then." He holds out a hand between them. "It is an honor to meet you, Just Anna, Friend of Silas."

Anna puts her hand in his, his palm warm against her own. Something in his crystalline eyes—a spark of mischief—is her only warning before his grip tightens and he *pulls*. She stumbles toward him, Khiran's snarl echoing in her ears as Cassius' mouth covers her gasp.

It's a fleeting touch, too unexpected to even fully register it. She jerks away, relieved to find his hold on her loose enough to escape.

Khiran's hands are already at his throat, his knuckles white against the dark silk of the other man's shirt and his fury electric. "Undo it," he growls. "Undo it *now* or I promise you, death will not come swiftly enough."

Cassius doesn't seem at all intimidated—he's too busy staring at *her*. "There's nothing to undo," he murmurs, his brow lined with shock. "What have you done?"

Heat blossoms in her chest, vivid and sweltering, the lingering shock melting away like a candle in a blaze. Anna has no idea what he was trying to accomplish—she's not sure it matters. Not when he tried to use *her* to do it. She stalks toward them, spine straight as she pushes Khiran aside. She thinks she hears her name on his lips as his grip loosens from the other man's shirt. It sounds like a question. Anna can't be sure, not when the blood is rushing in her ears.

Her palm stings with bitter satisfaction as it connects with Cassius' cheek.

There are so many emotions clamoring in her chest, tangled in knots on her tongue. She spits out the one that rings loudest; the one too tough to swallow. "Silas calls you a friend," she fumes. "He would be *ashamed*."

Cassius sucks in a breath, so soft she almost misses it. The way he stares down at her, shock twisting into something she can't recognize. Maybe it's guilt. She hopes it is.

The pain in her palm is already gone. She almost wishes it wasn't. It would help distract her from the disappointment, the *worry*, that's creeping in and slowly suffocating her fury.

Khiran's hands cradle her jaw, turning her to face him and searching her answering stare for something she doesn't recognize. When Anna reaches for his wrists, a gentle hold, the sigh he breathes is full of relief. His lips kiss her forehead, more firm than tender. Anna can feel the lingering traces of fear in it.

"Come," he murmurs, fingers threading through her own. "We'll find somewhere else."

"No," Cassius says, cutting in. "Stay."

The look Khiran shoots him is as sharp as murder. "You tried to influence her."

"And it didn't work," Cassius snaps, hand gesturing to her. "What *is she*?"

Khiran doesn't answer. Anna watches the muscles in his jaw strain, but there's something in the way he looks at her... the starting thread of a question he's too afraid to unravel.

He doesn't know.

It dawns on her, then. The level of fury in his voice—the *relief* when he looked in her eyes and she was still herself. Whatever Cassius had been trying to accomplish, whatever magic he attempted to snare her in, Khiran had fully expected him to *succeed*.

The Heartsinger. He's The Heartsinger.

The realization is jarring. His hold on her hand tightens. A warning. Whatever the answer is, it's for them to figure out and Cassius to wonder.

Only, they don't take more than two steps before he's shouting at their backs. "Do you think you're the only one who opposes him?! The only one who wishes to see him gone?!"

Khiran's shoulders stiffen, his answer tired. Resigned. "I'm not fighting for a side. I'm fighting to *keep her safe.*"

"One doesn't exclude the other! You wish her to be safe? *Destroy the threat.*"

Khiran laughs.

Anna finds no joy in the sound. It's dark and twisting, settling like a cold stone in her gut. Goosebumps prick her skin, a chill tracing up her spine like a caress. There is something desperate flirting at the edge of his voice. She's afraid to wonder how hopeless the suggestion has to be to inspire such a sound.

Cassius glowers. "It's possible. If we—"

"Stop," Khiran says. "Just stop. We're leaving. Feel free to fight your war without us."

"Silas is more than a friend to me," he calls out, voice ringing across the empty courtyard between them. "He has been for centuries. You are not the only one hiding to protect the person you love."

Anna draws a small breath, her steps faltering, because *of course he is.* The way Silas' voice dipped lower when he said his name—the unwavering faith that it was true. Then she remembers the night they shared conversation over the fire during those years Khiran adamantly refused to share his secrets with her.

How Silas agreed, to her great disappointment, that she was safer not knowing.

She can tell the exact moment when Khiran realizes they aren't leaving. The tension in his shoulders shifts, disbelief temporarily smoothing the angry crease in his brow. "Anna, *no.*"

But they *must.* She can feel it, down to her marrow, that staying is the right choice. The *safest* choice. It screams in her ears like cicadas in a Louisiana summer and, for a moment, she's back on that creaking front porch with Silas' words nagging at her heart.

It's you. You're the secret.

A secret Silas kept, even when it meant keeping it from perhaps the one person he cares for most.

"I'm not mortal," she confesses. Khiran's jaw flexes, as if he's biting back a curse or six. Anna's sure she'll hear them later. "I haven't been for over eight centuries."

A moment, no more than a few seconds, of silence. "He stole a peach for you," Cassius breathes. His focus shifts, landing on Khiran with new understanding. "No wonder you're running. The First must be furious."

Khiran doesn't meet his gaze. "I'm not convinced he knows."

The word *yet* hangs between them, ominous and sharp. A blade still sheathed, but there's the sense that an executioner's hand is ready on the hilt.

Cassius nods, expression solemn. "I see. Then I vow to do everything in my power to keep it that way." He makes a sweeping gesture to the grounds behind him. "Please, stay. I apologize for my behavior, but please understand the position I'm in as well. Hard to trust a garden snake when surrounded by vipers."

Anna gives Khiran's hand a squeeze. A message of support and perhaps a hint of an apology. "Thank you. I understand."

Khiran's expression twists into something dark. "No, you *don't*," he growls. "He tried to *possess* you. You would have been hanging on his every word, love-drunk and stupid. If he asked you to jump, the only question that would break through the magic is *how high*."

Cassius rubs the back of his neck, cringing. "For the record, I had no intention of doing anything untoward. I simply needed assurances of your honesty."

"You had no right," Khiran snaps.

"My lover's name left her lips. His safety weighs more than my morality. Surely, you can understand that?"

When Khiran remains stubbornly silent, Cassius sighs. "Things aren't as they were before you left. This past millennia... you can't take a moment to look at the stars without fear of someone going for your throat."

Frowning, Khiran scoffs. "It's always been like that."

"Maybe between his favorites, but the rest of us? Those that were content living on the outskirts? Brother, something is happening. The Tree—"

"Is dying," Khiran finishes. "I've heard."

Cassius raises a brow. "And the fruit?"

"What of it?"

"They're gone. Each one rotting from the inside, slowly. He's tried, several times, to increase our numbers over the years. The magic didn't take." He looks to Anna, studies her as if she holds all the secrets he covets. "Eight-hundred years you said? Strange that you just happen to be the last to receive its gifts. Don't you think?"

Anna inhales sharply, the shock of it like ice water. Beside her, Khiran has gone stiff. It's only the intensity of his stare, the way he searches Cassius' expression for any sign of falsehoods that convinces her that it's news to him as well.

"A coincidence. It has to be." Khiran shakes his head, his hold tightening on her hand. "I stole a peach. Nothing more, nothing less."

"Come now, Brother—"

"Stop calling me that."

Cassius continues as if never interrupted. "We're too old to believe in coincidences."

"I didn't do anything to the damn tree."

"I didn't say you did."

"Then *what* exactly are you accusing me of?"

"Of stealing a peach. *The* peach." Cassius makes a wide, sweeping gesture. The smile he wears is sharp. Ready for a battle neither of them are prepared to face. "There's only one that left The Tree without The First's blessing. One. And she just happens to be immune to my gifts? Don't you see?! You set it all in motion, whether you realize it or not. We are going to rip the throne away from him, and she's going to be the reason we succeed."

"You're still a fool," Khiran sneers, but it sounds more tired than sharp.

"Funny, because I don't remember you being such a coward."

"I could kill you."

"And I could kiss you," Cassius counters, "but that would be incredibly rude being that you're spoken for." His eyes linger on her, bright with hopes and sharp with vengeance. "I suggest we behave ourselves, at least for dear Anna's sake."

CHAPTER EIGHT

He has every reason to distrust him—has carried the burden of his betrayal longer than Anna has drawn breath. He had come, prepared to sacrifice his pride and consider the possibility of forgiveness. Such generous intentions shattered when the fool pressed his lips to hers and tried to lure her into a war that isn't hers to fight.

Istanbul, Turkey
Summer 1958

"You shouldn't have agreed to stay."

They're in the private rooms Cassius has lent them, surrounded by delicate silks and plush velvets—brass and marble. Their host seems to have more opulent tastes. Comparatively, it makes the treasures Khiran has collected over the years look more sentimental than lavish.

Anna shrugs off her jacket, feeling oddly out of place as she hangs it on the gleaming scrollwork that makes up the coat rack. She's missing her wooden pegs and the painted leaves that weaved between them. "Where else would we have gone, Khiran?"

"Anywhere." He doesn't bother hanging his coat, instead tossing it over the arm of a marble statue that looks like something a museum would spend a good amount of money on to add to their collection. "He wants to start a war," he growls, the soles of his shoes slapping against the polished stone with every pacing step. "Worse, he's got it in his head that you're going to magically seal his victory."

She takes a seat on the red velvet sofa, reaching down to remove her shoes. "Maybe I will."

His head snaps toward her, steps faltering. A second, perhaps two, and his searching look hardens. "Don't joke. Not about this."

Sighing, she leans back into the cushions. It's uncomfortably stiff, built more for looks than for comfort. "Would it be so terrible?" she asks. "Standing up to him?"

"You can't *possibly* be asking me that. Anna, victory could be written in the stars, and it still wouldn't be enough to convince me to risk *you*."

For a moment, she says nothing. Her fingers busy themselves with tracing looping designs in the velvet before chasing them away with a swipe of her hand. "Do you think he's right?" she murmurs, breaking the silence. "About me being different?"

"We're all different."

"You know that's not what I mean." When he doesn't answer, she continues. "Silas was surprised when I told him I didn't have a gift beyond immortality, but you never mentioned it."

"I thought the peach must have been weakened," he admits, running a hand through his hair. "That perhaps the magic in it faded the longer it was plucked from the branch."

"And now?"

"My opinion hasn't changed." He glances at her hand, resting on the ring encircling her finger. "There are other factors to consider."

Anna reaches for it, running her thumb over the shallow etchings. The only jewelry he ever gave her. The one he insisted she never try to remove. Out of habit, she starts turning it and watches the way the light catches on the designs. "You said it hid me from their sight."

"Marcia—" he cuts off, but Anna hears the rasp in his voice and thinks of ashes on the breeze. Thinks of how Eira's last word was *run*. He clears his throat. "The ring masks your magic with my own."

Her fingers slow to a stop, his meaning sinking into her like ink bleeding across a page. "You think in hiding me, it's suppressing whatever gift I may have."

There's an apology in the way he flinches. Looks away. "It's possible."

Possible, because there's no way to know for sure. Not unless...

Her grip on the ring turns tight. She can feel the etched edges pressing against the pad of her thumb. She hadn't felt any different after she tasted immortality, but how would she if she didn't know to look? Khiran had told her the magic was something that was discovered, maybe in the scant amount of time between burning on a pyre and slipping the ring of bone on her finger, she had a subtle power that was all her own, but never knew to look for it.

The only way to know would be to break free and sever the tie.

Khiran must see her thoughts, because his expression darkens. "It's not worth it."

"I know," she murmurs. The words feel honest even as she says them. Perhaps there is some unknown power buried within her, strangled into quiet submission by the ring of bone that sits, snug on her finger. It wouldn't be worth trading what she has for it.

The thought of being separated, of him being unable to find her, terrifies her in ways she's never had to think about. She's not sure there is a power worth trading that for.

"I would be lying if I told you I wasn't curious—that I didn't wish to know where your power ends and mine begins—but it doesn't matter," she says, hoping he hears the truth in it. "Not when the cost is you."

He softens, the grim warnings in his scowl melting into something tragic and warm. The space between them shrinks into nothing as he kneels in front of her, his hands folding over hers on her lap. "I would give it all up, Anna. My immortality, my gifts, all of it. If it meant you would be safe. If it meant we could greet every morning without fear of what the day might bring." His hands slide forward, arms wrapping around her waist. Anna mimics the motion, pulling him closer, closer, until his face is cradled in the crook of her neck and her hands tangle in his hair. His words are a whisper over her heart. "I would give it all."

Anna knows. She knows, because she feels the same way about him.

THE DINING ROOM IS AS LAVISH AS THEIR ROOMS. THE MOLDINGS ARE gilded in gold and frame the floral murals decorating the ceilings in soft pastels. A crystal chandelier hangs over the long polished wood table, its warm light illuminating a feast ill suited for only three people.

Cassius plucks a grape, his mouth curving into a sly smile. "I admit you've surprised me, Brother."

"Stop calling me that." The sharp edge of Khiran's voice is dulled by the way the words echo around the brass goblet at his lips. It's his third helping. Anna has no doubt he'll be going for another refill before their meal is finished.

Tsking, Cassius sends Anna a conspiratorial look. "You see, this is why the idea of him settling down with someone as lovely as yourself is a struggle to wrap my mind around. He can be so terribly stubborn."

Anna bites back a smile, helping herself to some pheasant. "I'm afraid we both are." She sends Khiran a fond smile. He doesn't return it, but she can see the subtle softening of his expression. "Sometimes I think that's why we work so well."

Popping the grape into his mouth, Cassius looks between them curiously. "You must tell me, Sister—may I call you Sister? I feel like we're already family, at this point." He plucks the carafe of wine from the table, ignoring Khiran's glare and reaching over to refill her goblet despite it still being half full. "Was it love at first sight? It must have been, surely?"

Anna blinks, uncomfortable. A quick glance proves Khiran intends to offer no help in answering. He's too busy taking a long drink. "No... I—we weren't..." She flushes, heat prickling her cheeks. Picking up her glass, she takes a quick drink to hide her embarrassment. "It took a while."

"Oh? He courted you as a human, then?" He tips his drink in the other man's direction in a casual sign of respect. "Bold choice, Brother. You know how fragile they are. Smart, though, taking your time before committing to eternity. Very thorough of you."

Khiran refills his glass, pretending not to notice Anna's pleading looks and ignoring Cassius altogether. "He was a stranger, actually," she says, irritation smothering whatever embarrassment she felt. "I'd never seen him before."

"Really?"

"I saved his life. It was all very heroic."

"She *thought* she was saving me," Khiran amends. Strange how the conversation suddenly interested him enough to contribute to it. "Obviously, I was fine."

"He made a very convincing damsel in distress."

"I think love at first sight was an easier explanation to believe," Cassius murmurs. There's a frown pulling at the smooth line of his brow. "You truly gave the power of a god to a stranger?"

Khiran looks at her, gaze softening. "She was worthy of it. More so than any of us. She still is."

A soft laugh, more whisper than sound, escapes him. "My, perhaps you're a romantic after all, Brother."

To Cassius' obvious delight, Khiran only responds with another swift glare.

"What about you and Silas? He never told me," Anna asks. In truth, she's a little hurt that he didn't. She would have thought that having their secret entrusted to him would encourage trust in return.

"Ah," Cassius murmurs, setting his drink down. "You mustn't blame him. We made a promise to each other, Silas and I." He hesitates, as if weighing how much of himself he wishes to show.

"Having the rest of our twisted family knowing... well, let's just say it hasn't worked well in the past."

Khiran's gaze snaps up, interest piqued. "Psyche?" Cassius doesn't answer, not with words, but the way he flinches is telling. "I thought it was just a story."

Anna's gasp is small and silent, a breath of recognition. Psyche, the mortal woman who married a god she was never supposed to see. Who had to earn her husband back, prove her love for him, through trials after she gave into the temptation of gazing upon his face.

Cupid. She was married to Cupid.

She tries to remember the details of how the story ended, but all she can recall is that it was happy in ways few myths are. Psyche was given immortality as a reward for her loyalty, so she could remain at Cupid's side for all of eternity.

"Everything is a story, you know that. Just as you know they're usually more fiction than fact," Cassius says, watching his wine swirl in his cup. "You were right to hide her, Brother. Right to give her immortality without asking for it. The First does not care for any love he cannot claim."

There is a subtle shift, a softening in the line of Khiran's shoulders. "I'm sorry. I didn't know."

Cassius scoffs, the sound bitter and dark. Jealous. "No, you wouldn't. You've been free to roam the world as you see fit, so long as you follow the simplest of rules. Do you know, I tried for decades to follow in your footsteps? No matter how much I enraged him, he wouldn't cast me out. Why is it you always seem to get away with what I cannot?"

Leaning back in his chair, Khiran sighs. "My strength, my power, is influence. Even without his shackles, I cannot control others the way you can." A scoff escapes him, bitter and curling at the edges. "What good is influence to him, when he can utilize force?"

Cassius hums into his cup. "He never has been one for subtlety."

"No," Khiran agrees. "He hasn't."

When Cassius looks up, there is a sharpness in his gaze that Anna recognizes all too easily. A hunger for a war that has yet to begin. "All the more reason to rid ourselves of him."

"And I suppose we'll accomplish world peace while we're at it? Solve world hunger?" Khiran challenges, the words dripping in sarcasm.

"Be serious, Brother."

"*Stop calling me that!*" Khiran snaps, standing. Violently, his fists meeting the table with enough force to make the plates and silverware jump. An apple, polished and red, falls from the fruit bowl and rolls across the table. "We are not *brothers*," he growls. "There are precisely three people in this world I consider family. One has been slain, burned from this world so thoroughly that I don't even have ashes to remember her by. Now, you sit there, calling for a war we cannot hope to win, and asking me to risk the one person I would die before losing." He shakes his head, disgust twisting his features. "You are not a brother. You are not even a *friend*."

Cassius stands, blue eyes darkening. "You are still that self-centered, selfish little boy I watched grow into a stubborn man who thinks only of the consequences for himself and not others. Do you think I propose a war because I have nothing—*no one*—to lose?!"

"Whether you want to claim me or not, *Brother*, we have tasted immortality from the branches of the same tree. We are bound by the same poisonous hand. What can we possibly be, if not family?"

"You, all of you, are the cowards who stood and *watched*."

Anna doesn't understand, but the way Cassius blanches—the way the fight drains—makes it clear that he *does*. "You're right," he says, voice trembling. "You're right, and I'll never stop being sorry for it, but I am trying to be better than I was. To do better."

"How touching," Khiran sneers, the words barbed like wire. If he was to stretch any tighter, she thinks the coil would snap. Khiran tosses his napkin to the table. It lands, wrinkled from how tightly he strangled it in his grasp, on his untouched china. He offers her his hand, eyes silently begging her to take it, so they can leave.

Anna does, her eyes flitting between the two men carefully.

"Wait," Cassius calls out. "At least stay the night. Have breakfast in the morning. Gather your strength before you leave."

"Thank you," Anna says, before Khiran can decline. She can feel the tension in him, coiled tighter than a spring. She doesn't trust that his answer would be inspired by logic instead of emotion. "We'll see you tomorrow at breakfast."

Gratitude colors Cassius' expression. "I'm glad to hear it. Please, sleep well. If you have need of anything, you have but to ask."

Anna nods, unable to meet Khiran's gaze as they turn to leave. She can feel his glare burning into her cheek. His grip on her hand is tight enough to bruise, but she doesn't flinch away from it. She lets the pressure steady her as they walk across the courtyard, the breeze cool against her face and the sweet scent of ripe figs and apricots perfuming the air.

"You're angry with me." The words are an offering. Not quite an olive branch, but an invitation for him to say what she knows must be burning on his tongue.

"Yes," he growls, but another two steps and he shakes his head. "*No*. It's smart to stay." His jaw flexes, his gaze dark with an ancient anger. "I'm just furious that we must."

She squeezes his hand. It's supposed to be a sign of support, but his grip immediately loosens as if taking it as a hint. Anna uses it as an opportunity to lace their fingers. "We'll make a plan in the morning," she promises. "About where to go next."

He brings her hand to his lips. The kiss on her knuckle, just above her ring, feels like an apology. "I cut your dinner short. Did you have enough to eat?"

"Says the man who only had wine," she chides, sending him a pointed look.

Khiran's lips thin. "I found myself without an appetite."

They reach the door to their suite. Khiran dutifully holds it open for her. Anna's fingers trail over a marble bust that looks suspiciously like it might have been made in Cassius' image. She waits for the door to close before she asks, "What happened between you two?" Looking up, she tries to untangle the emotions playing across his face. "You were reluctant to come here from the beginning and just now, at dinner—"

"He is one of the favorites," he says softly, as if the words were a confession. "When I was too young to know better, I used to hate him for it. When I grew old enough, I learned to fear it. Cassius wants to start an uprising, but what he hasn't told you is that he isn't the first."

Anna's hand falls to her side limply. She thinks of all the times he told her he had fallen out of favor. Thinks of lavender fields in France, the names he claimed as his.

I am Loki, the god of Lies. Eris, the goddess of strife. Lucifer, Wisaked-jak, Eshu, Anansi, Hanuman.

Lucifer.

The angel cast from Heaven. Only it wasn't Heaven he was really cast from, but Edun.

"It was you," she breathes. Searching his face, she knows she's right. Anna frowns, teeth biting into her lower lip in thought. "Cassius... he didn't want to join you?"

Khiran's laugh is soft but sharp. A needle hiding beneath a layer of wool. "No, but I could forgive him for that." He shakes his head, mouth twisting in a sneer. "It was his kiss that exposed me. All my plans, my ambitions, laid bare at The First's feet. Cassius watched me fall, knowing he was in part to blame, and he did *nothing*."

THE MORNING IS COOLER THAN THE DAY BEFORE, BOTH IN WEATHER AND in tempers.

Gunmetal clouds sit, heavy and brimming with a summer rain yet to fall. Anna almost wishes the sky would open up and let a river of water wash them all away. It would be a good distraction and an even better conversation starter. Sitting at the table, the array of food ranging from the simit she tried yesterday and filled pastries called börek, to fresh fruits and a spread of different cheeses. The silence weighs heavier than the clouds outside.

She lowers her eyes to her plate, pretending to concentrate on the way her knife slices through her baked fig drizzled in honey and clotted cream. It's only the sound of silver on china that assures her that the two men she's sharing a meal with are eating at all. Even with the palpable tension, she feels a small amount of relief at the sound. At least Khiran is eating this time.

Cassius is the first to break the silence. "You're wrong, you know," he offers quietly. "It's not that I'm eager, it's that I'm desperate." His gaze drifts to her, heavy with the kind of grief Anna recognizes in herself. The dull ache of someone long lost.

His eyes drop away, finding Khiran's once more. "Silas and I— it's just a matter of time before we're discovered. It's a small miracle we have hidden our affections for as long as we have." He takes a bracing breath, releasing it slowly. "When we are, I imagine we will find ourselves much in the same position you find yourself in now."

Cassius sighs, resting his chin in the curve of his cupped palm. "I understand your reluctance. You have every reason not to trust me. Why would you? But right now, as it stands, we are fighting for time. I only suggest that, if we must fight at all, we should fight to win."

Khiran's stare is long, weighted with a history so much older than herself. Finally, he puts his silverware down and asks, "Do you know why I stole it? The peach?"

"I assume it was your way of getting back at him."

Khiran's scoff is colored with dark amusement. "Perhaps in part. Mostly, I just wanted to know if I could. Was ready to pay the price if I couldn't."

"What are you trying to say?"

"I have been expecting the end for over a thousand years, Cassius. The only thing I want now is to live the last of the time I have left with the person I love most."

"You'll spend the rest of your time running until she catches you?"

"If I don't use my magic, she'll have nothing to trace."

Cassius frowns, but it's not judgment clouding his eyes so much as bafflement. "You'll live as a human?"

"Why not? Anna has managed to do it for centuries." Under the table, his fingers tangle with hers. "It is a worthwhile trade, if it means spending our remaining time together, in peace, instead of risking everything in a war I know we cannot win."

Cassius' breath leaves him, long and deep. Anna can see the way his chest sinks around it. "I disagree," he starts, carefully mapping out his next words, "but I understand. Whatever you need, to get you to that peaceful place, say the word, and it is yours."

Khiran tips his chin. "Thank you." He twists the stem of his spoon between his fingers, the metal flashing with every turn. "What makes you so confident that we stand a chance?"

The grin that spreads across his face is sharp, forged with spite and dripping in secrets. "Silas and I have been working together on something. You'll forgive me for not disclosing what."

Khiran stares, searching, before he shakes his head. "It's not enough," he says, the words soft enough for Anna to hear the honesty in them. "I'm sorry."

Cassius nods, raising his glass in a solemn toast. "May our futures shine more brightly than our pasts, my brother." He takes a long drink, a sigh escaping him as he sets it down on the table. His finger traces the rim. "You should know, before you leave, The Bladesmith is dead."

Khiran's hand stills, an olive halfway to his mouth and his voice breathy with disbelief. "*What?*"

Cassius' pale eyes are sharp with warnings. "It happened years ago. The First believed she was conspiring against him."

Anna looks between them, her own meal now forgotten. "The Bladesmith? Isn't that—"

Khiran's expression darkens, returning the olive perched between his fingers to his plate. "Ying. In her hands, with her blood, she forged weapons capable of killing gods." A muscle in his jaw strains. "What was she accused of?"

"Attempting to forge a weapon with enough blood that it could even kill him."

"Was she?"

Cassius scoffs. "Does it matter? She's dead. I watched her burn, myself." He pours himself a glass of something pale and frothy over ice. "After centuries of trying to increase our numbers, *he burned her.*"

Khiran weighs his answer carefully. "I'm sorry to hear it, but Ying's death doesn't change my priorities."

"I didn't tell you in hopes of changing your mind. I told you so you would understand what you're up against."

It's the wrong thing to say. Khiran's gaze turns sharp. "Between the two of us, I think I'm more than aware of the cruelty The First is capable of."

Cassius rolls his eyes. "He's *unhinged*. Whatever cruelty he dealt you before was calculated. Controlled." Around his cup, his knuckles are so white they match the milky liquid frothing behind the glass. "I am trying to tell you to abandon any expectations you have, because he has gone beyond any semblance of reason. I am trying to tell you that, whatever the cost, do not let him *catch you*."

Setting his glass down, he sighs; the sound tight and ragged at the edges. "He burned Ying over baseless suspicion. Imagine what he will do to someone clever enough to steal the power of a peach from under him? Imagine what he will do to *her*."

Anna feels her pulse quicken, loud in the silence that descends over the table. There is a message behind those words, an unspoken threat that makes the gravity of their situation turn from smothering to poisonous. It rattles in her lungs, a sick promise of what their failure could cost.

Whatever the cost, Cassius had said, but what Anna hears is, *do not let him take you alive.*

She looks to Khiran, seeking answers in his eyes, but he doesn't meet her stare. He's too busy looking at the man across the table, a terrible look of resignation softening the line of his jaw. The muscles in his throat move as he swallows, his eyes momentarily shuttering closed. "I know."

Cassius nods, but there's no victory in the somber edge of his gaze. "Where do you plan to go?"

Khiran glances away. "We have yet to decide."

"Travel far from here. Once Marcia figures out that you're purposefully withholding your magic, she'll have to track you the old-fashioned way. The more difficult the location, the less likely she'll think to look for you there."

"I have a place in mind," Khiran murmurs, his brow creased in thought.

"Good." Cassius tips his chin to the marbled sideboard. "If you could fetch a pen and paper from that cabinet, Little Bird. There's a letter you need to write."

Anna frowns, curious, but removes the napkin from her lap and pulls her chair away from the table. She shares a glance with Khiran as she stands, but he seems as bemused as she is. She finds thick sheets of paper and a fountain pen finer than anything she's ever held in her life in the top drawer. "Who am I writing to?" she asks, moving her plate aside to make room for the paper.

"Silas." When Anna's head snaps up, he smirks around the rim of his cup. "Write to him, tell him where you're going, and seal it. I'll ensure he receives it."

Anna looks between them, confused. "I don't understand."

"It's a fail-safe," Khiran says, his finger drumming on the table as he studies the man who calls him brother. "If there's word that Marcia is on our trail, Silas can shepherd us to safety before she closes in on us."

Cassius' smile is crooked. "Precisely."

The fountain pen feels heavy in her hands as she stares at the blank page in front of her. "Then the letter…"

Cassius finishes where she trailed off. "It's so Silas knows where to find you, but I *don't*." He leans back into his chair, watching her over the rim of his glass as he takes a long drink. When he sets it down, it's empty. Standing, the chair screeches against the polished tile as he stands. "I'll give you privacy. There's a wax seal in that same drawer. Once you're done, seal it and leave it on the table. I'll have my assistant deliver money and supplies to your room. Take it and buy passage away from here."

Khiran stares. "What guarantee do we have that you won't open it and give our location to Marcia the moment it benefits you?"

"There are no guarantees, Brother. Only my promise. After what I've put you through, that may not be worth much, but you can trust that I want to be deserving of Silas' love almost as much as I want The First in the ground."

"Almost?"

Cassius' grin is wicked and sharp at the edges. "I'd sacrifice my soul if it meant the pleasure of watching him fall."

He pushes his chair in, walking away. But when he reaches the doorway he pauses, hesitating a moment before turning to look back over his shoulder. Maybe it's the shallow smile haunting his lips, or the memories darkening his eyes, but Anna is suddenly struck by how lonely a picture he makes. "Actually... one more thing." He meets Khiran's eyes across the room, a shared connection mapped out in spider silk. "Her name wasn't Psyche," he says. "It was Selene."

A moment of silence, a few heartbeats, before Khiran asks, "Why are you telling me this?"

"Because she mattered," Cassius says, and in it Anna can hear lifetimes of grief. Crystalline eyes catch hers, the implication of his words like a knife in her chest. "Because she's gone."

And then he leaves—walking away before Anna can fully process what has happened. The pen still sits in her hand, its tip poised over the empty page.

Khiran leans heavily into his seat, staring at where Cassius left. "You were right," he breathes. "About staying. About trusting him."

Anna doesn't need to ask what changed his mind. She's certain she wasn't the only one to see the regrets and warnings dancing around a ghost of a name; not the only one to draw the parallels between the circumstances of the love they share now to a love that lived and died before Anna ever drew breath.

She writes her message, hopes her gratitude is felt in the flow of ink, and silently passes it to Khiran so he can add their destination before sealing it.

CHAPTER NINE

It is harder than he expects, living without his magic. The instinct is there, stitched into the fibers of his soul with thread strengthened by time. There are moments where he finds himself blindly reaching for it, flinching away just before he can grasp it. Fear is a tangible thing. He coils it around his wrists, binds his hands with it. He will gladly live in shackles, if it means she remains free to fly.

KARACHI, PAKISTAN
SUMMER 1958

THEY WASTE NO TIME.

Once the letter is sealed, purple wax bright against crisp folded paper, they gather their supplies and leave without looking back. Cassius doesn't see them off, but Anna's not surprised. There was a finality to the words he left them with in the dining room. The kind that makes her suspect that goodbyes were an art he never bothered to learn. She wonders if that's because he's said far too few of them over the centuries or because the ones he's been forced into still carry scars.

Their bags are heavy with clothes and food as they purchase boat tickets to take them to the Port of Karachi. Khiran has already warned her that they won't stay there. Cities may offer a level of camouflage, but they're easier to travel. He has no doubt, Marcia will jump from city to city searching for a trace of them to hunt.

Seagulls squawk overhead as the small passenger ship pulls away from port. A group of young men throw day old simit high into the air and watch the birds swoop and dive for the bits of bread, their yellow beaks snatching it up before it hits the water.

There's salt on the wind, tangling in her hair. Anna unties the scarf at her neck to wrap it over her head, the knot sitting under her chin. The breeze nips at the exposed collar, but it's better than combing through matted hair.

A glance proves that Khiran is facing a far more troubling battle.

His knuckles are bone white with how tightly he grips the rail, his skin sallow and jaw tight with stubborn determination. He looks a breath away from heaving his meager breakfast into the churning waters below.

Gently, she covers his hand with her own, his name a question on her lips. "Khiran?"

"Is it always this miserable?"

Anna hesitates, casting a look over the relatively calm waters. "Are you certain you still love my honesty?"

Khiran groans, the stiff line of his spine bowing. "I think—" He doesn't finish, interrupted by his own body.

Anna rubs his back as he heaves, frowning at the way he quivers under her touch. She waits until his stomach is empty and the only thing passing his lips is his trembling breath. "I didn't know you could get motion sickness." The way he travels, lurching himself from one end of the world to the next, felt far more violent than the seawater breaking over the bow. Her brow creases, thinking of another boat in another sea. "You didn't seem affected on Ching Shih's ship."

"Magic," he groans, leaving it at that. "To think I was impressed by these metal monstrosities. Can make steel float but they can't make it comfortable? Absolutely ridiculous."

She doesn't have the heart to point out that he seems to be the only one struggling—or that her journeys across the ocean have fared far worse. Instead, she gently folds her arm into his and coaxes him away from the railing. "Let's get you inside. Sometimes these things don't feel quite so bad below the deck."

He lets her steer him towards the stairs. "My mouth tastes disgusting."

Anna presses her lips together, a poor attempt at smothering the smile threatening to break. "That's part of it, yes."

"We're never traveling like this again."

One of the crew steps aside in the hall, his bearded face blossoming into a huge grin. He laughs, full-bellied, and claps Khiran on the shoulder with enough strength to make him stagger. Anna can't understand what he tells them, but she can tell his amusement comes at her lover's expense.

The glare Khiran shoots him is sharp enough to kill, but with the pallid look to his skin, Anna thinks he's more likely to curdle milk. As they open the door to their room, he grumbles under his breath. "If you ever loved me, you'll push that man overboard at the earliest opportunity."

"Don't be petty. It's not his fault you're sick." She gets him into bed and brings the covers up to his shoulders. The material is scratchy and stiff, far from the silks they slept in last night or the luxuries he would have provided for himself. It dawns on her that he has never looked so human as he does now—brow damp and face pale with seasickness while laying in a cot he wouldn't have been caught dead in.

It's a sobering realization.

For all her amusement at watching him suffer the menial labors of mortals, Anna can't help the twinge of sympathy for him. It's hard, having to reinvent yourself. She knows, perhaps more than anyone, the struggle that comes with having to hide the parts of oneself.

First, her skin. Then, her immortality. Later, her knowledge.

It must be so difficult for him, denying himself the power he's wielded for over a millennium. And now, to be brought down by something as mundane as a rocking ship…

"Scoot over," she says, more a request than a demand. He shifts until his back presses against the wall, his arms open in invitation. She curls up next to him on the cot, their knees knocking and their arms draping over each other to fit. She tucks her head under his chin, fingers playing with a loose thread dangling from the blanket's hem.

"I'm sorry," she murmurs.

He sighs into her hair. "It will pass."

The seasickness will. Even if his stomach never settles, they're meant to reach port in a week. That's not what she's apologizing for. "Is it difficult?" she asks. "Not reaching for your magic?"

For a moment, only the subtle groaning of steel and the clumsy set of footsteps traversing the hall fills the silence. If it wasn't for the tightening of his arms around her, she would almost believe he hadn't heard the question. His throat moves as he swallows. "Yes."

Anna's fingers trail over his wrist before lacing with his. "Do you want to talk about it?"

"I don't know if I could explain it properly," he admits. "I have the world at my fingertips, but now I can't use it." He flinches, shooting her an apologetic look. "How spoiled I must sound, mourning privileges you never had."

"No," she murmurs, squeezing his hand. "Not spoiled." The look he wears is skeptical and lined with resignation, and she chokes on a laugh. "Well, maybe a little, but not in a way I find offensive."

He sighs, bringing their clasped hands to his lips so he can place a kiss to her knuckle. "If you weren't so difficult to offend, I might take comfort in that."

The smile she gives him is soft. "You lost a lot this week, Khiran. You're allowed to mourn."

His eyes are searching, heavy with heartache and sharp with understanding. "My grief doesn't outweigh yours, Anna."

She shakes her head, recoiling. "Of course it does." He lost the woman who raised him. Lost his home. Lost his power. How could she possibly feel sorry for herself when she lost so little in comparison?

A gentle kiss to her forehead, his lips whispering against her skin. "No, Anna, it doesn't. We both lost. Don't let my pain prevent you from treating your own."

"That's not what I'm doing," she grumbles, but in her chest her heart gives a traitorous squeeze. The truth is they've been so busy running—so busy trying to determine their next step—she hasn't dared study the lingering grief hiding in the shadows of her heart. Even now, safe in the hull of a ship sailing far from Marcia's reach, she still can't bring herself to pull it into the light. If she looks too closely, she's bound to feel it too deeply. Khiran's words have become a mantra, something she holds so desperately it's become an imprint on her soul.

It can't be for nothing.

She can't afford to let the grief swallow her, and she can't trust herself to be strong enough not to let it. Not now. Not yet.

Khiran hums, a low sound full of more understanding than she deserves, his nose tracing her own. "Must be my mistake, then."

Anna's throat goes tight, her eyes burning the longer she holds his stare. Sometimes she hates that he sees her so thoroughly. "She was your mother," she whispers, the words strangled and hoarse.

"Yes," he agrees. "And she was your friend. The pain is different, but one does not outweigh the other."

She wants to argue, but the ache in her chest has grown so heavy it's suffocating. If she speaks now, she'll be left breathless. Instead, she curls into him, her head tucked under his chin and his arms wrapped firmly around her body. They fall asleep, the rocking of the ship lulling them through their shared grief.

It's raining when their ship docks in Karachi.

The dark clouds hang low in the heat, the air so humid Anna feels like her skin is damp before she even sets foot in the light rain. Beside her, Khiran looks all too relieved to disembark. Anna can feel the rain sliding down the collar of her coat as they follow the line of people off the ramp and onto dry land. He murmurs a few choice words under his breath.

Karachi rises up to meet them. Wide, clean streets host a variety of different modes of transportation. The bell of a trolley car trills, ringing high over the noise of car engines. In the middle of the inter-section, a policeman directs traffic from a pedestal with his arms. Anna spies a camel pulling a cart. She has only ever seen one in a zoo. On the sidewalks, the people seem to be just as varied. Some wear western styled collared shirts and slacks while others wear long tunics with their heads covered with turbans or small hats in what Anna imagines must be the traditional style.

Khiran's hand hovers over her lower back, guiding her forward and into the crowds. She hadn't realized her steps had slowed as she took it all in. "Do you know where we're going?"

"Karachi sees a lot of tourism. We'll have no problem finding accommodations." He adjusts his bag over his shoulder, frowning up at the rain. "I'm afraid we'll need to stop by the bank before anything."

She nods, understanding. They had taken stock of their supplies during a lull in Khiran's seasickness. While Cassius had been kind enough to include cash along with food, the lira doesn't do them much good in a country that deals in rupees.

Khiran leads her down the street, his eyes scanning the store-fronts as if filing the knowledge away for later. Anna suspects she's not entirely wrong, and she takes in the shops and the advertise-ments. There seems to be a mix of the local dialect and a smattering of English decorating the signs and posters. "How long will we stay?"

"Just the night. We'll take the first train in the morning."

Anna frowns. "Is that necessary? I thought she couldn't track us so long as you withhold your magic?"

"I'd prefer to avoid testing her capabilities. Besides," he winces, glancing at her. "Pakistan only recently gained independence. Tensions are still high and its future still uncertain. Without my magic, I am as blind to what could be coming as anyone else. I won't risk the possibility of you getting caught in a conflict."

Anna sobers, threading her arm through his. "It wouldn't be the first time I've lived through one," she says softly, a gentle reminder.

"No," he agrees, expression dark. "But it would be the first time I couldn't use my magic to save you if things became too dire."

A breath, short and strangled, passes her lips, because he's *right*. Over the centuries, she had come to rely on the knowledge that he could rescue her if she ever came into too much trouble. It hadn't dawned on her, until this moment, how much she took comfort in his unspoken promise to never leave her to suffer—that safety was always just a blink away. Now, fleeing by anything but mortal means could cost their lives.

Swallowing, Anna finds the courage to ask the question despite dreading the answer. "How long would it take her to find us? If you had to use it?"

Khiran's lips thin. "Moments."

The word lands like a bomb, shrapnel rattling in her lungs.

Moments—not even minutes.

Moments.

Khiran sees the way she pales, must feel the echo of her fear in his chest. He stops, hands settling on her shoulders and bending to meet her gaze. "We will not give her a scent to trace. We will live by mortal means, and we will be fine."

Anna searches his face. It's been so long since he's lived a life without magic. She's not entirely sure he understands what it will look like, but there's a determination honing the green in his irises and sharpening the line of his jaw. And Anna knows, with everything she is, that it doesn't matter how ill prepared he is.

He would throw himself to the fire before leading The Huntress to their steps.

THE HOTEL ROOM KHIRAN SECURES FOR THEM ISN'T LAVISH, BUT IT'S clean and within the city center. After they drop off their bags, he leads her to a shop to purchase clothing in the local style. While Karachi seems to host people in all sorts of dress, Khiran insists they'll want something more traditional to blend in where they're going. He speaks in Urdu to the clothier, haggling the price down, as Anna trails her hand over the colorful cottons. Outside, the sun is beginning to dip below the horizon and the sound of jazz music is filtering from the clubs while the casino slot machines ring with the sound of coin.

Khiran touches her elbow, distracting her from her thoughts. In his other hand is a bag full of clothing—mostly long sleeved kurta and kurtis with some traditional trousers called churidars. "Come, we'll find something to eat and return to our room."

Anna's stomach gives a hollow pang of approval at the thought of food. Their last meal was on the ship that morning. Considering how little Khiran was able to keep down the past week, she's certain he must be starving. "Did you have somewhere in mind?" There certainly seems that there's no shortage of choices.

Khiran's gaze travels the busy street, reading the signs. He must find one appealing, because he takes her hand and leads her across the street. "What's the phrase? When in Rome?"

Anna is hit by the smell of spices the moment they enter the small, unassuming restaurant. There are only a dozen tables, but most are already taken. If the scent hadn't already convinced her that Khiran chose well, the amount of people certainly would have.

He leads her to a small table in the corner, barely large enough for them both. "Any requests?"

Shaking her head, Anna's eyes travel to a plate being served to the table adjacent to them and her stomach gives a hungry lurch. "Surprise me."

He orders nihari, a hearty stew slow cooked with lamb shank and served with a side of naan. Anna lets the flavorful spices sit on her tongue, memorizing the taste. She tries not to think about how much Jiro would have enjoyed it, or how he would have asked Khiran a dozen questions about where and how it's made.

Chicago, Silas had said. That's where he took him. Anna wonders if he has a warm meal in his belly while listening to jazz, too.

AFTER THEY FINISH EATING, THEY START THE WALK BACK TO THEIR HOTEL. The sun has set during their meal, the bright hues of sunset darkening to an inky black swathed in stars. Anna catches sight of a low hanging crescent moon peeking between the buildings as they walk. The city was beautiful during the day, but it absolutely thrives at night.

Music spills out onto the street, notes of jazz and rock and roll reaching her with every door they pass. Despite the late hour, there seems to be just as many people on the street as when they pulled into the dock that afternoon. It reminds her of New York, the way this city doesn't seem to have any intention of sleeping. Khiran tells her it's known as the City of Lights. She can't help but feel that the name is fitting.

Ahead of them, a large group of people spill out onto the sidewalk, chatting animatedly. It's only once they get a little closer that she realizes it's a theatre of some kind. Anna pauses in front of a poster, the bright colors and the woman's printed stare snagging her attention. The words are not in English, but the letters *are*.

Intezaar.

Khiran follows her gaze. "It's a film." He gestures to the printed face of the woman. "That's Noor Jehan. She's made quite a name for herself. They're calling her the Queen of Melody."

Anna has never heard of her, but she wants to. She is a world away from home and she wants to learn what this new landscape looks like. What it *sounds* like.

She takes Khiran's hand, walking backward and leading him toward the theatre with a smile. "Let's catch the next showing. We've never been to the movies together." Her eyes gleam.

Khiran hesitates. "We have a long journey ahead of us. You should rest."

"I can rest anytime. Who knows when I'll be back here?" She tilts her chin, adopting the impish smile he used to wear so well. "Besides, what better way to start our new mortal lives than with a first date?"

He looks more insulted than compelled. "If memory serves, I took you dancing for our first date."

"In another life," she says, squeezing his hand. "Don't you want to romance me in this one, too?"

Khiran's expression softens, his gaze adoring. "You won't understand it. It's in Urdu."

"Then explain it to me afterwards," she murmurs, lacing their fingers. "Tell it to me like a story when we lay down in our bed for the night." Her smile falls, a desperate longing taking its place. "Please. Let's just forget that we're running. Even if just for a few hours."

He reaches for her, fingers brushing her chestnut hair from her face. "How could I possibly deny you?" He sighs, but there's a fondness in it. "Let's see when the next showing is."

Her answering smile is as bright as the street lamps lining the sidewalks.

LANGUAGE IS A FASCINATING THING.

Throughout the film, Anna doesn't know what's being said, but she understands what's happening well enough. Some things need no interpretation. The way the music swells and dips, the facial expressions and hand gestures, the way the camera zooms and pans, is a language of its own. The details may be lost to her, but the story is not.

In the static filled frames of black and white, Anna can tell it's a love story. Knows that the beautiful woman is blind and waiting for her childhood love in the rural town of their youth. Feels the longing in her dark stares, feels her grief.

Anna understands why Noor Jehan, the woman whose face is printed on the movie poster that snagged her attention, has earned the title Queen of Melody. Her voice is melodious and haunting; ringing like a bell while the notes fall like bright colored confetti on the breeze. A combination of lively and soft that Anna finds captivating.

She understands the shadows in Khiran's eyes when the story ends in flames.

THE NEXT MORNING, THE TRAIN STATION PROVES TO BE JUST AS BUSY AS the city it caters to. People board with their luggage at their hips, shuffling down the narrow aisles as they search for a seat. Anna and Khiran manage to sit together despite how full the car is, but only because he was able to convince an older gentleman to give up his seat. Judging by the congratulatory smile behind his salt and pepper beard, Anna suspects Khiran told him they were newlyweds. She finds it fitting, being that they decided to celebrate this new mortal life they're embarking on.

The train moves through the city, buildings rushing past. Anna knew Karachi was large, but she hadn't understood the full scope of it until the beautiful architecture failed to give way to open fields. Instead, she watches as the streets become narrower and the buildings grow closer. Watches as shops give way to street vendors and food carts. Then, she sees the tents.

Khiran follows her gaze, a regret lining his expression. "Refugees. The partitioning of India brought a mass migration, both in and out of the country." There's a cadence to his voice, an undercurrent. Anna has been sheltered from more current events, but she understands what kinds of horrors accompany upheaval.

"There's so many…" Anna murmurs, her breath fogging up the glass. She leans back, her hands fisting in her lap. It's such a contrast to the part of the city they enjoyed last night, a study in opposites. Of haves and have-nots.

Khiran puts a hand over hers, speaking low. "You must let it go. You cannot help anymore than I can. Not anymore." He waits until she meets his gaze, his eyes shadowed. "You can't go back to saving others at the sacrifice of yourself, Anna. Promise me."

Everything that she is recoils, bitterness coating her tongue in words that are better left unsaid. She swallows them down instead, looking back out the window. Khiran has sacrificed his magic—his very nature—to stay by her side and keep her safe. She owes him the same level of dedication. Even though the thought makes her stomach go sour.

"I promise."

CHAPTER TEN

It's not the kind of life he cares for. He misses traveling on a whim, of tasting foods from every corner of the world whenever he fancied it. He misses feeling like the world is his playground instead of his cage. It's only her smile, her happiness, that makes his self-imposed prison bearable.

PHUKTAL GOMPA, ZANSKAR VALLEY
JANUARY 1959

ANNA IS FREEZING.

The snow is fresh, more powder than ice. With every shuffling step, she finds herself trudging through knee-high drifts. It's exhausting. She's sweating in her coat from the exertion, but with every gust of wind she feels the chill. She understands now why Khiran was so eager to hurry. Wherever it is they're going, can only be reached on foot. Had they made it a few days earlier, they would be hiking over rock instead of snow. It's been at least an hour since she's been able to feel her toes, her only consolation knowing (from unfortunate experience) that she's immune to frostbite.

"Where are we going?!" she shouts, fighting to be heard. It feels like the storm smothers the words the moment they leave her lips, but Khiran must hear enough. He points, his hand rising impossibly skyward. Anna's gaze follows, her steps faltering.

It is nothing but a shadow in the storm, a hazy outline blurred by snowfall, but it's enough to make out the flickering lights winking like eyes in the dark. Windows. Hidden in the mountainside, seemingly carved from the very same stone, are buildings.

"Phuktal Gompa," Khiran says, the wind almost swallowing the words entirely. If he hadn't leaned down, close enough for her to feel the heat of his breath on the shell of her ear, Anna's not sure she would have heard him at all.

His hand catches her elbow, steering her closer to the cliff face. It looms over them like a guardian, blocking the wind the closer they get. By the time Anna is able to touch the rock, she's not sure if the low whistle in her ears is real or an echo.

"There's a small cave up ahead," Khiran assures her. There's a carefulness in the way he watches her, concern warring with reality. "We will rest there until the storm passes."

Anna knows, without asking, that he came to the decision for her sake rather than his. His hair is windswept, his cheeks flushed pink, but he doesn't tremble from exhaustion or shiver from the cold the way she does. She leans on his offered arm, happily letting him bear some of her weight as her feet fumble. The cave, to her great relief, is closer than she imagined.

Unfortunately, it's also far smaller—barely enough room for them to tuck their bodies in. No room for a fire.

Khiran motions for her to climb in first, before following behind her. The ceiling is so low, Anna has to crawl on her hands and knees to get to the far end. She lays on her side, watching Khiran inch towards her. When he lays down, facing her, she understands why he wanted her to go first. His back is to the opening, bearing the brunt of the chill.

When he opens his arms, Anna doesn't hesitate to fold herself into them. "Are you warm enough?"

No, she thinks, but it tastes unappreciative despite it being the truth. Instead, she says, "I'm getting there."

"Many make the pilgrimage here, but I've never made the journey myself," he confesses. "It is more taxing than I imagined."

"I'm sure the snow isn't helping."

His answering hum is dark with grudging agreement.

She tucks herself fully against him, the tip of her nose brushing his throat. Her face is so cold, his skin burns in comparison.

"You're freezing," he mourns, reaching between their bodies to unzip his coat. He holds it open, an invitation she can't refuse. She curls up against him, their knees knocking and her hands soaking up the warmth of him.

She sighs, cocooned in his arms and folded into his coat on top of her own. Outside, the wind whistles. Not an echo, after all. "Tell me about where we're going," she murmurs, trying to fight the heaviness pulling at her eyelids.

He knows her too well. "Sleep, Anna."

She could argue, insist that she's fine. Any other time, she probably would have. But there is a song in the way the wind whistles, a melody that feels as old as the mountains themselves. Anna lets it sing her to sleep.

It's the silence that wakes her.

She turned sometime during the night. Her back is warm against Khiran's chest, his coat draped fully over her. A sliver of light plays on the back of the cave wall, rising and falling with Khiran's breathing. She knows, because she can feel it in time with the breath tickling the back of her neck.

"You're awake," he says, but there's no accusation in it. Only warmth. "It's midmorning."

Anna shifts, turning so she can face him properly. "I must have been more tired than I thought." She looks over his shoulder, peaking at the tiny glimpse of blue sky. "It looks like the storm passed."

"It stopped a little before dawn. It will still be difficult with the snow, but at least we'll be able to see properly. Are you ready?"

Part of her wants to beg for five more minutes, knowing the warmth she has now will be long gone once she's back to shuffling through the snow, but her joints are stiff from sleeping on the hard ground. Begging for movement. "Let's go."

They crawl out, Khiran offering her a hand. In the daylight, the opening looks even smaller than the tiny cave felt, but she doesn't dwell on it long. Outside, the world is white framed by blue skies. Pristine in ways that feel increasingly rare. Below them, a river so blue it almost looks otherworldly cuts through the landscape. She looks up, trying to find the windows she had spotted through the storm, but they're too close to the cliff face to see it.

"What did you say it was called?"

"Phuktal Gompa," he answers, walking ahead of her. Anna follows, trying to step in the tracks he's already made. "It's a monastery."

Anna thinks of Venice—of the years she lived as a nun, just so she could be permitted to heal without risking accusations of witchcraft. "What religion?"

"Buddhism." He looks back at her, a thoughtful frown creasing his brow. "Which I'm now realizing you probably know very little about."

She shrugs. "Only the bit I read from that book you have on religions. It gave some information on the origins but very little about the practice itself."

"I have a book on religion?"

Anna's certain he probably has a book on just about everything spread throughout all his little hideaways. Artfully bound in leather and pages gilded with gold. He's always seemed to have a penchant for hoarding things he finds valuable but never really *looking* at it.

"You do—did," she corrects, stomach twisting. "I suppose it depends on if our home is still standing."

Khiran says nothing. Anna appreciates that he doesn't try to ease the ache in her heart with false optimism. Even if the house still stands, they will likely never be able to return to it.

They continue on in silence, slowly scaling the mountainside until Anna spots the first glimpse of red-tiled rooftops. She thought it had been an optical illusion when she had seen it through the haze of wind and snow—that they couldn't possibly be built into the rock —but in the daylight, she's only more convinced. The buildings stagger, following the slope of the ridge of the mountainside, and seem to be built of the same stone it stands on. As they draw closer, Anna spots the round mouth of a cave perched at the back of it, spies the hint of steps leading in. "Does it go into the cave?"

Khiran nods. "Yes. The Tibetan monks have been here since the 15th century, but the caves are thousands of years old."

Anna traces the lines of the stepped roofs. "Why here?"

It's beautiful. Peaceful. She knows that can't be why he chose it. There were plenty of smaller, unassuming communities they passed and could have stopped in. None of them would have been even half as difficult to get to.

"I'm acquainted with one of the monks." He flinches. "Not that he'll recognize me. He's a good man… he'll take us in and ensure that we have food and shelter."

"What language is spoken in this area?"

His eyes slide to hers. "Tibetan is most common."

She nods. "You'll help me learn?"

Khiran's face softens. "Of course."

They continue to climb the zig zagging path. Anna bites back a curse when her foot catches a spot of ice buried beneath the snow—Khiran's grip on her hand is the only thing that keeps her from tumbling. Even still, the leg of her trousers bears the brunt of her misstep, sticking wet and cold against her skin for the rest of the hike. By the time they finally reach the monastery, Anna is happy just to be back on level land.

She immediately feels the eyes on them, but a quick glance

proves there is no unkindness in their stares but, rather, surprise. Anna imagines how haggard they must look—how *foolish* to brave the Himalayas in the middle of winter—and feels herself flush as deeply as the sea of maroon robes staring back at her.

One of the monks steps forward, his face round and his eyes concerned beneath his mustard yellow hat as he looks over them. He's young, certainly no older than Jiro. She can see the youth in the lankiness of his limbs, as if he's still growing into himself. He seems to be searching for words, but Anna doesn't understand why until Khiran speaks to him in the local language and relief colors his face. She doesn't know what he's saying, but she can hear the request in his inflection.

The boy looks between them before giving a sharp nod and gesturing for them to follow.

Anna and Khiran walk a few paces behind him through a maze of narrow footpaths, steep stone carved staircases, and tunnels held up by wooden trusses. Her eyes travel over the small buildings constructed of mudbrick and wood that would blend almost seamlessly into the mountainside if not for the colorful square-cut banners strung over the arches and doorways. "Where is he taking us?" she asks, smiling at a group of curious children watching them from around the corner. Some of them shriek, giggling. One boy answers her smile with one of his own that's so wide it shows off the gap of a missing front tooth.

"I asked him to take us to Master Tenzing." He glances at her just as she waves to the children, lips stretching into a shadow of a smile. "He's the acquaintance I spoke of."

Anna glances over the faces of the people they pass, noticing a commonality that makes her stomach sink. Those that aren't men, are boys. "Are you sure he'll let us stay?"

He follows her gaze before looking out over the snow filled mountains rising like pale giants on the other side of the winding turquoise river. "For now, at least. He won't turn us away when doing so would spell most people's deaths."

Anna nods, pulling her coat closer to ward off the chill. Their guide brings them deeper into the monastery. Pale white-washed walls give way to buttery yellows and rust reds that are nearly hidden in the shadow of the large yawning mouth of the cave's entrance.

"Shoes must be removed before entering," Khiran murmurs, his voice soft. "It is against their religious vows to be alone with or touch a woman. If something needs to be passed between you, I will do so. Out of respect, do not turn your back to the statues of Buddha."

Anna glances at him, worry gnawing at her stomach. "I'm not supposed to be here at all... am I?"

Khiran doesn't return her gaze, nor does he meet her eyes. It's enough an answer as any.

The young monk pauses at a doorway, gesturing with an open hand and soft words that Anna understands in context alone.

Khiran responds with what must be a thank you, but instead of reaching for the door, his feet remain planted while their guide enters. He must feel her questions because he answers before she can speak them. "Dawa will return to tell us if the master will see us."

"Is there a reason he wouldn't?"

The stretch of silence is as telling as the last. "Outsiders are unwelcome at the moment," he mutters, wincing. "If I didn't know him personally, I wouldn't have chanced coming."

Except, he doesn't know him. Not in this body. Not with this face. She wonders how much a name could be worth. Wonders if it will be enough. Thankfully, Dawa returns before she can dwell on it for too long. Khiran nods, reaching down to unlace his boots in what Anna interprets as a sign that they've been granted an audience. Anna follows his example, sighing in relief when her foot escapes the confines of leather, and follows Khiran through the door.

Master Tenzing is older than she expects.

He stares at them with milky eyes, pale shadows of cataracts so thick they obscure the color beneath. With how advanced it is, she expects he sees the shape of them more than anything. Still, his eyes follow as they take a seat on the floor across from him—linger in the direction of Khiran as he speaks in low tones.

"Welcome," he says, in accented English.

Khiran pauses, unsure. "I am fluent in Tibetan. There's no need—"

"But your wife is not, correct?" His pale gaze stares through her as his lips pull into a smile that deepens the laugh lines on his face like folded paper. "It is a lonely thing, being talked around."

The tension coiled in Anna's chest loosens. "Thank you."

He dips his chin, sweeping a sun spotted hand over the three steaming cups of tea between them. "I took the liberty of asking Dawa to pour for us. I'm afraid my eyes and joints are not what they used to be." He wraps an arthritic hand around one of the stoneware cups, offering it to Khiran gingerly. Once he passes it to her, he repeats the motion again until they all have a cup warming their hands. "I find conversation to be much like cold mornings. A cup of chai goes a long way to ward off the chill."

The spiced aroma is warm and smooth, the heat of it spreading in her chest after the first few sips. "Thank you," she says, an echo of Khiran's gratitude. "It's wonderful."

Tenzing smiles, delighted. "I'm glad. Now, Dawa tells me you are friends of Daivika?"

"Yes," Khiran answers. "When he discovered we needed shelter, he suggested we come to you."

"Shelter?" he echoes, turning the word over as if it holds the key to their secrets. He turns his face toward the window. "I assume you mean more than the weather."

"Yes."

His lips thin around a low hum. "You come at a troubling time."

Khiran cringes, hands fisting on his lap. "I'm aware."

"Yet you still decided to brave the journey." Master Tenzing's head tilts. "Why? What does this monastery have that your home does not?"

Khiran holds his milky stare, as if willing the elderly man to hear the truth in his words. "There are few people I trust. Daivika knew you to be a good man. A *fair* man. I trust you to hear our request for sanctuary and judge it with your heart above all else."

Silence falls between them, but Khiran doesn't drop his gaze. Then, a chuckle falls from Tenzing's aged lips. Rough as gravel, it escapes him like a landslide—building in momentum until his rasping laughter fills the room. "You must have known Daivika quite well. If your voices weren't so different, I'd mistake you for him. Very well, then. You are welcome to join us."

Relief is instinctual, but the grave expression on Khiran's face stills it before it can take flight. "Thank you, but I'm afraid we misunderstand each other." Gently, he sets his cup on the floor. "I am seeking shelter, not religion. I will not sacrifice my marriage to devote myself to a belief I do not share."

Tenzing's thin brows rise. "You understand that we practice celibacy here? You put your marriage above your faith?"

"For me, they are one and the same," he says, turning to face her. His eyes are warm, his smile soft. "Loving her is the closest I will ever come to enlightenment."

"I see…" Tenzing frowns, the furrows in his brow deepening. "So you wish only to be guests here?"

"No," Khiran says, without any hesitation. "We wish to live here, contribute to the wellbeing of the monastery and respect your traditions while being allowed the courtesy of our beliefs within the privacy of our own quarters."

A gong echoes, sounding closer than it should. Anna's eyes follow the sound, spotting an open pipe in the wall. She wonders if they run throughout the entire monastery.

Tenzing taps a crooked knuckle thoughtfully against his chin. "There is so much suffering in the world. To relieve us from these ills, we choose a monastic life," he murmurs. "But, there are many different paths. Even if ours lead in different directions, I suppose it's still possible to end up in the same place." He rises, joints creaking but spine straight. "I will have Dawa show you where you may stay and where we take our meals. Feed your body and rest your mind for today. Tomorrow we will come to an arrangement."

Khiran goes lax with relief, his words tight with emotion over his pressed palms. "Thank you."

IT'S SURREAL, FALLING INTO SLEEP NEXT TO HIM EVERY NIGHT AND waking to him every morning.

There had been a time when she longed for a reality where he could stay more than a few days at a time. One where he didn't feel forced to leave for the sake of maintaining the fragile illusion of safety. One where she didn't have to let him go. Sometimes, he kisses her goodbye and she has to remind herself that he's only going down the mountain and not across the world—that he'll return faster than the sun sets.

Being able to keep him close, to share his days and nights, brings her as much joy as it does guilt. When he comes home in the evenings, she sees the cost as easily as if he were wearing it around his shoulders.

Khiran is tired.

Anna can see it in the way his spine bows and his feet shuffle. While her days are spent between sitting in on lessons with the youngest monks and assisting in the kitchen, Khiran's responsibilities have taken him away from the monastery. The monks live entirely off a system of gifts—no money, no bartering—is to exchange hands with laypeople. The food they eat, the clothing on their backs, is all donated.

Tenzing has expressed no qualms about the monastery sharing their food, but Anna and Khiran both feel uncomfortable eating what was never gifted to *them*. Khiran spends his days traveling down the mountain and collecting donations so the people of the village do not have to brave the trek. He makes a point of purchasing food and cloth with their own money to contribute. Then he returns, donations strapped to his back and his hands rough from where the rope bit into the soft skin of his palms. The first day, he collapsed into bed, eyes closing, with barely a word to her.

The next evening was the same, and the night after that.

Concern rises like floodwater; the rushing sound of warnings before the levee breaks. She knows this isn't what he's used to. Knows that a life of hard labor and simple blessings isn't one he's lived since he was just another mortal boy in Eira's care. He's had thousands of years of freedom—of enjoying everything the world has to offer without living the realities of it.

She's determined to do what she can to make it easier on him. So, when he comes home from the hike, she's ready for him.

"Sit," she says, gesturing to the wooden foot stool. For a moment it looks as if he'll refuse, but she tips her chin challengingly. When she repeats the word, there's a command threading her voice. "*Sit.*"

Khiran sighs, but does as he's told. She kneels in front of him; helps him unbutton his top, peels the fabric from his shoulders. Her fingertips brush over his chest, muscle flexing beneath the skin. "Where does it hurt?"

He tips his head back, face to the beamed ceiling, and closes his eyes. The flickering light of the candle dances along the planes of his exposed neck. "Who says I am?"

Her answering stare is steady. "You promised me honesty in all things."

A moment of silence, a sigh in the dim. "*Everywhere.*"

Anna nods, knowing he cannot see it. She pours a small amount of oil on her palms. "Give me your hand."

Eyes opening, he studies her face for a few moments before doing as he's told. Anna massages the oil into his palm, her thumbs catching on calluses that weren't there a week ago.

She knows his body heals faster than a mortal's, but she's also painfully aware that when it comes to injuries, he's just as fragile as anyone else. It hadn't occurred to her until today that he would suffer muscle strain like one, too. That every day he was breaking down muscle and healing it in a cycle that would take any mortal man a week. It's no wonder he's as tired as he is when he finally comes through the door.

Her thumbs run along the lines of his palms with diligent pressure, massaging the muscles in his hand. He groans, the sound low and deep as if rising from the very bottom of his lungs. "You should have told me it was bothering you," she chides softly, turning his wrist and starting on the sinewy lines of his forearm. "I would have done this for you sooner."

"Careful, my love," he murmurs, eyes hooded and dark. "You may find yourself growing weary of my whining if you continue to reward me for it."

Anna smothers a smile. "I think I'll manage just fine." The curve of her lips falters. Fades. "Is it harder than you thought it would be?"

Khiran's sigh is so deep she can almost feel it. "In some ways, it's exactly as I expected." He glances down at his arm, tendons flexing beneath her fingers as he clasps his hand. "I admit I didn't factor in the physical toll. I'll adapt. Another week or so and it won't be so taxing." She moves to his upper arm and his sigh stutters. "I can't tell if you're incredibly good at this or if I'm just desperate."

"Perhaps both," she offers.

"Dare I ask where you learned to do this?"

She shrugs. "I picked a bit up here and there, but I suppose I improved the skill during the First World War. They used massage therapy to help with the rehabilitation of nerve injuries. I was never officially trained in it, but one of the girls was kind enough to show me a few basics."

He hums, eyes slipping closed and leaning towards her, his forehead resting in the curve of her neck and shoulder and his hands cupping the curve of her hips. "I hope she's living a long and prosperous life."

For the next fifteen minutes, the silence is broken only by her soft instructions and his breathy groans that flirt at the edges between pleasure and pain. Anna's hands knead at his flesh, working away the stiffness that has settled in the knotted muscle of his shoulder. "I'm sorry." The apology slips from her lips like a confession, soft as a secret and heavy with regret.

His huff of laughter fans over her collar. "Don't be. You've done nothing to warrant it."

Her fingers trail up his spine, sinking into his hair as she tries to arrange her feelings into words. "When I asked you to stay, I didn't know it would cost you so much."

A beat of silence, heavy enough for her to feel it, and he pulls away. "I did," he says, the words as firm as the hands on her hips. "I knew. And I chose you anyway. I would make it again, a hundred times over."

Her heart sinks. Twists. "But—"

Khiran reaches for her, his hands framing her face. Anna can feel the calluses lining his palms. She knows they'll be gone by morning, and he'll have to earn them all over again. He holds her gaze, his eyes dark and warm in ways that make her melt into his touch. "Stop trying to shoulder blame that isn't yours."

THERE'S A COMFORT IN ROUTINE.

During the early mornings, she shares a cup of chai with Master Tenzing and one of the younger monks to act as chaperon as he teaches her Tibetan. When the gong rings, she sits with the children during their classes and picks up what she can until the language becomes easier to follow. Soon, she's able to listen to the lessons instead of handfuls of disjointed words.

At night, Khiran teaches her the art of silence—silent gasps, silent pleas for more. In the privacy of their room, they practice their own way of worship, whispering devotions against each other's skin and finding salvation in each other's touch.

CHAPTER ELEVEN

*There is a blade hovering over his heart, ready to pry it from his ribs like a trophy, but it's her fear that he feels, a bolt of lightning to his chest, that terrifies him. He told her to run. Why didn't she just **run**?*

PHUKTAL GOMPA, ZANSKAR VALLEY
SUMMER 1962

THERE IS SOMEONE NEW IN THE TEMPLE.

Anna only knows because the children are abuzz about it. They whisper amongst each other, mouths stretched in grins so wide Anna can see their ears perking with the strength of it. She's curious, of course. The temple receives few visitors, and the ones they do receive are usually expected: monks journeying from other temples, the usual travelers coming to give donations. Anna can tell this is different. The children are too excited, too enamored, for it to be anything other than unexpected.

Then she catches snippets of their conversation.

"He's so tall!" one says. "His skin is like the ink Master Kulo favors," says another. Anna feels the tug of recognition, of hope, in her stomach. She has every reason to believe it's a coincidence, that it's just her heart hoping, but she scans the temple grounds just the same. Chasing that little thread of hope, she almost gives it up as a silly wish when she sees him.

Across the courtyard, talking with Master Tenzing, is Silas.

Anna stares, her smile growing as she watches her old friend's cheeks dimple with laughter. He towers over the old master by a foot at least, but the height difference is even more pronounced by the way Master Tenzing's spine curves over his cane.

As if feeling her gaze, Silas' head turns, eyes catching hers. He raises his hand in greeting. The smile he gives her is bright enough to chase away the darkest of shadows.

She runs to him, heart skipping in her chest. Silas folds her into a hug once she reaches him, his tall frame dwarfing her small one. "It is good to see you, my friend."

"You as well." She hugs him back, an appreciative squeeze, before pulling away. Anna swallows, preparing her heart for the possibility of receiving an answer that could break it. "Did Jiro...?" She trails off, unable to finish the question. Silas understands it anyway.

"He's safe. We made it to Chicago with no troubles. It wasn't until the path didn't reopen, that I realized something was wrong." Grief clouds his gaze, softening his strong brow. "Eira will be missed."

Anna's chest goes tight, heart stuttering painfully behind her ribs. "Yes," she agrees. "Very much so."

Silas looks over her shoulder, a subtle frown pulling at his mouth when he doesn't find what he's looking for. When his gaze returns to her, his voice dips low. "How is Khiran faring?"

Anna shifts, aware of the eyes on them. The children in particular seem entirely too curious. She can see their faces peeking from behind the stone terraced roof above them. "As well as expected," she answers, sending Kipu a pointed look and shaking her head when he giggles and waves in response. Anna is finding it increasingly hard to smother the urge to smile back at his antics. "Why don't we talk over tea?"

Silas' mouth curls, his eyes straying to the youthful faces above them. "Tea would be lovely."

ANNA PLACES A TEAPOT FILLED WITH WATER AND SPICES OVER THE FIRE so the chai can brew while they speak, the smell of cloves and cardamom warming the air. Folding her legs, she sits on the rug across from him.

His eyes are honey soft, sweet and warm in ways that remind her how much she missed the gentle companionship they share. "You look well, my friend."

Her answering smile is as honest as her words. "I am."

He glances around the small room pointedly, a thread of concern tightening his mouth. "And Khiran? I expected him to be at your side."

"Oh, he's helping some of the farmhands down the mountain. He should be home soon."

Silas' brow ticks, a subtle sign of skepticism. "Khiran?"

Anna understands. She had some doubts about how he would handle this part of mortal life. Labor, physical or otherwise, is not something he would have subjected himself to in the past. "It's been an adjustment for him."

"I am sure," Silas murmurs.

She hears the low bubble of water, the telltale current of steam moments before the whistle, and stands. She takes a moment to add milk to the kettle, letting it come back to a boil and simmer before straining it into two cups. She offers one to Silas before returning to her seat across from him.

"Thank you." He admires the glazing of the ceramic before taking a sip. The cup looks much smaller in his hand. "Cassius told me Khiran's plan. To deny his magic and hide as a mortal. To be truthful, I wasn't sure I believed him capable of it until now."

"Then you don't give him enough credit," Anna says, looking down at the tea in her hands and admiring the way the steam curls. "He would deny himself of every good thing this world has to offer if it meant keeping me close and keeping me safe. Just as I would do the same for him." A gentle smile curls her lips, and she lifts her chin to meet Silas' stare. "It was nice to meet Cassius—to know that you have someone who loves you so deeply. I'm happy for you."

Silas returns it, cheek dimpling and eyes softening. "We are so very different. It felt strange at first, but we fit where it matters."

She thinks of the swamps of Louisiana—of the meager meals they shared and the simplicity in which they lived. It is a pale comparison to the marbled halls and spread of delicacies that lined Cassius' table. She sobers, mind drifting to the last conversation they had with the blonde. "He tried to convince Khiran to fight."

Silas sighs, the sound so deep and tired Anna can nearly feel the weight of it. "So he's told me. I must apologize. I'm certain the conversation was held with much more animosity than what was admitted to me."

"There was a lot of yelling back and forth," Anna admits, the smallest of smiles kissing the corner of her lips. "I'm afraid Khiran wasn't on his best behavior, either."

He gives a somber hum of understanding. "They have a history."

"So I've heard," she says, an almost echo of his words.

"Have you?" Silas murmurs, his head tilting in thought as he studies her. "He tells you more now." An observation, not a question. Anna appreciates how much he sees her. How much he cares.

"He does."

"I am glad. The lives we lead are fuller, brighter, when we can share them completely."

Anna agrees, wholly and without question. "What do you think of it, Silas? Cassius' wish to fight?"

"I think it's as reckless as it is inevitable, but it is my greatest wish that the day the war starts is far in the future."

Anna nods. In her stomach, the truth of it coils and twists like the desperate thrashing of a viper with its head pinned, its fangs made useless. Helpless, but still fighting. "I feel the same."

A moment of silence. Anna gathers her courage to ask the question that's been haunting her. "Tell me, what is happening in the world? We're so isolated here, I'm afraid most of our news is limited to what the merchants bring with their wares." She frowns, fingers twisting in her lap. "There have been troubling stories about the state of China."

It's an understatement. Tensions between Tibet and the People's Republic of China had been high since they arrived at the monastery. An uprising in the capital city of Lhasa had erupted when fears of the Dalai Lama being arrested by the Chinese government spurred protests. It ended with clashes escalating into violence, thousands of Tibetans dead, and the fourteenth Dalai Lama escaping before Lhasa was retaken. Lately, she's been hearing whispers about the poor state of those within China's borders.

Silas' expression darkens. "I'm afraid they're likely true. The famine the citizens are enduring is as vast as it is cruel. I've been trying to shepherd those I can, but without Eira..." His voice trails off, an old pain shadowing his expression. Anna can feel the echo of it blooming over her chest like a cage of thorns. "I'm afraid my efforts do not go as far as they once did."

Anna's gaze travels to the window, noting the way the colors of the sky warm into hues of pinks and oranges. "Back home, there were nights I felt so guilty, I stayed awake with the weight of it on my chest. No matter how many times Khiran assured me that I deserved to rest—that I wasn't responsible for the lives lost."

Silas looks at her, the depths of his gaze as ancient as he is. "Khiran is right."

"Yes, but knowing it never erased the guilt." She faces him, her lips turned in a somber shadow of a smile. "I suppose what I'm saying is that I expect nothing we do will ever feel like enough."

"You're wise to understand it. It takes strength to witness horrors for as long as we have and feel anything but apathy at the end of it. In this, my friend, your strength outshines us all."

Anna laughs, the sound trembling and weak, as she shakes her head. "I'm younger. I've seen less. *Endured* less."

"You're wrong," he murmurs, bringing his cup back to his lips. "But I can forgive you for not seeing how brightly you shine."

It's more than two years later when Silas returns. Spring is nearly upon them, the air still cold but the snow only dusting the valley like powdered sugar. She's hanging bits of laundry in front of the communal fire, a few of the children play a game of Sho behind her. Kipu has already roped her into agreeing to play a game or two once she finishes. The six-year-old has become increasingly aware of how easy she is to charm with a dimpled smile and sweet words.

The boys squeal, delighted when one of them has a particularly good roll of the dice. She looks up, basking in their giddy laughter, when her eyes catch sight of Silas' tall frame in the doorway behind them.

Her smile dies, quick and without sound, when he doesn't return it. "Silas?"

"Where is Khiran?" he asks. The urgency of his voice sets her on edge. On the floor, the children go silent—looking between them.

Alarmed, she drops the laundry back in the basket without hanging it, searching his face as if she could find answers in the crease of his brow. "He's at home."

He crosses the room, barely sparing the children a glance. There are warnings in his eyes, trepidation in the heaviness of his steps. When he reaches for her, his hand settles between her shoulder blades, the pressure warm and urgent. "We must hurry."

Anna doesn't ask why. She can feel the truth pressing on her chest like a stone, pinning her breath in place. She plasters on a trembling smile for the children, tells them she'll be back even though the promise tastes like a lie. She keeps her expression calm, her stride even, but once she follows Silas past the doorway and into the courtyard, her steps quicken until just shy of a jog. Silas is a comforting shadow beside her. When they finally reach her door, her pulse has become a beat in her ears.

Khiran looks up, the iron kettle in his hand. His gaze shifts from her to Silas over her shoulder. "Another visit so soon," he says, pouring the hot water over his tea leaves. Steam curls over the rim of the cup. "How lucky for us."

Any other day, she might scold him for being rude, but Silas' urgency weighs heavier than decorum. She steps aside, letting Silas enter and shutting the door behind him. She's a moment away from suggesting they sit when he speaks the words she's been silently dreading.

"She's coming," Silas says. Even though Anna was expecting it, even though she had mentally prepared herself the moment she saw the gravity in his gaze, the words still land like a bomb. She can feel the world rocking beneath her feet, feel the percussion of it in her chest, when he adds, "Marcia knows you're in the Himalayas."

Anna is already mourning the lives they've built—the peace they've found.

Khiran pauses in his pouring. Slowly, he sets the kettle down. Anna can smell the cast iron burning into the wood of the table. The table he'd surprised her with last summer, because she had mentioned on a whim how she missed eating meals together at their little kitchen table back home. He'd bartered weeks of work for it. There are a hundred questions in his eyes, but the only one he voices is, "How?"

"She's tracking you."

Immediately, he shakes his head, frustration curving his spine as he splays his hands over the table. "It's not possible. I've been living —*suffering*—like a mortal since we left," Khiran snaps. He straightens, running a hand through his dark hair as his lips pull into a grimace. "There is no magic for her to trace. There can't be. If there was, you and I both know she wouldn't bother with subtlety," he sneers. "She'd follow the magic right to me and damn everyone else unfortunate enough to witness it."

"Yet she knows to look *here*," Silas stresses. "This is not an accusation, it's a warning. She has no reason to be here, except for *you*."

"Right. You're right. I just—" Khiran brings a hand to his temple, folding himself into a chair as his fingers drape over his eyes. "I've been so *careful*."

Anna winces, because she *knows*. She's seen it. Every day is another sacrifice he wouldn't have had to make had she not convinced him to stay. She turns to Silas, her question as fragile as her hopes. "Does she have another way?"

Silas shakes his head, his brow furrowed. "None that I know of." His dark eyes slide to Khiran before settling back on her. "But for her to find you all the way out here... she must." He seems as disturbed by his answer as she is.

Khiran scoffs, hand sliding away and eyes staring up at the ceiling. "That would be my luck." His head lulls to the side, pinning the other man with a dull stare. "Isn't that right, Shepherd?"

Pity softens Silas' expression. "You need to leave now if you are to escape."

Anna wets her lips, already making a mental tally of what to pack. What to leave behind. "Where should we go?"

A pause, so heavy it's frightening.

She looks to him, alarmed by everything his silence speaks. The pain reflected in his eyes, the uncertainty, makes her stomach drop. "Silas?"

"He doesn't know," Khiran answers for him. The words fall between them, leaden and lifeless. A shell of the hopes they harbored only days ago.

"Oh." The air tastes thin, the room tilting under her feet. She sits, hands gripping the table with a desperation that leaves her knuckles as white as the ring encircling her finger.

"Luck is fluid. It changes. Not knowing the destination only means the where doesn't matter. Not yet." Silas brings his hand to rest reassuringly on her shoulder. Anna tries to focus on the warmth of his palm to help distract her from numbness threatening to swallow her whole. "What I do know, with certainty, is you can't stay here."

Anna nods, forcing a deep breath into her lungs before breathing it out. She lays a hand over his, hopes he can feel her faith in him despite her fears. "When do we need to leave?"

"Now." The word sounds sharp. Final. "We need to leave now."

Another nod. This one feels stiffer than the last. "Do we have time to say goodbye?"

"My friend, you barely have time to pack."

THEY REACH THE BASE OF THE MOUNTAIN JUST AS DAWN STARTS BLEEDING across the sky. Anna mourns the goodbyes she didn't get to say— imagines the monastery waking to the bells and finding them gone. She wishes she could have at least thanked Master Tenzing for all his kindness.

Silas leads them as far as the next town over before he stops, his head tilting as he listens to the whispers the world delivers to his ears alone. "You need to go to Jammu Tawi. Board the train."

Anna swallows, mouth dry. She knows how far Jammu Tawi is. It had been their last stop before they left the train tracks and continued by foot and good samaritans who were willing to let them ride in the back of their cars and carts. It would be a journey just to get to the station, but she doesn't dare doubt Silas' word. Not when they had proven to be right so many times before. "Where do we go from there?"

Silas shakes his head. "I don't know." He pauses, his brow furrowed. As if he's struggling to interpret something she can't hear. "It's too convoluted—from there, the outcomes lean too heavily on your choices."

Khiran rips the seam of his coat, his nimble fingers fishing out a small nugget of gold from his collar. "No time to waste, then. We'll hire someone to drive us."

He approaches a middle-aged man busy unloading the back seat of his car. Anna can't hear what's being said, but she can tell by his expression and hand gestures that he must be in the middle of deliveries. Khiran holds out the gold piece in offering and the man's uncertain smile shifts.

"Will you be joining us?" Anna already knows the answer—can feel it curling behind her ribs, a quiet regret, but she asks anyway.

"No," Silas answers, voice soft. "I will serve you best if I continue to listen for danger at the source."

Anna nods, suspecting as much. "How will you find us?"

"Our paths will cross, just as they did a century ago." He takes her hands, folding them between his own. "Have faith, my friend."

She smiles, but it feels as weak and trembling as her heart. Khiran waves her over, their ride secured, and Anna's chest aches. She turns back to Silas, a goodbye resting on her tongue like bitter medicine, when he takes her hand in his—turning her wrist until her open palm faces the sky.

He places a blade in her hand, sheathed in leather but its handle a raw unfinished tang where a handle was never fashioned. It's old, crude iron she hasn't glimpsed the likes of in centuries. "One of Ying's blades," he murmurs, holding her stare.

The Bladesmith. The one who forged weapons capable of piercing gods.

Anna's fingers fold over the leather, gripping it against her chest to hide the tremors in her hands. As unfinished and crude as it is, she knows the value of what she holds. The implication that they'll need it is terrifying. Swallowing past the knot in her throat, she forces herself to speak. "Thank you. I'll make sure Khiran gets it."

Silas pauses, that strange concentrated look in his eyes as he studies her. His dark brow furrows. "No," he mutters, as if the word comes as a surprise to him as well. "It needs to stay in your hands." He grips her shoulder, the weight of his palm as heavy as the gravity in his gaze. "Do you understand?"

The iron bites into her palms, freezing against her heated skin like a bad omen, but she forces herself to nod despite the fear prodding her heart. "Yes."

THEIR DRIVER'S NAME IS AKAR.

Anna had expected the long drive to be smothered with silence, but Akar is full of stories. She didn't realize Khiran had known him from a few odd jobs around the village, had worked with him in his family's fields only last spring. Anna suspects that he might not have been convinced to take them, gold or not, otherwise.

He tells them about his two daughters, seven and nine years old, and all the trouble they get into. The smile he wears when he talks about them helps to soothe the sharp edge of fear she's been carrying since they've left. She still feels it, lodged between her ribs like the blade in her pocket, but as the minutes pass it becomes easier to breathe around.

Khiran sits, stiff and silent, beside her as she answers Akar's questions and makes small comments just to show she's listening. His hands are fisted in his lap, tendons straining as his eyes flit over the moving landscape. The twisting mountain roads have given way to a level stretch of dirt and rock, the lingering dusting of winter snow slowly melting as they lost altitude. They make it an hour before everything goes wrong.

There is a woman in the road.

Khiran curses, his arms wrapping around her, cradling her head to his chest just as their driver shouts. Swerves. The tires skid on the gravel before they lift. For an extended moment in time, gravity becomes more theory than law. She is suspended, lap belt cutting into the tops of her thighs as the world outside the windows goes upside down.

The roof hits the ground first, steel crunching and windows shattering. Glass showers over them, pelting her skin and tangling in her hair like crystal confetti. The car rolls again, and again, and again. It rolls enough times that the movement stays with her like an echo even after everything goes still.

For a moment, everything is suspended. Quiet. When she looks,

Anna finds Akar dead. The roof is crushed in, jagged steel pinning him to the seat, his eyes open and sightless as the blood saturates his shirt. Anna thinks of the picture of his children that was on the dash, placed with care beside the speedometer. The two girls he took this job for. The two girls who will never again welcome their father home.

Anna forces a breath, the air rattling in her lungs, as shaky as she feels. She's not sure what's happened—not sure whether to feel shocked or afraid—not until the feel of Khiran's grip registers. When she looks down at the hand clutched in the fabric of her shirt, his knuckles are white and his expression is frantic.

Anna does not bleed. She does not bruise.

She knows it's not her physical wellbeing that has made his face pale and his eyes wild.

Beside her Khiran, wheezes. "The belt," he urges, his hands already fumbling with the catch. "Undo the seatbelt!"

It's the pain in his voice that startles her back into the moment. She turns to him so quickly, it takes a moment for her vision to catch up and her palms to find his cheeks. There are a dozen tiny cuts on his hands and face. One at the hollow of his neck bleeds enough to stain the collar of his kurta. His fingers are slippery with it as he finally succeeds in unbuckling the latch. "Khiran—"

"Later," he hisses. "Right now, we need—"

A voice calls out to them from outside the wreckage, familiar in ways that haunt Anna's nightmares. "Khiran, I'm surprised at you!" Marcia croons, a cruel tsk sharpening the edges of her voice. "It's not like you to miss an opportunity to run. You must be getting rusty. Living like a mortal the way you've been."

He curses under his breath, eyes flitting over the crushed interior of the car, before winding his arm around her waist. "Hold on!" The words are a harsh whisper against her ear, the only warning she receives before the pit in her stomach drops, and the crushed steel shell around them twists, threads of color spinning until there is only open sky above them. Anna recognizes this feeling, can almost taste his magic on her tongue.

Her vision doesn't have time to settle before Khiran jerks back—a blade a hairsbreadth away from her face.

Marcia laughs, deep and rolling as thunder, pale blonde hair framing her angular face like a storm.

Anna fears the strike of lightning that's sure to follow.

She thumbs the blade of her dagger, her flinty eyes alight with the thrill of the hunt. For every cautious step they take back, she saunters forward with a feline grace. There's a promise in the way her mouth curves, sharp and wicked, that she's here for more than their death. She's here for their *pain*. "That's more like it."

Khiran says nothing, but his arm tightens around her as if he's a moment away from fleeing. The line of his jaw is rigid, his stare cool and calculating in ways that contrast the heart beating wildly beneath Anna's palm.

Marcia's eyes roam over him, tongue rolling over her teeth. "I admit, I thought that was rather clever of you—giving up your magic. It took me a few years to figure it out. I thought I might be losing my touch. So did The First, for that matter. You know how I hate disappointing him. I'll be making sure you pay for the embarrassment you caused."

Her gaze slides to Anna, the edge of her smile growing feral. "Tell me, do you really think this human girl will be worth it?"

Khiran shoves her further behind him, his chest rising and falling and his lip curling in a sneer. "She has nothing to do with this."

A lie, but he still manages to make it sound like the truth. Even if The First doesn't realize it yet, Anna knows she has *everything* to do with it. In her coat pocket, her hand curls against cold iron—ready to free the blade from its sheath.

Only, the longer Marcia stares at her, the more her serrated smile dims and her eyes narrow. Anna can practically see her mind turning —cataloguing her lack of injuries and tallying up the years and trying to make them match the youth still lining Anna's face. It's only been six years since she first saw her face; six years since Eira's heart and home burned to ash in front of their eyes. It shouldn't be long enough to suspect the absence of crow's feet and laugh lines…

but it hasn't been *just* six years. It was six years of running—of living a life that should have turned her skin leathery and her hands rough.

Anna sees the exact moment Marcia comes to the same conclusion.

She bristles, lips pulling back into a snarl. *"No."*

It's the only warning Anna gets before Marcia rushes toward them, her blade drawn and her eyes lit with fury. Khiran grabs Anna by the waist, blinking them out of Marcia's warpath only for her to follow the thread of magic faster than Anna can get her bearings. She doesn't know what's happening—can only make out the flash of her blade and bits of earth and sky before Khiran flits away again.

And again.

Again.

Again, until Marcia screams. "You filthy *coward*! It's been you all along! You've ruined everything!" Her blade comes down, the tip aimed at Anna's throat before Khiran physically shoves her back.

The blade nicks his raised forearm before he tackles Marcia to the ground, grappling with the knife in her hands as he shouts over his shoulder. "Run!"

Anna staggers back, still dizzy from his magic, and her heel catches on something—sending her to the ground. She yelps, her shoulder crashing painfully against a strip of steel. It takes another moment for her vision to clear enough to realize where she's landed.

Train tracks.

Staggering, she gets back on her feet, searching both sides of the track until she spots the train station in the distance—smoke curling lazily from the smoke box as it boards. Anna thinks about how many times Khiran blinked away from Marcia's strikes, despite knowing how easy it is for her to follow his magic and knows it can't be a coincidence.

Run, he'd said.

He wants her to run for the train.

Dust kicks up like a whirlwind, a storm of sand and grit that stings her flesh and robs her of her vision. One of Khiran's illusions, cast with so much magic it feels real. A smokescreen to shield her while she flees.

He should know better.

Nearly a decade ago she had stood in front of him, the barrel of a shotgun pressed to her chest and Jiro's finger trembling on the trigger. Nearly a decade since he asked her to never put herself in harm's way for him again.

Nearly a decade since she told him that she can't (that she won't) make such a promise.

Anna can barely make out the shape of them on the ground—can only tell Marcia is on top of him because of her halo of hair whipping around her face. As Anna stumbles closer, she can hear the other woman's voice over the roar of sand.

"I told him! I told him he should cull you from the beginning! You've never been anything but a filthy liar and a thief!" she snarls. Her hand is around Khiran's neck pinning him to the ground effortlessly as he writhes beneath her. His arms tremble, fighting against the blade pressing dangerously close to his chest.

Over his heart.

Fear is a fire in her chest, striking her with molten heat and crackling beneath Anna's skin. Khiran's head snaps in her direction, pulled by the emotion lancing her heart. His eyes are wide with a horror that matches her own. He doesn't speak—can't with the hand around his throat—but Anna doesn't need words to interpret the look he gives her.

You were supposed to run.

But she *is* running. Has been from the moment she saw how close she is to losing him. The blade in her pocket burns like a lifeline—*his* lifeline—the edge of unpolished iron biting hungrily against her palm as she grasps it. Ready to unsheathe it. Ready to *use* it.

Khiran's expression twists, desperation fueled fury momentarily eclipsing the fear. A blink and he's gone, Marcia's blade stabbing through empty air and into the earth.

Anna's steps falter, waiting for the inevitable moment Marcia follows his trail to wherever he's gone. It's not until the fair-haired woman screams, hands tearing at her eyes, that she sees the cobra coiled and spitting venom beneath her. Scales ripple back into flesh, Khiran's hand grasping the blade Marcia abandoned.

He drives the steel between the cage of her arms and into her stomach. Marcia's savage howl is equal parts pain and outrage. Khiran blinks away a split second before she strikes, the force of it making the ground tremble and leaving a crater in the shape of her fist. He reappears at Anna's side, grasping her hand with an unspoken command.

Run.

Marcia screams at their backs. *"You sniveling coward! **Face me**!"*

Anna can hear the train. Hear the wheels on the track and the clunking heartbeat of pistons before she sees it. The beat is steadily increasing, the slow buildup of momentum before it goes barreling full speed down the track. The last car is in sight, a beacon of hope if only they can reach it.

The stitch in her side protests angrily, but she only pushes herself to go faster. They're almost there. The pain she feels is only temporary. A lie when the threat behind them is terrifyingly real.

Khiran reaches it first, hoisting her up onto the platform. Anna grips the railing, turning to offer him her hand and pulling him up. She looks up, sees Marcia staggering after them and then the flash of a blade, bloody metal winking like death in the sunlight, a moment before Khiran cries out and falls at her feet. There is a knife lodged between his ribs, its polished handle gleaming in the sun and blood blossoming, wet and hot and crimson, over his kurta.

Anna shouts his name, dropping to her knees.

He answers by pulling the knife out himself, biting back a curse and eyes flashing. Pressing his hand over the wound, blood seeps around his fingers and paints his pale knuckles red as he throws the blade from them as if it burns. Above them, the metallic chink of metal on metal cries out a warning. The train is putting distance between them and the threat, but they aren't out of range. Not yet.

Shelter. They need shelter before another blade finds its mark.

Frantically, her hands scramble for the door latch as she winds her arm beneath Khiran's shoulder. She ignores the way his lips twist in agony. Ignores the way his blood drips from him like rain. Another flash of metal, a stinging pain at her calf where the point sharpened edge kissed her skin. Anna ignores that, too. There's only a few feet and a door between them and safety, and she's determined to meet it.

Khiran's shaky in her arms, but he helps her drag his body through the threshold. Anna takes one last look, meeting Marcia's rage filled stare just as her knees hit the dirt. Anna tips her chin up, hopes the other woman can see the victory in her eyes despite the distance between them, and closes the door.

CHAPTER TWELVE

Nothing could have prepared him for the emptiness. He searches for a trace of her, reaching out in the hollow of his chest, desperate to feel the echo of her soul respond. He's met with only the heavy, lonely beating of his own heart.

Indian Railways, India
February 1964

THE TRAIN CAR IS OCCUPIED.

A horse paws at the ground, ears pinned to its skull and snorting at the scent of blood. Its salt and pepper coat shines in the low light from the open slots as it pivots anxiously, tail high. It's only the lead rope tied to the opposite end of the car that prevents it from moving any closer.

Carefully, Anna guides Khiran onto a stretch of straw far enough away from the hooves beating against the wooden subfloor and coaxes his hands away from his wound. The blade had nestled itself neatly between his ribs. Heart in her throat, she tears his kurta open, sees the bubbles in his blood, and her fears are confirmed.

His lung. It's pierced his lung.

"Khiran?" His name escapes her like a question. A prayer for guidance and assurances.

There's so much red.

The same color as any of the thousands of patients she has treated over the centuries. Anna knows that wound, without the extensive treatment only a hospital can provide, would be a death sentence to anyone else. She puts her hands over his own, adding more pressure. Sweat beads down her neck, rolling down her collar. She can taste the salt of it on her lips. "Khiran, I don't—"

"It will heal," he assures her, but he sounds winded. Out of breath. When he coughs, the sound of it rattles in the cage of his chest. "Slowly, but it will heal the same as everything else. Don't worry, I've suffered worse."

She wants to believe him. Wants his reassurances to be spun more of truth than thinly veiled comfort. She looks down at her hands, at the blood—his blood—smearing over her skin. Darkening the etchings on her ring.

Her ring.

Blood and bone.

His blood. His bone. His *magic*.

The horror she feels is as sharp as the blade in her pocket. "Khiran…"

"I'll heal," he repeats, quickly. It's meant to reassure her, but all Anna can hear is the wheeze in his breathing. His head lulls to the side, eyeing the blood coating her fingers with a level of detachment that scares her.

"I know what she's tracking." She swallows, closing her eyes. "You told me it was born of you and you alone. Your magic." She looks at him, watches the understanding reach his eyes and the horror part his lips. "It's the ring, Khiran. That's how she's tracking us."

He swallows, breath coming faster. Anna can't tell if it's because of the panic rimming his gaze or because his undamaged lung is now doing the work of two. "I—" A cough cuts him off, wet and bloody. He cringes, red coating his lips and staining his teeth. "When I regain my strength. I'll find a way to remove it."

Find a way. Find a way because he can't. Doesn't know how.

Anna does.

The solution is heavy in her pocket. The blade Silas insisted she needed to hold on to. The blade she never had the opportunity to use. Anna pulls it out, unsheathes it, and stares at the chipped edge. A blade forged with the blood of a god for the sole purpose of cutting through divine flesh. And she knows—she *knows*—it wasn't meant for battle.

It was meant for *this*.

Khiran follows her gaze, his brow furrowing in confusion. "Anna," he breathes, "Where—"

"Silas gave it to me," she says, voice thready and weak. Her eyes lift, meeting his stare. "He told me I'd need it."

He must see the apology in her expression, see the way she holds her ringed hand to her chest in a final goodbye. "Anna, *no*."

But she has to. Marcia will keep hunting them for as long as she has a scent. Anna doesn't know how fast she heals, but she can't help but remember the way she hobbled after them—the strength in which she threw her daggers—despite an injury that should have left her bleeding out over the earth. Too fast. She heals too fast. She's probably chasing their train even now. Preparing to wait them out at the next stop, ready to ambush them the moment the engine slows.

Khiran is in no shape to run. He won't be for days, at least. Anna needs to throw her off the trail *now*. Needs her to believe they've already jumped the train so she won't be there at the next stop.

He lunges for the blade in her hand, a pained shout passing his lips.

Anna is quicker.

She raises the blade above her head, splays her hand out over the straw like a sacrifice, and brings it down with all her strength.

KHIRAN IS SILENT AS HE WRAPS HER HAND.

The rest of his kurta lays, cut into strips by the same knife that severed the ring finger on her right hand. Anna stares at the empty space that remains; watches the blood seep through the cotton. The flow has slowed to barely a trickle as it clots. Another ten minutes and it should be done completely. She wonders if Marcia has found her finger and the ring encircling it, caked with dirt and dried blood, where she threw it from the train car. Better yet, maybe a stray animal picked it up before she could. Maybe she'll spend precious hours searching and find nothing but a scavenger for her trouble.

Khiran ties it off, tucking in the loose end neatly. It's surprisingly well wrapped. Anna wonders if he'd learned from watching Eira or if it's a skill he was forced to learn from attending the wounds The First and his followers have dealt him.

"I would have found a way," he says, the words soft with regret. His hand lingers on hers, thumb brushing the edge of the bandage, hesitating over the knuckle missing its limb.

Anna stills his hand with her uninjured one, fingers curling around his palm. "I couldn't risk you." An echo of the words he spoke to her a lifetime ago. She's not sure he recognizes them.

He flinches. "I made it to protect you."

"It did. For eight hundred years, *it did*."

"It used so much magic—was a piece of me. I should have realized—"

"Don't," she says, a gentle command. "You told me to stop shouldering blame that wasn't mine to carry. So stop blaming yourself for something I wouldn't have changed."

She waits, patiently, for him to meet her gaze. Tries to soothe the guilt she finds there with a smile. "Eight centuries ago, you gave a piece of yourself to protect me." She reaches for the star-shaped scar along his ribs, resting inches below his wound, feeling the shape of it. "Now I've given a piece of myself to save *you*."

He takes her hand, kisses the fingertips that traced the edges of his scar just a moment before. "I won't be able to find you," he murmurs, voice soft. Anna can hear the fear in it—can feel its echo reverberating in her own chest like a warning. She breathes deeply, concentrating on the way air fills her lungs and rushes past her lips so she can ignore the gnawing pit weighing heavy in her stomach.

She straightens her spine and pulls her shoulders back. As if looking confident holds the power to make her feel it. "I wasn't planning on letting you leave." She leans toward him, their foreheads touching. "Together, remember?"

His sigh is pained. Weighted. She can feel his worry as easily as she feels the tremble in his breath. "Together."

The word tastes like a promise. Anna makes sure to seal it with a kiss.

EVERY TIME THE TRAIN SLOWS TO A STOP, ANNA FINDS HERSELF HOLDING her breath—her ears straining and her body ready to flee. By the time the metal wheels begin turning beneath them again, her lungs burn and her chest aches.

They're unloading cargo now—she can hear them a few cars down. She glances at the mare, finding the animal's dark eyes staring back at her as she lays in the straw. She's a beautiful creature and obviously well taken care of. Anna imagines she must have been sold as a broodmare for a hefty sum. Khiran insists they wait a few more stops until they reach Delhi. A city full of people makes a better hiding spot than a village. Anna only hopes the mare's destination proves to be farther than theirs. Charming as he is, she suspects even Khiran would struggle to explain the bloody mess they've made.

Khiran studies her, his body slouched against the train car wall. "Do you feel different?"

It takes her a moment to understand what he's asking. Then she remembers Cassius' theory and the conversation that followed in the privacy of their room. She looks down at her hands, gaze snagging on the missing piece of her. "No."

Power wasn't the reason she wielded the blade, but it doesn't stop her from feeling disappointed. Bitter, even. She gave up their connection to protect themselves. Having any semblance of power would have made it all the easier to stay safe—to spare Khiran the burden she knows he shoulders alone. The only one of them with magic as a last line of defense to save them both.

She wishes, fervently, that she could lift some of that weight from him.

There is a subtle shift in his eyes, a sigh that feels a little too long, that makes her think he might feel as disappointed as she is. Still, he forces a smile and holds his arms up in invitation. Anna accepts, curling into his uninjured side and resting her head on his chest. His heartbeat is a steady rhythm against her ear.

He kisses her crown. "It's alright," he murmurs into her hair. "It's not something we were counting on."

"Still would have been nice," she grumbles.

She can feel his huff of laughter. "I couldn't agree more."

Beneath them, the train starts creeping forward. Anna can feel the vibrations of the wheels on the track through the floorboards. She holds her breath as it gains momentum, releasing it once they're closer to normal speed. Khiran's fingers play with the ends of her hair, coiling and uncoiling a lock around his finger. She tilts her head, her cheek resting against his collar and her eyes tracing the line of his jaw. "Do you think she'll still find us?"

The corded muscle in his throat flexes as he swallows. "Eventually." A kiss to her forehead. "But it will be harder—take them longer. You have bought us time we didn't have before."

Anna wishes it felt like enough.

CHAPTER THIRTEEN

He's been doing it all wrong—living like a mortal. He'd resigned himself to hardship and monotony, had been at peace with it so long as it meant falling into her arms once night fell. It took seeing her bathed in color and laughter for him to realize that, with her, their world could still shine just as brightly.

DELHI, INDIA
FEBRUARY 26TH, 1964

AFTER SPENDING YEARS IN A MONASTERY, GETTING OFF THE TRAIN IS LIKE stepping into another world.

The station is packed with people, shoulders touching just to get anywhere. It isn't just the crowd that feels different, though. There's an energy, an excitement. Despite the jostling and the permeating smell of sweat, everyone seems to be in good spirits.

Anna catches little snippets of conversation, but there's a set of words that seem to spring from so many lips. Beside her, two older women greet each other, hands clasped warmly. "Holi hai!" one says before the other mimics and the conversation moves on to admiring the other's sari.

Happy Holi.

Anna keeps close to Khiran's side, trying to shield him as much as possible from the crowd. The day of train travel had allowed the wound to heal over enough for the bleeding to cease, but she can tell by the way his face pinched getting off the train that it still pains him. "What is Holi?" The question is meant just for them, but between the trains and people she still has to raise her voice just to be heard over the noise.

He blinks, as if coming back to himself. Anna doesn't ask where he's been… she suspects it was somewhere between the pain in his ribs and the boxcar stained with a mix of their blood on the floor-boards. "It's a Hindu festival."

"What does it celebrate?" she asks, her eyes roaming the crowd. "Everyone seems so happy."

A soft breath of laughter leaves him, something she feels more than hears. It gets swallowed up in the noise. "The triumph of good over evil," he says, the words weary. "They'll be lighting bonfires tonight, to chase out the evil spirits."

Anna scoffs; she can see the irony. "Let us hope it works."

Lips twisting into a wry grin, he tips his chin in agreement. "Indeed."

"Is there a story?" At his questioning glance, she shrugs. "You said it was a Hindu festival. Is there a story behind it?"

"There is always a story."

She fights the temptation to ask him to tell it. There's a stiffness in his gait, she can feel it every time she maneuvers around the crowd and is forced just a little too close to his side. They need to find lodging, the stories can wait until later.

The streets of New Delhi are still crowded, but it doesn't feel nearly as suffocating as the train station behind them. Anna has no idea where they're going, but Khiran walks with a determination that says he clearly does. Anna follows his lead down the bicycle lined streets, trying to keep up even as her eyes wander. The city still holds scars leftover from Britain's colonial rule: a plaque here, a statue there. At one point, they walk past the entrance to Coronation Park. The statue of the British King George the Fifth rises up like a pale spear jutting from the landscape. It looks entirely out of place here, where saris fill the streets with color and the scent of spices perfume the air.

She catches the subtle tremble in Khiran's frame, despite his valiant efforts to hide it from her. "Is it much farther?"

"Another few yards," he promises. Anna can't seem to tell if the words are meant to comfort her or himself. In the end, she decides it's likely a touch of both. He pulls them into a tiny alley, checking over his shoulder to ensure they're alone. "Do you still have those gold pieces sewn into your clothing?"

"Yes." Her hand automatically finds the hem of her collar, feeling the bits of gold between the cotton.

"Good," he murmurs, his fingers replacing her own. He pulls a small silver knife from his pocket. Anna recognizes it as the one Silas used to carry. He used to whittle tiny wooden figurines from branches for the children. The blade cuts a small opening in the seam before being folded away. Khiran diligently works the nuggets of gold from the hem, his knuckles brushing her collarbone. "We'll need to get more funds."

"Where's the closest hideaway?"

He grimaces. "Geographically? Too far."

Anna's not sure what he means, but he doesn't allow her the opportunity to ask. He ushers her forward, his hand on the small of her back, leading her back into the busy street. The lodging he brings them to is more beautiful than Anna expected considering their limited budget. The doors and windows stand tall, ornately carved and painted a bright, welcoming blue. Surrounding the entry, flowers carved in stone twine up the columns and arch over the doorway. They remind Anna of the trailing vines she painted with her own hands in the home she can't return to.

Yearning unfurls in her chest, an ache so soft she feels guilty feeling it at all.

She swallows, smothering the feeling of homesickness with reminders of her reality. "Can we afford this?"

The door creaks on its hinges as Khiran opens it. "We're in the older part of Delhi," he answers, in French, as his other hand gestures for her to go in. "Our gold will go far enough to get us settled."

"And after?" she asks, matching his choice in language. Her eyes drift around the lobby. The host is walking towards them, eyeing them curiously.

He doesn't answer. Instead, he presses his palms together in front of his chest and dips his head in a slight bow. "Namaste," he greets, switching to Hindi.

The middle-aged man mirrors the greeting, bowing his head to each of them in turn as he addresses them. He looks over his shoulder, gesturing a young girl with a tray forward. His hazel eyes dip, a not so subtle glance at their travel worn clothing stiff with dirt and streaked with blood.

Anna follows little of the conversation, but she gratefully takes a glass of water from the girl when offered. The glass sweats in her hands, cool against her palms. When she takes a deep sip, the taste of coconut lingers on her tongue like a promise.

Khiran has bartered one of their last pieces of gold for not only lodging and meals, but supplies as well. Anna wasn't sure how far the gold would really take them, not until the young girl—the host's daughter—delivers a box full of essentials to their room four hours later.

When Anna unpacks it all, she finds close to everything they could need: three sets of clothes for each of them, sets of underclothes, two toothbrushes, dental cream, and a bar of soap. She even included sanitary pads. Anna has no need for them, but she appreciates the thought all the same.

She runs a hand over a sari, admiring the feel of the emerald silk. The other two are cotton—far more practical for their budget. Before they had gone up to their room, Khiran had lagged behind to discuss final payment. She suspects that must not have been the only thing that was said. "This is finer than we can afford."

Khiran hums from the bed, an eye cracking open drowsily. He's sprawled out over the mattress, enjoying a patch of evening sunlight in a way that reminds her of a cat. He's still wearing the hotel bath robe he found in the bathroom after they scrubbed the dirt and blood from their skin in the large sunken tub. The bathwater had turned such a filthy shade of rust, they emptied and refilled it once more before they felt entirely clean.

"Consider it my gift to you then," he murmurs, closing his eyes once more. "To celebrate your first Holi."

Her fingers drift, tracing the hem of the matching blouse. "My arms will be exposed," she says softly, old fears robbing her voice of volume. Even if she wraps the sari in a way that hides one arm, the other will be on full display. Not long ago, this wouldn't have worried her, but they don't have Khiran's magic to fall back on. Not anymore.

He sits up, leaning against the headboard. The drowsy sleep-soaked look in his eyes is gone. "Are you worried?"

"Should I be?"

He gives her the courtesy of considering the question before he answers. "You will receive stares, but it will unlikely lead to any violence." His gaze drops to her chest, where a pale sliver of one of her larger patches peeks between the folds of her robe. "Many will have seen it before. It is more common here than most."

The admittance makes her interest pique. "Is it?"

His chin dips in a nod. "Not enough to be considered common, but yes."

She picks up the sari, holding it against her chest. "So, in theory, I should be able to wear this without fear of being accused of being a witch or possessed by evil spirits?"

A smile pulls at his lips. "In theory."

Her own falters. "You're sure it wasn't too much? When I asked, it seemed like your other safe houses might be farther than we can get to with what we have."

"They are," he admits, sobering. "The closest is in Kolkata to the east, but I'm not sure if it's worth trusting. Not when Marcia knows we're somewhere in the country."

Anna thinks of how quickly they had to leave the temple—how they barely escaped on the train. It wouldn't be a stretch for her to suspect they're desperate enough to risk it. "And the next closest?"

"We're going to Mumbai."

Where they are going isn't what she asked, and Anna is far too old and knows him far too well to believe the deflection wasn't purposeful. Brows rising, she pins him with her stare. "Is your gold in Mumbai?"

He reaches for her, fingertips trailing the inside of her arm before curling around her palm and tracing her heart line. "The ocean is."

Anna frowns, shifting her hand until their fingers lace. "You have gold in the ocean?"

"Yes," he murmurs, bringing her hand to his lips and placing a kiss to her knuckle. "Though likely not in the way you're thinking." His gaze lifts, snaring her in a stare as searching as it is gentle. "I ask that you permit me to withhold the rest of the details. Not for the sake of secrecy, but rather to let you experience it for yourself. Some things are better when approached without expectations."

Anna tries to smother her smile but fails tremendously. "I'm a little old for surprises, don't you think?"

"Never," he answers, and in that sighing breath is a reverence that attests to the truth in which he holds it. He nods toward her other hand, the one still wrapped in his crude bandages. "Let me see."

She offers her hand without protest. As he unwraps the cloth, she's unsurprised to see the skin has already healed over—the base of the amputation shiny with scar tissue.

Khiran runs his thumb over the stump so gently, if she closed her eyes she might think she imagined his touch. His eyes are dark with grief. "Does it still hurt?"

"No," she answers, relieved that it's the truth. "The pain stopped before our train did."

He nods, gaze turning thoughtful. "You heal faster than I do."

"Your wound was considerably more serious," she reminds him, her own eyes drifting toward the side he's been favoring. "If you were human—"

He doesn't let her finish the thought. "I'm not." He places a gentle kiss to her scarred flesh, his eyes lifting to meet hers. "Neither are you."

It feels like an echo of his old assurances—that fear is for mortals and not for them. In this, it still rings true. Death isn't something they need to concern themselves with. Silently, they agree not to think of the ways in which it feels like a lie.

THEY DON'T LEAVE THE ROOM UNTIL DUSK. WHICH, IF ANNA IS BEING honest with herself, provides a small amount of relief. She was determined not to let her condition prevent her from going out (especially after Khiran's assurances) but it still feels immensely easier when she knows the low light will help shield her from stares. She thinks of her conversation with Jiro in the garden she's homesick for—how she tried to capture in words the difficulties that come with being different. Of being *other*.

The world has come a long way from where she started. A few hundred years ago, she wouldn't have risked leaving the privacy of their room without the pale patches of her skin carefully hidden. Maybe, she thinks, there will also come a day where she won't have to fear the stares or the disgust. For tonight, she will trust the night to mask her differences.

Khiran seems more relaxed than when they arrived. Anna

suspects the four hour nap has helped his body heal enough to make the pain more manageable. He's certainly moving more like himself —less guarded as they weave their way through the crowded streets. It helps, she thinks, that everyone seems to be going in the same direction.

A bonfire has already been lit, the flames high and as bright as the smiles of the people dancing around it. The beating of drums fill her ears, a lively pulse, as they find a seat at the edge of the festivities. Anna watches the flames grow higher as they feed it, her throat tightening with a pang of grief.

"They light the fires to drive out the evil spirits," Khiran explains, the reflection of the flames casting shadows in his eyes. Anna wonders if he's thinking of Eira, too, then wants to shake herself. Of course he is. How could either of them think of anyone else when the fires burn this brightly? "And to celebrate the burning of the demoness Holika."

"You did promise me the story," she reminds him, leaning her head against his shoulder.

"There are different versions, different customs even, for this particular one."

"Mm," she hums. "Tell me your favorite then."

The short, few seconds of hesitation make her think the one he tells her is easily his preferred version. "Once, there was an evil king who coveted power above all else. He was gifted immortality. No man nor animal could hope to kill him. Arrogant, he forced his people to worship him like a god."

Anna scoffs. "Sounds familiar."

Khiran's mouth twitches into a smile. "Prahlad, his son, refused and continued to worship Vishnu. His father was furious, of course, and bid his daughter to trick him. His daughter, Holika, being impervious to fire, tricked her brother to join her on a pyre as it was lit. But in a twist of fate, Prahlad emerged from the flames unscathed and Holika was reduced to ashes."

"And the king who believed himself to be a god?"

His eyes gleam, wicked and violent with fantasies he'll never share out loud. "Slayed."

Anna tips her chin to the sky, eyes tracing the familiar shapes of the constellations hiding there. "I hope our story has a similar ending."

The frown he wears is immediate. "You sound like Cassius. Don't let his optimism blind you to the reality of our situation."

Anna shrugs. "Hope costs nothing."

"Nothing *now*," he grumbles. "It can cost you everything, if you aren't careful where you place it."

"I placed my hopes in your hands." She turns her face away from the stars to look at him, her smile soft and teasing. "I think it's gone pretty well, so far. Don't you?"

Khiran is clearly not amused, but the irritated glare he answers with only makes her smile grow wider. She stands, dusting off her sari before holding a hand out to him in peace offering. "Dance with me."

There's a thread of laughter in his sigh, amusement in the way he shakes his head, but he takes her hand readily.

The warm light of the bonfire flickers over his face. His eyes are dark, but sometimes they catch the reflection of the flames just right and she spies a hint of blue. She thinks of the night they danced to Ray Charles in their living room—of how far away that life feels. She won't admit it out loud, but she understands Khiran's hesitance. A tiny part of her had hoped the peace they found at the monastery would last. It wasn't the home she left behind, but it was home enough so long as he remained beside her. She won't tell him that it hurt her to leave it. Won't admit that, in the end, it was that shard of hope that cut the deepest.

She'd rather hold those painful truths close to her heart if it means sparing his.

MORNING BRINGS LAUGHTER.

It filters into their room from the streets, the sound stirring her

R. RAETA

from sleep. She looks over to Khiran, but his eyes are closed and his breathing remains deep and even. Carefully, she untangles herself from the sheets and manages to leave the bed without waking him. She pulls the robe over her body and shifts the curtain aside to look out onto the street.

There is music and color everywhere—plumes of pink, blue, and green rising up over the street like a fog. Laughter spills between the notes, cutting through the powdered air, like an instrument all its own. Anna watches, fascinated, as a girl smears a handful of vibrant green powder over an elderly woman's graying hair. She suspects they must be related, a grandmother perhaps, because the older woman only laughs before returning the favor. They, like everyone else, are covered head to toe in a kaleidoscope of color. The whites of their eyes, their smiles, the only part of them that escaped.

She feels Khiran at her back, the warmth of him the only warning before his arms wrap around her waist. His chin rests on her shoulder, his eyes taking in the scene with her. "The day changes every year," he murmurs, his voice still stained with sleep. "Lucky that we were able to be here during the celebrations."

"What is this?" Her voice is breathy with her awe.

"Holi," he answers, kissing her temple. "Would you like to join the celebration?"

She's certain he already knows her answer. Still, she hesitates, turning in his arms and pulling his robe aside. Her fingers trace over his ribs, gently investigating. She tries not to let herself dwell on how gruesome the scarred nub of her finger looks in comparison to the smooth stretch of skin of his torso. The evidence of his wound is gone, but she knows better than to trust it. The streets are crowded with people. She won't let him suffer for her curiosity. "How are you feeling?"

He covers her hand with his own, bringing her palm to his lips in a fleeting kiss. "Slight pinching," he admits. Anna appreciates the honesty. "Nothing unbearable and certainly nothing worth you fussing over."

She looks over her shoulder, teeth sinking into her lower lip. "It's daylight."

170

"It is."

Rubbing her arm with her free hand, over the pale patches of skin she knows will be entirely too visible. She looks up at him through her eyelashes, her smile timid. "You're certain I won't cause a scene?"

Khiran's eyes soften, his palm cupping her cheek. "I'm certain the opinions of strangers weigh less than the joy you would be robbing yourself of if you let yourself fear them."

She holds his gaze, a stubborn smile pulling at her lips. "That seems like a very roundabout way of saying no."

"An answer so simple would have felt disingenuous." He kisses her softly, his words a murmur against her lips. "I promised you honesty, Anna. It's not a vow I've taken lightly."

Sighing, she lets her forehead touch his. "You're right—I know you're right. It's just…" she trails off, the words escaping her.

As always, he's there to save her. "Forever is a double edged sword. It allows us all the time we need to change. In the same breath, it allows the opportunity for our fears to be justified again, and again, and again." He shakes his head, empathy curling, soft and warm, in his gaze. "I do not fault you for fearing the kind of treatment the world has already proven itself capable of. I only suggest that you are above their insipid opinions."

Laughter sharpens her exhale and she leans back to look at him fully. "You always know what to say."

"Only because I know your heart as well as my own," he murmurs, a promise and a prayer. "I see your scars. I know where you hurt." His eyes drop to her right hand, thumb stroking her knuckles and pausing over her scarred flesh. He swallows, shakes his head, before lifting his gaze. There's a determination in the firm set of his jaw. "I don't need magic to see you."

Anna's breath leaves her, chest aching. She knows the words are as much for himself as they are for her. A reminder that the bond they share is one that goes beyond magic peaches and rings of blood and bone.

THERE IS SO MUCH POWDER IN THE AIR, IT'S AS IF A FOG OF COLOR HAS settled over the narrow streets. Khiran steers her through the chaos, keeping them off to the side and towards a stall. A few people watch them, as if considering whether they're out to celebrate or simply go about their business. Anna suspects they wouldn't have hesitated if they weren't clearly foreigners.

Khiran reaches into his pocket, fishing for some rupees their host provided along with their other necessities as he trades words with the vendor. The older gentleman's face is lined with days spent under the sun, evidence of a life of laughter lining his eyes. When he sees her hovering at Khiran's elbow, the friendliness of his smile dims. Anna can feel his gaze dropping to the exposed skin of her arms.

Anna stills, fighting the urge to flinch away.

The merchant says something as a bag of colored powder and rupees exchange hands. The twitch in Khiran's jaw and the man's continued blatant stare means she doesn't need to know Hindi to know that she's the subject. She swallows, throat dry. "What did he say?"

"He said his sister has your condition; that you're brave to show it."

It's meant as a compliment. There's no disgust in the merchant's gaze, but Anna can't help but feel the sting of it. Wearing her skin shouldn't be an act of bravery—shouldn't be an obstacle to overcome —but it is. It *still* is.

She holds the man's gaze and gives a silent nod in acknowledgement. Bitterness sits on her tongue, tar-thick. Any words she says now will be coated in it.

Khiran offers some parting words that sound neutral to even her ears, before leading her away. Long, tapered fingers open the bag, his fingertips coming back red as he coaxes her left hand into an empty cradle and tipping the bag until she holds a pyramid of red powder in her palms.

Anna takes a pinch of powder, feels how fine it is between her fingers. When she looks up, Khiran paints her cheek in red. For a moment, she merely gapes at him, but the crooked smile he wears is as infectious as the energy around them. He leans toward her, tipping his chin in offering. Anna's answering smile is blinding.

Her fingers drag across his face—smearing the red powder from his brow down to his chin and delighting in the way his eyes spark. In her chest, all the worry and fear she had been carrying the past week unravels, and she gives a shriek as he dumps a fistful of color over her head. She retaliates by throwing what's left in her hand at his chest. It's all the invitation the locals seem to need before Anna and Khiran are bathed in color from strangers' hands.

Anna is surrounded by smiles, by shouted bursts of laughter and colors so bright she feels like her world up until that point was seen behind tinted glasses. It's so overwhelmingly *wonderful*. Her cheeks ache with the force of her smiles and as a handful of blue powder dusts the side of her head and neck, she laughs.

A true laugh. The kind that rises from her chest like it's a living, breathing thing. The kind that begins and has no expiration, because even when there's no more air in her lungs she can still feel it in her heart. She laughs like they didn't nearly lose everything. Like their future isn't still uncertain.

Anna laughs, because in the narrow streets of Delhi, she feels like the festival is doing more than celebrating new beginnings; it's *creating* them.

She turns to Khiran, to see if he knows—to see if he *feels it too*—but his expression catches her off guard. His pupils are blown wide, swallowing the blue. When he reaches for her hand, fingertips tracing the lines of her palm, the touch feels charged. Electric. "You're beautiful."

Breathless, she smiles. "Is that what you're thinking?"

"More or less." His gaze dips lower, to her lips. "I'm afraid the rest is not suitable for public."

It's a statement, but all Anna hears is the unspoken promise in it. "Maybe we should go somewhere more private, then?"

The grip he has on her hand tightens, before he releases her to reach for her face. When his thumb traces the ridge of her cheek, powder in his touch, his eyes follow the motion as if he's under a spell.

Pulse fluttering, she holds his stare. There's something in his expression—something too weighted for a festival of light and laughter. "What's wrong?"

The muscles in his throat work as he swallows, gaze dropping to her lips. Then his hand drops from her cheek, tracing the inside of her arm before lacing their fingers. "Come with me?"

There's a question in the request, which is ridiculous. She would follow him into the fire if only it meant staying by his side. "Anywhere." The word holds the weight of a promise despite how softly it leaves her.

He squeezes her hand, leading her into the twisting side alleys. It's only when they find themselves alone that he stops. Anna's lips part, ready to pry, when he turns and silences her before the first word can escape.

His hands tangle in her hair, his lips slanting over hers with a hunger that arouses her own. Anna can taste the tart edge of the hibiscus coloring the holi powder in his kiss, but she's too hungry for him to care.

"I wasn't prepared," he breathes, teeth dragging over her lower lip. His hand glides over her skin, fingers fanning over her waist. A trail of color follows his touch, the powder from his hands mapping her body like breadcrumbs.

Anna gasps into his mouth, fingers clutching the fabric of his kurta. She can feel his heartbeat thundering beneath her closed fist. "Prepared for what?"

"To see you in full color," he breathes, the words an aching sigh against her lips. His hand cups the back of her neck, fingertips threading through her hair. "To watch you experience something beautiful and *new*. I want to show you every corner this world has to offer and watch your face light up in wonder." His forehead touches hers, noses brushing. "I want more *time*, Anna."

She understands—*oh* does she understand. Because she has lived more lifetimes than any mortal could dream, but today has reminded her that there is still so much left for her to see. To experience. She has lived for centuries, but the years they've had together feel so heartbreakingly short.

Anna also wants more time. Needs it the same way she needs air to breathe.

She kisses him, the burning in her heart transforming from want to *need*. "Me too," she murmurs, the words so heavy she feels like she could break beneath them. "I want that, too."

Her back meets limestone, his body pressing against her and drawing a whimper from her throat as he traces her bottom lip with his tongue. "I want to watch your face as you discover the northern lights—watch the way it reflects in your eyes as colors move across the sky," he breathes, moving to the line of her jaw, a gentle torment as his words brush over her pulse. "I want to watch you crane your pretty neck trying to catch a glimpse of where the waters of Kerepakupai Vená start and the clouds end."

Anna swallows, eyes dark and nerves thrumming beneath his touch. "So take me," she whispers, a dare and a promise. She doesn't need to be seduced, but his touch and his words are doing a fine job of it. There is a humming beneath her skin, a warmth settling so low she *aches*.

A storm is building, darkening eyes, electricity in his smile. She can feel it traveling between them, an invisible heat that courses through her with the barest of touch.

A chorus of giggles is all it takes for the heat in her veins to change from hunger to embarrassment. Three young girls, no older than thirteen, peer at them from around the corner, laughing behind their hands. Anna hides her flushed face in Khiran's chest.

He laughs under his breath, his lips so close to her ear she can feel the heat of it. "It seems we've gained an audience." He pulls away from her, his hand sliding from her hair, fingertips a whisper against her jaw. He brings the hand to his chest, facing their onlookers and addressing them in Hindi.

The girls squeal, equal parts embarrassed and delighted that he knows the language, before scampering off.

Anna raises a brow. "What did you say?"

His grin is crooked at the corners. "Only an apology and that your beauty overcame me. I find that charm does wonders when it comes to avoiding trouble."

She hums. "Particularly when you're the one causing it, I imagine?" She hasn't been blind to the looks they've been receiving. Even their holding of hands seems to have attracted some disapproving looks. Anna imagines being caught kissing in public would be met with an unwelcome response.

He takes her hand, thumb brushing over her knuckles. "You know me well." A quick squeeze and he releases her. "Shall we rejoin the festivities?"

Anna smiles.

SHE DIDN'T KNOW IT WAS POSSIBLE TO WEAR SO MUCH COLOR. EVERY visible inch of her is saturated in a mixing of hues. It's as amazing as it is wonderful. She needn't have worried about the pale shadows on her skin, not when everyone in the street is so thoroughly covered in powder. She laughs as a stranger, dark brown eyes shining as brightly as Anna's own, smears a handful of blue into her hair before darting away.

The street, the people, are all a pallette of color—a painting without the constraints of a canvas. It's hard to tell where the body of one begins and another ends in the crowd. She turns to Khiran, another handful of powder at the ready, and her heart drops.

He's not behind her.

Frantic, she searches for him, but there's so many people and they wear the color like a mask. She can't even scan the crowd for the purple of his kurta because she knows it stopped being that color hours ago. In a sea of moving bodies, she spins, panic rising. If they're separated he can't find her. What if—

A hand grips her shoulder, fingertips biting into her flesh like teeth, turning so quickly she nearly trips over her own feet. Khiran stares back at her, face a mural of purple where the red and blue powder mixed. The breath she releases is stuttering, sharp in ways that prick her lungs like glass.

"I have you," he assures her, his voice nearly drowned out in the crowd. It doesn't matter, she can see the promise in his eyes even though it's tangled with a fear that mirrors her own. "I haven't taken my eyes off you." The hand at her shoulder drops away, reaching for her right hand. It feels like his fingers folding over her palm might be the only thing grounding her. He ducks his head, their faces level. "I won't lose you, Anna."

There's something unsaid in the words, a trembling edge to his voice that tells her he's shaken, too. She swallows, nods. Her finger burns where his ring used to sit, a scarred reminder of how fragile things have become. In her mind, she knows being separated in the street is easily fixed. She knows it would only be a matter of meeting him back at their room.

Her heart doesn't feel it.

Fear beats in her chest, a tattoo against her ribs she knows she may never shed.

Khiran's hand squeezes hers before lacing their fingers. Ghosts of what could have been darkening his gaze. "Would you like to go back to our room?" Anna can hear the wish straining the edges of the question.

"Yes," she breathes, eyes closing as she wills her heart to calm. To be *sensible*. Slowly, the drumming in her ears recedes as they push against the crowds. Khiran's hold on her hand never falters, as if seeing her is no longer enough. Compared to what they had, to the promise of magic melded of blood and bone, Anna's not sure if having him in her sight will ever feel like enough.

THEY RINSE IN THE TUB, COLOR COMING OFF THEIR BODIES UNTIL THE water turns a shade of purple so dark it's nearly black. They wash until the water runs clear and only the stubborn stains are left behind. There is a trail of Holi powder retracing their path across the floor of their room.

Khiran's chest is warm against her back as she reclines against him, her head cradled in the curve of his shoulder as he diligently massages coconut oil into the stains on her arms to coax the color from her skin. She can still hear the excited chatter of people outside the stone walls of their room, the sound of their laughter filtering in through the cracked bedroom window.

"It's terrifying." The confession is a sigh, shaky and warm against the shell of her ear. He coaxes her hand to turn, his thumb tracing the stained lines of her palm as if he could read their future there if he only looked hard enough. "Not being able to feel your fear. I thought the idea of not being able to find you scared me, I didn't realize… When I saw the fear in your eyes and I didn't feel the echo of it in my chest… I never recognized it for the gift that it was—knowing you were safe with a certainty I could feel as easily as if it were my own."

He swallows, pressing his cheek to her temple. "Anna, I cannot lose you. I cannot lose you and not know if you're safe or if you're in pain. There would be no greater agony."

Grief is a vice. It coils like a noose around her heart, her throat. The finger that used to wear the ring that tied them together aches with a phantom pain, burning with accusations. She hadn't been prepared when she drove that knife into her flesh—she hadn't thought about the after. She hadn't had *time* to. Their lives were in danger and she did the only thing she could to protect their future.

She hadn't been prepared for that first blinding moment of panic. Hadn't been ready to face the fear that came with knowing he only has mortal means to find her.

There's an apology on her tongue, barbed and bittersweet, that she refuses to part with. It tastes too much like regret, and she is too old to mourn what she cannot change. She turns in his arms, kneeling between his legs. Water sloshes along the sides of the tub as she moves. His face is as stained as her own, a watercolor of purple and pink, the blue-green of his eyes vivid. She dips her fingers into the bowl of coconut oil beside the tub and traces the shape of his brow, his nose, his lips.

She massages it into his skin, the color swirling beneath her fingertips as she draws it to the surface. When she wipes it away with a dry cloth, most of the stains lift away. Some remain stubborn shadows. "Tell me where you'd take me," she murmurs, washing away a smudge of color lingering on his chin. "If we weren't running, if we could go anywhere, what wonders would you show me?"

He kisses her, his lips warm and tasting like coconut as his palms cradle her jaw. "I would show you shores made of pearls of salt instead of sand," he breathes, the words whisper soft against her parted lips. When his mouth slides against her own, the touch is so light it teases. "I would show you a forest beneath the waves, trees of coral and fish so bright they look like jewels scattered in the light."

Anna swallows, breath hitching as his hands travel lower—tracing her breast and settling in the curve of her waist. "All of it," he breathes. Gently, he coaxes her knees apart, straddling his thighs, while he whispers promises against the beat of her pulse. "I would show you *all of it*."

She sighs, melting against his touch. "Tell me," she urges, *commands*, her hands mapping over the lean lines of his chest and her fingertips grazing the star-shaped scar along his rib cage. The reminder of the magic, the connection, they've lost. "Tell me more. Please."

More, so her pulse races because he's too close instead of too far. More, so she can drown the fear of losing him by being lost *with him*.

He tells her of cenotes with water so blue they feel crystalline as his lips map out the rise and fall of her chest. As her hands thread into his damp hair, he describes a desert so full of color it looks as if it was painted by the brush of an artist as her body arches in an invitation to travel the length of her neck with his teeth. Her hips roll over his, the sweetest of friction, and his words stumble, twisting into a breathy curse as he grips her—long fingers fanning over her hip while the other cups her breast.

His tongue curls against her collarbone, shoulders straining beneath her fingers, as he tells her of an island of lizards so large, people call them dragons. Of rolling green mountains that reach up like fingers to touch wisps of cloud. Turquoise oceans dotted with islands so alive and green they look more like paradise than a place. The words hitch in his throat as she sinks down on him, pulling him close and taking him in.

His touch shifts from gentle to desperate, his hands dragging over her back as she decorates the smooth skin of his shoulders with crescent moons in the shape of her fingers. He breathes her name into her skin, a rasping prayer, and Anna whimpers—buckling under the adoration in his voice. She is rising and falling like the tide, water lapping at the sides of the tub as diligently as the fingers slipping between their bodies and stroking her.

A mewling whine rises from her throat, sweet and warm as honey. Khiran's hand travels from her hip to tangle in her hair, tilting her head, so he can taste the sounds falling from her lips. Underwater, her toes curl as her body tightens around him. A coil wound so tightly she can feel it humming under her skin, ready to spring loose and *sing*. Her thighs tremble, weak with need, but Khiran's hips move beneath her, his fingers still stroking.

He speaks against her mouth, lips brushing over hers with every syllable. "I would give you the world, Anna."

Maybe it's the shape of her name, or the whispered touch of the promise. Or, maybe, it's just *him*. Anna only knows that the tension coiling in her lower stomach has snapped—her spine arching and her hands grasping. Later she'll feel guilty for scratch marks along his back and shoulders, but right now all she knows is pleasure and the sense that, if she doesn't latch on to him she may float away.

She curls into him, gasping as he continues to move beneath her. *Inside* her. His hands glide over her skin, gripping the undersides of thighs and lifting her from the sunken tub. The tile is shockingly cold on her back and shoulders against the flush warming her skin. He hovers over her, droplets of water dripping off his body onto her own as he curls a hand around her hip, coaxing her back into motion. The desperation in his movements is gone, replaced with a deep and gentle rhythm, but the heat in his eyes burns bright.

"We aren't done," he murmurs, stare hooded and drunk off the feel of her. He reaches up, lacing their fingers above her head, the tile cold against the back of her hand. "Not yet."

Anna knows the promise extends far beyond the ways he's touching her.

CHAPTER FOURTEEN

It's been too long since he's seen her. Too long since he let himself be soothed by the sounds of her oceans and comforted by the soft curve of her crescent smile. The memory of flames, of cornflower eyes burning with forgiveness, is crushing. He knows, before he even says the words, that the news will break her heart.

MUMBAI, INDIA
MARCH 1964

IT'S A MONTH-LONG JOURNEY FROM DELHI TO MUMBAI ON FOOT. IT would be faster to travel by train, but the rupees they have remaining feel ominously light in their pockets. Better to brave a longer journey than to risk being stranded.

In an effort to conserve their funds and spare their feet, they slip some rupees into the hands of merchants in exchange for allowing them to ride in their boats and carts. They travel south down the Yamuna River, the current in their favor.

Raj, the merchant guiding them down the river, has agreed to take them as far as Etawah, where he will unload his wares. She's grateful that Khiran's weak stomach seems to be behaving itself on the calm waters. He sits beside her amongst the crates of silks, their shoulders brushing as they look out over the water. People bathe along its banks, purifying themselves in the holy waters—freeing themselves from the fears of death.

They pass an older man paddling a coracle, the circular basket frame weighed down with sacks of rice and grains. His beard shines white against his sun drenched skin. A monument rises in the distance, pale stone gleaming in the afternoon light. Anna recognizes it almost immediately from pictures she's seen and the articles she's read.

"Are the stories true?" she asks, nodding toward the Taj Mahal. "That he built it for his late wife?"

"Favorite," Khiran corrects, his gaze sliding to hers. "She was his favorite wife, but one of many."

"It's beautiful."

He hesitates, weighing his words as he follows her gaze. "It is hard for me to see beauty in many of man's wonders," he admits, voice haunted by memories. "I was there when it was built. I saw the lives its foundation was built on. It only stands because a great many suffered. The same with so many of man's marvels—the pyramids in Egypt, the Great Wall in China, the Colosseum in Rome."

He shakes his head. "You see a marvel, but I still see the blood those stones were baptized in."

Anna's gaze lingers on the pale towers, tracing the curve of its arabesque domes. She slips her hand into his, lacing their fingers. "Maybe it's both," she murmurs. He looks at her, his dark brows furrowed. The smile she offers is somber, heavy with the weight of all the ghosts that haunt his eyes. "A marvel and a grave."

ANNA'S NOT SURE WHAT KIND OF SURPRISE SHE EXPECTED WHEN THEY reached Mumbai, but it's certainly not this.

They don't linger in the city, don't find lodgings. Khiran leads them straight to the ocean. When the sand begins to sink beneath their steps, they remove their shoes, carrying them at their sides. They walk for hours, Khiran's eyes flitting over the landscape and lingering on every stranger they see. It's only when the sand turns rocky and they find themselves entirely alone that he pauses.

He issues one final surveying look, assuring himself that they don't have an audience, before Khiran hands her his shoes. "Hold these for me?"

She nods, still baffled, as he turns his back to her and walks into the ocean. Anna watches the waves lap at his ankles, his knees, his hips. Deeper and deeper he goes until the tide rises to his chest. His hands rest, open and floating on the surface as if feeling for something spiritual.

Anna feels the trembling beginnings of concern. "Khiran?"

He turns his face toward her, grin teasing the corners of his mouth. "Don't worry. It will only take a moment."

"As comforting as that is, what are you *doing*?"

"Calling on an old favor." It's the only answer he gives before the rest of him slips below the surface, disappearing from her sight.

She waits, her eyes lingering on the spot she last saw him. The ocean is calm, but it does nothing to ease the frantic beating of her heart when a minute passes, then two, and he has yet to emerge.

The waves stutter. Shift.

Instead of crashing on the shore, the tide recedes until she sees Khiran's dark head. The sea *parts* around him, a wall of water on each side. Seawater drips from his hair as he plucks a piece of seaweed from his shoulder, lips thinning in irritation, before he flicks it away. The wall of water devours it eagerly.

"Come," he says. "Kaia's waiting for us."

Kaia, the woman who once stepped from the depths of a river when he was a boy instead of a god. The one Eira once called friend.

Anna tentatively steps forward, heart in her throat and pulse drumming in her ears with such volume that it drowns out the tide. There are few things Anna fears anymore—she has lived through burning pyres and bombs of war and walked away unscathed.

The thought of drowning terrifies her.

A fire will eventually burn out and a dropped bomb only goes off once, but the sea... the sea is endless. If these walls of water crash around her, if the current sweeps her away, there is no limit to how many deaths she will suffer. A never ending cycle of choking, her body fooled into gasping for air even when she sees nothing but water. It's the worst torture she can imagine.

When Khiran had left her on that island so many years ago, she thought she might lose herself in the fight between starving and drowning. Sometimes she thinks the only thing that kept her from giving up and going into the ocean was the fear that he might never be able to find her at the bottom of it. Being that she never learned how to swim, drowning was as good as guaranteed. It was safer to stay and starve.

Warily, she eyes the wall of water as it rises the farther in she walks. When it grows taller than her head, she hesitates.

Gently, Khiran folds his hand over hers, easing it away from where she has it tucked to her chest. "Don't be afraid. Once we go a little deeper, the path to shore will be swallowed back up by the ocean, as will the open sky above us. It can be an unnerving experience, but I promise there is nothing to fear."

Nodding numbly, Anna squeezes his hand with more force than needed, and allows him to lead her deeper. As he had warned, the path behind her is slowly washed away with a gentle sweeping of the tide. Anna's surprised by how gentle it is. She had expected it to be crashing, a show of power. Instead, it's like tucking a child into bed, the smooth sweeping of a blanket being pulled up to a little one's chin.

Then the water spills over their heads, an invisible ceiling holding it up, and Anna has to close her eyes and stop. Khiran, ever patient, waits for her to collect herself.

Finally, when she feels she can breathe without the risk of hyperventilating, she reopens her eyes. It's darker now that there's no unobstructed view of the sky. When she looks up, she can still make out the distorted light of the sun bathing her face in rippled sunlight. A school of fish darts over their head, casting dappled shadows.

She releases her breath, but it barely touches the tightness in her chest.

Khiran reaches for her hand, lacing their fingers. "It can feel overwhelming."

Swallowing, she confesses, "I don't think I've ever felt claustrophobic like this."

"I understand." He squeezes her hand. Right now, it feels like he might be the only thing tethering her to the ocean floor and keeping her from being swept away. "Would it help to close your eyes? I could guide you."

Anna thinks it over before shaking her head. "No. I think—I think that might be worse, honestly. Let's just walk. Maybe moving will help. Just, please don't ask me how I'm doing," she says, because she knows without a doubt that her answer will only serve to remind her of how very *not* fine she is.

"As you wish." Gently, he pulls on their connected hands, subtly guiding her into taking those first few steps.

She only manages three before the wall of water shifts, wicking away from the path ahead of them, but to Anna the movement feels like a warning that all of it will come crashing down.

"Breathe, Anna."

She is, isn't she? Her heart is hammering against her ribs with enough strength that her entire chest feels like it rattles with every beat. No, he's right. There's no air in her lungs. She takes a breath. Holds it. Forces it out. Again. Again. Again. But the panic isn't receding. It's rising up and over her head, the strength of it sweeping her away, crashing down on her until—

"Look at me."

She does. Because it's a command. Commands are easier to

follow than the twisting, dark thoughts screaming at her to run, hold her breath, dig her hands into the ocean floor so she can claw her way back to shore.

Khiran's eyes look darker here in the deep, the blue and green drowned by shadows, but they're calm. Controlled. Anna seizes it with the same desperation as she does his offered hands. It is only feeling the steadiness of his touch in her white-knuckled grasp that makes her realize she's trembling.

He takes a step backward. Over his shoulder, the water ripples. "Don't look behind me," he scolds, his grip on her sliding up her palms until his fingers snare her wrist.

Anna likes it. The hold he has on her feels stronger, less likely for her to be ripped away from him. She mimics the motion. He's sure to sport bruises and the imprints of her fingernails later, but she can't bring herself to loosen her grip.

"Look only at me. Do you understand?"

Tightly, she nods, forcing the breath in and out of her lungs and pinning her gaze to his.

"Good," he soothes, taking another step back. And another. She follows. "Just keep looking at me."

She wets her lips, following his every step, and tries not to think of how the light is fading because the water above their heads is growing deeper. "I hate this."

"I noticed."

"Please tell me this is a short trip."

A moment of silence, a skipped heartbeat. "Khiran?"

The tiniest hint of a smile plays across his lips, eyes shining despite the dim. "Kaia's magic works in similar ways to Eira's paths. It will be far, but it won't be long."

"Good. Because I *hate* this. It's terrifying."

Khiran glances up, thoughtfully. Anna has to force herself to focus on the hollow of his throat instead of following his gaze. "I can't say I disagree." His eyes meet hers. "I was afraid the first time, too." It shouldn't, but somehow the confession makes her feel a little bit better.

After a few minutes, her heart gradually slows to a pace that is *almost* normal, and the crushing weight on her chest floats away. In a moment of bravery, she begins glancing over Khiran's shoulder as they walk. Testing the strength of her courage.

Goosebumps dot her arms, her breath fogging. "It's getting colder."

"Yes."

"Is that because of the depth or the destination?"

He thinks about it. "Both, actually."

The sand under her feet has turned rocky and slick. She's not entirely sure when that happened. With a feeling of unease, she realizes it's slanting down instead of up. "Does... does she live *under* the water?"

"Yes." At her look of alarm, he chuckles. "Magic, Anna. You'll feel perfectly at ease once we get there." His eyes crinkle in the corners, mischief in his grin. "Other than the feeling of thousands of tons of water being magically suspended over you, it'll feel just like you're on land."

She glares. "Mean."

"A taste of how I felt on that disgrace of a ship."

"There was nothing wrong with the ship," she huffs. Her breath curls into clouds with the force of it. "You just have a frighteningly weak sto—" Movement catches her eye, a shadow moving through the water just over his shoulders. Large and getting larger. Colossal.

The hands around her wrist tighten. "Anna—"

"I'm okay," she murmurs. And, for the first time since watching the tide rise around her, she truly feels it. As the shadow comes closer, the details the water masks become clearer and wonder overshadows the fear. It's not one creature, but many. A pod, her mind supplies, fishing the word from somewhere in the corner of nearly forgotten bits of knowledge.

They swerve, the pod splitting around their bubble of air, swimming through the wall of water on either side of them. So close, Anna could reach out and touch their white and gray mottled sides if she were brave enough. Flashes of tusk, a wand of spiraled ivory on some of their heads.

"Narwhals," Khiran says, standing beside her, shoulder to shoulder, as he watches them glide past. "Unicorns of the sea."

Anna wonders, awe stricken, how an everyday creature could feel more magical than the forces allowing them to walk the ocean floor.

ANNA ISN'T SURE WHAT SHE WAS EXPECTING, BUT IT CERTAINLY WASN'T this.

The mouth of the cave yawns open, icicles lining the top like rows of teeth. Perhaps it is Cassius' influence, but part of her had expected something more opulent. Which is silly, really. Eira and Silas hardly lived in luxury.

Khiran prods her forward, shaking his head. "We still have a little ways to go. The caves are part of the journey, not the destination."

"Caves," she echoes, under her breath. "There's multiple?"

"It's an entire system. A labyrinth for anyone she wishes to keep out." His hand goes to the small of her back as they step through the entrance, his eyes raised to the icicles above them until they've safely stepped past. "Before I became immortal, I'm told she drifted much like Silas. Traveling between the seas, slumbering on the isles, as it pleased her."

Anna watches a crab scuttle across the cave floor, pincers searching for its next meal. "Why the change?"

"If I had to guess?" He sighs, eyes clouded in memory. "I always thought it might be for Eira."

Anna frowns. "I don't understand."

"Eira's meadow, it was fixed. Once Marcia forced an invitation from her, there was no going back. No locking her out. Kaia... her gift isn't tied to a place. She doesn't *need* a home at all. I think... I think this place was an apology. Maybe even her repentance. If Eira ever needed a place to run to where she couldn't be found—"

"She'd at least have here," Anna finishes, heart aching. "Did Eira ever forgive her?"

"In her heart? I like to believe so. In the ways that mattered?" Khiran shakes his head, a scoff laced with fondness escaping him. "And now she's gone, and it's too late."

Time is a fragile thing.

Once, Anna had a better sense of just how fragile. Those years she struggled to find her next meal. The nights that were so bitterly cold, she wasn't sure she'd wake come morning. Then Khiran placed that peach in her hand, and she stood in the flames but did not burn. Years turned to decades and decades into centuries, and somewhere along the line Anna forgot how it felt to feel afraid of running out of time.

It wasn't until she took Piers under her wing and called him son —when the years became a countdown instead of a tally—that she had a taste of that feeling again. Being immortal, having forever stretched before her, robbed her of that. How easy it must be to hold on to an apology when you think you have an eternity to make it.

Anna leans her head against his shoulder. "Do you think she knows? About Eira?"

A moment of silence, filled only with their breathing and footsteps. Then, so quietly she nearly misses it, Khiran answers. "No."

He doesn't offer any further explanation. Anna doesn't ask for one. There's a hollowness to his eyes that indicates he's more focused on his thoughts than what's in front of them. She wonders if he's going over the dozen different ways that conversation will go, the way *she* is.

If he's right—if Kaia truly doesn't know of Eira's passing—then she will soon. As much as she's sure he hates to be the one to tell her, she knows Khiran will. Sometimes, lies can feel kinder than truths, but secrets can fester—a bitter, subtle poison. He won't risk silence when he knows it will only sharpen the lancing pain of the truth.

Anna can't help but wonder why he didn't call on this favor before, when they were in Istanbul—a city settled on a strip of land cradled between the Black Sea and Marmara Trough. It would have been so easy to run straight from the temporary shelter of Cassius' generosity to Kaia's uncharted fortress protected by the ocean itself. She wonders, but she doesn't ask.

How can she when the answer wears the shape of Eira's parting smile?

THE TEMPERATURE CONTINUES TO DROP.

Soon, Anna's jacket doesn't feel nearly warm enough to protect her from the cold. Her teeth chatter, the sound obnoxious even to her, but she can't bring them to stop. Khiran gives her his coat, but it still doesn't completely shield her from the chill. She tucks it around herself firmly, ducking her nose and chin under the collar so she can at least feel the warmth of her breath.

"Almost there," he promises. The cold barely touches him. It's only the goosebumps dotting his arms and the breath curling like smoke from his lips that convinces her that he feels it at all.

"Will it b-be warmer?"

"… Do you want the truth?"

Her answering glare is as bitter as the cold.

Khiran chuckles, pulling down the collar of his coat just enough to place a kiss on the reddened tip of her nose. "Don't fret. Kaia would turn me out before she let you freeze. Some of the rooms are colder than others, but she'll have some spare furs for you to wear to ward off the chill."

Anna nods, ducking her face back into the collar of his coat. It's hard to gauge how far they've traveled—the cave walls leave little room for landmarks, but they walk another fifteen minutes when Khiran's steps slow and Anna realizes the tunnel has opened up into a cavern. At its entrance, a woman who can only be Kaia stands as if she'd been waiting for them.

She's beautiful.

Her thick, black hair gleams. Even braided, it's still long enough to reach past the woman's lower back. Then she turns, and Anna sees her face. She understands how a young Khiran would see the moon in her. Her face is full, glowing and soft. When she smiles, her dark, hooded eyes are like twin crescent shadows.

"Khiran." She says his name like a song, her voice melodic and deep. Ancient. "It has been many years since you journeyed here."

"I'm afraid mortal perils rarely find their way this deep." The corner of his lips curl, a subtle smile that feels as tired as she feels. "Hello, Kaia."

When she walks, she's so fluid and silent she almost floats. Intricately carved hooks pierce her ears, flashing pale and iridescent against her tan skin. Shells, Anna realizes, they're carved from shells. As she gets closer, she gets a closer look at the design and notices that the carved scrolling framing her face looks like waves.

Kaia reaches up, placing a hand on Khiran's cheek. A string of shimmering shells dangle from her plump wrist, ringing out like the world's only wind chime beneath the waves. "I'm happy you're here." Her eyes slide to Anna, head tilting. "And not alone." The pleased smile she gives is as soft as she is. "My, things must be changing in the world above."

Khiran's knuckles brush her own. "This is Anna, my..." he falters, eyes meeting hers. "My person," he says, voice soft. "My heart."

Once, Anna would have only seen the romance in such a statement. But for all the love he holds for her, the adoration lining his voice like velvet, there are flames haunting his eyes like ghosts. His heart. His weakness. Burn her to ashes and he will float away with her.

Subtly, she laces their fingers and hopes he catches the echo in her eyes. In her smile. He is her heart, just as much as she is his.

Anna lets her eyes drift back to Kaia, momentarily alarmed to find tears dripping from her chin.

"Oh," she sniffs, hands clutched to her chest. "Your love for each other is so...so *beautiful*." Another sniff and the tears come faster, her face crumpling. "I am so **happy**."

Khiran sighs, but there is a fondness in it. He releases Anna's hand to ease the clasped ones away from Kaia's chest. "Thank you, truly, but I'm afraid I'm not here for the sake of visiting."

She blinks up at him, the top of her head barely reaching his shoulder. "What—"

"Once," he starts, bracing himself with a breath before starting again. "Once, you offered me a favor. I'm afraid I've found myself in need of it."

Kaia stares at him, the softness of her expression hardening. She wipes the stubborn tears clinging to her cheeks with the palm of her hand. "I see. I will start the fires. You know how I feel about bad news on an empty stomach."

"I do," he assures her. "Is everything where it was when I last visited?"

She nods. "It is. Please, make yourselves comfortable." Her gaze shifts to Anna, eyeing the way she's drowning in what is obviously Khiran's coat. "There's some warmer clothing in the wardrobe you're more than welcome to. I'm afraid the rooms stay rather cold."

Anna tips her chin in gratitude. "Thank you."

Kaia offers her a warm smile before heading down one of the long corridors. Anna assumes it must be the kitchen. Once she's out of sight, Anna leans into Khiran's side, her voice soft. "Is she alright? She seemed—" Anna's not sure how to describe the swing of emotions without it sounding negative instead of concerned.

Khiran huffs on a laugh, his fingers pulling the collar of his coat more securely around her neck. "Kaia feels things a little more deeply around this time." When he catches Anna's questioning look, he makes a vague gesture to the ceiling. "Full moon."

"Oh," she murmurs, eyes lingering on the hallway. She thinks of how the phase of the moon affects the tides, the relationship between the two as old as the oceans themselves. "Is it like that with all emotions or...?"

"I have yet to make her angry and I don't plan on testing it anytime soon," he answers, a wry smile curling the corners of his mouth.

Anna's teeth worry her bottom lip. Khiran had requested a favor, but never made any mention of the bad news he carries with him. "Will you tell her?"

Khiran's hands still, a soft intake of breath passing his lips. He swallows, eyes closing. Pained. "Not yet."

She wants to ask when, but she holds back. There have been so many times she's had to break the news that a loved one was lost. It was never easy, even when they were nothing more than strangers. She knows it will hurt Khiran to tell the news just as much as it will hurt Kaia to hear it.

He must see something in her expression, because he glances up at the ceiling as if looking through the stone and ice and to the sky itself. "The moon... it would be cruel to tell her now."

Anna can't help but feel that there's a cruelty in waiting, too.

ANNA IS A LITTLE RELIEVED TO SEE THAT KAIA'S MEALS ARE MORE IN line with what she's used to. Less long tables lined with velvet cushioned chairs and more home cooked meals served around a low table on the floor. Anna tucks her feet beneath her wool skirts, the fur trim brushing her ankles and tickling her collar. The creamy fish soup Kaia shares with them smells as rich as it tastes. Anna lets it sit on her tongue, savoring the flaky texture of the fish and the way it warms her from the inside out. "This is delicious," she compliments. "Thank you."

Kaia beams. "It was always one of Khiran's favorites when he came to visit. I'm pleased that you enjoy it as well."

Khiran hums in agreement around his spoon, eyes closed as he savors. "No one makes it quite like you do."

Kaia smiles, her cheeks flushed with her joy. "So you've told me every time I've served it."

"It has always been true."

Kaia chuckles, her laugh deep and melodic. If Anna listens closely, she can hear the echo of it ringing off the stone walls. "Your home is impressive," Anna says, eyes tracing the gentle slope of the ceiling. It should be rough and decorated in jagged edges, but it's perfectly smooth. She can't even see any tool marks. "Khiran said you built it?"

"Ah, he gives me a little too much credit. The caves were here before, I merely made them my own." She shrugs, following Anna's gaze with a fondness. "Water has a strength most take for granted. They forget that it is water that cut fjords and carved canyons. They forget how easy it is for bodies to freeze and for lungs to drown."

Anna understands what she means but she can't relate. Not when the feeling of walking beneath the shadow of the ocean still makes her skin prick. She would face the fire before she'd dream of taking on the ocean and its depths.

Khiran's eyes are searching as he looks at her—as if following her train of thoughts. "Most would be quick to change their mind after a stroll on the ocean floor."

Kaia's brow furrows. Then, understanding, her lips pull into an apologetic smile as she turns to Anna. "I'm sorry. I forget sometimes how scary it can be to travel here when you're so used to land beneath your feet and sky above your head. Khiran once struggled with the trip, as well. He's always been more involved in the world above—has always had a hand in shaping the myths humans surround us in. Eira and I have always done things more quietly and from within the comforts of the places we call home."

The table goes quiet. Anna can feel the weight of it on her chest, the words unsaid so heavy they're suffocating. She looks to Khiran, gauging his expression.

Slowly, he sets his spoon down, his hands moving to his lap. Anna can see the way they clench beneath the table. She reaches for him, folds her hand over his own.

Kaia looks between them, a frown forming between her brows. "I apologize, did I say something—"

"No," Khiran interrupts, wincing. His throat moves as he swallows. "Nothing like that. It's only—there's something I need to tell you, but I know it will hurt. And with the moon—I thought if I waited perhaps you wouldn't feel it so sharply."

She sits back, her dark eyes searching. "Pain is pain, whether I feel it now or later. You know that." She folds her hands over her lap, chin tipped proudly. "Tell me."

"She's gone," Khiran murmurs, as if saying the words softly could ease the blow. For the first time since Kaia said her name, he looks up and meets her stare. "Eira is gone."

For a moment, Kaia only stares. The corners of her mouth twist into a gruesome smile as she shakes her head. "Gone?" she echoes. "Don't be ridiculous. You know she—"

"Malik burned the meadow, Kaia. The house, *Eira*, they're both gone. They killed her."

Her smile wanes, the playful light in her eyes turning dark and cold. Kaia stands, backing away from the table but never dropping Khiran's gaze. "No." Her voice is deceptively calm; the warning groan ice gives seconds before it cracks.

Khiran flinches, his own pain twisting his expression into one of regret. "I'm sorry."

"No," she repeats. There's an unsteadiness in the way she stands, a sway, as if she's caught in a current of her own making. A whirlpool of every regret. She repeats the word, again and again, the volume and the despair mounting with every cry until it is a scream.

Around them, the ocean freezes—ice branching out like lightning and expanding in the cracks and crevices of the earth. Above them, the land shakes and the ocean swells. For four minutes and thirty-eight seconds, Alaska is reshaped by fissures and landslides in what will become known as the most powerful earthquake recorded in North America.

Only three souls will ever know it was heartbreak that made the earth split.

CHAPTER FIFTEEN

*He worries. His distress split between two different women for two entirely
different things: one drowning in despair and the other too beautifully
optimistic to admit that loving him—staying with him—is bound to drag
her into those same depths.*

ALASKA, UNITED STATES
SPRING 1964

THE ROOM IS DARK, A SINGLE CANDLE BURNING ON THE NIGHTSTAND. IT
casts long, flickering shadows along the cave walls. Anna waits until
they're curled up in bed, warm and wrapped in each other, before
she speaks. "Will she be alright?"

Under her cheek, she feels a stutter in Khiran's sigh. "I want to
say yes, but..." His words trail off, but Anna doesn't need them to
understand.

The pain in Kaia's scream will haunt her for lifetimes. In it, Anna heard the echo of her own fears mirrored back at her—a glimpse of what the future could hold if they aren't careful. Her hand curls against his chest, searching for comfort in the steady beating of his heart. "She loved her."

He covers her hand with his own, his thumb brushing over her knuckles. "She used to say they were soul mates. That, even though Eira refused to speak to her, they would always carry a piece of each other." He turns his head, lips brushing her crown as he murmurs into her hair. "That piece of her died tonight."

Tilting her face, she studies the heaviness in his answering stare. "I'm sorry you had to be the one to tell her," she whispers. He looks so fragile in this moment, as if the weight of her words could break him.

He breathes a sigh so soft, it *aches*. Gently, his hand lifts to her brow, fingers tracing the shape of her face. "It felt like I was mourning her all over again," he confesses, his eyes shutting as he presses his forehead against her own. His voice is fragile—riddled with a pain she can feel echoed in the hollow of her chest. "Anna... I cannot lose you. I couldn't bear to live in a world that doesn't have you in it."

She wants to assure him, assure *herself*, that he could. That it would hurt, but he would still have a life waiting for him after the pain settled into an ache. She wants to, but she doesn't. How can she, when the fear of losing him is crippling? Instead, she holds him close and lets the sound of his heartbeat soothe the fears she's afraid to speak out loud.

Kaia doesn't leave her room for four days.

Khiran brings her meals and sits with her. Anna wanders the cave system as far as she dares to pass the time. Sometimes she hears Kaia crying, the sound of her heartbreak echoing off the walls. Anna can feel it in her heart, a crushing weight on her chest, as her own grief answers back. It's a strange kind of torture. Anna thought she was done mourning Eira's death, thought she had come to terms with never seeing her again, but Kaia's despair reignites her own. The pain she thought she moved past creeping back with a choking grip, her throat tight and her eyes aching.

At night, she dreams of her.

Sometimes it's an echo of a memory. Sometimes it's a nightmare. They all feel too real. Too close to the truth. When she wakes, she's dizzy with trying to comb through the tangled threads of memory and dreams. Some of them are so fragile, they break away like spider silk in her grasp—sticking to her skin, but unrecognizable. A handful of splintered, tangled strands without a full picture.

She doesn't know where one ends and the other begins anymore —doesn't know where that line is drawn in the sand because the tide of grief has washed it away. All she knows is that it hurts in ways she wasn't prepared for. Anna has had centuries worth of loss, but she had always been prepared for it. Her eyes were open and her heart was guarded. Every relationship she forged was tempered with the knowledge that it would only ever be temporary—a fleeting chapter in her everlasting life.

Eira was different, because Anna believed her story would last as long as her own. She had never considered the possibility of losing her when they had been gifted with forever. She's still not sure which hurts more deeply—knowing time is short or never knowing to say goodbye.

On the fourth day, Khiran finds her curled up in the sheets of their bed with a book in her hand. "I want to show you something."

Anna looks up from the yellowed pages. Kaia's book collection isn't nearly as expansive as Khiran's had been, but there were a few she recognized and more she didn't. The tome she holds in her lap is leather bound, its pages whisper thin and brittle with age. The graceful looping language is one she doesn't recognize, but she was content appreciating the illustrations until she could ask Khiran to interpret it for her.

Leaning against the doorway, his arms crossed, Anna can see the fatigue lining his smile despite the warmth in his eyes. She frowns, closing her book with gentle hands. "But Kaia—"

"She was the one who insisted on it." He pushes himself from the frame, crossing the room and cradling her face in his palms. For a moment he only stares down at her, searching, before leaning down to press a kiss to her forehead. It feels like an apology. "You've been stuck here, alone, for the better part of a week. I've been suitably reprimanded for failing to properly host in her stead."

Towering over her, he brushes the hair away from her face, fingertips brushing over her skin. "Besides," he murmurs, his voice as soft as a confession. "I'm not certain my presence is helping anymore."

Anna nods, understanding. In grief, there are times where being alone feels like being untethered. Sometimes, though, losing oneself in mourning is exactly what's needed in order to face it. She sets her book on the bed. "Where are we going?"

"I thought I'd show you some of the connecting caves—help you get your bearings." He flinches, his smile apologetic. "I realized you've probably avoided exploring them too closely for fear of getting lost in them."

He's right, of course. What little investigating she'd done had been kept close to the main branch of tunnels that connected to their room. She hadn't even trusted herself to try and find the kitchen. His warnings about the tunnels had stuck with her and now, without his ring to tether him to her, she wasn't willing to risk what getting lost in them might mean.

She follows him out of their room, their hands linked as he leads her through the maze of tunnels. Lights line the walls, their glow otherworldly. Ten minutes of walking, and she realizes that the temperature has risen, the air more humid. It's the scent that gives it away. "Is that sulfur?"

"There are a few underground hot springs," he confirms, eyes sliding to meet hers. "We can start there, if you'd like?"

"Is that what you wanted to show me?"

His laugh is breathy, spun of wishes and weak hopes. "Have you forgotten, Anna? I want to show you *everything*."

In her chest, her heart gives an answering hum. "Is that what you wanted to show me *today?*"

"No," he admits, gaze soft. "What I had in mind is a bit farther down."

She gives his hand a gentle squeeze. "Let's start there, then."

He squeezes back, warmth in his answering smile as he leads her farther into the tunnels. She unbuttons her coat as they walk, the chill fading faster than should be possible. Another few minutes and she's removing it entirely, draping it over Khiran's offered arm.

"Are these tunnels...?"

"Kaia's magic branches out differently than Eira's. Her pathways travel the same distances, but they remain open."

Anna frowns. "How does she keep mortals from stumbling on them?"

"They're connected by water." He tips his head, gesturing to the network of tunnels they've already passed through. "Dive deep enough, and those hot springs will lead you to Japan."

No wonder she doesn't have a problem with strangers roaming her halls. The entrances are too deep for most to find. Even if they did, very few would be foolish enough to risk entering an underwater cave without knowing what's on the other side of it.

He takes a final right turn, the tunnel opening up into a yawning cavern and a large underground lake that looks deep enough to swim in, but it's the light scattered like stars across the rocky walls, the reflection of them on the still water, that robs Anna of her breath. "How?"

"It's not quite as romantic when you know the truth of it." His eyes, dark in the dim, drink in her awed expression. Savoring her wonder, the way he promised he would. "Let yourself believe it to be magic for just a little bit longer."

It's not a hard ask. Anna is almost convinced that it *is* otherworldly. "It's beautiful."

His smile is soft as he kisses her knuckle. "Come, let us get closer." Khiran leads them to the water's edge, pausing only a moment before releasing her hand. He pulls his shirt over his head, leaving it to the rocky shore at his feet, before starting on the button of his pants.

Anna watches the way the muscles of his back and shoulders move and flex. "What are you doing?"

The pants join his shirt, leaving him in nothing but a pair of pinstriped boxers Anna recognizes as having come from the drawer in their borrowed dresser. Not for the first time, she wonders if that room has always been his. "Swimming," he answers simply, casting her a look over his shoulder. There's a playful challenge in the way his brow rises, the corner of his mouth hinting at a smile. "Are you coming?"

She hesitates, her gaze lingering on the star dappled water. "Is it cold?"

The laugh that leaves him is deep and throaty as his hands settle at her hips and pull her closer. "Would I invite you to swim if it was?" he asks, the question a breath at her ear. He pulls the coat from her arms and drops it to the rocks at their feet, before his fingers play with the buttons lining the front of her dress. "Come into the water with me, Anna. Help me remember the beauty of it all."

She swallows. Wets her lips. The warmth he inspires wars with the nervous fluttering of her stomach as she reaches for the top button. "I won't go in all the way," she warns, but the words sound too breathless to be taken with any seriousness. Khiran is too distracted undoing the remaining buttons, watching her dress fall from her hips to her feet. The satin slip clings to her skin, offering enough coverage for her to feel like she's not entirely exposed. Despite having these caves entirely to themselves, she still feels a little less vulnerable with it on.

He takes her hands, walking backwards into the water. Anna follows until the bottom half of her slip sticks wetly to her thighs. She expects him to stop, or at least slow, but he continues leading her deeper without any hesitation. It dawns on her, then, that he doesn't know her panic a few days ago was born from more than the disconcerting feeling of being surrounded by ocean, but the fear of *drowning* in it. "I can't swim, Khiran. I don't know how."

Finally, his steps falter. The playful curve of his lips wavering. "You've walked this earth for eight centuries." There is no cruelty in the words, only bewilderment. Anna sees it for what it is: a reminder of their differences.

She kisses him. Sweet and soft and forgiving. "It wasn't on account of not having the time," she says, brow arching. "I move through the world differently than you do, remember? Things are far better than it was, but I'd still attract all the wrong kinds of attention if I showed up to a public pool in a swimsuit."

His expression softens, eyes and fingers tracing a pale patch at her shoulder before sliding down to her palm and lacing their fingers. He brings her hand to his lips, kissing the inside of her wrist and leading her farther from the shore. "I won't let you drown."

The water rises around her, lapping at her skin. Goosebumps dot her arms, a shiver dancing up her spine when it reaches past her navel. Still, she holds Khiran's gaze as she follows him deeper; counts the stars-that-aren't-stars reflecting there. It is only once the water kisses her collar that he stops. His hand slips beneath her hair, cupping her neck, while the other releases her hand to rest on her hip. Water slides down her nape, his fingers cool and patient.

His lips brush over her face, his words a warm murmur against the ridge of her cheek. "Lean back for me, my love."

It is unnerving at first—the feeling of weightlessness.

Water fills her ears, dampening the sounds of the world above. Khiran's hand settles, a comforting pressure at the small of her back. His thumb strokes the base of her skull soothingly and Anna relaxes against him. The cave air feels colder than the water now. She can feel it trembling against the exposed skin peeking above the surface. The gentle currents from their movements lap at her sides in a way that almost tickles.

"Take a deep breath and hold it in your lungs."

She follows his instructions, feeling her body gently rise from his hands until only the gentle assurance of his fingertips remains like an unspoken promise. If she sinks, he will catch her.

"Good girl," he praises, the words sending a shiver across her skin for reasons that have nothing to do with the cold and everything to do with the darkness of his gaze. "Control your breathing, just like that. If you ever feel overwhelmed or like you're sinking—if I'm ever too far to help you stay above the water—just turn your face to the stars and take a breath."

A laugh, more breath than sound, leaves her. "As if there is a universe where you would not catch me."

The corner of his mouth curls, a smile so adoring she can feel the warmth of it nestling contentedly beneath her ribs. Nudging against her heart with an almost feline purr of approval. "Best to practice anyway," he says, eyes dancing. "Are you ready for me to move my hands?"

He's barely touching her, just a mere graze of fingertips between her shoulder blades. Still, she appreciates him asking. Appreciates that he understands how terrifying *new* can be to those as old as they are.

She wets her lips out of habit and tastes a drop of water clinging to her upper lip. "I'm ready."

His touch falls away, leaving her to float on the surface by her power alone. Patiently, he watches her. Waiting for the slightest sign of distress. When moments pass and it doesn't come, he shows her how to cup her hands and kick her feet. Shows her how to tread water. Soon, she is swimming beside him into deeper waters, her strokes clumsy but effective. Her pulse speeds up, a shallow drumming, but the blood pumping through her heart isn't encouraged by fear.

Khiran's smile dimples, his eyes bright as he swims beside her—never too far to save her.

THEY LAY AMONGST THE ROCKS, LETTING THEIR HAIR DRY AS THEY admire the way the lights reflect off the water. Anna breathes her question into the dim, afraid to disturb the peace of the moment. "What are they really?"

Khiran chuckles. "Are you sure you're ready for the magic to end?"

"I'm not sure there is an explanation that would take away the magic," she confesses, her smile soft as she admires the would-be-constellations. "It's just a different magic, is all."

It's obvious he disagrees. The bridge of his nose wrinkles, voice deadpan. "They're worms."

Anna's smile only widens, eyes tracing the little flecks of light with new appreciation. "How amazing," she murmurs. "That something so small can shine so brightly."

He stares at her, his expression one of hope and agony. "You are brighter than this world deserves. Than I deserve." He shakes his head, leaning over her and pressing a kiss to her forehead with a reverence that aches. "And yet, we both need you."

She frowns. "We *deserve* each other. *Need* each other," she reprimands. "As for the world, it needs you far more than it needs me." Her heart twinges at the truth of it. She wonders how many lives have been condemned because she couldn't let him go. How many he could have saved if her selfishness hadn't cost him his freedom.

"You're wrong," he whispers. Another kiss, this one placed at the corner of her mouth. "It needs you desperately. You change people, Anna. Inspire them to be better just by being yourself." His fingertips brush damp hair away from her temple before traveling down, his palm cupping the line of her jaw. "Giving you that peach was the single best thing I've ever done for this world."

Anna's laugh is breathy and wet, her love for him so heavy she can feel it like a gentle, aching weight on her chest. She folds her hands behind his neck, pulling him closer until their lips brush. "That last part, I think, we can agree on."

Shadows chase the color from his eyes. "Does it still feel like a gift?"

Anna knows what he's really asking. Knows his insecurities as well as if they had been inscribed on her own heart. His question isn't about the magic she'd bit into or the immortal life she's lived. It's about the decision made in the garden she cultivated in front of the home he gave her. The one they made together after he cradled her face in his hands and begged her for an answer.

What am I to do, Anna?

It's about the choice she made when she answered, *You stay.*

Anna kisses him gently, a balm for the tender scars lining both their hearts. She waits until she feels the tension melt from his shoulders, feels the long sigh escape his lungs, before pulling away. She needs him to see her eyes when she tells him. Needs him to know the truth of it so he'll never carry the weight of his doubt. "It will be a gift for as long as you're with me."

KAIA COMES OUT OF THE SHELTER OF HER ROOM TWO DAYS LATER.

Her face is sallow—pale like paper instead of the radiance that reminded Anna of a full moon in a dark sky. There are no bruises marring the fragile skin under her eyes, but with the grief that burdens her dark gaze, Anna is certain there would be if Kaia were anything less than divine.

Khiran stands from the low table, taking her arm and helping her take a seat beside him. Kaia doesn't need the help, but she covers one of Khiran's hands with her own, thankful for the comfort that comes with his touch. She looks at the meal lining the table, curiosity breaking through the dark waters of her sorrow. "What's this?"

Anna ladles soup into a bowl, offering it to their host. She doesn't know if Kaia has been eating, or if she even feels hunger the way she and Khiran do, but she knows there can be magic in a meal. A comfort. "Clam chowder."

Gingerly, Kaia accepts the bowl with a weak smile. "Thank you. I assume you cooked?"

"It was a joint effort."

"Ah." Her eyes flit to Khiran, a bit of warmth returning to her expression. "He must adore you as much as he claims if you were able to get him to step foot in a kitchen. I've been trying for centuries."

Khiran scoffs, but there's a gentleness to the sound. More sweet than bitter. "Don't give me so much credit. I only helped gather the clams and shelled the meat."

"It's more than you would have done," Kaia says, her expression clouding. "You've changed."

Khiran's smile goes soft. Gentle in ways that carry the power to hurt and heal. "Everything changes."

"Yes," she murmurs, eyes searching his face as if she can find all the ways he's grown written there. "The world does that, doesn't it? And yet, this feels like more. Tell me, how long have you been running, Khiran?"

He pauses, indecision pulling at his brow. Kaia sees it for what it is. "Don't try to spare my feelings. I may never again be whole, but I am not *broken*." She softens, like wax brought too close to a flame, as she folds her hand over his. "You are the last thing I have of her. Tell me your struggles, so that I may do what I can to ease them. Allow me to find a glimpse of happiness in your own."

Khiran cringes. "Six years."

Kaia nods, her fingers playing with the handle of her spoon. "When did Eira—" her voice breaks. Closing her eyes and taking a deep breath, she tries again. "When did it happen?" Khiran's silence is deafening, guilt lining the omission. Kaia wilts. "I see."

He swallows, hands fisting under the table. "I'm sorry."

She shakes her head, the carved shells in her ears catching the light. "I don't agree with what you did, but I understand it. If the roles were reversed—if I was the one forced to tell *you*... well, I would have wanted to run, too."

Gingerly, she picks up her spoon and stirs the contents of her bowl. "Now, let's try this meal you contributed to." She brings a spoonful to her lips, chewing thoughtfully. A smile lines her eyes as she sends Anna a knowing look. "I see you kept him away from the spices."

Anna sees the change of subject for what it is: the opening of a path they can travel together without the weight of having to look back. Kaia's own way of running. "He's ruined a few too many meals that way."

There's a relief in Kaia's eyes, warm with gratitude. For the rest of the meal, they talk about everything but the past, sidestepping its existence despite its presence hovering at the edges of their conversations. When Kaia asks what they plan to do next, it hangs over them like a shadow hungry for its next meal.

There's a question in Khiran's eyes when he looks at her, one that echoes her own. They could stay here, in Kaia's labyrinth of caves. So long as Khiran doesn't use his magic, doesn't open up a path for Marcia to follow, there is probably no safer place. Anna thinks of a cave made of dreams and starlight—thinks of the way he promised the wonders of the world while washing colored powder off her skin. She holds his gaze when she asks him, "What would you show me first?"

He stares at her from across the table, eyes full of so much emotion she's drowning in them. Something has shifted in him since leaving the mountains of the Himalayas. He told Cassius he would be content to run—to live as a mortal for the sake of gaining as much time with her as possible—but it's not enough.

It's not enough to breathe and eat and sleep.

It's not enough to be alive.

Not for him. Not anymore.

I want to show you every corner this world has to offer and watch your face light up in wonder.

Slowly, his lips curl into a smile.

A WEEK LATER THEY'RE SWIMMING IN THE WARM WATERS OF Cenderawasih Bay in Indonesia, snorkels in their mouths and goggles strapped to their faces. They float on the surface, their fingers tangled and the sun on their backs with another world teaming with life beneath them. Reefs stretch out before them, a patchwork of movement and color Anna never knew existed beneath the waves.

They drift farther, the water growing deeper. Shadows of shipwrecks rise up from the depths, memorials of a world war that feels more recent than the rusted metal hulls look.

Her ears full of water, she hears them before she sees them. A creaking echo that pierces the depths, punctuated by guttural clicking that sounds almost like a growl. It's a song more ancient than anything she's ever known, and as her vision fills with gray and white spotted skin she's never felt so small.

Khiran squeezes her hand—an unspoken promise that there's nothing for her to fear—but Anna isn't afraid. The whale shark is a goliath, but it moves through the water with a grace that feels more gentle than predatory. She stares, heartbeat in her throat as it swims so close she's able to reach out and brush her fingertips against sandpaper skin.

She doesn't surface until the ocean swallows its silhouette, pulling her mask and snorkel from her face. Khiran mirrors the action, his smile wide as his eyes memorize her expression.

When she kisses him, his lips taste like saltwater and hope.

CHAPTER SIXTEEN

There are so many things this century has shown him that his younger self wouldn't have believed. How do you explain hearing a voice from a world away? Or a picture made with light and chemicals instead of paint? How could he have fathomed the possibility of man touching the heavens, and believed it to be anything but a dream?

VICTORIA, AUSTRALIA
JULY 21, 1969

THE EXCITED CHATTER OF TEENAGERS AND A DOZEN STAFF FILLS THE auditorium like an endless echo. A small school for a small town, but there is a buzz in the floorboards. Anna can feel the hum of it burying beneath her skin like static. Outside, she can see the swaying of eucalyptus against a gunmetal sky through the windows and wonders if the high winds will affect the television signal.

Giving a disgruntled sigh as her class files onto the bleachers

213

behind them, Susan sits beside her on the lowest bench. The older woman's gray hair is pulled back into her customary low bun, but there are some stray wisps escaping the pins. She looks more irritated than usual. Anna wonders if the assembly disrupted the cigarette break she usually sneaks between classes.

"Well, they landed the thing," Susan says, voice rough as gravel. She raises a thin brow, brown eyes looking at her over the thick red frames of her reading glasses. "You watch it this morning?"

"Of course." Anna doesn't know of anyone who *didn't*. It seems like the entire world has their attention on the heavens. Khiran had sat beside her on their tiny yellow sofa, their coffee cold and their fingers entwined, watching history being broadcast on their tiny television. Anna didn't understand most of what was being relayed between NASA command and the Apollo 11—the jargon too unfamiliar for her to untangle, but it hadn't stopped her from hanging on every word.

"Longest fifteen minutes of my life," Susan quips. "Thought they were going to end up like all those poor bastards that came before them."

"Susan!" Anna hisses, reprimanding. A quick glance shows the nearby students as being too preoccupied with their own conversations to have noticed.

"Please," she drawls. "Like you weren't thinking the same thing."

Anna won't admit it—not to Susan, anyway—but she's been carrying dread around like a weight for the past *week*. Hard not to, when humanity's adventures into the galactic unknown have been marred by more failures than successes. This morning, when the countdown changed from moments till landing to how much fuel remained, her heart had seized—prepared to mourn yet another catastrophe. They waited, air stale in their lungs, until the moment the long empty stretch of static made way for words.

The Eagle has landed.

A laugh, breathless and full of wonder, escaped her. The feelings that clamored inside her chest too great to hold. Khiran had kissed her—picked her up and twirled her around their tiny living room and laughed in ways she hadn't heard in years. But, for all the excitement, she still can't seem to shake the dread that had taken root. Getting there is only half the journey—there is still so much that could go wrong. Being lost in space… well, Anna thinks it must be a different kind of drowning. One where the ocean is without end and no shore to wash up on.

Susan leans her chin on the heel of her hand, glancing at the empty seat on Anna's other side. "Where's tall, dark, and handsome?"

Anna shakes her head, amused despite herself. "That *is* my husband you're talking about, Susan."

She shrugs a bony shoulder. "Just be grateful I'm saying it to your face." There's a distinct implication that there are others that *don't.*

Sighing, Anna glances toward the auditorium doors. For all Susan's teasing, it *is* strange that he hasn't arrived yet. Stranger still that Principal Merryweather is also missing. She frowns. "Hey, Susan? You're pretty good chums with the secretary, right?"

"Course I am. Small town like this? Gotta get my bit of gossip somewhere." The corners of her mouth lift into a smirk, nudging Anna's side with a sharp elbow. "Why? You worried your mister might be sticking his hands where he shouldn't?"

Anna shoots her a dry look, more exasperated than angry, and Susan clucks her tongue approvingly. "No, I suppose you wouldn't, would you? You got him so wrapped up in you, he's damn near blind to everything else. Between you and me? I hear the way he shut down that hussy from the admin office was a bona fide work of art."

Anna's smile goes tight, her laugh hollow. She knows exactly what incident Susan is referring to. The woman—Carol—had been a little too forward with her flirting, and Khiran had been all too happy to retaliate by shamelessly broadcasting his disinterest in front of his entire class. The poor woman had felt so humiliated, she'd refused to show her face on campus since.

"No, I don't see those hands straying," Susan hums, glancing pointedly at her watch. "Now, if you could manage to do something about that *mouth* of his."

Anna's stomach sinks, resisting the urge to rub her temples. "What did he do?"

Susan leans close, her whisper sly. "Word is he went off lesson again. Mr. Merry ain't living up to his name about it."

Anna cringes—recognizing the probability of the accusation. Mr. Merry is the nickname the staff call Principal Merryweather when he's out of earshot; an entirely too ironic jab at his surly demeanor. Khiran's consistently proven to be a thorn in the administration's side and not just because he insists on sharing bits of history the textbooks like to gloss over or outright ignore. Anna still doesn't understand how he managed to keep his job after the incident where he told a student his father was an idiot after regurgitating some of his parent's talking points.

If they let him finish the school year, it will be a small miracle.

The auditorium door opens, Khiran walking in and looking entirely unfazed. Anna wishes that soothed her nerves.

He's been happy these last few years—learned how to navigate his mortal limitations and still find fulfillment. Yet, he never bothered to invest himself in any kind of relationship outside their own. He plays his part well: goes to the pub to have an occasional drink with some of their male faculty members, tells jokes and stories in the break room. He has fun with it, but he always stops just short of *caring*.

It's all just a game—this play pretend mortal life. Like children playing house, immersed in their roles but ready to let them go once the dinner bell rings.

Anna understands the instinct. She has had to restart and abandon more faux lives than she can count. It's easier to say goodbye when you know from the beginning that people are temporary. What she struggles to comprehend is his utter disregard for causing *trouble*.

Khiran's sleeves are rolled up to his elbows the way he knows Merryweather hates (and she secretly admires). His eyes scan the bleachers, grinning when he finds her. Anna's more focused on the fact that the principal walks in right behind him.

Definitely not a coincidence that they were both missing, then.

Susan gives a huff of laughter, the sound smoky at the edges. "Well, speak of the devil." Anna can't be sure if the devil she's referring to is her husband or their boss, but Susan stands, knees creaking, before she can ask. "Well, while you grill your honey, I'm gonna go get the scoop from Cathy." She gives Anna a wink before leaving, but pats Khiran on the shoulder, chuckling, as she passes him.

He gives the teaching veteran a curious look, but says nothing as he sits beside his wife. He's so close, his arm brushes hers as he reaches up and loosens his tie. Anna catches Merryweather's scowl at the action. "Sorry, I got held up. Has it started?" he asks, eyes flitting around the auditorium. "Looks like we're still waiting on the television?"

Anna scowls at him. "How much trouble are you in?"

He blinks, startled, before his gaze flits to her accomplice on the other side of the auditorium. Sighing, he runs a hand through his hair. "Susan?"

"Susan."

"Old bat could run an entire business on selling secrets," he muses. "If it weren't so aggravating, I'd find it impressive."

"Khiran. How much trouble?"

"Two weeks suspension," he grumbles, but there's a spark of laughter in his eyes. "Or, *would* have been. Thankfully, your husband is incredibly charming, and I got off with a metaphorical slap on the wrist." His grin is teasing, but when she doesn't smile back, he sighs. "A few parents didn't appreciate my commentary on certain current events."

Anna's heart sinks. There is no shortage of topics for him to choose from with the anti-war protesters demanding an end to military presence in Vietnam to civil and land rights for Indigenous Australians. "Khiran—"

"I'm not sorry for it," he says, voice as low and level as his stare.

"I would never ask you to be," she murmurs fondly, expression softening. Discreetly, she leans closer until her knee touches his. One of the reasons she had suggested he try this field was so he could see there were ways he could still make a difference in the world. That he is just as capable of inspiring change as she is.

She won't scold him for teaching the truth.

"You worry over nothing." His fingers curl along her palm, coaxing her hand open until he can trace her heart line. There's a warmth in his eyes, sly and brimming with mischief. "I have everything handled."

It's a bit of a game they play—subtle touches stolen in the teachers' lounge and between their classes. Little things that wouldn't go so far as to get them in trouble should they be caught, but not so innocent that their students are blind to their affections.

To her (and she suspects, Merryweather's) disappointment, their relationship had quickly become one the school's favorite topics. Her students would often teasingly offer to pass notes to her husband, and every Friday there always seemed to be an inquiry on whether she and Khiran had any romantic plans for the weekend. Anna can't quite say she minds it too terribly. Even if they've become a bit of a joke on campus, it feels more friendly than anything. Just a few weeks ago, she had a student confess that she thought it was sweet that they still loved each other despite working together.

Still, Anna tries to focus on teaching her students French and not encourage it.

Khiran, of course, has no such reservations.

Some days he sends his students over with little mundane gifts like erasers with little hearts penciled in at the corners or tiny stems of bluebell flowers he plucked from the track and field on his off period. The week he sent along little bits of poetry scribbled on scrap pieces of binder paper had her entire class of teenage girls swooning and giggling the entire period. She had to forbid him from sending more, just so she could get them to focus on her lessons instead of her marriage.

She knows for a fact that he wasn't at all sorry, but she also might have saved those little scraps of paper, too, so perhaps she wasn't really either. Even if it meant suffering Principal Merryweather's reprimands the next day.

Though, she supposes taunting their employer has become a game in and of itself to Khiran. Her husband's subtle jab at retribution for all the hours Merryweather has complained to him about his failing marriage. He doesn't say it, but considering his distaste for the man, Anna suspects he had a lot more to say about her gender in general. None of it, she expects, is good.

"I thought the plan was to save before picking up and going to another town," she says, keeping her voice low. "At the rate you're going, Merryweather will be happy to chase us off the continent himself."

"Merry and I have come to an understanding," he says, too cryptic to trust.

"Which is?"

His voice drops, the curl of his mouth turning wicked. "He keeps me on till the end of the year, or I tell his wife and the entire school he's been having an affair with his neighbor."

Anna's head swivels to face him. "What?! How long have you known about this?"

"Since I caught her bringing him a plate of cookies."

"That doesn't mean they're having an affair!" she hisses.

"Merry is one of the most miserable human beings on this side of the continent. Why *else* would she bring him cookies? Homemade at that. I might have snatched one while he wasn't looking—don't worry. Yours are better." He looks entirely too proud of himself. "Besides, you should have seen his face when I threatened to expose him. I didn't know people could go so purple."

Anna brings a hand to her mouth, not entirely sure if she's hiding her horror or her amusement. She has to fight the urge to glance at the man in question. "You *blackmailed* him?!"

The grin he flashes is crooked and sharp. It reminds Anna of the god he once was—someone who plucked and pulled at strings as effortlessly as a pianist plays keys. She supposes he still is, even if it is on the small scale that is their mortal lives. Somehow, she can't fault him for it—for taking this small amount of control back.

But perhaps that's just her dislike for Mr. Merry speaking.

Mr. O'Connelly backs into the auditorium, wheeling the school's sole television on a cart across the wooden floors. The students whoop, clapping, and the red-headed man pauses long enough to take an exaggerated bow. The janitor polishes his nails on his coveralls, just under his name tag as he basks in the applause before continuing to roll the cart to the middle of the center of the floor. "Where do you want her, Mr. Principal, sir?"

Merryweather's thick jaw clenches around words he doesn't dare speak in front of the students. Jack O'Connelly is the only one who refuses to call him by name (Anna suspects it's because he's the one who dubbed *Mr. Merry* to begin with). "There's fine," he answers, lips forced into a smile and words slipping between his teeth.

Mr. O'Connelly gets to work plugging it in and setting up the antenna. Around him, the volume rises as he works—excited chatter filling the empty spaces of the large room. A low static sounds from the television as he moves the long metal rabbit ears until, slowly, the hum of static is replaced by voices, and the fuzz on the screen sharpens into grainy black and white images of lunar craters and voices break through the static.

Within seconds, the voices that once filled the auditorium go silent. Anna leans in close, her eyes never leaving the screen as she whispers in his ear. "Do you think they'll really do it? Walk on the moon?"

Khiran stares at the picture, his fingers lacing with hers. "I think it will either be a success or another tragedy and nothing in between," he murmurs, lacing their fingers. Anna would chastise him, but she's fairly certain there's not a single pair of eyes that aren't glued to the screen. "Either way, we're watching history."

For the first ten minutes, they watch as the broadcasters show snippets of the reel she and Khiran watched that morning before cutting to the NASA control room. When the first live footage comes in, the picture is upside down before it's corrected moments later. Then Neil Armstrong comes down the ladder, his fuzzy form in the shadow of the lunar module. She listens as he says the words that will be remembered by the world and recognized for generations. "One small step for man, one giant leap for mankind."

Khiran stares at the screen, eyes wide and lips parted in breath-less laughter. "The *moon*, Anna. There are humans walking on the moon, right now, and we're *watching* it."

In that moment, Anna is taken back to those alley streets in Delhi.

Only, this time, it's him who wears wonder as visibly as if it were colored powder. She's never seen him wear such an expression, has never watched awe and amazement mingle into something that almost looks like *hope*.

She has known him for nearly a millennia but has only spent decades at his side. Anna mourns all the moments she's missed—regrets that their history has been built more on the world's tragedies and so few of its triumphs. Did his lips part around an open smile the first time he heard a faceless voice on a radio? Did his eyes shine with questions when he first watched a plane take flight?

Silently, she makes a promise to herself to memorize this moment —both the achievement of man and the wonder in her lover's expression. To hold it close to her heart, so she will never forget what she's fighting to keep. They're safe for now, enough for even Khiran to relax into a mortal life, but they both know Marcia won't give up the hunt. Even if she wanted to, The First would demand their capture from his throne—too insulted to think of letting them go unpunished.

On the seat of the scarred wooden bleachers, Anna kisses him and doesn't care who's watching.

She doesn't look at the night sky the same way after that. Doesn't see the moon and the stars as something out of reach and unattainable.

CHAPTER SEVENTEEN

He's lost her. Ashes sting his eyes and blister his tongue as he screams her name again, and again, and again. His lungs ache with the soot that lines them, but he can't stop. He can't lose her to the fire, too.

NORTHERN TERRITORY, AUSTRALIA
JUNE 1975

MAYBE IT WAS A MISTAKE, MOVING THEIR LIVES FROM A SMALL TOWN TO the bush.

She had wanted a bit of quiet after living within a community—longed for the peace that comes with a simple life and solitude. Part of her never stopped missing the home they left behind... of silly luxuries like fresh eggs gathered by her hands or honey milked from her hives. Of speaking loudly and freely because there are no ears to hear them for miles and wearing her sleeves short without feeling the stares.

So they packed their things and took their wages and bought a tiny ranch swallowed by dust and sunsets. It lacked every convenience living in town has to offer—no grocers, no shops, no banks. But in the absence of nosy neighbors and thin walls, they found a night sky that looks the same as the one they once stared up at centuries ago, surrounded by sounds that feel as old as they are.

It's all on fire now.

The smoke is what wakes her. Anna doesn't have nightmares often, not anymore, but when she does it is usually of flames licking at her skin or of the ashes pulled from Eira's smile. So when she wakes up gasping, it takes her a moment to realize the smell is more than whispered echoes of her dream.

"Khiran!" She shakes him awake, her pulse thundering in her ears. The scent isn't overwhelming, but it's heavy enough to warn her something is desperately wrong. The bushfire season had been horrendous this past year, leaving more than fifteen percent of the continent scorched, but most of it had slowed to an end with the Australian summer. It seems the Northern Territory, with its arid heat and thick grasses, doesn't seem to have been gifted such a reprieve. "Khiran, wake up!"

He jerks awake, gripping her wrist with a strength that would bruise mortal flesh. It's only once he finds they're alone that his hold softens, his chest rising and falling as his breathing slows. Anna wonders if there were smoke-fueled nightmares playing behind his eyelids, too. "Anna, what—"

"I smell smoke." Her voice trembles with implications.

Khiran frowns, momentarily lost, before looking to the window. He throws off the sheets, the lines of his bare back and shoulders flexing in the dim light as he stands. Anna follows, her hand brushing his arm and taking comfort in his touch. Past their fields and fence lines, an angry glow lights the horizon. Red and urgent, like the flash of warning lights amid disaster.

His jaw flexes. "We need to go." He turns from the window, going toward their dresser. His hands rifle through her drawers, pulling out a change of clothes and tossing it to her before pulling a t-shirt over his head.

Anna grips the dress he tossed her, hands trembling. It's the one she likes to wear when she's gardening because the black cotton is breathable and easy to work in. Easy to run in. She glances over her shoulder, back to the window. "You don't think it's them... do you?"

Pulling up a pair of slacks, his fingers still as he registers her question. His eyes meet hers. "There's nothing unnatural about a bushfire."

He's right—she knows he is—but she can't shake the feeling that there's something sinister hiding behind the smoke. She shakes her head, changing into her dress. It must be the painful echo of the past poisoning her present. There's no reason to believe Marcia would have traced them to this little corner of the bush. Khiran's ring is gone, and he's been carefully living a life without magic. Without it, Marcia would have to be within miles of them before even sensing his presence.

The odds of it are incredibly low, but when Anna glances back out the window, the eucalyptus sway, silver green leaves rustling in warning. *Run,* they whisper.

Run.

Paranoid. She's being paranoid. A bushfire gives her plenty to fear, but it isn't an obstacle they can't overcome. They'll flee before it catches up to them. The old utility truck the previous owners left in the barn, the one Khiran drives into town with his bootlegged driver's license, is a temperamental thing, but it should still make it.

Anna stares at the exposed skin of Khiran's arms as he pulls on his boots. Skin that will burn if he's caught in the flames.

Outside, one of the sheep gives a panicked bleat and Anna's gut sinks. "I'm going to let the animals loose," she says, breathless with urgency as she slips her feet into a pair of shoes. "Give them a fighting chance."

Khiran's jaw strains, the muscle jumping, but he nods. "Be quick —it moves faster than you think. I'll grab our things and get the truck started."

They don't waste any time. While Khiran grabs the emergency bag from the top of the closet, Anna runs out the back door. The sheep are frantically pacing along the fence, screaming. Her hands fumble with the lock on the gate, the clip slipping between her fingers. When she finally gets it open, the herd runs out of the pen and into the yard. They hesitate on the driveway, their ears swiveling anxiously and their trembling bodies stiff. Instinct is telling them to run, but they don't know where to run *to*.

Anna knows she doesn't have time to help them. She goes to the chicken coop next, throwing open the door. They stare back at her with dark eyes from their roosts, but it's three in the morning and the late hour holds them still—the burning light on the horizon isn't enough to coax them into wakefulness. She leaves the door open and hopes for the best before running to the barn.

She can hear the old truck's throaty hum, smell the gasoline puffing from the exhaust like a chain smoker. Her nose wrinkles at the smell as she opens the passenger door, and freezes.

The driver's seat is empty.

Her heart crashes, knocking into her ribs with enough force to leave her momentarily breathless. In her hand, the metal handle bites into her palm as she frantically searches the barn. "Khiran?" His name trembles on her lips, a question she's afraid to know the answer to. She can't stop looking at the keys dangling from the ignition, from the emergency bag set on the cracked leather seat.

He was here. He was here, and he'd had everything they needed to flee.

Why wasn't he *here*?

"**Khiran**!?" Her voice breaks as she screams his name, her hand leaving the handle to run back into the yard, into the house. His name keeps falling from her lips like a prayer, a fragile, desperate hope made sharp with fear. He's not in the yard. Not in the house. She can hear the fire now—hear the mighty cracks and pops of the eucalyptus as they burn and crash.

Anna stands on the front step, paralyzed as she watches the flames grow higher. Grow closer. Her ears strain for the sound of his voice in the chaos, but there's nothing, nothing, nothing—

Movement from the corner of her eye, a glimpse of a humanoid shape she shouldn't have seen in a landscape of flames and shadows.

The trees are thrashing now, the heat of the flames spiraling through the branches.

Run, the leaves hiss.

Run, the branches groan.

RUN, the trunks howl, wood splitting.

She bolts from the house, runs past the truck, and chases the shadow. She swears the trees are screaming at her as she weaves between their pale, peeling trunks. The flames haven't touched this part of the bush, but it's quickly creeping closer. Anna can feel the threat of it on her skin, hot enough to sting and coaxing sweat from her pores. Smoke surrounds her like a fog, thick and suffocating, but in it she can see the shadow of a silhouette.

It's not Khiran.

The figure is too small. A child. Oh, god, it's a *child*.

Anna rushes forward, a different kind of urgency flooding her. She reaches out; the smoke thinning enough to make out the curled figure of a little boy. His knees are folded up to his chest, his arms hugging his legs and his head bent.

The moment she touches him, his head jerks up—staring at her with large eyes that shine like amber in the firelight. There's soot streaking his olive skin, ashes tangling in his dark hair, but there's no fear in his expression. No red eyes or tear tracks. Only a calm surprise that sets her on edge. He can't be older than four; he should be terrified. Smoke is curling in her lungs, making her throat itch and her chest ache. She coughs around a breath, still staring at the boy, and understands that something *isn't right*.

"You're not human," she murmurs. He looks down at her hand, still gently cupping his shoulder, but shows no sign of understanding her.

She thinks of the story Khiran told her, of the boy turned god who was too dangerous to roam free. The one of fire and fury. The one no one could touch without being burned. A child, Khiran had called him. She had never stopped to question if that changed, if he grew the way *Khiran* grew. She never realized that when he said child, he meant child then and a child forever.

This is the god they treat like a bomb waiting to go off.

This is the boy they fear.

In her chest, her heart splinters. How long has it been since someone touched him? Held him? How could they treat him as an adult when he was still imprisoned in the mind and body of a child?

Her hand falls from his shoulder, but she lets it hover between them—palm up—in offering. "You can come with me, if you'd like."

He stares at her hand, one moment, two, before his amber eyes return to her hazel ones. "I'm not supposed to leave. I'm supposed to make sure it keeps burning."

He sounds as young as he looks. Anna swallows, lets her hand fall. A quick glance proves the fire is getting closer. The heat of it makes her skin damp, sweat rolling down her collar and between her shoulder blades.

"You should run," he says, but the warning falls flat. As if he doesn't believe it will really make a difference if she heeds it or not. "They're going to come for you, too."

Anna's heart stutters.

They.

Her knees tremble as she straightens, retreating a step. There are shards of bitter truths in her throat, cutting like glass when she swallows. When she speaks, the words are shredded and metallic on her tongue. "Where's Khiran?"

The boy—Malik—doesn't answer, not in words, but Anna can see it reflected in his eyes. It's just as destructive as the fire surrounding them—just as deafening. Anna's chest rises and falls, gasping, but she can't find her breath.

The key was in the ignition.

The key was in the ignition and their bag—their bag was on the seat.

She sways, stumbles. Malik watches her with detached curiosity as she sinks to the ground, but she doesn't care. She is unraveling, fragile satin threads of control slipping between her fingers and curling in the heat. Ready to blacken. Ready to burn.

A thought echoes like a nightmare in her mind, over and over, until Anna can feel the cruel cut of the truth.

Khiran would die before he left her.

Together. They promised each other that they would face what-ever came *together*.

"Aren't you going to run?" Malik asks.

Anna's fingers curl against the ground, ash and earth burying beneath her nails. She stares at the furrowed grooves her hands leave behind. Run? Where would she run to? Khiran is gone. "No." She lifts her head. Meets Malik's concentrated stare.

He's waiting, she realizes. They'll come for him, pluck him from the chaos he's created, and take him home.

Home.

They would take Khiran home, too. Home to The First.

If she waits here, they'll take her, too.

Malik only watches as she folds in on herself, drawing her trem-bling arms around her chest. "You'll burn," he murmurs. Anna could almost believe it to be a warning if not for the confused inflection marking it as a question.

A laugh, bitter and pained, claws up from her throat until it twists into a sob. If there are tears streaking her cheeks, she can't feel it. The heat of the fire makes her skin prickle and her eyes sting. It won't be the first time she's burned.

Maybe it will be her last.

In another life, Khiran had spun her stories of this boy while her hands tended to her garden. The Calamity. The boy with a short fuse and scorching power. *None of us are immune to his flames,* Khiran had said. Anna doesn't know if that's true for her or not. She only knows the risk of burning is worth the chance of being brought back to him.

Anna breathes deep, the air laced with soot and heat, as she lifts her head. Studies the boy described as a bomb. Marcia had enjoyed their fear—had drank from it as if it were the sweetest of wines. Anna sees none of that cruelty in him. There is no wicked, cutting smile. No sadistic pleasure in his dark gaze, only apathy.

A voice—her name—so soft she barely catches it. It slips through the static humming in her ears, the roaring rush of flames. She stands, soot darkening the front of her dress, and strains her ears. She's scared it's not real. Scared her heart is meddling with her mind, but she hears it again and the relief is so great she almost collapses with it.

Khiran.

She runs. Towards the sound of his voice. Towards *him*.

It's impossible, but she swears the trees sway away from her. Their flaming branches parting to make a path she can travel without fear of being tangled in them. She follows it, even when the splitting of limbs and the screaming whistle of steam becomes so loud she loses the sound of his voice. There is something else there now. An urgent buzzing under her skin telling her to listen. To trust.

She doesn't know what she's hearing, what she's feeling, but she's too desperate to question it. Her pulse drums in her ears, blood rushing beneath her skin. There's a wall of fire in front of her, but she turns sharply, following the instinctual pull of her heart. A clearing, not yet touched by the destruction, opens up ahead.

Khiran's there, his back to her and his eyes wild and searching as he screams her name into the chaos. Looking for her.

She answers, his name cracking with the weight of her relief. He turns, just in time to catch her as she launches herself around his middle. Shaking, his hands are on her face, her body, checking her for burns. Her fingers tangle in his soot stained shirt, gripping him with an urgency that borders on desperation. Anna can't tell where his trembling begins and hers ends.

"Anna," he murmurs, a choked breath. "I thought—"

He doesn't finish—can't. She doesn't need him to. She holds him tighter, because even though the world is burning around them, she still needs this moment to convince herself that he's real. "You were gone." Her voice catches, words tangled and barbed in her chest.

Khiran pulls away, his hands anchored on her shoulders. "Marcia is here."

She swallows. Nods. "I know." There's a bruise blossoming along his jaw, circling his neck like a shadowed collar. Her hand reaches between them, tracing the damage. Blood smears across his skin. Her hand is covered in it. "You're hurt—"

"It's not mine." His brow furrows, searching her face with growing trepidation. "Anna, how did you know?"

Her eyes meet his. "Malik."

Khiran pales, his grip on her tightening. "You saw him?" His eyes flit over the flames, a bitter laugh staining his lips. There's nowhere for them to run. The fire has encircled them. "Of course. That's why she didn't follow. They're burning us out..." He shakes his head, hiding his face behind his hand.

The wind shifts, smoke stinging her eyes and clouding her lungs. She coughs into her sleeve and blinks back the tears trying to clear her eyes. Her throat aches with it. The expression Khiran wears is nothing short of tormented. Anna understands why.

I'm supposed to make sure it keeps burning.

They've been forced into a corner they can't escape—not without magic. If they stay, Malik's flames will devour them. If they leave, Marcia will follow the thread of magic, ready to draw blood on the other side. Only one of the options provides them with a chance.

Anna suspects that's just how Marcia wants it.

"We can't face Malik," he murmurs, hand dropping from his face. His skin looks sallow, wrung of hopes and sharp with bitter realities.

Anna studies the shadows lining his eyes. "He's a child." Her voice still shakes with the horror, the heartbreak, of it. "You didn't tell me he was still a child."

Khiran scowls. "He *isn't*. He's older than I am—don't let his appearance fool you into believing otherwise."

Anna thinks of the look in his eyes when she touched his shoulder. Thinks of how similar it looked to another boy all the way in California who was only ever angry because he hurt. "You're wrong."

He doesn't argue with her, but she can see his doubt. It doesn't shake the conviction she feels in her heart.

KHIRAN PRESSES THE HANDLE OF A BLADE INTO HER HAND. ANNA instantly recognizes it as the one she used to cleave her finger from her flesh. It's stained with blood—Marcia's, he tells her. He managed one good hit before he'd fled into the fire. He has some burns on his legs and scorched clothing to show for it, but the gamble had paid off. Marcia refused to risk following him. Why would she, when all she needed to do was wait? Drawing on Khiran's magic is the only option left to them.

He holds her close to his chest, his arms a vice binding them together. "Are you ready?"

Anna wets her lips. The heat of the flames surrounding them makes her thoughts muggy. Their plan is more thin hopes than a strategy—travel to the other side of the world and hope the distance causes enough of a delay that they can slip into a crowd before Marcia can catch them.

Khiran's hand slides along her jaw, tilting her face to his. "Anna?"

There's a determined edge to his stare, rimming his eyes and tightening the line of his shoulders. Anna tries to draw courage from it, swallowing the fear suffocating her. Her eyes drop to his lips, heart splintering.

These could be their last moments.

She leans into him, her fingers tangling in his shirt and the flat of the chipped blade pressing over his heart, and brings her lips to his. Soft and reverent, as if kissing him slowly could delay the inevitable. His mouth slides against her, fingertips burying in her hair at the nape of her neck and the hand on her hip holding her flush against him.

When he pulls away, his forehead pressed intimately to her own, Anna feels the loss as keenly as the scorching heat stinging her skin. She has so much to say to him, so many feelings she's never found the words for. Finding them, *saying* them, now would feel too much like a goodbye. Instead, she grips the knife until her knuckles go white and holds his gaze. "I'm ready."

His chin dips, pressing one last kiss to her trembling lips, murmuring against her parted mouth. "Hold on to me. Don't let go."

It is, perhaps, the easiest thing to promise. Still, she repeats it like a mantra. Winding her arms over his shoulders, she holds him so tightly her chest aches with the pressure and her muscles tremble with the strain. His hold is equally fierce, a protective cage she's terrified of escaping.

The world folds around them, violent and crushing like a ball of paper in a clenched fist. It *hurts*. It feels like she's at the center of a storm, centrifugal force tearing pieces of herself in every direction, until the only thing that feels real is the press of Khiran's body against her own. She's screaming, she thinks. Her mouth is open and her lungs are empty. The sound of it is lost, pulled from her lips and smothered in the weight of the universe.

Darkness creeps at the edges of her vision, spreading like an oil spill. She's suffocating in it. Drowning.

Hold on. She has to hold on. She promised.

But it's too much.

The last thing she's aware of is the sound of her name, the breath in her ear, before she passes out.

CHAPTER EIGHTEEN

He can see it in her eyes — a last, wordless appeal to leave her behind and save himself. To run. As if he could ever find peace on a path she didn't share.

NEW YORK, UNITED STATES
JUNE 1975

SHE'S BEING HELD.

It's the first thing she registers when she comes to—the feeling of movement, the press of hands cradling her to a firm chest and her legs draped over a lap. The next is the sound of traffic: car horns, the throaty purr of engines, and a kaleidoscope of voices. The smell of trash and sewage is heavy, the air humid. Stuffy. Anna's stomach revolts, clenching painfully, but she doesn't have time to be sick. The world won't stop spinning, but it doesn't matter, because she has to run. She has to—

"Shh," Khiran soothes, his gentle voice tangling in her hair. It settles around her like the comforting weight of a familiar blanket. "It's alright. Breathe. Nice and slow."

A voice, one she doesn't recognize, to her left. "How's she doing there, boss?"

That accent. She recognizes that accent—has heard a version of it fifty years ago in the Bronx. New York. They're in New York. She swallows down her nausea, closes her eyes and concentrates on the press of her ear against Khiran's chest and the heart beating beneath it. Alive. They're both alive. Her tongue feels like cotton. "What—"

"Later, dearest," he soothes, his voice soft but still loud enough to carry. Words that aren't meant for her ears alone. "We're in a taxi. Pete here was kind enough to offer us a ride. You've had a nasty fall during our walk in Central Park."

Her face is tucked into his neck and shoulder. Opening her eyes, she's relieved when her vision remains steady. She pulls away to look at his face, but the movement makes her head throb. Her limbs feel heavy, but she can feel the buttons of his shirt digging into her palms. Even unconscious, she'd managed to keep her promise. She held on.

Acid is rising in her throat. "I'm going to—"

"Got some puke bags on the car door there, boss." That voice again. The one she doesn't know. "Good stuff, too. Wife's a nurse over in Manhattan. She brings 'em home for me. Night shifts can get a little crazy, if ya know what I mean."

Khiran hands her a bag, plastic crinkling. His fingers brush the clammy skin at the nape of her neck as he pulls her hair back, and Anna's stomach surrenders. She heaves, gagging on the rancid taste coating her tongue. Her chest aches with the force of it, her throat burning. Traveling alongside him has never crippled her like this before. She supposes that must be the difference between crossing continents and going to the other side of the world entirely.

He takes the bag from her, carefully tying the top closed. Anna wipes her lips with the back of her sleeve, cringing, before the sight of it makes her falter. The ash stained dress she'd been wearing is gone. In its place is a belted green skirt that kisses her ankles and a white blouse with long airy sleeves that cuff at her wrists. She reaches for her neck, fingers gliding over a silk patterned scarf. She glances at Khiran, noting that his t-shirt has been traded in for a collared button up and a vest.

He catches her eyes, gaze flitting towards their taxi driver pointedly. Anna bites back the question she wants to ask, chews on it until it resembles something safe. "How long was I out?"

"Only twenty minutes, give or take," he murmurs, studying her. "How are you feeling?"

She swallows, wincing at the taste still coating her tongue. "Better."

"Ya know, the wife says vomiting after head injuries can be a big deal," the voice—Pete, she reminds herself—chimes. Anna meets his reflection in the rearview mirror, his blue eyes flicking between her and the road. "You sure you don't want me to take you to the hospital?"

Khiran pipes up before she can, the lie slipping off his tongue like dark chocolate—smooth with a bitter edge. "Thank you, but I'm afraid my wife has had this sort of episode before. It's chronic, you see." His eyes meet hers. "A bit of fresh sea air and she'll be right as rain."

The sea.

Of course. If they can reach the sea, they can find safety beneath the waves with Kaia.

Pete's pale brow furrows under his cap as he stops at a light, but it's followed by a shrug of his hefty shoulders. "You're the boss. Though, you know, I wouldn't say Coney Island's ideal for R and R. You sure you won't want to go somewhere quieter?" Outside, a breeze snakes between the buildings, stirring up a bunch of pale pamphlets littering the sidewalk. Anna watches as they float on the wind like stiff-winged butterflies. One of them catches on Pete's windshield, causing the middle-aged man to curse. "These damn flyers. Gonna drive off all the tourists and then where am I gonna be, huh?"

He continues to grumble complaints as he cranks down the window, but Anna's too focused on the image staring back at her to register them. Above a black and white illustration of a skeletal grim reaper, his mouth grinning and his eye sockets dark and empty, read the words: *Welcome to Fear City.*

Anna almost asks, but there's a sudden shift in the air. A pause.

In the rearview mirror, Pete's expression is frozen, his lips pursed around a sentence he can't finish. Outside, suspended and motionless, the pamphlets float as if pinned in place by an invisible force. Anna's eyes slide to the traffic light. The red has turned green, but the line of cars doesn't move. Everything is still. Everything is silent.

Every thing, every *one*, is suspended.

Her lips part around a quick intake of breath, fear swelling in her chest.

Khiran curses, grabbing her arm and pulling her from the taxi. "She brought Dante. Time to go."

Time.

Dante must be The Timekeeper.

Khiran swats at a pamphlet, the littered paper still suspended as if on strings as he helps her out of the bright yellow cab. He steers her down alleyways, twisting and turning in ways that make her dizzy. She doesn't know this New York. It's been too long since she's walked these streets, and the decades have changed the city into something she struggles to recognize. Another turn, and suddenly they're back on a main street. There are dozens of cars on the road, hundreds of people lining the streets. They're all motionless. Soundless. Anna's not sure she's ever seen anything so disconcerting, so *unnatural*, in her entire life.

"Why aren't we suspended, too?" she asks, struggling to keep his pace while her eyes drink in their surroundings. Recognition nags at her, but it isn't until she sees the pale columns of Federal Hall looming across the street that she understands why. The last time she was here, shattered glass littered the ground like confetti while her ears rang with the echoed blast of a bomb. Her hands were soaked red with the blood of a paperboy while she begged Khiran for help he could not give.

"If he gets close enough, we will be," he says, weaving them through the crowd of stilled lives. "The more he has to stop, the harder it is to chain us down. He won't be able to hold it for long, not in a city like this, but he won't be alone."

Marcia.

Suddenly, Anna realizes how empty her hands are. "The blade—"

"I have it," he assures her. "When time restarts, we need to be ready." The words are little more than a breath, but it sounds so loud in the silence. Anna catches him snatching a charcoal fedora off a young man's head. There's construction scaffolding up ahead, draped in canvas to keep the dust off the sidewalks. Khiran makes a beeline towards it, stopping only once they're safely hidden behind the cloth. A group of workers sit along the benches, their laughter paused, dinged metal lunch boxes at their feet, and their half-eaten sandwiches still in their hands.

Khiran shrugs out of his vest, letting it fall and crumple to the ground. In the shadowed corner, Anna thinks it almost looks like the carcass of an animal. He puts the fedora on his head before his hands reach for the silk scarf at her throat. She can feel him tugging at the knot, the cool fabric sliding along the back of her neck as it slips away. Folding it in half, he covers her hair with it. "We want to make it as hard as possible to pick us from a crowd," he murmurs, his nimble fingers retying the scarf under her chin.

All at once, the city outside the canvas turns loud—cars honking, people shouting on the streets. Behind them, the construction workers laugh. Khiran grabs her hand and leads her back onto the streets just as one of the crew notices them. His pace slows once they're back on the sidewalk, matching a group of friends ahead of them. He stares straight ahead, expression blank. The grip on her hand, white-knuckled and trembling, is the only outward sign of fear.

Anna can feel her heartbeat in her throat, the flush of it making her feel hot. She wants, desperately, to look behind her. To see if she can find the face of the stranger looking for them. She resists the temptation and follows Khiran's example.

For an excruciating ten minutes, they blend in with the crowd.

She can see the bay. Anna leans in close, their shoulders brushing, and keeps her voice low. "Does it have to be Coney Island?"

"No, but jumping into the bay would cause too much of a scene. We would be caught before Kaia's path could open."

Anna nods, understanding. Coney Island isn't the closest to the water, but it is the closest public beach. In the middle of the humid New York summer, its waters are sure to be full of people trying to beat the heat. She thinks of how carefully he searched for a secluded stretch of beach back in Mumbai, the minutes she waited before the tide shifted, and frowns. "How will we avoid being seen?"

Khiran cringes, guilt flashing across his features. "We don't."

Her heart stutters over the implication. "It will cause a panic."

"Let it." The words are as tight and unforgiving as the line of his jaw. "If that is the cost of saving you, I will pay it a thousand times over."

"Khiran—"

"We have done enough for this world. Sacrificed enough," he snaps, his hand flexing against hers. "Let it save us for a change."

It's a terrible idea. The sea parting is bound to cause chaos of biblical proportions, but Anna swallows the weak protest sticking in her throat. She's not sure she believes the world owes them this—not convinced that kind of debt is something that is reimbursed so much as paid forward—but she loves him too much to deny them this chance. She holds his gaze, offering the smallest of nods. The world isn't ready for proof of the divine, but she's not ready to lose *him*.

Khiran hails another cab, pulling bills from his trouser pocket. "The Brooklyn Battery Tunnel is closer than the bridge," he murmurs, subtly glancing up. "Marcia will likely take the high ground, especially since Dante is with her to stop the clock. It will offer us some coverage as well."

As the taxi pulls up to the curb, Anna frowns at the sight of the American currency in his hand. She suspects it must have come from the same place as their fresh clothing—magic spun into existence those split seconds between one continent and the next. She's relieved he had the foresight, because she certainly hadn't.

They climb into the cab, Khiran handing the driver a generous wad of cash to take them to Coney Island and to keep the change.

Anna had heard about the Brooklyn Battery Tunnel when it was built back in the fifties; the papers had celebrated it as a feat of American engineering. The longest underwater tunnel. It's disconcerting, driving down into the earth and under the bay. Pale tiles line the walls and ceilings, reflecting the light cast by the twin rows of bulbs lining either side of the tunnel. Anna grips the fabric of her skirt, trying not to think of the weight of the water above them.

The road levels out, a sign that they are fully beneath the bay. Anna swallows, trying to find comfort in the fact that the tunnel is only a little over a mile long. Then the taxi slows to a stop, the sound of horns echoing off the tiled walls as the traffic creeps to a standstill, and her pulse jumps. She looks to Khiran, the tunnel lights casting shadows over his face. He looks as worried as she is.

The driver curses, voice raspy and his salt and pepper brows furrowed in irritation as he fiddles with his radio. "Oy, anyone got eyes on what the holdup is in the Battery Tunnel?"

Static fills the cab as they wait for an answer. After a few seconds, a new voice filters through the speakers. "Strap yourself in for a wait. There's a five car pile up blocking the southbound." Another curse, this one longer and in Italian. Anna chooses not to embarrass him by disclosing that she understands every filthy word.

Khiran opens the car door.

"Hey! Hey, you can't do that!" their driver shouts, twisting in his seat. Khiran doesn't spare him a glance, but Anna murmurs a soft apology as she slides across the leather seat and takes Khiran's offered hand. He slams the car door behind her.

The sound echoes, sharp in the sudden silence.

Anna's heart stills.

She ducks her head, looking through the passenger window, hoping to find movement. The cabbie driver stares past her, unblinking and lips pulled back in frustration beneath a thick mustache. She faces Khiran, his name a breath on her lips.

He isn't looking at her, though. His eyes dart between the cars, searching for something Anna doesn't have a name for. A sound, a rhythmic clicking, echoing off the tiled walls.

It sounds like footsteps.

There is no warning. One moment he's waiting, the next they're fleeing. Urging her, with his fingers on her pulse, to *run*.

Run and don't look back.

A laugh, cutting and cruel as a nightmare, surrounds them like a flood. Filling her ears and drowning her hopes. She watches Khiran reach into his pocket, drawing the divine blade from its sheath. His lips pull into a sneered grimace, eyes electric and ready to draw blood as he turns—

And stops.

Snared in the web cast by the Timekeeper's hand.

Anna falters, her hands ghosting over his arms, his chest, as if she could coax movement from him. "No—no no no!" Her voice cracks, harsh in the silence despite how quietly she frets. There's a trembling against her palms, it takes her a moment to realize it's not just the shaking of her hands but *him*. Frozen as he is, he's still fighting the bonds keeping him still.

A different set of footsteps, heavy and flat compared to the clicking of Marcia's booted heels, sounds behind her. Anna stills, pulse beating in her ears like an executioner's drum. A looming presence behind her, a deep voice accented with the graveled edge of time itself. "So," he drawls, his fingers trail over the ends of her hair escaping her scarf. "You're the one causing all this trouble."

Slowly, Anna's hand slips down Khiran's arm, carefully unfolding his fingers from the blade's handle and taking it into her own. She wills her hand to stop trembling as his words breathe across the shell of her ear. "It will be fun, watching Marcia break you."

The handle of the blade bites into the palm of her right hand, scar tissue brushing against the iron that put it there. Her eyes lift to Khiran's frozen expression.

She isn't ready to lose him.

Anna turns, barely registering the surprise flitting across Dante's chiseled features, before she plunges the blade into the soft tissue of his muscular throat—feels the snap of bone as the tip drives into his spinal cord.

Blood coats her hand. Warm and wet. Anna can't bring herself to look away from the face that stares down at her. His thick, dark hair is past his shoulders, his beard a shadow around the full lips parted around a final breath. She pulls the blade from his flesh, more instinct than thought. He buckles, dropping to the ground like a puppet with cut strings. All joints and limbs, splayed over the road and blood pooling beneath him.

Dead.

He's dead.

She killed him.

Noise returns. Car horns and shouts swelling like a tide, but Anna already feels like she's been swept under. The blade slips from her fingers, the iron clang against the brick almost lost amidst the noise. More shouting. She thinks she might recognize the echo of her name in the chaos. A familiar arm wraps around her waist. The feeling of the universe folding—

A collision, arms slipping away from her and air whistling past her ears.

She's flung from Khiran's arms, body landing with bruising force. Her fingers curl against the soil, dry grasses slick against her bloody palm. They're in a field, snow-capped mountains dotted with evergreens on the skyline and the air thin. The sky is blue and cloudless. Blindingly bright compared to the dimly lit tunnel they came from.

It takes too long for her eyes to adjust. Too long to register the feeling of a body behind her, an unfamiliar arm caging her in, and a blade at her throat. She's caught—a fly in the web, unable to escape and waiting for death to descend. Anna's eyes find Khiran's, the fear clamoring in her chest sharpening into regret. He's on the ground, paused mid crawl, as his terror rimmed eyes flit between her face and the knife at her throat.

"Don't," he says, the words strangled, "Marcia, *please*—"

"Reduced to begging now, are we, Liesmith?" Marcia mocks, pressing the blade closer and nicking Anna's skin. She winces, feeling a bead of blood run down her neck. Marcia's porcelain cheek brushes hers with enough friction to feel like a threat, her voice a venomous purr. "Try *harder*."

"Take me." Khiran pleads, his hand splayed over his heart. "That's what you really want—what you've *always* wanted, right? She is nothing to you."

A pause, and then Marcia laughs. The sound of it cutting through the mountain air. "You would have known better once." The cruel curve of her mouth presses against Anna's cheek as she gives a taunting hum. "Do you always make him so stupid, I wonder?"

"Please—"

"Dante is dead," she croons. "His mistake, really. He was a fool to think your kitten didn't have claws." There's no grief in the words. No regret. There's a trilling note to her voice, like they've given her an unexpected gift wrapped in blood and sacrifice. Her blade traces over Anna's pulse, so close Anna need only swallow for it to cut. The sadistic grin pressed against her skin feels just as sharp. "Not that it matters. The First is going to be *furious* with both of you."

Khiran could still run, Anna thinks. The only thing tying him here is her. He would get so much farther, move so much quicker, without her weighing him down. She wants to scream the word, but it catches in her throat.

She knows his heart the way she knows her own. There is nothing she can say, nothing she can do, to convince him to save himself. They had promised each other, in her garden under the summer sun, that they would face what came together. Had the knife been pressed to his throat, had the opportunity to save herself been placed on her, she would do no different. They are too tangled, too crucial to each other's happiness, to walk away now.

Still, her eyes beg him. A silent, heart wrenching plea her parted lips can't speak.

Run.

Even though she knows he won't.

Run.

Because she has to try, anyway.

In his answering stare, she sees his answer reflected back to her. *I won't. I can't.* And Anna feels her heart crack, her lungs burning around a sob she can't shed. She can't let him see how much she hurts, can't let him carry the weight of her heartbreak when he's being crushed by his own. Tears slip down her cheeks before she can stop them.

"Oh, she is a pretty crier, isn't she?" Marcia croons, tongue dragging over Anna's tear stained skin. "How *delicious*." She shifts, the arm caging Anna in, extending out with a closed fist. "What will it be, Liesmith? Do you yield, or will you give me the pleasure of breaking you?"

There are apologies in his eyes when he looks at her. Anna doesn't believe she deserves them. Softly, his answer leaves his lips with the weight of all their shattered hopes. "I yield."

Marcia opens her palm, golden threads spinning from her fingertips like silk—coiling and twisting around his neck, his wrists, until they've braided into a rope as thick and heavy as chains. When her fist closes, the rope tightens, binding his hands together and drawing them to the noose around his throat with enough force that Anna can hear the aching thump his fists make against his chest.

"Would you like to know something funny, girl?" Marcia's mouth twists into a razor wire smile, her free hand sliding down Anna's right arm before grabbing her hand with a bruising grip. She forces it up until the scarred tissue of her missing finger fills her vision. "I may need to touch you for my magic to learn your signature, but it doesn't require your body parts to be attached. You threw that finger of yours out to throw me off the scent, but all you did was give me another one to track. Like a bloody, fleshy breadcrumb."

She drops the blade from her neck, spinning Anna around to face her, Marcia's bruising grip goes from her hand to her face—cold fingers digging into her jaw. She towers over her, pale blue eyes as hard and honed as ice as she holds up her hand, gold braided magic connecting her to Khiran's bindings. She pulls, and Khiran staggers forward, landing amongst the weeds with a grunt. "I want you to remember that while you watch him suffer. Remember that his death and all the pain that leads up to it is entirely *your fault*."

CHAPTER NINETEEN

True hatred is a rare thing, but he feels it rushing through his heart like a poison. A vicious venom that burns his veins with a fury that blisters. If not for Anna, for her fate balancing on his every action, he would let it consume him entirely.

EDUN
JUNE **1975**

THERE IS NO PATH.

Anna doesn't have time to wonder how it works, though. Not when Marcia's blade presses between her shoulder blades, urging her forward. She shadows Khiran's steps, the golden rope binding his hands swaying between him and the caster as the landscape changes. The rocky mountainside surrenders to lush greenery, tall evergreen trees slowly disappearing into a patchwork of flora. Lacy ferns brush her ankles, the pale twisting trunks of banyan trees creating a canopy so thick, Anna can barely see slivered bits of sky between the branches.

Then the ground beneath her shoes changes from rich forest underbrush to snaking roots. Anna watches where she steps, trying not to trip over the increasingly thick tangle lifting from the soil. Between the trunks, she catches glimpses of moss covered rock rising around them and realizes why the air feels different and the light seems dim. They're in some sort of sinkhole. One large enough to house an entire ecosystem.

Abruptly, Khiran stops, and Anna nearly collides with his back. Then she follows his gaze and understands what made him falter. Rising before them is a tree larger than any giant.

The one from which their immortality stemmed. The one that made a god of man.

It is both everything and nothing like she envisioned. It climbs higher than the skyscrapers that gather in the heart of New York, its trunk surely just as wide. At the base, the roots lift from the earth like giant hands cradling the world. It would be beautiful—*should* be beautiful—but for all her awe, Anna can't fight the sense of wrongness. Because the tree Khiran spun stories about was vibrant and full of life and magic.

The tree in front of her now looks closer to death.

Its branches are barren—skeletal arms reaching across the sky like lightning captured mid strike. The breeze moves through its limbs, a deep and subtle moan that echoes in her chest like a low note held too long. The bark is cracked, sap dripping from the wounds like an infection. In the center of it all is a mass of gnarled roots twisted into a throne. In its seat, a pale shadow of a man stares down at them. Silas, Cassius, and Malik line up at his left hand side.

Cassius and Silas stare back at her with masked detachment while Malik sits at their feet, his tiny fingers drawing looping patterns in the dirt, seemingly uninterested. Remembering the apathy in his expression, the shadows in his eyes as his flames surrounded them, he probably thought their capture was inevitable.

Her eyes lift, catching Silas' dark gaze, and sees the warnings hiding in his eyes. The First cannot know of their alliance. Any association to her would put both him and his lover in danger. For now, it must be as if she is no more than a stranger.

When she looks to the man on the throne, he's already returning her stare with quicksilver eyes. He's a portrait in grayscale; as if time has bled him of all color. Pale skin as smooth as one of the Roman statues lining Cassius' garden, his gray hair so light it looks like strands of silver hanging below the lithe line of his shoulders. There is a power to him. Anna can feel the weight of it bearing down on her, a shiver trailing up her spine. It isn't until his gaze slides away from her that she realizes the air in her lungs has turned stale.

"Where is Dante?" he asks, voice rumbling like thunder.

"Dead," Marcia chirps. The blade at Anna's back retreats, replaced by a rough push of her hand. Anna falls forward, catching herself on her hands and knees. Anna can hear the cruel enjoyment in her voice when she says, "She killed him."

Alabaster lips twist into a scowl, his hands gripping his throne with a strength that makes the roots groan in protest. At his feet, Cassius and Silas share a silent look. "Is that so?"

Marcia's grin is feral. "She had one of Ying's blades." Her eyes slide to Khiran, lip curling in disgust. "Apparently, the Liesmith thought to hide one away before he faced banishment."

"It is not the only thing that's been stolen." He says, standing. The First walks toward them with a grace—a *strength*—that seems at odds with the silver in his hair and the paper thin wrinkles lining the corners of his eyes. He stops in front of Khiran, towering over him once Marcia delivers a kick to the back of Khiran's leg, forcing him to kneel.

He hisses as his knees crack against the roots blanketing the earth, wincing.

The First reaches into the pocket of his pale robe, retrieving something. It isn't until he lifts it up to the light, holding it between his thumb and forefinger, that Anna realizes what it is.

Her ring.

The one Khiran sacrificed blood and bone to make, all so she would remain hidden to the eyes bearing down on them now.

Anna's heart gives a painful lurch, her sharp intake of breath rattling in her lungs. The etchings are dark against the pale bone; stained where her and Khiran's blood had settled and never flaked away.

"An interesting piece of magic," he says, studying the runes etched into the bone. "It must have hurt terribly." He drops the ring to the ground, his boot grinding it into a patch of earth nestled between the maze of roots. "Imagine my surprise when Marcia dropped it in my palm with news that the girl you ran off with has tasted a peach from **my** tree."

"Be honest," Khiran mocks, glaring up at the pale god, "are you angry she tasted it, or are you just pissed it was taken without you—the great, all seeing First—ever noticing?"

The First's eyes narrow, veins mapping the pale skin of his neck like roots. "Still don't know when to hold your tongue, I see." His eyes slide to Anna, gaze dragging over her as if there are secrets buried beneath her skin, waiting to be carved from her flesh. "Ah, but maybe I give you too little credit. Perhaps you know exactly when to let that mouth of yours run."

Khiran's gaze doesn't drop, but Anna catches the way his jaw strains. He hasn't looked at her once since they left the mountains behind them. As if his glance alone could condemn her. "Credit is something you've never been generous with."

The words effectively snare The First's attention, but there's a dark amusement pulling at the corners of his mouth that spells danger. "I suppose not. Perhaps, in the end, you've done me a greater service than you intended. The Tree is dying, our numbers dwindling. And you come bearing fresh blood."

Khiran's teeth grind, his hands trembling in their bonds. "She's of no use to you. She—"

A bored flick of his hand, and Khiran's voice is gone. Silenced with no more than a thought.

"My," Cassius hums, leaning against one of the larger roots, "I think this is the first time I've seen him speechless."

The shapeshifter's responding glare is murderous. Anna reminds herself that the amused tipping of Cassius' lips is part of his mask.

The First looks over at the small group nestled between The

Tree's great roots, his eyes darkening. "I see Kaia has still failed to heed my call."

Marcia scoffs, as if the shape of the other woman's name brings a bad taste to her mouth. "Kaia is as much a traitorous coward as he is. It's no surprise she chooses to hide despite your summons."

His lips twist into a smile so sharp, Anna can feel the edge of it like a blade against her pulse. "She will come," he says, grabbing Khiran by the back of his neck, dragging him away. Khiran fights his hold, his mouth moving around a silent snarl, but there is a strength in The First that is deceptively subtle. For all of Khiran's efforts, feet planting into the earth, body twisting, The First seems entirely unfazed.

Then Anna sees where he's taking him—water, crystalline blue against a forest of green off to the side of the great tree. A pond, its waters deceptively deep judging by the way it darkens as it pulls away from the shore.

Anna fights against the hands that hold her, blood rushing in her ears like a riptide fighting to drag her under. "Stop! Leave him alone!"

His steps don't falter as he walks into the water. He doesn't even give her the dignity of his attention, only stopping once the still water reaches his hips, before forcing Khiran's head under. "You make things hard for yourself, Kaia!" he calls. "Come now and come quickly or I'll hold him under until there's nothing left for him to scream."

The magic that had silenced Khiran earlier is gone. Anna can make out the garbled sound of his voice as he thrashes against the hands holding him down. Her efforts to get away from Marcia's iron grip doubles, desperate to reach him, but her strength is unyielding. A mountain she can't move. Shackles she can't escape.

Khiran stops screaming, out of breath, and Anna is losing herself in his silence, because she can't sit there and watch him drown. She can't. There are begging words in the shape of promises on her tongue—anything, she will do anything, just please stop hurting him—but the water recedes from the shore before she can speak them.

A wall of water rising, rising, rising. The First stands, small but without fear, in the shadow of a tsunami waiting to fall. His hold on Khiran's neck goes lax, the shapeshifter falling to the shallows. The impact, and perhaps Kaia's magic, pulls the water from his lungs in a guttural cough. The First doesn't drop his eyes from Kaia's. "How kind of you to join us."

Kaia's gaze is deadly. Cold enough to burn.

The First meets it without flinching. "I'm sure I don't need to remind you how Marcia's binds work? Try to whisk him away and that lovely noose will tighten." He turns his back to her, returning to his twisted throne and flicking a hand towards the others. "I trust you remember your place, Kaia?"

"I remember much more than that," she hisses, her round face pale with quiet rage. She kneels in the shallow water, helping Khiran up as he finds his breath. He leans on her as they leave the shore, the wall of water dropping with the subtlety of a door slammed shut behind them.

The First sits, his gaze falling squarely on Anna as he motions for her to approach. "Let us have a look at you, then."

When she doesn't move, Marcia pushes her toward him, threats falling from her lips like barbs. Anna stumbles forward, feeling the weight of everyone's eyes. Emotion clashes in her chest, fear and fury twisting until they feel like two heads on the same snake. For a moment, she thinks she might suffocate beneath the weight of it.

Then, between one breath and the next, it eases. Spilling from her until the beat of her heart slows, the pulse in her ears fading until a new sound snares her attention.

There is a whisper disguised as wind slipping between the skeletal branches. Anna feels it more than hears it. It's a storm—a demand, a plea.

Anna stares, the echo of it robbing her of breath. She can feel it curling against her heart, the way a newborn curls its fist around a finger. The way Piers once hugged her as a child, with his entire body and no reservations. The way Eira took her hand in her weathered ones and called her Child.

Child.

Anna is just a child. Her eight centuries are a mere stitch in the tapestry compared to the canopy looming over them.

The branches groan and Anna hears the wordless songs mothers hum to their children. Comforting. Soft. A stark contrast from the cold edge in The First's gaze.

"I'm afraid your lover has put you at a disadvantage," he says, voice booming over the courtyard. "Entry into this family is normally by my invitation only."

Anna looks at him with new understanding.

She thinks of the hives she abandoned on the California coast. Hives that thrived under her care, but were more than capable of surviving without it. She thinks of the bees, the intricately simple way in which they work together as a collective for the good of the many instead of the individual.

She thinks of what happens to an unfit queen.

The First grips her chin with bruising force, his long fingers a vice along her jaw. "What gift do you possess?"

So close, Anna can feel his power humming against her skin. The split second of electricity in the air before lightning strikes. She should feel terrified, but her heart is calm, her pulse steady.

"She doesn't have one," Khiran says. His voice is rough, an avalanche of sleet and stone. Bitterly cold and hardened by hatred. "She is of no use to you. Let her go. Let her be."

The First's stare is piercing. "Marcia." The sound of knuckles cracking against flesh, a pained grunt that sounds too much like Khiran to be anyone else. "Since your first warning didn't seem to take, speak again and I'll slit her throat. Now." The First's fingers bite into her jaw as she tries to look. "You'll find I abhor repeating myself as much as I do interruptions. Tell me. What is your gift?"

Stubbornly, Anna repeats what Khiran has already told him. "I don't have one."

He looks down at her a few seconds longer. "I don't believe you." His hold on her face softens, fingers assessing the line of her jaw. "No bruises. You're less prone to damage than your lover." He grabs her right hand faster than she can pull away, evaluating the nub of flesh that used to be her finger. "But not impenetrable, I see." He turns her wrist, catching sight of the pale shadow on her forearm and pulls up her sleeve. "What is this, then? Do you change your skin like he does?"

The flush that spreads over her chest is far from embarrassed. It's *angry*.

Eight centuries ago, Khiran knew with only one look what the patterns on her skin were and were not. He knew because he had seen it before—because he cared enough about the world to want to be a part of it. The ignorance of someone who has had lifetimes on top of lifetimes to learn, who has decided the world is beneath him from a throne of roots and ruin, is infuriating. "It's *mine*."

His lip curls. Whether it's in distaste or disappointment, Anna can't be sure. "Cassius." He says the name like a summons.

Anna has to force her expression to remain neutral, but her heart stutters. She knows why The First is summoning him, but she can't be sure if his kiss will yield the same results as last time. The empty space between her middle and pinkie finger stares up at her.

She still doesn't know if it was Khiran's magic or her own that saved her from succumbing to his gift.

Cassius hesitates, his eyes finding hers. For a split second, his horror is an echo of her own. Then his expression goes carefully blank. Guarded. She can see his mind working behind his passive expression.

Anna realizes with a sinking heart that whatever plan he's making is contingent on her being immune to his charms. He doesn't know about the ring. Doesn't know she is probably as susceptible to his kiss as any of the others. They never told him. Never told *anyone*. The only one who ever had an idea of the ring's origins—of its importance—is gone. Anna thinks of all the secrets Eira kept, from *her*, for Khiran's sake and knows with certainty that this was guarded just as carefully.

The First gestures to her with a flippant hand, leaning back into his throne. "I've grown impatient. Force the answers from her."

"Very well," Cassius says, tipping his chin in mock deference before stepping towards her. His hands, smooth and unblemished, cup her jaw with the gentlest of pressure—a cage in appearance only. There's a message in his eyes, begging to be read.

Pretend.

The strain on Anna's heart doubles, fear spiking. She doesn't have any way of telling him she may not have to.

The kiss is as chaste as one can be, the mere brushing of lips.

Anna waits, breath held so long her lungs burn with it, as he pulls away. His dark blue eyes search hers. She stares back, relief slowly unknotting the worry snaring around her heart.

She is still herself. Cassius' kiss no different to her than any mortal. The immunity to his charms was hers.

Only hers. Her gift.

"What power do you possess?" Cassius asks.

"I do not have one." Her answer is breathy, drunk without her having to bother faking it. A lie has never tasted so sweet. It coats her tongue, makes her giddy. She is a mouse in a den of snakes, but they've been robbed of their venom without their knowing it.

There is a shadow of a smile hinting at the corner of Cassius' mouth. Anna thinks it says, *well done.* "Is that all you wished for, oh exalted one?" The mockery coating the words is so thick it drips.

The First's glare is full of warnings. "Careful, Cassius. I'm not in the mood. If you wish to keep your tongue, I advise you *still it.*" Anna can feel his gaze burning into her cheek, but she doesn't dare look away from Cassius. She remembers how Khiran described it to her—of being enamored. Obsessed. As if there were no one else in the world but him and his words. "Ask how she got the peach."

Cassius turns back to her, trying to look admonished and failing spectacularly. "Who gave you the peach?"

Who not *how.* The difference strikes her as an important one. A hint of a plan laid out in the meager offering of a few words.

Who?

It's not what the First asked. The who is already—no. Not known. *Assumed.* They all believed it to be Khiran, because who else would risk taking a peach, of angering The First, than the one who once wished to overthrow him? Anna understands the difference between knowledge and assumptions. Understands that the latter holds room for doubt.

"A woman gave it to me," she answers. "She—"

"I don't care what form The Liesmith took," The First interrupts, frowning. "Ask her how he got it."

"How did Khiran get it from The Tree?"

"It wasn't him. It wasn't Khiran." She can feel the ripples of shock, hear the murmurs, but she doesn't pull her gaze from Cassius' face. She thinks of another pair of blue eyes, one's cold with cruelty. "It was the one you call The Huntress."

The reaction is immediate, but it's the shine of approval in Cassius' gaze that she focuses on. In them, she sees the same wickedly sharp edge as the moment he looked at her across a court-yard and realized she was *different*.

"She lies!" Marcia shrieks. From the corner of her vision, Anna can see her draping herself at the feet of the throne. "He must have stolen my face! My love for you is endless. No one has ever matched my devotion to you! The girl is a liar. A *snake* just like her maker! You mustn't—"

The First strikes her, the back of his hand cracking against her cheek with enough force to send her stumbling. "You presume to tell me what to do?!"

"No! No, of course not. I wish only to serve you. To *protect* you."

His pale hand wraps around her throat. "And yet, Cassius' charms point to the opposite," he says, thumb stroking the line of her jaw. He looks down on her, contemplates her fate with as much emotion as one decides on what animal to cull for their next meal. "Release the girl, Cassius. I have questions for Marcia that require explicitly honest answers."

Cassius' hands slip away from her face, his finger tapping against her jaw. Anna knows it's a signal, but she doesn't know how to inter-pret it and she's too afraid she'll ruin everything by dropping the act too soon. Cassius chuckles, a dark purr in his voice. "How sweet. She still can't seem to keep her eyes off me! Do you like what you see, Little Bird?"

Anna ducks her head. To anyone else, it must look like embarrassment, but the truth is she fears her expression might give her away. Her blood is thrumming in her veins; her pulse so quick, she feels like her entire body is humming with it.

She remembers the secretive smile Cassius gave the morning Khiran asked him what had changed—what could give them a chance at winning a war so stacked against them. Anna had no idea what it could be, not until she saw the flash of satisfaction the moment The First called out Marcia's name.

He tried to possess you. Khiran had told her. *If he asked you to jump, the only question that would break through the magic is* **how high**. Anna saw the power such a gift could wield, but didn't share Khiran's fear. Her hands close into fists, her knuckles pale against the rich earth.

Cassius said he had been working with Silas. Silas who loved him—who trusted him completely. Who would be willing to submit himself to his kiss, again and again, if it meant his lover could twist his gift into something *else*. Something darker than obsession. Something that skipped the question, the order, entirely.

Anna knows, even before his lips touch Marcia's, that it won't be the truth that springs from her lips. It will be his words in the shape of her voice. His will disguised as her actions. With just a kiss, he will have her power at his disposal.

She looks up just to see Cassius pull away, watching the hatred in Marcia's eyes soften into dough for him to mold. Anna holds her breath. Counts.

One.

Two.

Three.

Marcia's hand shoots out, snaring The First's wrist in her grasp while the other plunges her blade straight into his heart.

CHAPTER TWENTY

Something gives. Snaps. Maybe it's hearing their screams or maybe it's watching the woman he loves risking everything to end it all. He's tired of running.

EDUN
JUNE 1975

A CRIMSON STAIN IS BLOOMING OVER HIS CHEST. BLOOD SOAKING INTO the pristine white fabric, dripping, thick as sap. The First looks down, staring at the blade with a furrowed brow. Cassius' grin is vicious, more bared teeth than a smile as Silas draws to his side.

Then the growing red stain stutters. Shrinks. The blood is spilling back into the wound as if time is nothing but a word. The First turns his head, calm in ways that promise pain. Marcia's hand is still wrapped around the hilt, as if holding it there will make the blood spill once more. The First's hand wraps around her wrist. There is a sickening snap of bone, the end that held the knife now bent back in an angle so unnatural it makes Anna's stomach churn, but it's the lack of scream—the lack of *anything*—reflecting on Marcia's face that makes her blood run cold.

The First meets the blonde's darkening gaze. "Dear Cassius, I do believe you've finally made yourself more trouble than you're worth." He charges forward—faster than Anna's eyes can follow. His fingers wrap around Cassius' throat, lifting him with a strength no mortal should possess, the hilt of the blade still protruding from his chest as if it were nothing. The tendons in his forearm flex, a map of veins and sinew leading to the hand tightening around Cassius' throat. "Fear not. I will find another use for you. It will be curious to see how much this body of yours will take before it breaks."

Cassius' hand wraps around the blade's hilt, pulling it free from The First's flesh just as Silas draws his own. The glint of smooth metal is the only warning before he stabs the arm choking his lover. It slices all the way through; the tendons snapping and his grip going lax. Cassius falls to the ground, dragging air into his lungs with heaving, wheezing breaths. Silas immediately goes to his side, herding him away and placing himself between the threat.

The First looks at his arm, lip sneering as the blood drips from his fingers. "You too, Shepherd?" He grabs the hilt, pulling the knife slowly from his flesh. Anna can hear the agonizing scrape of blade against bone, but The First gives no indication of feeling any pain. He tosses it aside, the steel clattering amongst the roots. "Here I thought you realized your place. Did you forget you are expendable?"

The blood recedes, just as it did when he took a blade to the heart. He holds his hand up, flexing his fingers into a fist as if testing how well the sinew has knit itself back together. "It seems I have been too lenient with you. All of you. I will be certain to avoid such mistakes in the future."

Silas scowls, his eyes melded with a fury Anna has never seen him wear. "You are undeserving of your gifts. Of your power. I will see you stripped of them, or I will die trying."

"Die?" The First scoffs, his silver eyes gleaming, molten with a simmering fury. Dark tendrils spill from his fingers, translucent as smoke and rising above him until the wisps meld into a singular form. A shadow. "Pray that I will be so merciful."

The shadow strikes, spilling across the ground like ink, dark hands reaching towards Silas—

"No!" Cassius shouts. Driven by his will, Marcia throws herself in front of his lover, her body a shield. The shadow reaches her, siphoning into her veins and branching out over her pale skin like an infection. Like *poison*.

Cassius' kiss held the power to turn her against her master without so much as a flinch. The bones in her wrist had snapped beneath The First's fingers without a whimper. Whatever the shadow is, it must be made of the worst the world has to offer—a blend of agony and nightmares—because Marcia's mouth parts around a scream.

Anna has spent lifetimes around the sounds of the suffering, but nothing compares to what she's hearing now. Sharp and guttural, it claws its way into her chest like a howling beast, thrashing behind her ribs and clashing with the strangled beat of her heart.

This is more than pain, more than suffering.

It's as if every one of Marcia's nightmares have become real and they're feasting on her—breaking and burning her from the inside.

Part of the shadow remains, spilled limply over The Tree's roots. Sluggish and a few shades lighter, it reaches for Silas and Cassius's ankles as they rush around it. Marcia falls, her lungs emptied of air but her mouth still yawning open around a scream she can't give sound to.

Cassius slashes at the god's throat, but The First leans back and the blade's tip only nicks his skin—the wound healing over before the bead of blood can roll down his pale neck. The god's hand lashes out, aiming for Cassius' face, but Silas lands a stabbing blow to his side, first—the knife slipping between his ribs and puncturing a lung.

Anna is horrified at how little it slows him.

The lovers move as if it is a dance: parry, block, strike. The flashing of steel, the wet glint of crimson as it arcs like ribbons each time a blade tastes flesh. The First heals fast, but they aren't giving him time to breathe between blows. Frustration pulls his lips over his teeth, snarling. A flick of his hand, and his shadow trembles, reaching for Marcia. The toxin fades from her veins, soaking back into the shadow. It grows darker, faster, as her tortured expression smooths back into apathy. She stands, released from her nightmare as the shadow rushes to its master's aid.

"The *binds*, Cassius!" Khiran yells. The rope twining around his neck and wrists flicker as he fights against its hold. Beside him, Kaia sidles closer to the water's edge. Her eyes, dark as the deepest parts of the sea, follow The First's movements with a determination that promises action.

Marcia's body stills, gaze empty as her hand reaches out towards Khiran. The golden threads around his wrist and throat unravel, floating on the air like spider silk, before winding around The First. He snaps them as if they are as brittle as glass.

Khiran's hands are cold against her shoulders as he tries to draw her away, but his touch feels more like an echo than reality. Anna hears the sound of her name, the sounds of battle, but there's something else gnawing at the edges of her sight. A vision pulsing under her open palms, carried by the roots the way veins carry blood to a heart.

A vision of flames.

Of a canopy of branches alight with a fire so consuming, the smoke blocks out the light. Of smoldering ashes, an emptiness where a magnificent tree once stood.

Anna knows why The Tree has been dying. Knows it has been in preparation for this exact moment. The barren branches creak, the dried out limbs rubbing together like kindling without a match. There is no water, no life, there. Just the spirit, urging her to burn it to the ground.

One look at Marcia proves she is still under Cassius' possession. Her gaze is clouded, her body a weapon under his control. She fights beside the lovers, her movements more fluid than any puppet has a right to be as they dodge fists and shadow. Cassius, bruises ringing his throat like a necklace, must have given the silent order to protect, because when she isn't attacking The First, her body is shielding them from his wrath.

Anna's eyes slide to Malik, to the anxious sparks lighting his hands as they flex at his side. He looks lost. Unsure. No one has given him an order. Anna knows he won't get one. Not here. Khiran's words from decades ago ring in her ears.

He's a bomb waiting to go off.

A bomb. The Calamity. The bringer of the end for whoever is unfortunate enough to be there when he detonates.

Khiran is still pulling at her, urging her up. "We have to run," he says, his eyes wide and frantic. Water still drips from his hair, his face pale with pain. "Go to Kaia. While he's distracted."

Anna's lips part around an apology she can't bring herself to make. It sticks in her throat, stubborn and honest. He sees it—she knows he does—because the desperation rimming his eyes blurs into fear.

"Anna—"

She kisses him. Hopes he tastes apology mixed with the goodbye. Then she does what he asks:

Anna runs.

But not toward the water. Not toward Kaia and the escape she offers, but toward Malik. The child with a temper faster than reason because he was never given the opportunity to grow old enough to control his impulses. Anna is counting on that temper, that lack of control, now.

He's so focused on the battle, he doesn't see her until a split second before she collides with him. They're on the ground, roots digging painfully into her hip as she scrambles to get up. Malik's complexion is so red it's beginning to bleed into purple. Fire flares from his fingertips, licks of it slipping between his clenched teeth.

The First catches her gaze, snaring her between dodged blows. There's a furrow in his brow—disapproval—but he must see something in her. A determination. A confidence. Then his eyes slip to Malik, and he bares his teeth around a snarl. "No!" Abruptly, his shadow abandons the battle and reaches towards them, clawing over the tangle of roots with a frenzy that feels reckless.

It's too late.

Malik's small mouth is already parted in a scream full of flames and fury, leaving his hands with such force that Anna can *hear* it. The roots at their feet catch, the flame traveling faster than should be possible—as if The Tree itself were urging it along. It sweeps over the network of limbs and branches over their heads, the wood groaning and cracking. Malik stares up at the burning canopy, the fire reflecting in his wide, terrified eyes as he realizes what he's done.

The First is yelling, furious, but Cassius and the others don't give him the opportunity to come forward. Someone has landed a blade behind his knee, cutting through the tendons and crippling him, but he isn't given a moment to drop his hands long enough to remove it. He turns to Kaia, his eyes wild as he continues to block their blows. Gone is the calm, confident control—burned away like the branches raining ash and embers over their heads. Gone is the god, exposing the desperate man beneath the power. "Don't just stand there! Put it out!"

She steps back, drawing herself closer to the shore. Behind her, the water ripples as if in anticipation. Her answering stare is as frigid as her answer. "No."

He growls, blocking Silas' attempt to cleave his hand from his wrist and backhanding him with enough force to send him hurtling into the throne—smoldering roots snapping on impact. Anna cries out, ready to run to him, but a hand clasps around her wrist, stopping her.

"Don't," Khiran begs, a hiss in her ear. She doesn't understand why he's stopping her, not until she notices the erratic twitching of the shadow mere feet from the boy curled on the ground, his hands over his ears and his face burrowed in his dirty knees. It shudders in indecision, as if torn on who to punish, before retreating from the shell shocked boy and racing back towards its master.

Silas stands, embers falling from his broad shoulders, and dodges the pale hand shooting for his throat, sweat slick on his brow—

And steps on the hungry shadow waiting for him.

He drops, screaming, as his veins blacken and his eyes roll back until all that's visible are the whites. On instinct, Cassius reaches for him.

A mistake.

Tendrils of shadow claw at his wrist, poison seeping into his skin. His knees crack as he kneels, dull nails clawing at the dark lines spreading over his flesh. His pain is only drowned out by Silas' continued scream.

Chest heaving, The First pulls the blade from his leg, blood splattering across the pale, broken and burning roots of his once mighty throne with a hiss. He towers over them, flames reflecting like embers in his pale eyes and the blade's hilt strangled in his blood soaked grip. "Do you have any idea what you have *ruined*?!" he thunders, delivering a swift kick to Cassius' prone form. The blonde wheezes as the foot connects with his stomach, the air expelled from his lungs. Beside him, Marcia stands listless—strings unplucked.

Pushing his pale hair away from his face, he whirls on Kaia with new fervor. He steps toward her, made all the more terrifying by the backdrop of smoke and flames. "Put. It. **Out**."

She returns his stare, flames reflecting in her eyes as the water rises around her. It moves with her when she takes a slow step forward, coiling like a snake ready to strike. "No."

"Don't be a fool!" he rages, but his tirade is interrupted by a jab to his neck. Blood gushes over Marcia's fingers.

From the ground, Cassius grins through his pain. His jaw clenches so hard, his gums bleed from the force—staining his smile red. What was left of the shadow after infecting Silas must not have been potent enough to debilitate him completely. His glare is as sharp as the weapon wielded by Marcia's puppet hands. He's in too much agony to speak, but there are volumes in that stare. Chapter after chapter detailing all the ways The First has wronged him; all the ways in which he would see him *pay*.

The First draws the knife high, blood still dripping from the steel and eyes rabid, and Anna knows he's aiming to kill.

Her heart drops, scrambling toward them despite knowing she's too far to stop its descent in time—

Before she can even register the loss of his hands on her shoulders, Khiran teleports to the god's side, tackling him to the ground before his blade can taste Cassius' flesh.

The First howls in rage, slashing at the shapeshifter's face and missing when Khiran blinks away and reappears at the water's edge beside Kaia. "*You.*" The First spits the word as if it is something foul. Something poisonous.

Marcia's blade glints, aiming for the stretch of spine between his shoulder blades, but he turns, catching her wrist before she can meet her mark. He doesn't settle for snapping the bones, not this time. His other hand raises to her throat, his long fingers curling around the back of her neck, and crushes her spine.

She goes limp. Lifeless. The knife in her hand drops to their feet half a second before her body joins it amongst the roots. For a moment, The First stares down at her crumpled form, something that almost looks like regret flashing over his face, before he turns back to Khiran.

"This is *your* fault," he fumes, walking toward them. "I could have ended you—I *should* have—and this is how you repay my mercy?!" A crack in the flaming canopy of them, a thick branch crashing to the ground and erupting in a storm of embers. "Do you want to know a secret, boy? Why I bound you with the promise not to meddle in the lives of mortals? Why the terms were loose enough for you to walk among them, but never save them?" His lip curls into a vindictive smile that looks so much like the one Marcia wore, it's staggering. "It's because I knew you would *fail*. You and Eira were always so keen on helping those who are beneath our notice, fools that you are. I knew you would get too close, too attached, and every time you broke your vow would mean I would have the plea-sure of *breaking* you."

Kaia's eyes flash, her voice a hiss. "How dare you say her name?!"

Beside her, Khiran's face is dark with contempt, but Anna is increasingly aware of the rising heat making her sweat—the smoke tainting her lungs. Silas and Cassius are still lying amongst the roots, prone to the flames. The blonde is crawling towards his lover, who is dangerously close to the fire, but the shadow's weight pins him down.

The First laughs, cruel and mocking. "Had I known what ruin her choices would bring, I would have killed her before she brought this bastard into our midsts."

Anna ignores the clenching of her heart, muscles straining as she pulls Silas away from the flames. His body is taut with pain, making it harder for him to drag, but she's not willing to give up on him.

Hands.

The ones she knows—the ones she loves—wrapping around her waist and winding beneath Silas' arms. Magic pulling at her stomach, blurring her vision, and they're at the forest's edge. Far from the flames and far enough from The First's reach. Khiran blinks away, gone for mere seconds before returning with Cassius.

"I loved her," Kaia says, and the words are enough to draw Anna's gaze. The calm Kaia exudes is deceptive. There's danger lurking beneath the words; rows of teeth gnashing beneath still waters, waiting for the moment they can sink into flesh. A wall of water swells behind her, towering like a giant and trickling beneath The First's feet. It rises up to his ankles, his calves, wicking up his pale robes. Then it freezes, anchoring him in place.

"I loved her, and now she's gone. Extinguished by the same flames devouring your beloved throne." A shadow moves in the mountain of water behind her. "She burned, and for that, you will *drown*."

Tentacles break through the surface, coiling around The First's wrists like ropes. He growls, fighting the creature's pull into the unnatural tide. "You cannot kill me," The First spits, but there is an edge of desperation to his voice. His shadow spills from Cassius and Silas' veins, reforming and racing towards the woman in the water. "I am a *god*."

"Even gods can drown," Kaia promises. "I will drag you down so deep, you will beg for death to take you."

There is too much distance for the shadow to cross, it only makes it halfway before the water crashes over Kaia and The First's heads; the tide pulling away from the shore as quickly as it met it. Anna watches as the shadow seizes, shivers and shrinks. By the time the tide recedes, only Kaia remains. Anna knows, without a doubt, that she has fulfilled her promise. That her currents have swept the self proclaimed god into the rivers and out to the deepest, darkest parts the ocean has to offer.

A crack, louder than a gunshot. A scream sticks in Anna's throat as she ducks, hands flying to protect her head on instinct. When she looks up, the main trunk is split—yawning open like a hungry mouth.

A screech rings in Anna's ears, high pitched and urgent. It drowns out everything and everyone else.

Distantly, she registers Khiran is yelling her name, but there's something she has to do first. She can feel the demand squeezing her heart, its hold so tight it's almost suffocating. There's something in the trunk. Something she has to get.

She pushes forward, the heat almost unbearable. The pain of it feels worse than she remembers. Worse than when it licked up her dress and left her in nothing but ashes. She bites back the urge to scream, gritting her teeth as tears track over her face. They evaporate before they have the chance to fall.

Her hand reaches, blindly, into the cracked wood and grasps something hard. It burns in her palm, but it's a different kind of heat. One of magic. Of success.

Anna tears herself away, tripping over the roots in her haste to get away. She can't see. The smoke is burning her eyes, making the world blur. She closes them against the pain, eyelashes wet. Arms wrap around her, guiding her. Khiran. It has to be. No one else has ever held her so close.

But the arms feel different.

They don't sit as high up on her shoulders, don't engulf her in the ways her heart intimately remembers. When he's guided her far enough from the fire, she falls to her knees, eyes still screwed shut as she coughs so violently that her entire chest aches with it. For all that she gasps, she can't seem to find the breath her lungs are starving for. Khiran's hand rests on her back, a comforting weight.

Someone hands her a flask. Shakily, her hands close around it, feeling the stitched leather pressing into her fingertips. "Drink," he says, voice deep and familiar. Silas.

Anna is relieved to find it's water.

She takes a long drink, blinks her eyes open. They still ache, but the tears have lessened enough for her to make out Silas' face. He's kneeling in front of her, soot streaking his cheek, his clothes. "You had us worried, my friend. What possessed you to run into the flames?"

Her right hand still grips the treasure like a lifeline. Anna looks down, trying to uncurl her fingers with a wince. She sucks in a breath, reveling at the jolt of pain. The back of her hand, her fingers, are burnt. The skin blistered and raw. She can't bring herself past the point of pain to open it. Someone shouts for water, but she's too engrossed in the sight of the burns across her knuckles to pay attention.

Her healing is gone.

Mortal. She's mortal again.

She turns, searching for Khiran's gaze. For his comfort. But when she looks, it is the face of a stranger that stares back at her. His eyes are too dark, his hair a dark blonde that is a dozen shades too light. He's thin and sallow, like a wisp. All sharp lines and swollen joints. He looks nothing like the man she loves. Nothing like the face that stars in all her favorite memories.

Anna recognizes him anyway.

Her empty hand traces the gaunt line of his cheek, leaving a trail of ash in its wake. She breathes his name between them. A question. A confirmation. "Khiran?"

A scream pierces the air, shrill in ways only small bodies seem capable of accomplishing. Malik lays on the ground, face and clothes streaked in ashes and soot, his small fists and feet striking the ground in a tantrum. The words that leave him are so tangled up in emotion, it takes Anna a moment to decipher them. When she does, her heart gives a painful twist, regret coating her tongue in bitter understanding.

"My fault," he screams. "It's all my fault!"

Anna knows she's to blame for it—that she used him the same

way The First has for thousands of years. As if he were a weapon instead of a boy. Instead of a child.

Anna stands, her burned hand curled protectively over her chest and feeling every bruise and scrape with a permanence she hasn't felt in nearly a millennium. Strange how something so universal can feel so new. She wets her dry lips, tasting ash, and steps toward him.

A hand on her wrist, gentle and unfamiliar, stops her.

"Leave him," Khiran says, but his voice is as foreign to her as his features. He winces, as if the change surprises him, too. Frowning, he releases her wrist to look at his hands, leaving a smudge of ash where his fingers curled around her pulse. A shadowed bracelet forged from everything she's destroyed.

Slowly, his fingers close into a fist. The sinewy tendons of his arms flexing just beneath his skin.

Over his shoulder, Anna sees the look in Kaia's eyes. The same frozen promise as the moment the tide swept The First to his end. Anna's not sure how fast or how far her current traveled before the magic burned from their veins, but she doesn't doubt that Kaia's delivered on her threat. Somewhere, The First's screams are being swallowed by an ocean, his lungs filling with salt water. Anna has always feared drowning—feared the agony of it. She thinks it's a fitting end for a man who would happily let the world burn.

But not for Malik.

She steps to the side, putting her body between the boy who has nothing and the woman who has lost everything. "He's a child," Anna says, looking between all their faces. She expects to find sympathy, to find an *ally*, but even Silas averts his gaze.

Cassius is the one bold enough to voice what they all must thinking. "He's a monster, Anna."

"Only because he was never given the chance to grow into anything else!" She looks to Kaia, but she won't return her gaze. She's too busy staring down at the child pounding at the earth, body pale with ash, as if he's an obstacle to overcome. It may have been on The First's orders, but it was Malik's fire he weaponized. Malik's hands who killed Eira. "Kaia," she says, a plea threading through the woman's name like a prayer. "He never had someone like Eira to teach him. To *love* him."

Anna takes a deep breath, hands fisting at her sides. "He deserves that same chance. Please."

Cassius shakes his head, his arm cradled against his chest. The First must have landed a blow before Kaia's waters swept him away. "You're a few thousand years too late, Little Bird."

"You're wrong." Anna looks to Khiran, her gaze steady and her voice strong. "Time touches everything. He deserves the chance to grow. To *change*."

He can't hold her stare, his eyes dropping. Anna feels his doubt like a betrayal.

"He killed Eira," Kaia says, but the edge in her gaze has dulled into something thoughtful. Pain mixed with reflection.

"Yes." She won't deny the truth of it, as partial as it is. Anna glances at the smoldering ruins around them. A throne of roots and ruin smoldering into ash. "In a way, he helped you kill The First, too."

They all go silent—Malik's tantrum and the hiss of the waning flames the only sound between them. Khiran wets his thin lips, shaking his head. "Anna's right." He looks over at the boy, measures the way his tiny fists and feet beat against the ashes of a stolen temple. "If oppression can breed cruelty, then perhaps empathy can heal it." He reaches for her, fingers trace the line of her jaw and meeting her gaze. "He suffered as we did, but without the freedoms. Without the friendships. He deserves a chance, and we owe it to him to give it."

Silas' expression is weighted with understanding. "I agree."

Eyes rolling, Cassius does little to rein in his skepticism. "That's all very touching, but that doesn't really solve anything. Which one of us is actually willing to *take him in*." He looks between them, his uninjured hand splaying over his chest. "Because I'm certainly not. I refuse to be responsible for a child, let alone one with thousands of years of emotional baggage."

"I'll do it," Anna offers. "I'm the one who hurt him—who used him. The least I can do is try to teach him how to live a normal life."

"No," Silas murmurs, a furrow in his brow. "That's why it shouldn't be you. He's been angry for so long... looking at you is more likely to remind him of what he's lost instead of the freedom he's gained."

Anna winces, hearing the truth in it. "But—"

"I'll take him."

The words are quiet, but they ring in Anna's ears like a promise. When she looks, Kaia doesn't meet her eyes. She's too busy looking at the boy.

Khiran is the first to react. His brow creases, his dark eyes anguished. "Kaia, you don't—"

"I do," Kaia says, cutting him off. She turns to him, her face softening in ways Anna hasn't seen since their time below the waves. "I need to be the one to take him in. I need to be the one to ensure something good comes of all of this. So *I* can heal, too." Her hand rests over Khiran's gaunt cheek, her eyes glassy. "It's what Eira would have wanted."

Her hand slips away, her gaze resting on Anna. Something passes between them, so heavy it takes Anna a moment to put a name to it. It's more than understanding; more than something shared.

She remembers the feel of warmth from the hearth, the way a quilt stitched by her hands covered their bodies and Khiran's fingers trailed over the patterns on her skin. Remembers the way he told his and Eira's story and Kaia's mistake. Remembers the reasons Kaia gave him for interfering.

She confessed to me, much later, that she was a mother before she was a god.

The tension spills from her chest like coiled wire set loose, tangled and chaotic. A mother. Kaia was a mother. Of everyone here, they are the only ones who understand what parenthood means. The only ones who understand the pain and joy of it. The responsibility.

And Anna knows, with a certainty that leaves her breathless, that Kaia wouldn't offer to take in a boy with bloody hands if she didn't believe there was room in her heart to forgive him.

THE HAVE TO PRY HER FINGERS AWAY FROM HER PALM.

The pain is unspeakable, a scream in her lungs and a sob sticking in her throat. Khiran murmurs apologies as he carefully peels each finger away from the burnt and blistered skin. Then her hand opens, and she sees what she burned for—what she could have *died* for—and feels her heart race with the implications.

In the blistered cradle of her palm is a peach pit.

Cassius stares down at the grooved and pitted seed, a crooked smile dimpling his left cheek. "I knew it. I knew it chose you." He looks at Khiran with a teasing glance. "Oh, I will most certainly enjoy holding this over your head for the rest of our pitiful mortal lives, dear Brother."

Silas shakes his head in disapproval, but there is a fond smile pulling at his lips. He still wears it as he places a kiss to the blonde's temple.

Cassius stares at her as if she is a dream made reality. Then his grin falters. Fades into something soft. Something warm. "Well done, Little Bird."

Anna barely hears him. Her eyes are on the pit in her palm with giddy relief. Hope unfurls in her chest, fragile as a sparrow's wings and ready to soar.

CHAPTER TWENTY-ONE

*His fingers rake through the remains, soot blackening his nails and ashes
smearing gray shadows over his skin. This body feels strange—as alien to
him as the lingering, aching pain. Hiding somewhere beneath the cremated
remains of the great tree is a piece of himself.*

EDUN

JUNE **1975**

THEY LINGER.

Mend their wounds and still their hearts while the flames slowly
perish, embers glowing like eyes in the pitch of night.

Anna often finds her hand slipping into her pocket, closing her
fingers around the seed just to assure herself that it's still there.
Sometimes, when everyone else has fallen into sleep, she'll close her
eyes and hold it for hours just to see if she can feel the hum of magic
against her palm.

She never does.

Whatever magic it holds is now beyond her reach, but she knows with a certainty that only faith can inspire that it's there. She can no longer hear the whispers or feel the tug on her soul, but the moment she saw the pit in her soot-streaked palm, she knew what she was meant to do with it.

Plant it. Care for it until it grew into its magic like a phoenix made stronger for having been burnt down to ash.

She had considered letting it grow in the ashes of its mother. It would be poetic, she thinks, but ultimately it didn't feel right. This paradise has been tainted. The roots twisted and forced into the unnatural shape of an unfit throne while its gifts had been exploited. Sometimes it's not enough to rise from the ashes. Sometimes one has to start somewhere new to grow.

Anna suspects that sentiment will ring just as true for all of them.

Sometimes she catches a stillness in Silas. One she recognizes as the same faraway look he would get when the world whispered its secrets to him. Anna knows he's listening for something that will not come.

When she asks, he offers her a smile, but it's weak at the edges. "The world is so quiet now that it no longer speaks to me. Sometimes I find myself forgetting that there are no longer whispers for me to hear."

She sits beside him, drawing her knees to her chest. There's a sliver of regret lodged in her heart. It twinges every time she's reminded that they bear the burden of her choice. "Do you miss it?"

He looks down at his hand, somber gaze tracing the lines of his palm as if they could spell answers. "It feels like a piece of myself is missing."

Cassius sidles in on his other side, their shoulders brushing as he gently places a plate of food into his lover's hands. "Worry not, my love," he soothes, lips curving into a smile as honest as it is playful. "Now that there's no one to stand in our way, we will build a life together that fills the parts of us that feel empty."

Silas' answering smile is as warm as the fire reflecting in his dark eyes. "That we shall."

Cassius' gaze lifts to hers, his head tilting as he studies her. There's concern chipping away at the curve of his lips. By the time he finishes chewing on his words, his smile has disappeared entirely. "Should I be worried?"

Anna winces, the empty space beside her chafing.

Khiran isn't acting like himself—hasn't been since the moment The Tree went up in flames.

He's been quiet and withdrawn. Given the circumstances, she can understand why he might feel the need to pull away from the others —to recenter himself in his new reality. It must be hard, suffering under their gaze and being reminded that the body he's come to know as *his* has been stripped away. What worries her is the way Khiran seems to be distancing himself from *her*.

Once, he'd told her he'd give everything if it meant they could hold each other without the fear of The First hanging over them. Now, she worries the realities might cost more than he imagined when he murmured the promise over her heart.

He keeps going back to the spot where The Tree once stood—his eyes measuring. Anna can't be sure what kind of answers he's searching for and she's too afraid to ask. It's been at least an hour since he told her he was going for a walk. She knows where his feet must have taken him.

Her hand goes to her pocket, fingers tracing the curve of the pit, trying to draw a bit of comfort from the hope it holds. Cassius' question feels like a weight she can't escape. "I don't know."

She hates that it's the truth.

Silas must hear the pain lacing her voice, because he shares a look with Cassius before setting his plate aside. His hand is warm, reassuring, when it settles on her shoulder. "Why don't I go tell him the food is ready?"

Weakly, Anna nods. "Thank you."

Cassius studies her a moment longer while Silas walks away, before dropping his gaze to his plate. The First, she learned, hadn't felt hunger for food or drink, but a larder had been kept with some basic staples for Malik and Marcia's sake. Kaia had found enough to make rice to go with the fish they'd caught that afternoon. Taking a bite, Cassius chews thoughtfully before speaking. "You'll get your happy ending, Little Bird. You've fought too hard to accept anything less."

She shakes her head. "I haven't—"

He pins her with a knowing look. "You killed Dante."

Anna recoils, heart giving a stuttering whine in her chest. She hadn't had a chance to process the blood on her hands—hadn't *wanted* to. Better to bury it until she could afford to let the guilt cripple her. She feels it now, though. A burning under her skin. She swallows down the nausea rising in her throat. "Yes."

"Wish I could have seen the look on his face when he failed to still you," he says, voice lilting. "He always was an arrogant bastard."

"I've—before that—I'd never killed anyone before," she admits, staring at her hands. If she looks hard enough, she thinks she can still see the blood staining her pale skin. "Not directly. Not like that."

"I know." At her cautious, questioning glance, he smiles. A gentle pull of his lips that feels weighted, dragged down by memories she's not privy to. "We all had that look about us, once upon a time."

Anna swallows tightly. "I don't regret it," she whispers, the words an aching confession. "I thought I would."

"Why should you? The only thing you're guilty of is surviving."

Anna's heart doesn't agree, but maybe someday she'll feel it. Time changes everything, after all.

Her eyes drift across their meager campsite, lingering on the boy by Kaia's side. Malik's wrath had quieted into resigned silence. Sometimes Anna catches him watching them, his hazel eyes studying their more gentle interactions with a bemusement that makes her heart break. She's afraid to know what his life looked like under The First's care, treated like a weapon instead of a child.

Kaia must know some extent of it. She's extra gentle with him, soft in ways that soothe. She sings him songs and tells him stories; turns the shadows of her fingers into puppets. Now, she sits with him on the ground, showing him how to play a version of tic-tac-toe and drawing in the dirt with the pointed end of a stick.

Suddenly, the quiet peace is broken by Malik's scream. The sound blisters, so large for such a small body. Anna jumps up, running toward them. Malik is too caught up in his frustration to speak, his hand clutched to his chest. It takes Anna and Kaia a full minute before they realize the cause of his distress.

A splinter, big enough to hurt and small enough that Anna has to squint to see it in the firelight. She wonders how overwhelming such a pain must feel to a child who has lived too long to remember its bite.

She catches the moment Kaia reached for a magic that's no longer hers; sees how lost the older woman looks without it. For the first time, Anna sees them—beings thousands of years her elder—and finds her youth to be an advantage. She has not forgotten what it is to be human; to be powerless.

She's beginning to realize that they *have*.

IT TAKES THREE DAYS BEFORE THE LAST OF THE EMBERS GIVE UP THEIR stubborn spark. Anna finds Khiran in the ruins not long after.

He's kneeling, hands sifting through the ashes. It coats his arms up to his elbows like a ghostly pair of gloves.

"Khiran?" His name is a question she can't bring herself to ask. The more days pass, the more she's convinced that he's changed in more ways than just appearances. There's a pain in him, a quiet torment she doesn't understand. Even when they lay together, their limbs tangled and their breath shared under the blanket of night, he still feels far away. Lost in thoughts he either can't name or won't share. "What are you doing?"

For a moment, he gives no indication of having heard her. Ashes spill from between his fingers as he rakes his hand across the earth. Once, twice, before he answers. "Searching."

She kneels beside him, her bandaged hand reaching out to join him, but he grasps her wrist. Ashes smudge, ghostly and gray, over her skin as he meets her stare. His brown eyes still feel unfamiliar, but the look in them—the exasperation—is something she'd recognize anywhere. "Your hands," he scolds softly. "You'll get them infected."

Funny, she's forgotten to worry about infection even though her skin burns with a reminder of her newfound mortality. She swallows, throat dry, and nods. His fingers flex against her wrist, a gentle squeeze, before he releases her and returns to his previous activity.

Anna folds her useless, bandaged hand in her lap. "What are you looking for?"

The smile he gives is tender, tired and soft at the corners. "If I find it, I'll let you know." Briefly, he glances up at her from the corner of his eye. "You needn't worry about me."

She studies his profile, searching for cracks in his impassive expression. "Don't I?"

A laugh leaves him, raspy and full of whispered relief and tired regrets. "We're alive, Anna. I may no longer have forever with you, but the time we do have... it's enough."

Hesitantly, Anna relents and lets him dig amongst the ashes in peace. As she helps Silas and Kaia prepare dinner, she tries not to think of the heaviness in the words he left unsaid.

It has to be.

HE'S COVERED IN ASH AND SOOT WHEN HE FINALLY JOINS THEM. IT'S raining, the warm air humid as they huddle beneath a rocky overhang. Water drips down his jaw, his dark blonde hair dark with it. There's a reprimand on her tongue, a reminder that whatever he's searching for can't be worth the time and energy. Then he holds out his hand, a ring she'd recognize anywhere nestled in his muddy palm. The one made of him. The one made for her.

He slips it onto the ring finger of her left hand, and Anna chokes back a watery laugh as she curls it lovingly against her chest.

Khiran doesn't need his magic to see her, but it's a nice reminder all the same. Time changes everything, but the ring that once tied them together still fits like it was made for her.

Together is a promise that needs no magic to bind it.

IT TAKES DAYS TO CLIMB THEIR WAY OUT OF EDUN'S DEPTHS. ANNA'S NOT sure if they would have made it at all if it weren't for Malik and his knowledge of every cavern and limestone ledge. After thousands of years, the sinkhole was as much his home as it was his cage.

It isn't until they leave it behind them that Anna realizes they are as lost as she is.

The Tree's magic was a strange thing. None of them had ever bothered to learn where it stood in reference to the rest of the world. It had its own magnetic pull, its own magic that led each of them there in different ways. The desire to be under its branches had always been enough to gain entry from anywhere.

So when they make their way down the mountain and finally stumble on a rural Mandarin speaking village, it comes as news to all of them that the tree of legend actually hailed from the same region that told stories of gods and peaches that grant immortality. They're in the Guangxi region of southern China, surrounded by rivers banked by lush forests and towering karst formations that rise from the earth like slumbering stone giants.

Without money, it takes five days for them to travel to one of Khiran's hideaways in a small coastal town south of Nanning. The only thing they have of value is the golden hoops lining Cassius' ears. It's at least enough to trade for food and transportation part of the way.

To Anna's immense relief, the hideaway is stocked immensely better than the one in Sweden had been. Instead of a single tin of almond cookies, they find enough food to comfortably share. They're all in need of it. They are haggard and travel worn in ways that only mortality can bring. Anna had taken for granted the way her feet ached but never blistered; the way she felt the fatigue of a journey but not the bone deep throbbing of her muscles protesting every step.

She knows it's the same for the rest of them, too.

Malik had whined and whimpered, tears stubbornly clinging to his cheeks, until they took turns carrying him on some of the longer stretches. Cassius had grumbled about it incessantly, but he let the boy curl against his back despite looking as haggard as the rest of them. Anna suspects it was only watching Khiran stumble, his sallow face twisted into a grimace, when he had carried Malik the time before that prompted the offer.

They are all suffering under the constraints of their mortality, but Khiran seems to bear a weight that they don't. He doesn't utter a single complaint, but Anna can see the shakiness in his steps—can see the way his complexion pales with pain. And Anna knows, without him breathing a word, that he isn't fit to travel on foot.

It is with that thought, that *fear*, that she finds herself flooded with relief when Khiran pulls an old tin hidden beneath the floorboards and filled with small gold bars.

It's enough to send them all wherever they wish to go, in comfort.

CASSIUS AND SILAS LEAVE TWO DAYS LATER, BUT NOT BEFORE THE BLONDE scribbles an address on a piece of paper and folds it into her palm. It's in Istanbul—the home she and Khiran had taken shelter in those dark days after Eira's death. Silas makes her promise to write, his smile warm and dimpling in the corners when he reminds her that they've been friends too long to let something like mortality come between them.

His arms are warm when he hugs her goodbye. Anna finds herself blinking back tears. Strange how a farewell can hurt so much when forever is no longer promised.

Cassius' grin is crooked and teasing as he instructs her to make sure his 'brother' keeps in touch, but there's a storm darkening his blue eyes that tells her more than he can in words.

He's worried about Khiran, too.

Kaia fusses over him as much as she does Malik, mothering them both in equal measure. She has already told them she plans to stay. She likes the little house—likes that it's close enough for her to hear the crashing of the waves from the open window. Between the roof over their heads and the gold, they can live a modest life and give Malik the chance to grow into a person of his own making.

In the end, there is never really a question about where Khiran and Anna will go. In the safety of her pocket, she wraps her scarred fingers around the pit. She can think of no better place to plant it than the home—the *roots*—she'd left behind.

It turns out Khiran hates flying almost as much as he hates traveling by boat.

His hands clutch the armrests, knuckles white. "Anna?" Her name slips between his teeth, the muscle in his jaw spasming. "This is worse."

"Worse than what?"

"Anything. Everything. I hate it."

Carefully, she coaxes his grip from the armrest and threads his fingers through her own. His grip borders on painful, her fingertips prickling with the beginning signs of numbness. She's glad he sits on her left—her right hand is healing, but the burns are still tender. "It's the fastest way," she murmurs, studying his face closely. "Do you feel sick?"

"What I feel is *terrified*," he grumbles, a growl in his voice. "We're flying in a tin can."

Anna turns to the window, tracing the shapes of the clouds they're flying over. "You're concentrating on the wrong thing."

A moment of pause, filled by the idle chatter of the other passengers and the hum of the engines, before he gives. "What should I be concentrating on?"

Sometimes, Anna still catches herself expecting one face but finding another. Fleeting moments where she has to remind herself that there are no flecks of blue or green to be found in his irises, no dark curls of hair to twist around her fingers. Habits, she finds, are hard to change when they've had centuries to instill them. She finds herself thankful for all those years, all those different forms, he'd once visited her in.

Thankful for having already learned to recognize him no matter the face he wore.

Anna squeezes his hand, her smile soft. "That we're *flying*."

WHEN THEY FINALLY TURN THE CORNER AND SEE THEIR PALE YELLOW cottage off the California coast, Anna is surprised to find it in far better condition than she expected. The garden is in full bloom, tended and cared for. In the apiary, there are significantly fewer hives, but she spots at least four. The siding is still yellow, but the hue is just a touch brighter than she remembers it—indicative of new paint.

Someone is living here.

Her heart drops, thinking they've journeyed across the world for a home that is no longer theirs to claim. She wonders if they've kept the little treasures she's painted—the vines and flowers caressing the trim like a mother. Then the front door opens. A middle-aged man, familiar but not, pauses in the threshold. It's only when he smiles that Anna recognizes him.

"Took you long enough," he says. The years have added depth to his voice, sand shifting beneath the tide. There are wrinkles around his eyes, around his mouth, that she doesn't recognize—spoils of a life lived well. A life with laughter.

His name is a memory on her tongue, sweet and nostalgic. "Jiro?"

Maybe it's the question in her voice or the trembling beginnings of a smile, but his expression softens. "You told me once, that this place was your first home." There are so many missed years in his gaze, Anna only recognizes the shadow of who he was before—a boy angry at the world that turned its back on him. He pats the porch rail fondly, like a friend. "I knew you'd come back."

His eyes move to Khiran, a shadow of confusion passing over his face. It's not until his gaze falls to their laced fingers that he understands. His expression softens into something gentle, as if he can read all their scars in the gaunt lines of Khiran's face.

Her throat tightens, tears threatening to spill. "This whole time?" she asks, voice as weak as her heart. She repeats it, because it sounds as wonderfully impossible as it feels. "You stayed this whole time?"

He smiles, and it's so soft and warm—so at odds with her memory of him. No longer is he a lanky teenager with so much hurt it soured into rage. The man before her is content. Happy. "Welcome home."

CHAPTER TWENTY-TWO

His reflection is a patchwork of parts he didn't choose, his skin sallow and his body traitorous. It pains him in ways that go beyond physical—an ache made sharper with knowing he would choose to bear it all over again if it meant staying by her side.

CALIFORNIA, UNITED STATES
1976

ANNA PLANTS THE PEACH PIT IN THE HEART OF HER GARDEN.

It's the wrong time of year for it, but as Khiran helps her bury it one handful of soil at a time, she can't help but feel that it's right. Magic doesn't wait for seasons.

Off to the side, Jiro watches with his hands in his trouser pockets.

They had exchanged stories over wine the night before. Trading histories until they could see the framework of the tapestries Life had continued to weave while they had been apart.

He doesn't live at the cottage full time, but he drives up almost every other weekend to maintain the place. His home is in Santa Cruz, where his restaurant, his wife, and young daughter are. The three of them like to spend the summers up here. His daughter, Ami, took her first steps in the same kitchen he learned to cook in. She likes to play in the garden and listen to him tell stories about gods masquerading as humans between the stems of rosemary. Sometimes, he overhears her trying to retell the same stories to the neighbor's little boy.

They're only stories to her—myths and legends spun of the same magic as cursed princesses and magic spinning wheels—but sometimes he catches her on the front porch, staring out over the horizon with her favorite stuffed bunny in her hands as if she's waiting. Stories have a way of snaring hearts—of following children as they age into adults until they pass it down to the next generation. Jiro admits that was his hope—that the gods who gave him a home could live on in his daughter until they could return and prove themselves real. It's why he strived to leave their home unchanged.

Time has left a patina on every item within its walls, but everything Anna once cared for has remained the same. Her little murals still decorate the doorways and float down the halls. There's an entire corner of the greenhouse devoted to storing all the faded remnants of artwork she hadn't had the heart to get rid of. In the living room, Khiran's leather wingback sits in the corner, the shelves framing the fireplace still carrying the weight of all their books. Anna can even recognize some of the titles. By the record player, the Ray Charles album they danced to their first Christmas sits on top.

It feels, in all ways, like the home they left.

SETTLING BACK INTO THE LIFE SHE ONCE CHERISHED TAKES LONGER THAN Anna expected.

For as much as Jiro tried to keep things the same, it doesn't change the fact that *she* is changed. Sometimes she'll prepare a meal, the hilt of the kitchen knife pressed into her palm, and she'll remember how blood had spilled over her hands and the terror that had seized her heart. Last week, when Jiro helped her burn some of the waste from the garden, she had to fight to hide the way her body shook in front of the flames, the burns on her hand twinging with painful memories. Considering the concern she saw in his dark eyes, she's not entirely convinced that she succeeded.

In the garden, the pit has sprouted.

Its leaves uncurl and soak up the last offerings of summer, reaching up on a spindly trunk towards the open sky above it. It's already as tall as Anna, growing faster than her eyes can keep up. Some days it feels like it's gained a month of growth in a single after-noon. Whenever she feels shaken by old fears and past regrets, Anna takes a seat beside it and admires its green foliage with a gentle hand. It helps ground her; reminds her of the hope they've earned and the pain they've escaped.

Somehow, the threat of The First still lingers despite knowing it's no longer real. Anna worries that Khiran must feel it, too. When summer wanes into fall, the colors of the landscape turn warm and vibrant beneath its cool touch. It's beautiful—just like she remembers—but it means they've been home for months, and his face still looks gaunt. His skin still pale in ways that suggest sickness.

He's not gaining weight.

Anna starts adding more fat, more butter, more cream, to their meals. She can see the effects of it in the heaviness of her breasts and the softness of her hips and thighs, but when she explores the dips and valleys of his body at night, his ribs read like braille beneath her fingers, spelling out her failures.

She thinks of his beginnings. Thinks of the night they spoke of memories carried and memories left behind.

I came into Eira's care because I was unwanted. I never knew why—I was too young to understand.

He didn't understand then, but Anna does now.

There are days he spends more hours sleeping than awake. Days where his muscles ache and swell even when he's done nothing to warrant the stiffness. For all of Anna's experience, all her knowledge, she can't name what ails him, but she knows with a certainty that echoes in the hollow of her chest like a nightmare that his frailty was the reason for his abandonment. He was the mouth not worth feeding. The child they didn't expect to live.

She wonders if he's come to the same realization she has.

THE BATHROOM MIRROR IS SHATTERED.

Jagged pieces lay scattered in the pedestal sink, shining against the white enamel. On the floor, shards wink up at her like sharp confetti. With the way the evening light shines in from the window, tiny reflections cast out like stars around the room. It would almost be beautiful.

Almost.

There's blood dripping from sharp fragments, smearing across the mirrored surface like a stain. It matches Khiran's knuckles.

She calls his name, soft with concern and lined with questions.

He doesn't look up.

"It's not me." His voice is serrated at the edges. Raw. "This face. This body. It's not right. I can't—I'm *trapped*. I'm trapped in this form that isn't of my choosing and I *don't know the person staring back.*"

Anna doesn't know what to say, doesn't know how to fix it.

She thinks of Silas, of how he feels lost in a world that no longer whispers in his ear. Thinks of Malik and the way his anger bled away until all that was left was fear. Cassius, who's having to learn how to trust a world he can't seduce. Kaia, who lives by the ocean she can no longer call home. Each and every one of them are struggling to adjust to mortal life the same way Khiran was forced to.

A life of less. Less power. Less magic.

Somehow, Anna knows that's not the reason why there are shards of mirror littering the floor. The blood branching across the back of his hand and dripping into the sink isn't for feeling lost in the world, but being lost within himself.

Stepping into the tiny bathroom, pieces of mirror splintering beneath her slippers, Anna wraps her arms around his waist. Forehead resting between his bony shoulder blades, she can feel the way his breath hitches a moment before his uninjured hand covers hers. His thumb brushes over the ring on her left hand like a worry stone.

"Let's pick up some hair dye when we go into town tomorrow," she says, turning her head and pressing her cheek to his back so she can hold him closer.

One breath, two, before he answers, "What?"

She closes her eyes, wets her lips. "Last time I was at the drugstore, it seemed like there were a lot of different options for the home dye kits. Maybe you could try one out, if you'd like." Her fingers curl into the cotton of his shirt. "I know it's not—I can't give you back what you've lost. What I've taken—"

"Don't," he commands, turning in her arms until he's facing her. His palms cradle her face. She can feel his blood against her skin, wet on her cheek. "This isn't your fault."

Don't shoulder blame that isn't yours.

"This isn't that." She takes a lock of dark blonde hair between her fingers. "You're still Khiran to me. You always have been, no matter the form you take. But if wearing this face hurts you, it hurts *me*, too." His hair slips through her fingers and she traces the shape of his low brow before resting her palm on the hollow of his cheek. "Our happiness, our burdens, we share them. Remember?"

The muscles of his throat work around a swallow. "I don't know how to share this."

Her answering smile is gentle. Soft with empathy and brimming with hope. They both still carry their demons, but give them time, and they will rob them of their teeth. Wear them down until they're more memory than ghost. "That's okay. We'll figure it out. Together."

He stares at her with those eyes she still hasn't quite come to know. Give her a year and she'll memorize every fleck of amber; memorize how the shades of brown turn caramel in the afternoon light and chocolate at sunset. They don't have forever, not anymore, but Anna doesn't need eternity to learn this face, this body, as well as she knows his heart.

He echoes her, voice so soft it's more a whisper. She hears the promise in it, anyway. "Together."

It's almost winter when she wakes up to blood.

It's been so long, it takes Anna longer than it should to realize her thighs are wet with it. In her chest, her heart stutters—caught between the grinding gears of old regrets and current realities.

Her hand shakes as she reaches for his shoulder. "Khiran?" His name trembles on her lips, so weak Anna doesn't think it can wake him.

Maybe it's her touch, or the trace of fear threading her voice, but he rouses quickly. His eyes follow her gaze to the red stain smeared over the white sheets. Anna feels him stiffen beside her, his eyes wild with the same fears—the same questions—as her own.

She goes to the bathroom to wash. Once she's cleaned up, she drapes a blanket over her shoulders and sits on the back porch step. She looks out over the garden, at the willowy trunk of a once magnificent tree. Despite the layer of winter frost, its leaves still shine with bright new growth. Unbothered by the cold.

Khiran sits beside her, pushing a hot mug into her hands. "Drink."

Anna doesn't ask what it is. She's brewed enough menstrual tea for others to recognize the scent. She brings the steaming rim to her lips, taking a cautious sip. He's added honey to mask the bitterness. The ring of bone on her left hand clinks against the ceramic when she adjusts her hold. The warmth against her palms helps thaw the tension in her chest. "Do you—we've never talked about children." They've never had to. It was never within the realm of possibility.

He sits beside her, their shoulders brushing. "What do you wish?"

Turning to him, she studies his profile. If she follows his gaze, she knows it will lead her to the very same tree her own just left. "I asked you first." She means for the words to be teasing, but they twist at the last second. The weak joke souring until it sounds more like a plea.

His sigh is heavy, curling from his lips like smoke, but there's a shadow of a smile hinting at the corner of his mouth. "You didn't ask anything. Even if you did, it wouldn't matter." He meets her eyes, flecks of amber warm despite the chill. "My answer is dependent on your own."

Her heart aches. "Don't do that. Don't put it all on me. That's not fair."

Khiran hesitates, studying her as he measures his response. "It's not something I ever considered—it has never been a possibility before today," he admits. "You've raised children, Anna. You understand the weight of this decision, what it would mean for us, in ways I can't even fathom."

Anna understands—she *does*—but that isn't what she's asking. "Consider it now," she urges, lacing her fingers with his and squeezing. His hand feels cold against her scarred flesh. His skin is always cold, now. "This isn't a decision we need to make today, but it's something we need to talk about. I just—I want to know where you stand. Right now, in this moment. I just want to know how you're feeling—"

"Terrified," he says, the murmured word silencing her as effectively as a shout. Around her fingers, his hand tightens. "I feel terrified."

She swallows, mouth dry. "Why?"

There are ghosts casting shadows in his eyes. "Because you're mortal."

He doesn't elaborate, but Anna doesn't need him to. Medicine has come so far, the mortality rate for pregnancy improved so much, but there's always that chance that something could go wrong. The odds would feel small to anyone else, but she has spent so many centuries being untouchable that even the smallest of risks feels colossal.

She knows he feels it, too.

Khiran leans into her, forehead resting against her own. "There was a time when you wanted this, when you mourned the family you could never have," he says, and Anna knows he's thinking of their conversation on a grassy knoll overlooking a battlefield—the one where she grieved for the future dreamed up by another man. A future that was out of her reach. "How could I possibly live with myself if I denied you this chance? If I let my fear of being left behind strip you of the happiness you once wished for?"

She frowns, an uncomfortable truth tightening her chest. "It's been a long time since I wished for that, Khiran."

"Yes," he agrees, cold fingers tracing her brow before his palm cups her cheek. "That doesn't mean it's dead."

No, it doesn't.

Regrets are stubborn things. They sink their teeth and hold on even as other hopes and other dreams slip through her fingers. But that's all it is now, Anna realizes. A regret. A wish that soured, because she was robbed of the chance to *choose*.

"I'm not sure I want that anymore," she tells him. There's a twisting sensation in her chest, and she realizes that her words aren't entirely true. She shakes her head, hand curling over her heart just so she can take comfort in its steady beating beneath her palm. "No... I *don't* want that. It's an old dream, one leftover from who I was—who I wanted to be—before. I'm not that person anymore."

His stare is so weighted, so searching, she feels pinned by it. "You don't need to be certain, Anna. We may no longer have forever, but we still have time."

She knows, but it still doesn't change the answer she feels in her heart.

WEEKS PASS, A BLUR OF LITTLE MOMENTS THAT BUILD UNTIL THEY FEEL like something bigger.

The things she once loved—the slow, simple life she once craved —suddenly chafes. Time is moving differently, now. There is an hourglass in her mind, sand spilling through her fingers faster than she can catch it, reminding her that she no longer has forever.

Before, time felt like wading in cool, still waters, but now she's being swept away by the current—forced to swim with the tide or drown fighting it.

"You seem restless," Jiro tells her, a question disguised as an observation.

He drives her into town every other Saturday to run errands and deliver the occasional letter. He'd been kind enough to let her use his home address for corresponding with Silas and the others. There are no letters today, but the rolled paper bag from the pharmacy crinkles on her lap as her grip tightens—pills rattling as he stops at a red light.

It still feels strange, the way their relationship has shifted. He's no longer a boy looking to her for support, but a grown man—a *father*—trying to give it to her. In her mind, the sand spills a little faster. "I'm..." she trails off, searching for the word to describe the anxiety pacing within the hollow walls of her chest like an animal. The kind that knows when something is coming because instinct tells them to be afraid but not what to do. "Adjusting."

Jiro glances from her, to the bag on her lap, and back to the road as the light turns green. He releases the brake and steps on the gas. "I didn't think there would be much to adjust to," he admits, more curious than unkind. "The life you're living isn't all that different from the one we lived together, is it?"

She hesitates, but the silence that falls between them is patient enough to coax an honest answer. Looking out the window, she admires the way ordinary people walk along the sidewalks, unburdened by the weight of knowing how short their lives really are. "It's been seven hundred and ninety one years since I've been mortal," she says, the words leaving her like a confession. "I've lived more lifetimes than any one person should. I should feel satisfied—at peace—with however much time I have left."

She looks to him, her brow furrowed. "So why doesn't it feel like enough?"

Jiro is quiet, glancing between her and the road as he pulls over and parks the car. The sound of the engine fills the silence until he releases a heavy sigh and shakes his head. "I don't know."

There's an edge of regret in his stare that tells her he wishes he did. Anna closes her eyes, gathers her resolve, and forces herself to smile. "I don't think I expected you to. I just—sometimes feelings are easier to navigate when they're put into words." She shrugs, dropping her gaze. "Maybe I've been immune to death for so long, I've forgotten how vulnerable it feels to be powerless against it."

"You still have a long life ahead of you, Anna."

"Maybe," she says, her expression softening. "Maybe not. That's always been part of it, after all. The not knowing."

"Yes, I suppose it is." Jiro's fingers drum against the leather of the steering wheel. "Those pills… they're for Khiran, aren't they?"

Her chest tightens, heart squeezing painfully. Aside from her prescription of birth control, everything in the bag is over the counter pain medication.

"It's the cold," she murmurs. "The weather has been hard on him."

It's an understatement. Khiran moves around the house with a stiffness, his thin body shivering and his joints aching. She knows he's been struggling to sleep—can feel the way he turns in the night as if searching for a reprieve. Some mornings, he doesn't get out of bed until the sun sits high in the sky. Some days, he hardly leaves the bed at all. He'll lay, burrowed in their blankets, and drift between sleep and a level of glazed detachment that scares her.

Her heart gives a hollow ache, the paper bag crinkling in her hands. "I've been giving him what I can from the garden, but most days it doesn't seem to be enough."

She hates seeing him in pain. Hates that there's so little she can do to ease it.

Jiro frowns, rotating the wheel and taking a right turn onto the freeway on-ramp. "Ami mentioned he's been hurting."

The family of three drive up to the cottage every few weeks to visit. Sometimes they would stay the entire day, and Jiro and his wife Jenny would help her in the garden (Anna has learned that it is her touch that was responsible for it thriving while she was gone). Other times they stay only long enough to share a meal and a bit of conversation. Ami, their five year old, had taken an immediate liking to Khiran.

Wherever he went, she followed as faithful as a shadow.

Khiran had found it uncomfortable at first. He admitted, later and only to her, that he feels woefully unprepared on how to interact with someone so small. His only experience with someone her size had been Malik—a boy in mind only. The roles he took in the world's affairs had rarely merged with family life. Even when they did, it was hardly anything more than passing.

Jiro, absolutely delighted by his obvious discomfort, teases him mercilessly, but there's a warmth in his eyes when he watches them. Anna understands why. Ami, with her countless questions and insatiable curiosity, softens Khiran's edges in ways only Anna had once thought herself to be capable.

In the span of a few months, he seems just as fond of her as the child is of him. Anna's certain he wouldn't have burdened the girl with his discomfort, but children often understand more than they're given credit for. It is no surprise that she would have noticed the change in him, no matter how valiantly he tried to hide it.

Anna swallows the emotion lumping in her throat. "She's a smart girl."

The acknowledgement sits between them, loud in the silence. Jiro doesn't say anything else, but as he pulls back onto the road he holds out his hand between them in offering. Anna squeezes it, lets him tether her the way she once tethered him, the entire drive back.

"WE SHOULD PLAN A TRIP." THE WORDS LEAVE HER, MORE INSPIRATION than thought. It's been four days since her trip to the pharmacy.

Outside her window, frost glitters like a thin sheet of snow in the gray early morning light. Her mug warms her hands as they sit together on the couch. The smell of coffee reminding her of fresh figs drizzled with honey and the Bazaar she only ever saw a corner of.

Khiran's gaze slides to her, her thickest quilt wrapped around his shoulders. "A trip?"

"Yes." She shrugs. "We aren't running anymore. What's stopping us?"

His stare is searching. "You would leave The Tree?"

Anna tilts her head, thoughtful. "Jiro has offered to check in should we need it."

"He's only human."

Brows rising, she reminds him, "So are we." When his only answer is silence, she takes a sip of coffee as she studies him. "You think it needs protecting?"

He shrugs. "Is that not what it chose you for?"

"No," she says, her answer swift and sure in ways that only the truth can be. Her connection to The Tree is gone, but she still carries the echoes of its memory. Its wishes, her *purpose*, are as clear to her as if they were imprinted on her heart.

She shifts, facing him fully and settling herself more deeply into the cushions. "Silas told me a story once. *His* story." Khiran's gaze sharpens, curious despite his dark mood. "He thought he was dying until he followed a fox out of the desert and found his feet cradled by The Tree's roots."

"What's your point?"

"The First didn't choose Silas. The Tree, did," she says, holding his stare. "Don't you think it's strange? That he refused to leave his throne?"

Khiran scoffs, the sound bitter and dark. "He couldn't be bothered."

"No." She shakes her head. "He couldn't risk not being able to find his way *back*."

She offers him a smile. "The Tree doesn't need me for protection. It will hide itself and us until it's ready to help those who need it." She reaches over, takes his hand. "So, where should we go? What wonders will you show me? We should start planning now so we can go in the summer."

His eyes drift to the window, pulling the quilt more firmly around his shoulders. A grin pulls at his lips, crooked in ways that are so familiar, her heart stutters. "Somewhere warm."

ANNA WAKES MOMENTS BEFORE DAWN.

Beside her, Khiran still sleeps, his breathing even and his expression lax. Spring has finally brought warmer weather and a reprieve from the pain that haunted his nights. Everything is as it should be, but Anna has the strange sense that she didn't fall out of sleep on her own. *Something* woke her.

She slips out from under the covers, careful not to wake him, and threads her arms into her robe before slipping out the front door. The birds chatter from the branches in the gray predawn as she stands on the porch, eyes searching for something she can't place.

There's a feeling in her bones, a gentle nudge on her heart, telling her to *look*. Her bare feet lead her into the center of her garden, the ground damp beneath her toes. It's only as the sun peeks over the mountains in the east, bathing everything in dawn's warm glow, that she understands.

Hanging from The Tree's lowest branch, plump and ripe and *golden*, is a peach.

The breath leaves her lungs, her eyes tracing the gentle curve, admiring the morning dew clinging to the fuzz. Slowly, carefully, she steps closer. There are no whispers, no roots tangling and prodding at her heart. It is only her, standing in the garden she cultivated, in front of the tree she has dedicated the rest of her mortal life to nourishing. She cups her hands, wanting to feel the fruits of her labor.

It drops into her palms.

A message she doesn't need the whispers to understand. A gift. A nudge.

Anna sucks in a breath, her heart beating so fast it feels more like the humming of wings. She looks up at The Tree. The fruit in her hands feels as fragile as a bomb.

One. There is only one.

She swallows, regret sour on her tongue. "I won't do it without him. I can't."

A breeze whistles through the branches, sunlight glinting off the leaves. All Anna can think about is the shattered mirror on the bathroom floor casting blood-tinged reflections on the walls. Her fingers curl, fuzz tickling her palms. "I need him the way you needed me," she murmurs. "Please."

She receives no answer. She never will. Not until she accepts.

Teeth biting into her lower lip, she dips her head and tries to breathe through the heaviness weighing on her chest. That's when she notices it. The peach in her hand, the one she thought to be flawless, *isn't*.

A seam runs down the middle, splitting it into two perfect halves. Two buds, two peaches, grown so close together they've fused into one.

A gift, not just for her, but for them both.

A laugh escapes her, watery and bright as she holds it close to her heart. "Thank you."

She brings the peach into the kitchen, cutting it down the middle without resistance. When she pulls the halves apart, the center is hollow.

A gift that cannot be replicated.

CHAPTER TWENTY-THREE

"What's this?" he asks.
"A gift," she teases, an echo from their past.
"Is it magic?" He means it to be a joke, but there is a light in her eyes that
robs him of his breath. In his chest, his weak, fragile heart stutters when she
answers.
"Yes."

NEW EDUN
1977

SHE KISSES HIM AND HIS LIPS TASTE LIKE MAGIC—PEACHES DRIZZLED IN honey on a warm summer day. When she pulls away, his hair is dark and softly curled. His eyes, those eyes she would recognize on any face in any lifetime, smile back at her—blue on the verge of green.

THE END

ACKNOWLEDGMENTS

There are always so many to thank when a book is published, but when it comes to these characters and this world I find that the people I want to to thank the most are too great to number. This story was born from just a few snippets of dialogue about a woman who found greater beauty in the truth than in a mask ("I would rather see you as yourself") and evolved into a love letter to the everyday heroes of both the past and present.

Sometimes, I think of all the ways humanity has failed and the grief of it feels too heavy to breathe through. Then, I look and I see all the Anna's of the world—people who are strong because of their unwavering empathy and compassion—and things feel a little less hopeless.

Thank you.

Thank you for saving this world one person, one action, one protest, at a time. If I have one hope for this story, it is that these words helped you feel seen as the heroes that you are. If I have one wish, it is that this story inspires kindness in a world that is so, so desperate for it.

I would also like to take a moment to thank my family. I am so incredibly grateful to have you. From buying a copy for yourself, gifting paperbacks to friends and coworkers, to helping sew book sleeves for PR boxes, you have made me feel supported in a way I know so many people don't.

To Katherine, thank you for suffering the task of being the very first set of eyes on this book. Your input was invaluable in helping make this story shine.

To Krys, thank you for always cheering me on. I'm not sure I would have kept going if not for your friendship and your support. Also, thank you for saving me from what would have been an (admittedly) hilarious but very unfortunate cover mishap.

To Sarah, thank you for sticking with me since my fanfic days and for catching my more embarrassing typos. Thanks to you, readers are able to read about 'green grasses' instead of 'green gasses'. Your comments and reactions always bring me so much joy.

To Ash, thank you for always being so supportive and giving such beautiful feedback!

Lastly, the most heartfelt thank you to my readers. Your support has not only left me in awe, it has quite literally changed my life. It is because of your enthusiasm that when I'm asked what I do for a living, I can answer with confidence, "I am an author."

ALSO BY R. RAETA

A mortal love,

An eternal life.

Lily doesn't remember her death, or even her reawakening, but she knows this: the sun is to be feared, words are her salvation, and—above all—the bench facing the playground is hers.

Every night, she writes stories about the broken and abandoned things she finds littering the park. As the decades pass and the city skyline grows, her body remains immortal and unchanged… even as her mind decays. She is the pin holding the hands of the clock, fixed and entirely alone as the world moves around her.

Until Sam de la Cruz, a young man of summer smiles, takes a seat beside her and an unlikely friendship blooms. Months pass and their relationship grows, but her mind and memories continue to fade until Sam realizes the strange, lonely woman he's come to love is more than what she seems.

A story about love, loss, and what it means to live forever.

ALSO BY R. RAETA

5 Star Readers' Favorite

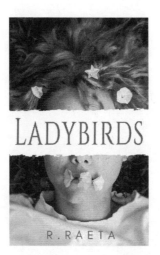

Miracles don't come free and words are binding.

His miracles have a cursed edge, but he's not the villain Sara expected. Still, she's not exactly thrilled about being stuck with a centuries old ghost with a flair for the dramatic and a nasty habit of pushing her buttons just for the fun of it. With his penchant for boredom—and the fact that she's the only one able to see and hear him—he's about as common as her shadow and as welcome as mold.

Even if he *is* pretty handy in her British Literature class.

ABOUT THE AUTHOR

R. Raeta writes slow burn love stories with splash of magic. She is a Readers' Favorite Gold Medalist for Literary Fiction and two-time IAN Book of the Year Finalist for her debut novel, Everlong. When she isn't agonizing over word choices, she enjoys telling the dog how handsome he is and sitting in on the nightly therapy sessions the cat so generously provides for her. She is a Trigiminal Neuralgia survivor, and believes in living your best life day by day.

If you would like to follow R. Raeta's future works, you can visit her website at www.rraeta.com or find her on the following social media platforms.

Made in the USA
Columbia, SC
10 March 2025

54995404R00190